FOG SI

"Deliciously fun, immersiv
complicated family loyalties,
packed with wonderful wom

Stephanie Burgis, author of Masks and Shadows *and* Snowspelled

"Patrice Sarath takes readers on a fine, twisty adventure with two determined young women who abandon their dutiful, well-mannered upbringing for drawing room gambling, dark alleys, and magic."

Carol Berg, author of The Sanctuary Duet *and the Collegia Magica Series*

"Patrice Sarath gives us a colorful Dickensian fantasy that leads the reader on an unpredictable path of murder, intrigue, and mystery, served up with her customary lively characterizations and pitch-perfect dialogue."

Louisa Morgan, author of A Secret History of Witches

"I loved the determination of the Sisters Mederos! Despite myriad setbacks, they return to the city that crushed their family a decade before, take on the corrupt guild, and bring their enemies to justice."

J Kathleen Cheney, author of the Golden City series and Nebula Award finalist

"Delightful and compulsively readable account of the escapades of two strong willed sisters determined to restore their rightful place though disreputable means."

Tina Connolly, Nebula-nominated author of Ironskin

BY THE SAME AUTHOR

The Sisters Mederos

Books of the Gordath
Gordath Wood
Red Gold Bridge
The Crow God's Girl

The Unexpected Miss Bennet

PATRICE SARATH

Fog Season

The Tales *of* Port Frey

ANGRY ROBOT
An imprint of Watkins Media Ltd

Unit 11, Shepperton House,
89 Shepperton Road,
London N1 3DF • UK

angryrobotbooks.com
twitter.com/angryrobotbooks
Doing it for themselves

An Angry Robot paperback original 2019

Cover by Paul Young/Shutterstock
Set in Meridien & Adobe Caslon by Argh! Nottingham

Distributed in the United States by Penguin Random House, Inc., New York.

ISBN 978 0 85766 777 9
Ebook ISBN 978 0 85766 778 6

Printed in the United States of America

9 8 7 6 5 4 3 2 1

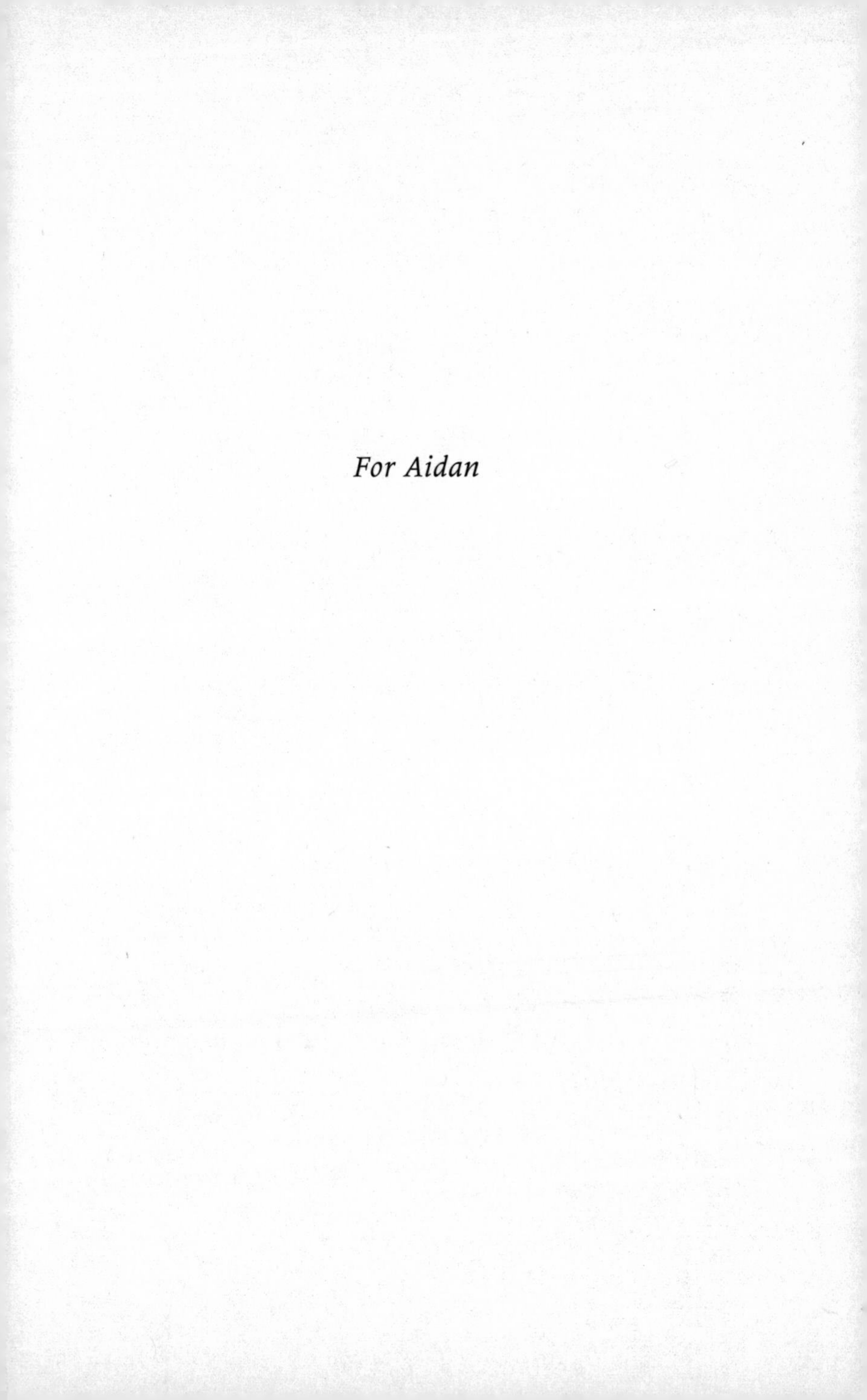

For Aidan

The coldest winter I ever spent was summer in San Francisco.

Attr. to Mark Twain

Chapter One

There was an air of festivity at the Port Saint Frey harbor, where Tesara Mederos and her sister Yvienne waited to send off their parents on a six-month voyage that, the entire family hoped, would restore their fortunes. Stevedores and sailors trundled up and down the gangplank of the clipper *Iderci Empress* with barrels and gear and supplies. The *Empress* was a fast, lean ship whose keel was laid eight months before; this was to be her maiden voyage. Her masts were black against the bright blue sky, her furled sails a fine white, and her balustrades and brassworks gleamed. She wanted only for passengers to come aboard with their luggage. Brevart was already on deck, asking dozens of questions of the captain and the first mate, and they were patiently answering him, though no doubt they had much to do before the ship left port.

Despite the sunshine, clouds massed on the mountains behind the city, and Tesara could feel a wetness to the air that had nothing to do with the sea. Her power felt dampened, and she gave a little experimental push, flexing her fingers. Down the dock, air pressure and then a gust of wind rattled the dockmaster's manifests, and the man and his apprentice scrambled to catch the pages before they flew off into the harbor.

Oops. A small surge of nausea struck her and she swallowed. Every time I use my powers, she thought. Each surge of energy caused a blowback. She struggled to keep her composure.

"For goodness sakes, Tesara, can you at least pay attention?" Alinesse said with exasperation.

"Sorry, Mama," she said, but Alinesse didn't wait for her apology and had already turned back to Yvienne. "Now, Yvienne, I've spoken with Albero about the broken dumbwaiter, but I'm leaving it in your hands to consult with the engineers. After all, you know the most about those things."

"Of course, Mama," Yvienne said, with a straight face. Tesara was impressed by her composure. "I'm as interested as you in determining why it's stopped – I mean, why it never worked."

It had certainly worked just fine the night they ousted their enemy, the nefarious Guild liaison Trune, from their family home. No doubt in a nasty fit of spite Trune had damaged the dumbwaiter, a parting shot at the family he had been determined to destroy. The whole house had needed to be made over when they moved back in, and Alinesse, though her nature was normally frugal, had spared no expense in removing "the stench", as she called it, of Trune.

"I must say that if the tradesmen who installed it say it has to be taken out, I will not be displeased," Alinesse said. She made a pursed-lip expression of disgust. "I am sure I could never be persuaded it was of any use. Finally, girls, you need to keep up with the household expenses and bills. This is your responsibility, Tesara. No, I will brook no complaint. Yvienne is busy with the office. You'll have to meet with Mrs Francini every morning and go over the accounts. And you do have a good hand (*said grudgingly*), so please take over the correspondence. And another thing – *no invitations.* I expect you to live retiringly. Perhaps the Sansieris can visit, but none other. I am sure the gossips in this town have nothing better to do than to find fault with your conduct in the worst way. *Where* is your father?"

They all looked up at the ship. Brevart followed after the captain eagerly, gesticulating. Surprising them both, Alinesse smiled, clutching her broad-brimmed bonnet. Her eyes were bright.

"I do love a sea voyage, girls. I wish it were for better reasons, but this is the first step in restoring our fortunes. What a stroke of luck that we got word that the *Main Chance* was sighted off the coast in Grand Harbor."

Tesara and Yvienne exchanged glances. Yes, thought Tesara. That was rather convenient. Six years after the ship allegedly went down with all hands, and six months after House Mederos was restored to her rightful place, the great flagship of the Mederos fleet turned up on the other side of the continent. That sort of luck made a girl suspicious.

Yvienne stepped forward and gave Alinesse a kiss on the cheek. "You have nothing to worry about, Mama. We'll take care of things here, and we'll see you in a few months."

"Or sooner," Alinesse agreed. She held out gloved hands to both girls and clasped them tight. "I know we can trust you. You have a good head on your shoulder and you, Tesara..." Tesara braced herself. Alinesse gave a smile that was half a rueful grimace. "You have hidden depths, my dear. If you but concentrate–"

Before Tesara could say something she would regret, Yvienne interposed smoothly. "It's time, Mama," she said, nodding over at the chaplain from the Church of the Sea. He and the acolytes were preparing the Service of Outgoing Ships. Already the voyagers and well-wishers moved in that direction. The sailors and the officers on board gathered at the rail above them, Brevart among them, hats and caps doffed and heads bowed. The sailor at the end caught Tesara's eye just before she bowed her head, and she turned to look at him as the priest began the ceremony.

The sailor at the end of the row, slender, slighter than the other men, and with a scant beard, was none other than Jone Saint Frey.

She gave a quite audible gasp. Yvienne looked at her in warning, and Tesara hastily bent her head and clasped her hands. But as soon as it was safe, and all had their heads bowed, she peeked again. Yes. She had not been mistaken. Tesara stared straight ahead, allowing the service to wash over her, mouthing the responses automatically.

Our Father in Heaven, our Mother the Sea, bless and keep this vessel…

At the last 'amen', she turned fully around and peered at the ship. Jone had already disappeared. The bustle around her increased, good-byes were said, people embraced their families. Brevart and Alinesse were two of eight passengers; a scattering of younger sons, amidst tradesmen from Ravenne. Tesara picked up her skirts and strode toward the gangway, ignoring her mother's exasperated, "*Tesara!*"

She pushed her way up onto the ship, shouldering past the stevedores carrying the last crates and luggage. Her father caught sight of her and waved her over to meet the patient captain.

"Ah, Tesara, have you come to see the ship? Captain, this is my youngest–"

Tesara bobbed a quick curtsey. "I would love to look around. May I? Thank you."

She went aft before they could say anything, threading between cargo and sailors, stepping over ropes and gear.

It wasn't hard to find him. He was coiling and securing rope on the deck. He looked up at her. She let out her breath, just then realizing she had been holding it.

"Hello," she said. It was wholly inadequate and captured none of what she wanted to say to him. They had not seen each other in the past six months – she had thought he no longer cared for her.

He gave his crooked smile, the one that transformed his face from ugly to charming. Now that she saw him up close, she realized that the slender boy she knew had filled out, his face reddened and browned under the sun.

"I wrote you a letter," he said. "I posted it. I didn't know your parents had booked passage, and I didn't expect to see you."

"I look forward to reading it. I... Does your mother know?" It was a terribly awkward thing to assume, she knew that as soon as the words blurted from her mouth.

This time he grimaced. "She thinks I'm in Ravenne, courting Mira."

Courting Mira. Had that even been possible? She felt sickened by the idea. *But you knew he could never love you. You could only ever be friends. You knew that. So why shouldn't he marry the sparkling, spoiled, charming, beautiful Mirandine Depressis?*

"Does *she* know?" And this time Tesara was ashamed at the jealousy in her words. If Jone heard that undertone, he gave no sign.

"It's all in the letter, Tes. I'm sorry – I know that was the coward's way out." He spoke in a sudden rush. "I spent my whole life being frightened and avoiding all unpleasantness. I knew if I gave in to my mother, I would spend decades and decades being pleasant and obedient, and never once feeling... anything. And then I would die. I needed to do what I was truly afraid of, and I couldn't tell anyone. I had to just do it."

"It's not being cowardly. It would have been cowardly not to do this." She said it with sudden, fierce urgency. "I'm glad you're going." She laughed a little, and he did too.

"I'll miss you, Tesara Mederos. That's in the letter too, but not this." He came to her and kissed her, first on the cheek, and then on her lips. For a brief moment, the kiss lingered, his lips salty and warm on hers.

"Tesara!" It was her mother, calling from the gangway. They both jumped back.

Tesara said in a hurry, "I have to go. I'll read your letter, and I'll write to you – but the post will take months."

He grinned, and he looked in that instant like a carefree young sailor. "Send it to the Cape – we'll pick it up on the return journey."

"Tesara!" Her mother called again with rising impatience.

She pressed his hand. "Good-bye. Good luck. Remember, there are no such things as sea monsters."

He laughed, and she hurried back to her parents.

All during their leavetaking, she couldn't help but think of the kiss. It was Jone Saint Frey. They had kissed. It had been lovely and unexpected, and so part and parcel of the new Jone, halfway to shedding the skin of the quiet, uncertain boy that wore him down. So why did she have such deep misgivings?

There are no such things as sea monsters. Except me.

The sunk fleet haunted her, and she knew she would not rest until her parents discovered the truth. And if that truth was that their daughter was an ungovernable monster, what then? Tesara pressed a hand against her abdomen, trying to quiet the ever-constant roil. Next to her, Yvienne, quietly noticing, gave her a quick side hug. Dear Yvienne, Tesara thought. She always knew when she was worried.

At last the lines were untied from the moorings and tossed back onto the deck of the *Empress*. The tugs, manned by twelve muscular longshoremen apiece, began the laborious task of towing the ship out of the harbor. Slowly she made headway. The acolytes tossed the flowers from the service into the water. The passengers clustered on the rail, waving.

"I don't really have to manage the household accounts, do I?" Tesara said, waving after the departing ship.

"I wouldn't dream of letting you near them," Yvienne promised.

Finally the order came and the sails unfurled, belling as they caught the wind. The ship began a slow, ponderous turn, and the tugs rowed out of her way. At the same time, the fog bank flowed over the mountains and settled onto the city, dampening the sun behind them, while the sea before them dazzled with freshening whitecaps.

The last sight Tesara caught of the *Iderci Empress* was of her gliding out into the sunlit sea, while all around them the docks and the city turned gray and wet.

Bother, she thought. Fog Season had come early this year.

Chapter Two

Yvienne Mederos, the unheralded savior of her family's trading House, once the most distinguished, ruthless, and successful business of Port Saint Frey, looked at her disreputable Uncle Samwell and wondered why she had even bothered.

"Why in the name of Saint Frey himself would you want to commit to such an unsuitable contract?" Yvienne said to that shabby, rotund gentleman. He blinked at her in surprise.

"Here now, missy, don't take that tone with me," he said, helping himself to coffee from the carafe on the sideboard, and adding a generous dollop of whipped cream. They were in the House Mederos offices on the dock, and the windows were wide open to the brisk, cold, wet air of the harbor, the smell of salt, dead fish, and cargo wafting in with the wind. Yvienne loved it. It smelled like money.

All of which Uncle Samwell was seeking to squander with the stroke of a pen.

One week, she thought. They've not even been gone *one week.* She took a deep breath, holding herself steady. She didn't want to shout, because she could see through the open door their two clerks bent over their tall desks, ostensibly handling the accounts, but clearly poised to listen so they could gossip on their dinner break at the coffee house later in the day.

"Uncle," she said, keeping her voice low. "Inigho Demaris gave you terrible terms on that contract. We would be on the hook for most of the costs, and we would have to sell at such a volume that the chance of making even a five percent profit is quite low."

"Oh, and I suppose that a slip of a girl like you understands better than an old salt like me? I've been making deals before you were born, young lady. We need to show this city that House Mederos is back and ready for business. Working with Inigho gives us credibility. Once the word gets out, everyone else will fall into place." He snapped his fingers.

How to make him understand? She put her hands on the desk and leaned forward to face him. Despite herself, her voice rose.

"We have credibility. We have the good wishes and fellowship of the merchant families. What we don't have is money. And this contract won't allow us to make any. Inigho Demaris is a shrewd businessman. He's not doing us any favors by agreeing to do business with House Mederos. He's taking advantage of our perceived weakness."

When she stopped, the usual work noises in the clerk's office were dead silent – and then with haste the men began to whistle and their adding machines clattered all over again.

She knew she had hit home though, because Samwell turned pouty.

"Just like your father. Always have to put down any idea that I have. Well, I won't have it, missy. You are not the boss of this House, for all you act like it. You should know, I'm the only one that kept us going in the bad times. *My* connections, *my* business deals. You keep this up, and there's nothing stopping me from starting up my own merchant house. The Balinchards were great once – we will be again. Then we'll see who has the business sense."

He stormed off, letting the door slam behind him. This time the clerks stopped work with no pretense. Yvienne couldn't blame them, though she made a mental note to move their desks into the records room, where they wouldn't be distracted by family matters.

She pressed her fingertips to her forehead, then pushed back wisps of dark hair from her temples. As always, the wind of the harbor tousled her careful bun, but she preferred the crisp outdoor air except in the coldest weather. It helped her think.

She looked once more at the contract. It was florid and well drawn, with the Demaris seal next to Inigho's signature, and the blank space waiting for a representative of House Mederos to sign and seal. She went to rip it up, then held off and reread it, shaking her head at the exorbitant terms. If Brevart found out his ne'er-do-well brother-in-law was trying to make yet more deals on behalf of the Mederos family, he would be livid. Alinesse, too, would be thoroughly annoyed that her little brother Samwell Balinchard was at it again.

A polite cough broke through her absorption. With a start, Yvienne looked up from the pages of printed contract. A strange man stood in the entrance of the office. He was short and stocky, in a tweed coat that had seen better days, and thick wool trousers, ditto. He was clean-shaven, his hairline receding for all that he was a youngish man, only six or seven-and-twenty. There was something about his expression – he had an appreciative look about him, as if he had been watching her for a good while and liked what he saw. Yvienne felt irked that he had spied on her while she was lost in concentration.

"I beg your pardon," he said. "I knocked, but you never acknowledged me."

"I do apologize, Mr–?"

"Fresnel. Abel Fresnel. Harrier Agency." He came into the office, hand outstretched.

She didn't take it. In Port Saint Frey, a man bowed to a woman. Maybe it was his frank appraisal of her that set her off, but she had no interest in schooling a stranger on customs. After a moment he fished in his vest pocket and stepped into the office, handing her his card. She didn't take it. He set it down on the desk. The card was smudged and bent at the corners. She read it upside down. Abel Fresnel. Detecting Man. Harrier Agency.

Yvienne remained calm. She gave him an inquiring look. "How may House Mederos help you, Mister Fresnel?"

"I've been hired by the Guild to investigate some doings early this year, and since your family was involved, I thought I'd start with you," he said. His accent had a trace of something she could not identify – a bit country, she thought. Unsophisticated. It set off alarm bells. The famed Harrier Detecting Agency did not hire country bumpkins. The accent was a lure, meant to reassure, before a trap was sprung.

"Goodness," she said, at her most neutral.

"The Guild was interested in your opinion of the matter," he went on. She raised a brow. That was an out and out lie; the Guild knew all about the Mederos opinions. She wondered why he told her that.

Mister Fresnel pulled a chair out from against the wall and sat across from her, crossing his leg and leaning back. He nodded his chin at the card. "That's me."

"I see. As you can see, I am very busy today. Too busy to offer my opinion. Good day."

He didn't make a move. She glanced over at the clerk room, and knew by the different quality of silence that they were gone to their dinner.

Mister Fresnel had no doubt waited until just that moment to enter.

"What do you want?" Her voice sharpened, and she cursed her temper that made her reveal her fear and discomfort. She kept her hands on the desk. If one didn't know to look at it, one would never see the outline of the small compartment built flush into the desktop, where a bit of pressure would release the catch. Father had stashed ready cash in the drawer; Yvienne kept her pistol there. This man had made no threatening overtures, but Yvienne had no doubts that she faced grave danger. If there was a Harrier nosing about, it could only mean the Guild had suspicions regarding last spring's activities.

"It was a sad business, that. The disappearance of Guild Liaison Trune and the merchant Barabias Parr, the fraud against the Mederos home business. A real mystery."

"It's properly called a House, not a home business," Yvienne said. He acknowledged the correction with a little nod and a smile. He had a distracting smile. She told herself to concentrate. "And our House was restored six months ago, the fraud revealed and the charges reversed. So we don't need your help, thanks."

"There's still the matter of the missing Magistrate and the missing merchant. Some might think that House Mederos would want revenge for his role in the downfall of your family's home… House… business."

"Goodness," she said again. "Of what are you accusing my family, Mister Fresnel?"

"Accusing? Are you feeling guilty, Miss Mederos?"

"I'm sorry," Yvienne said, letting her voice reveal her

temper. "Tell me again why you are here? Because, to recap – the fraud was revealed, the perpetrators punished, my family's reputation restored, and what you call a mystery was solved six months ago. You may now go, sir."

He sat still for a moment longer, regarding her with a quiet, piercing expression. He had dark brown eyes, a bit of shadow around his jaw, and a plain, angular face. He was entirely an unprepossessing sort of man, except for the impression of strength in his shoulders, and his battered hands. Had he been a prizefighter? she wondered, though he didn't have the broken nose or misshapen ears that classified that profession. No, he was not a brawler, and he was far more dangerous for all that.

She flushed, aware that he had been taking her measure as intently as she had taken his. Fresnel stood, taking his time. He nodded at his card on the edge of her desk.

"Keep it. I'm staying at the Bailet Hotel, on the Esplanade, if you want to tell me anything. I am sure we'll be speaking again, Miss Mederos."

He closed the door behind himself, and Yvienne was left alone in the office. With the imminent danger gone, she allowed herself to take a deep, shuddering breath.

Don't react. He's still watching.

She took the card again, as if curious, then stuck it in the small box on the desk where all the other cards were kept. She would take it home later. Still performing, she drew the contract to her, picked up her pencil, and began to jot meaninglessly on it. All the while her mind was racing as fast as her heart.

Calm, she ordered herself. Stay calm. The Guild doesn't know anything. As far as the Guild wanted anyone to think, the Great Fraud that embarrassed its senior executives was foisted upon them by the Guild Magistrate Trune – a loose cannon, and now a fugitive from justice. Ditto Barabias Parr; she had never liked the man, but she had no doubt that he had thrown his lot in with Trune. This was probably just a grandstanding measure, nothing more.

Foolish of them, she thought, her heart slowing. The Harriers had a fearsome reputation of always getting their man. If they weren't careful, they'd be hoist with their own petard.

Chapter Three

If you can't identify the mark at the table, you're *the mark.*

Tesara was reminded of the adage as she fanned her cards and looked over her hand at Lieutenant Anais, an encouraging half-smile tilting her eyes. He hesitated and swore, throwing down his cards on the green baize-covered table. "That tears it. My luck has been abominable tonight, and no mistake." He sat back in his chair, and tried to re-light his cheroot with a damp match, swearing when it didn't catch.

Tesara reached across the table, took one of Colonel Talios's matches from the silver case at his elbow, struck it, and held the flame out to the lieutenant. He gave her a startled look, but leaned forward, and puffed.

"It is too bad, sir," she said, shaking out the match and pulling her winnings toward her. "I thought you had that last hand. But you know what they say," she added. "No luck for the wicked."

The crowd at Fayres, a melange of officers, actors, heiresses, and dock lovelies, laughed, and the lieutenant scowled. Fayres wasn't the most exclusive casino on Port Saint Frey, but it had a devoted following because it was well-run and kept its customers' secrets. What happened in Fayres stayed in Fayres, even when wayward merchant daughters won a month's housekeeping money in one night.

And that reminded her of a second adage, by one Alinesse Mederos – *If you cannot be an asset, you must not yet be a liability.* Tesara was not Vivi. She had no head for business, no desire to run a great House and increase its wealth and holdings.

But she could fleece a cad of a lieutenant at cards, and do it with pleasure.

The lieutenant switched tactics. "Perhaps you could transfer some of that luck to me, Miss Mederos?" he said, and he kissed his thin lips suggestively.

The crowd ooohed, while Tesara hid her revulsion behind a smile. "Oh, and ruin a perfectly lovely friendship, Lieutenant Anais? I believe in a more spiritual connection over that of the flesh."

"And I believe five minutes in the garden with me will disabuse you of that quaint notion," he retorted, his hostility ill-concealed.

"Here now," Colonel Talios said, with an uneasy chuckle, as if remembering that he had once been interested in marrying Tesara and should still feel protective. The lieutenant ignored him. He flushed, and rose with an oath, pushing his chair back so hard it fell over. He stood up, and loomed.

Tesara felt the spark rise in her fingertips, and she concentrated on sorting her chips. When she had control over her dangerous emotions, she looked up at the lieutenant. She said nothing, merely gave him a level stare. He reached over and yanked her to her feet, chips flying all around them, his hand so hard around her wrist it would leave a mark the next day.

"Come with me, girl," he said, his voice slurred and guttural.

Everything happened at once. The drunken revelers were shocked and owl-eyed, blinking foolishly at the sudden turn toward violence. Two burly gentlemen, house peacekeepers, shoved their way through the crowd toward them. Bracing herself, Tesara gathered the electricity in her fingertips and pushed it out at the lieutenant. There was a fizz and a crack, the air smelled like a thunderstorm, and the lieutenant was suddenly sprawled on his behind, his mouth and eyes wide with shock and pain.

A woman screamed. Tesara put her hands to her mouth, feigning surprise. A new feeling of nausea came over her and lingered, then faded.

"Poor fellow," she said for the crowd's benefit. "He can't hold his drink."

"Here now, Ani!" said another reveler, his red officer's coat half-unbuttoned. He reeled but he managed to get his hands under Anais's shoulders, lifting the drunken man to his feet. "Behave, man. We won't get asked back. No, no, it's all right. I've got him," he said to the burly fellows. "Just a bit to the winds, but harmless, you know?"

The guards folded their arms across their massive chests, and didn't look convinced. The two officers stumbled away under their steely gaze. Tesara sat back down, maintaining her composure, and went back to gathering her chips.

"I can't abide a man who can't hold his liquor or his temper," she confided to the overdressed woman at her side. "So bad-mannered, don't you think?"

The woman gave her a sidelong look. "You're a cocky one, ain't you?" She tossed back her drink. "Table's too hot for me, Baby. Let's dice."

Baby, a dissipated young man half her age, with a dirty cravat and an overabundance of opinions, hastened to help her to her feet. He cast a glare at Tesara's chips.

"It's not fair, you know," he said in his reedy voice. "You know it's not fair to win so much. It is not a complaint. It is a fact."

She kept from rolling her eyes. Fair had nothing to do with it. *Don't play if you can't lose.* She wasn't cheating. She was just counting cards, and if they couldn't do it, that was their problem. And now the table was breaking up, leaving only Tesara, Colonel Talios, and the dealer, a silent and supremely competent man employed by Mrs Fayres. The crowd parted and Mrs Fayres came forward, laying a possessive hand on the colonel's broad shoulder. He reached up and patted it, but he gave Tesara an abashed look.

Oh, for goodness' sake, she thought. It had never been a real engagement.

"Miss Tesara," said Mrs Fayres in her melodious voice. "Are you ready to cash out?"

No more gambling for you tonight, was the message. Tesara stood.

"Thank you, Mrs Fayres. That would be lovely."

At a nod from Mrs Fayres, the dealer began totting up her chips, and with a quick tally wrote down her winnings on a tiny sheet of paper from the pad in his vest. He presented it to her with a flourish. Tesara ran through the numbers. Less the house's take, she cleared one thousand guilders. She tried not to smile with satisfaction. *And Mama says I have no head for business.*

"This looks satisfactory," she said. She initialed the receipt. "Mrs Fayres, may I buy you – and the colonel, of course – a drink?"

"Quite nice, quite nice!" the colonel boomed. Mrs Fayres smiled, but in a way that suggested that Tesara was being a precocious child.

"Thank you, Miss Tesara," Mrs Fayres said. "We'll place

your winnings in the safe, and if you like, tomorrow we can deposit your money directly in your bank account. You do have an account, of course?"

"Yes, thank you," Tesara said. She knew she could trust Mrs Fayres, the woman's louche reputation notwithstanding. Mrs Fayres was correct. An account had been opened for her when she was born, and she had been supposed to tithe ten percent of her allowance into it. That was a joke – what with Uncle Samwell winning all of her sweets money, her own profligate nature, and the reversal of the fortunes of House Mederos for six years, there was likely nothing in the account with her name on it other than cobwebs. So it was with relief that Tesara handed over the receipt.

Mrs Fayres stripped off a few engraved banknotes from the dealer's bank and handed them to Tesara. "Pin money," she said, as if she merely gave Tesara her allowance as a young, silly, merchant's girl. It stiffened her back even as she had to acknowledge there was some truth to it.

Tesara stood at the bar, flanked by Mrs Fayres and the colonel. Mrs Fayres signaled the bartender, and he brought them all drinks. Tesara leaned against the long mahogany rail and sipped her sparkling wine with punch. She looked around at the place. The gambling house was as elegant as a house of disrepute could be. That was Mrs Fayres's management, and Tesara could not deny that the woman had a head for business. The gambling tables were well-run, the liquor was top shelf, and the prices at the bar were high enough that drunkenness was discouraged, though it did not entirely keep the lieutenant and his ilk from becoming completely disordered. Mrs Fayres employed well-trained croupiers and concierges, and the burly gentlemen at the door and who walked the gambling floor were inevitably polite, even as they took a gentleman – or a lady – by the elbow and ejected them from the premises.

The parquet floor was inlaid with an elegant design of stained wood. There was plenty of light over each table, the red-and-black wheel, and the dicing table, and the house was humming. A haze of cigar and cheroot smoke hung mid-level in the air, the only drawback, she thought. She hated the way it stung her eyes and made her hair reek, and her gown always needed a thorough airing the day after. She and Mirandine used to complain, after a night at a fashionable salon, about the gentlemen's cigars, and how hard it was to get the stink out.

She missed Jone and Mirandine fiercely. Three disreputable comrades, and even though she knew they were playing at banditry, life had sparkled back then. It had been a brief, remarkable summer. Now Jone was gone for a sailor, and Mirandine – she hadn't heard from Mirandine in months.

If Mirandine had been there when the lieutenant grabbed her wrist, she would have stood up for Tesara and she wouldn't have had to use her powers. Tesara rubbed at her bruised wrist.

What time is it? she thought. There were no clocks, and she suspected that was deliberate on Mrs Fayres's part. One lost track of time, and one stayed – and stayed – until the money was all gone. Or, in her case, she was thrown out. Politely thrown out, yes, but thrown out nonetheless.

One of the burly gentlemen came up to Mrs Fayres and whispered.

"Thank you, Vere," Mrs Fayres said. She set down her small crystal glass of topaz liqueur. "I've taken the liberty of ordering a cab for you, Miss Tesara. At your leisure, of course – you are welcome to stay."

At the way the colonel gave his mistress a startled glance, Tesara recognized a polite fiction when she heard one. She smiled and set down her drink, gathering up her netted purse.

"That is most kind, Mrs Fayres. Thank you so much for an enjoyable evening."

"Darling love," Mrs Fayres said to the colonel, "would you be so good as to tell our friends that I will join them shortly?" She waved a hand at a far table. Tesara recognized Bunny and Firth.

"Of course, my goddess," the colonel said, capturing and kissing her fingertips. Tesara tried hard to keep from bursting into laughter. Had her parents ever been so soppy?

Mrs Fayres escorted her to the front door. A maid handed Tesara her silk shawl, and a manservant opened the door for them. The cold wet air of Port Saint Frey smacked her in the face, a welcome coldness after the close, smoky air of the casino. At the foot of the townhouse stairs, a fairly well-kept hack waited.

"Tha–" Tesara said again, when Mrs Fayres interrupted her. The tall woman never expressed anger, but by her face and her tone, Tesara could tell she brooked no discussion.

"Miss Tesara. I don't know what you did or how you did it, and I'm not saying the lieutenant didn't deserve everything you gave him. But I can't have talk about my business. It would be best if you don't return for a decent interval."

Tesara's lips parted but she couldn't speak. Mrs Fayres kept her steady gaze on her.

"I didn't do anything," she managed, but it came out as high-pitched and childish.

"Don't try that on me, Miss Tesara," Mrs Fayres said, and the woman's smooth facade slipped. She leaned closer to her, her voice a steel whisper. "You are a spoiled girl who is playing with fire, and I will not let your heedlessness ruin my livelihood. Is that clear?"

Tesara managed to nod. Mrs Fayres stepped back.

"You can expect the guilders in your account tomorrow," she said and turned back to the house before Tesara could say a word in protest. Flushing, she turned and walked down the stairs. The cabbie jumped down from the driver's seat and opened the door for her, helping her in. Tesara sank back against the uncomfortable upholstery, and the hack lurched off, to bump and sway over Port Saint Frey streets, from the bohemian part of town to the fashionable Crescent.

Well, that was a kick in the teeth to a blind man, as Uncle Samwell would say. That stupid lieutenant, she thought, bitterly. If she couldn't play among the real gamesters with their larger stakes, and if the first families of Port Saint Frey would no longer let her play at their fine salons, how could she make money?

She was back to being the family liability.

Six months ago, she had been welcome among the Port Saint Frey merchant families. To be sure, it was as a novelty, a subject of gossip, and mockery, but she had been a fixture of the gaming tables and won the ladies' pin money. Then the Great Fraud was revealed, and too many merchant families had been embarrassed by their complicity or, at the least, their determination to look the other way. On the surface House Mederos had regained its status as one of the first trade families of the city, but in reality a tinge of the disreputable still hung over the family. They had very little business coming in, as their old contacts and business partners always found a reason that it wasn't the right time to invest in a Mederos venture.

Tesara ran a fingertip along the window frame of the cab,

watching a tiny trail of sea fire curl into being and then fade away. So she had powers. It did little good, if she couldn't *use* them. Yes, she could do more, but it was too dangerous.

You didn't sink the fleet.

Sometimes that consoled her. At other times, when she was tired and despairing as she was that morning, riding home in a dirty cab that reeked of spirits, tobacco, and the stink of vomit, she didn't believe that was true. She remembered what she had done that fateful night, and she remembered the vision she had of the ships breaking apart in a violent storm. She could not dare to hope that the *Main Chance* had been found, and was safe at harbor three thousand miles to the east.

The hack arrived at the bottom of the Crescent. Tesara rapped on the ceiling to signal the cabbie to stop. No need to bring attention to her early morning arrival by having a hack drive right up to the house. She could let herself in through the side door. The rickety carriage jerked to a halt and tilted sideways as the cabbie climbed down. He opened the door and rolled out the step. From long experience Tesara knew his outstretched hand had nothing to do with helping her out of the cab and everything to do with her fare. She picked up her purse and her wrap and stepped down, holding the door frame. Safely on the ground she doled out the fare and a tip. Without a word the dour man made the money disappear, and climbed back up onto the driver's seat. He slapped the reins and turned his rig, soon swallowed up in the fog.

She waited a moment, weary. Then she gathered her strength and her skirts and marched up the steep cobblestoned street, wincing at the cold and wet that seeped through the soles of her thin evening slippers. It would be good to get out of her wet, smoky frock and wrap, and into a cozy robe, towel her hair by a fire in her room, and sleep in all morning. Yawning, Tesara made her way home, more by feel and memory, than by any attentiveness to her surroundings.

Chapter Four

Tesara slipped in through the side gate, latching it behind her. The rusty iron groaned in the wet, foggy air. She scurried to the servants' entrance. As expected, light spilled out of the kitchen into the dank hallway, a warm, cosy light from the whale oil lamps and the fire. Mrs Francini was hard at work. She could hear pots banging in the kitchen and masculine whistling coming from the butler's pantry. Albero, the young butler, was up and about. She could hear the homely kitchen clock on the mantel chime six.

Drat. She had returned home later than she expected. She had no wish to face Mrs Francini's or Albero's disapproval.

Tesara held her breath and sidled down the narrow hall past the kitchen. The lovely smell of porridge, sausages, and coffee wafted through the house. Even though it was just the girls and Uncle Samwell now, Mrs Francini put on a full spread. Tesara's stomach growled and she threw one more glance back at the kitchen – and ran smack into Noe, the new housemaid.

"Oh!" The maid, a thin nervous girl with stringy blonde hair and a small straight mouth, dropped her bundle of linens.

"Oh! Sorry!" Tesara whisper-shouted. "Let me help."

"Oh, no, Miss Tesara, I can do it."

"No, it was my fault, sorry."

They both knelt to pick up the linens and bumped heads. Tesara saw stars.

"Miss Tesara!" Noe snapped. "Let me do it, miss. You're a sight and you're getting everything all filthy."

Just like a rich merchant's daughter, to make more work for me, was the not-so-implied undertone.

"All right!" Tesara said, guilty and annoyed. She got to her feet, but the damage was done.

"Miss Tesara, is that you?" Mrs Francini said, coming out of the kitchen. She took in Tesara's bedraggled appearance, and her tight-lipped expression gave Tesara to understand that she was just – barely – holding her tongue on her opinion. Tesara was surprised at how low that made her feel, to have disappointed the kind cook. She had been so patient with Tesara when she had been impersonating a maid, and had forgiven her when it had all been found out. Had it been Alinesse, Tesara would surely have been impertinent with her. Instead, she said humbly, "I'm so sorry, Mrs Francini – and Noe – I didn't want to make a fuss and bother you."

Noe snorted and stomped off.

Mrs Francini sighed. "Change your clothes, Miss Tesara. Noe will see to your dress."

Tesara was in her dressing gown toweling her hair, the silk gown given over to Noe's capable hands and surly demeanor, when a quiet knock came at the door. Yvienne poked her head in.

"May I?"

Tesara nodded. Yvienne entered and sat down on the bed, leaning back against the headboard, hugging the pillow. In her dressing gown and with her loose braid, she looked shockingly young and far less severe than the face she usually presented to the world. When she spoke, though, she was her usual forthright self.

"How was your night?"

"One thousand guilders, clear," Tesara said. She met Yvienne's eyes in the mirror, and her sister was gratifyingly shocked. "Mrs Fayres is depositing it into my account tomorrow."

"Good God," Yvienne said, simply stunned.

"Unfortunately, there's bad news. I've been banned."

"What did you do?" Yvienne said.

"Vivi! I'm insulted."

"Tes..."

"All right," Tesara said with a sulk. She explained about the lieutenant. "He was abominable, Vivi. You would have approved."

"I do approve, Tes, but if people start to talk..." Yvienne stopped.

They would put two and two together, and soon it would get about exactly what happened the night Trune disappeared, and all the other strange things that happened around the younger Mederos girl. They would even, potentially, tie her back to the missing fleet. Tesara began to work a comb through her hair, studying her reflection in the shadowy mirror. "It doesn't matter," she said lightly, refusing to meet her sister's eyes. "I'll just find a new game."

"Is that wise?" Yvienne asked. "Mrs Fayres's establishment is one thing; she's a smart businesswoman. She knows what would happen to *her* if anything happened to you. But any of the other gambling dens or casinos – they're barely a step up from the docks."

Tesara rolled her eyes. "I'm not Uncle Samwell. I

wouldn't play on the docks. I'm just saying there are other establishments that are of a respectable level with Mrs Fayres's."

"And what if there's another lieutenant and another ban, and another? Word will get out, Tes. Remember Trune."

"Trune's long gone," Tesara pointed out.

"There will always be men like him, who seek to use your talents to their advantage."

"If it's all I have, shouldn't I use it?" Tesara said. At Yvienne's protest she lifted a hand. "I'm not like you, Vivi. I can do two things. I can make odd things happen, and I can gamble. I'd rather not do the first, and now I'm banned from the second. I'm not sure what else I can do."

To her credit, Yvienne didn't try to dissuade her. "You're right," she said at last. "I know. I just wish–"

The muffled sound of something dropping outside the door caught their attention. Tesara and Yvienne immediately silenced and looked at one another. Tesara gave a quizzical shrug at Yvienne's questioning look. She tiptoed over to her door, then pulled it wide.

It was Noe, scrambling to pick up the same armful of linens that Tesara had knocked out of her arms before breakfast.

"Oh!" both girls said. Yvienne came up behind Tesara.

"I can help now. I'm all clean," Tesara said, her voice bright.

"No!" Noe almost shouted it, and she gathered up the sheets in a careless wad. "Let me be to do my work, miss."

She hurried off, trailing a bit of sheet and treading on it.

"What was that about?" Yvienne said, staring after the departing girl.

"I didn't know there was that much laundry," Tesara said. She gave a guilty thought to the dress she had so heedlessly added to Noe's workload. "Maybe that's why she doesn't like me."

"Interesting," Yvienne said, lost in thought.

"What? Laundry?"

"Not that. And you're imagining things. She barely talks to me. No, I meant about the linens. All the sheets were changed and aired last night, and the linen warmer is downstairs by the kitchen."

That was true. "She had them this morning, too. I bumped right into her outside the dining room," Tesara said.

"Someone carrying an armful of linens could reasonably be considered to have legitimate business, going from one place to another in a household," Yvienne mused.

"So if she were found loitering outside a closed door, for instance, she was just walking past and could never be suspected of eavesdropping," Tesara finished. "What do you think she's plotting?"

"Whatever it is, she's quite inept," Yvienne said. "It rather makes me long for Mathilde. Now there was a conniving maid. We should keep an eye on her, nonetheless."

"Agreed," Tesara said. She stifled a yawn. The night's excitement and the morning's emotion caught up to her all of a sudden. "Sorry. Long night."

Yvienne gave her a teasing smile. "It's going to be a long day, too."

"What! Why?" Then Tesara remembered. With a groan, she flung herself onto her bed. She had been so looking forward to a long, leisurely sleep, rising only for tea... "Elenor Charvantes's luncheon."

"Indeed." Yvienne looked at the small watch pinned to her bodice. "By my calculation, you have time for a nap only."

"Oh, Vivi, must I go? I'm so *tired*." Tesara knew she

sounded much like her twelve year-old self but she didn't care. After last night, the last thing she wanted was to visit with merchant women and their daughters, all of whom would be angling for gossip about the two Mederos sisters and their errant parents.

"Nonsense. This is Elenor's first informal party as a married woman. Of course we're going. Better get some sleep – I'll wake you in time to dress."

Chapter Five

A knock interrupted Abel Fresnel as he finished tying his tie at the round mirror over the cheap deal dresser. He picked up the small pearl-handled pistol on the battered dressing table and palmed it. It was a lady's gun but no less dangerous for all that. He liked the way it felt in his hand.

He positioned himself behind the door, ready to slam it closed if he didn't like what was on the other side.

"Who is it?"

"Front desk, Mr Fresnel. You have two letters, sir."

Still cautious, Abel opened the door. The eager clerk waited with his post, his starched collar already wilting under the pomade applied to his hair. "And may I just say, sir, how honored we at the Bailet are–"

"Thanks," Abel said, taking the letters and closing the door on the clerk, with just enough time to see the man's expression turn from expectant to crestfallen. One of the occupational hazards of the Harrier profession was hero worship. The least the hotel could have done was put him up in a better room, if they expected to fawn over him, he thought. The space was small, cramped, and narrow. It was little more than a sailor's rest, but at least Abel had the place to himself. He could put the washbasin outside the door when he finished, and a maid came by and emptied it. There was a water closet at the end of the hall. Best of all, Abel was able to jigger the lock to his room so that the master key wouldn't be able to open it.

The first letter was an invitation to come to the Charvantes house for a meeting with the Merchants' Guild to:

discuss the tenor and direction of the investigation into the criminal and civil activities of former Guild liaison P. Trune.

The other note was a letter from his mother, to idle eyes anyway. Abel ignored the florid, breathless feminine script littered with phrases about how she missed her darling son, her rheumatism, and gossip about the neighbors. He ran his fingers across the rough paper, picking up the tiny pricks and bumps of a carefully lettered code.

Contact in Port Saint Frey has identified the younger Mederos girl as an unnatural. Find her and bring her in alive. Exercise extreme caution. She is believed dangerous.

An unnatural. No wonder Doc had a special interest. The Harrier Agency was always looking for unnaturals – and if Doc couldn't find them, he had ways to encourage the talents of his Harriers. Abel wondered if Doc had sent him to Port Saint Frey with this second job in mind or if it had come to his attention after Abel had been dispatched. The letter was undated and unfranked, meaning it hadn't come by the mail coaches that trundled along the coast. While that passage was secure, the mail took ten days and multiple stages to carry letters between Great Lake and Port Saint Frey. Doc had sent this coded letter via the express riders who galloped their spry, lean ponies down through the Chahoki empire and across the Desert Sea. The fearless riders were able to shave the time to five days, but they were expensive, and many a letter pouch languished under the bones of a painted pony and its orphan rider, shot down by Chahoki horse soldiers wielding their fearsome repeating rifles. Doc was lucky though; his letters always got through.

This was the first instruction he had received since he had come to town two days ago. Three weeks previously a request for the services of the Harrier Detecting Agency came to Doc Farrissey's offices in Great Lake. Doc had dispatched Abel alone, and he had made the journey via stagecoach westward through Chahoki territory and then down the coast through the Ravenne Protectorate. He had sent word to Guild headquarters that he had arrived and waited orders. This was the first time they deigned to reach out to him.

Abel had not been cooling his heels for the last two days. He was a Harrier, and a Harrier always got his man, and part of that success had to do with understanding the client as well as their target. He had the kind of unassuming demeanor that made people comfortable, and he listened – to the gossip, the constables, the gents o' the night who would ramble on for the cost of a glass of whiskey or a pint of ale. He had gleaned a lot in the past two days, and all of it would be enormously useful in both of his jobs – the one for the Guild, and the one for Doc. Because while Doc might have thought the two were completely unrelated, Abel had discovered that the Guild, the Guildmaster, and now the unnatural younger Mederos girl, were all entirely intertwined. And after meeting the self-possessed elder sister, he was more certain than ever that whatever happened during the Great Fraud, the girls had something to do with it.

When Abel was eight years old, nearly twenty years before, his father indentured him to Doc Farrissey as an errand boy. A roof over his head and a trade and not too many beatings – it was the best he could hope for. He liked being told to run fast on his deliveries, and he liked threading through the crowds, his wiry little body ducking and dodging, taking all the short cuts at a sprint. He didn't like the cursing and the beating, and he didn't like the fact that he never had enough to eat, and he missed his mother. Once he took time out after delivering a message to one of Doc's cronies to divert down a familiar alleyway to his old house. There he perched like a small gargoyle on top of a back wall and watched his mother hanging out clothes in the narrow strip of yard behind the house. He almost called out to her when his father saw him and gave a yell.

Abel had been so startled he fell off the wall, had the wind knocked out of him, and was caught by the old man. He got beaten twice – once by his father, who told him never to come back, that it was a breach of contract; and once by Doc.

When he was nine, he was summoned to Doc's office. Doc was a big man, with a big stomach and a big black beard. To a kid, he was a giant. He handed Abel a thimbleful of liquid and told him to drink. For all Abel knew, it was strong spirits. He drank eagerly, thinking it was a sign that Doc would treat him like one of the big boys, and almost immediately his throat and stomach burned as if he had drunk lye. He couldn't scream, just clawed and grasped at his throat, and when it was over and he was still alive, Doc knelt beside him and put Abel's limp fingers around his wrist.

"What can you tell?"

"Everything," Abel managed to whisper.

Doc chuckled. "I knew you had it in you, boy. Just needed to bring it out."

By the time he was fifteen, he very nearly didn't need to touch his target to know if they were hiding something. He could almost tell their very thoughts, but he usually didn't need that much detail. Emotion, unease, small tics and changes in expression – all were as revealing as a confession.

Doc always said it took an unnatural to find an unnatural. This wasn't the first time he had been tasked to bring in such a person of interest. Dangerous though she might be, the Mederos girl stood no chance against a Harrier.

Whistling, Abel sauntered down the stairs to breakfast in the hotel dining room.

Chapter Six

What Price Peace of Mind?

It has been six months since the scourge of Port Saint Frey, the so-called Gentleman Bandit, last terrorized the city. The Chief Constable and the city constabulary have pointedly said little about the progress of their investigation into the identity of the scoundrel and the likelihood of his capture, but their silence speaks volumes.

What is known is this – the Gentleman Bandit's career ended as abruptly as it began and it coincided with another disappearance, that of Guildmaster Trune, the mastermind and perpetrator of the Great Fraud. Rumor has it that the curious events at the address of One Hundred Fourteen High Crescent were enlivened by the presence of the bandit, and that his role was both pivotal and yet unexplained.

The city has a right to know. Who is this man? Why has he not yet been apprehended? If he has given up his life of crime, will he walk among us unmolested by justice, or has he fled the city to take up his career among other peaceful people?

We demand that the Chief Constable tell us what he plans to do to capture the Gentleman Bandit and bring him to justice.

Editors, The Gazette

Georges Kerrill, Head of House Kerrill, smacked the paper and threw it down on the gleaming oak table in Jax Charvantes's billiards room, where the board members of the Merchants' Guild met in conference with Abel Fresnel. "I'm telling you, Fresnel, you need to do something about this," he said in his bullying way. "The whole town is going to hell in a handbasket." He puffed on his cigar, blowing out a rich, acrid cloud. A golden brandy in a crystal snifter rested by his elbow.

Abel sat back, feigning ease to cover his irritation. Kerrill was one of those men he disliked the most – he had no understanding of power, and therefore wielded it like a bull in a china shop, rather than with surgical precision. Face it, he told himself. You just don't like being yelled at.

"First things first, Mr Kerrill," he said, his accent smooth and sophisticated, meant to intimidate. There was no point in laying on the country bumpkin routine he had tried on Miss Mederos. That would have been lost on Kerrill. "I've been hired to find your Guildmaster. Other crimes will have to wait."

"Don't groat and guilder me," Kerrill said. He settled back into his armchair with irritation, his striped waistcoat straining over his bulk. "We're paying you Harriers enough."

With no warning, his son Amos cursed a bad shot at the billiards table, and smacked the cue onto the mahogany edge. "You've a rotten bad table, Charvantes."

Abel didn't have to look at Jax Charvantes to feel his wince from across the room.

"Hold on, hold on," said another merchant, making a placating gesture. Abel identified him: Havartá, the mild-mannered head of House Havartá and a self-styled peacemaker. He had been at the house on that fateful night. So far he had ducked Abel's questions, telling him hastily it was never the right time, and to call at his office for an appointment. The spare, thin man went on. "Why don't we settle down to business, while the ladies chat in the salon? We've got a lot to cover, don't we?"

"Fine, fine. I don't know what we have to discuss. Let's just get on with it," the elder Kerrill said. "Put that damned thing down, Amos, and sit and be quiet."

Amos sulked some more, but they finally all settled, seven of the top merchants in the city, the cream of the Guild.

It was late afternoon, and while their ladies visited in the salon upstairs they had gathered at the home of Jax Charvantes to discuss the Guild and Trune. The luncheon had started at noon. Abel had been directed to come at two; and he had cooled his heels in the anteroom while the convivial crowd had their luncheon. He had caught a glimpse of the ladies as they followed the young Mrs Charvantes, the wife of the ambitious lieutenant who was their host, and he spied Miss Mederos and her sister.

And he continued to wait, while Amos Kerrill whined, his father blustered, and the rest of the merchants eyed him with deep misgivings.

For a group invested in bringing their errant Guild liaison to justice, they were acting as if they didn't want Abel to get started.

Finally, Mr Havartá managed to bring the group under his control.

"Our thanks to Lieutenant Charvantes for his hospitality," he said. "And welcome to Mr Fresnel. Your organization comes highly recommended, and no doubt you'll get to the bottom of this. Unfortunately, I myself am quite busy – we'll have to make an appointment – but I'm sure the others will be happy to discuss with you what they know."

Lupiere coughed, and TreMondi just rolled his eyes.

Abel took out his small notepad and pencil, and prepared to take notes. He had not been able to shake hands with any of the gentlemen – apparently in Port Saint Frey a merchant did not touch those of a lower class, but made a slight bow instead. It was a small setback. He could tell almost as much from what was unspoken as he could from his acute sense of touch.

"Very good, gentlemen," he said. "Now, tell me the last time you saw your Guild liaison Trune."

Kerrill leaped in with a snort. "This is a waste of time. Do you mean he doesn't even know what happened? What are we paying him for anyway?"

"Georges, Georges," Havartá said. "Patience. The man has to start at the beginning. Please. Just tell him what you know."

"I don't know anything," Kerrill said, truculent in his voice and expression. One of those men who is always apoplectic, Abel thought. "I wasn't at the last meeting. You – all of you – were there. But not I. So you can't pin anything on me."

"Georges, no one is pinning–" Havartá began. He controlled himself. "Please. If you don't care to speak, let someone else talk for now."

Kerrill subsided with another snort, and Lupiere spoke up. "We were invited to a meeting of the senior council of the Guild. Trune called us to dinner, we discussed Guild business, there was a disruption–"

Kerrill could no longer stay silent. "None of that is important. What's important is that the youngest Mederos sister was at the house that night, and we all know she did something. She can do things. We all know this. Amos, tell them." He smacked his son on his shoulder. The young man stumbled forward, his pugnacious face flushed.

"Dad, quit," he whined. His father made another threatening smack, and Amos shrank back. "All right! All right! She can do things with her hands – she makes these sparks and they go right through you."

Kerrill scowled at his son's inadvertent sexual innuendo, and the older men hid smirks. Abel just listened, drawing his tiny spoon through a delicate thimble of espresso. Kerrill made his useless son sit down, and Havartá said hastily, "Yes, well, we saw something too that night – the chandelier came down on us, and then Trune's man said there was an intruder. When he went out to confront the bandit, there was a great commotion, and then the girl and the bandit were gone, and when we got out of the dining room, Trune and his man were trussed up."

Abel spoke up. "And that was the last time you saw Trune?"

Everyone looked around at each other, awaiting confirmation. Once again, Havartá took the lead. "Yes, that is correct."

"Who untied Trune and his man?"

"Well – we all did," Havartá said, puzzled. "I mean, inasmuch those of us who were there. I don't know who specifically–"

"And he said nothing of who attacked him and rescued the girl?" At their expressions, Abel revised, "I mean, interfered by taking the girl?"

"He was shaky, as one can imagine," Havartá interposed. "Livid, too. Incoherent. He was berating all of us – his man, for allowing the intruder, and Parr for his attempting to help. I'm sure I've never seen the man in such a rage."

"Parr?" Abel said. He had not heard the name before.

"Barabias Parr," TreMondi said. He smirked. "A weak sort of fellow, no backbone or spirit. He was another one who said the girl could do things. He threw in with Trune and disappeared along with him."

"He was a friend of Samwell Balinchard, an uncle on the distaff side of House Mederos," Havartá explained. "He had special knowledge of the girl, and that was the sole reason he was at the dinner that night, as he was not part of the Guild board of directors."

There were a couple of chuckles around the room. Apparently the Guild held this Parr in low regard. Abel nodded and jotted meaningless notes. "So, including the Guild directors, Parr, Trune and his man, the girl, and this bandit – these were the only ones at the house that night?"

"And servants, of course, but we saw none but Trune's man," Havartá said.

There was another glance around the room. They were hiding something else about that night.

"The bandit who took the girl – he's the one referred to as the Gentleman Bandit?" Abel asked.

"He is," Havartá said, with some relief, now that they were off the subject of Trune's last day. "He rained terror upon the city for several weeks. The Kerrill house was hit during young Amos's birthday party, and many of the other salons."

"He'd fire one pistol, terrorize everyone, guests would hand off their money, and he'd be gone before you could call for your men," Lupiere said. He grimaced, his thin lined face tensing with memory, and Havartá patted him once on the shoulder.

"We almost caught him, right, Dad?" Amos said eagerly. His father scowled at him.

"Well, we didn't, did we? Idiot. You had to have a party."

Abel took a tiny sip. The coffee was rich and heady. "So, why was the girl at Trune's house?"

There was a vast, profound silence. Even Amos went dead quiet, although he looked uneasily at his dad.

"I'm not sure it matters," Havartá said, breaking the spell. He glanced around at the others. "You are here to find out only where Trune has gone. He has completely ruined the reputation of the Guild, not to say embezzled funds. That's your mandate, Fresnel."

Abel nodded again, but another gentleman spoke up.

"No, that's not all," Jax Charvantes said. The young lieutenant was flushed, and he stood soldier-erect by the sideboard, the crystal brandy decanter clenched in one fist. "Whatever happened that night, Fresnel, the Mederos girl is involved somehow. If you want to find out what happened to Guildmaster Trune, you need to investigate House Mederos. The entire family is a blot on Port Saint Frey. The girls and their uncle! I'm not saying they don't have a right to justice, but the way they went about it: using their daughter to play at cards – cheating, I'm sure of it! – and behaving most abominably; it was shameful. We'll all be better off if we get to the bottom of this."

Abel cocked his head. "Didn't I see the Misses Mederos among the female guests? I'm sure that I saw them while I waited in your hall."

The merchants exchanged glances, and Charvantes turned a deeper red. "My wife is naive and singularly forgiving. The girls were all friends as children. I see no reason to prevent them from knowing one another – that is, until you provide us with the evidence, Fresnel."

"Well, look at it this way, Charvantes. If the Mederos girl is visiting with your wife, she isn't engaging in immoderate frisks," Havartá pointed out. Charvantes made an impatient face, as if such logic were beneath him.

"I would like to help, gentlemen," Abel said, "but as I told

Mr Kerrill, I've been engaged to find Guildmaster Trune, not uncover the malfeasance of House Mederos."

"And I'm telling you, you won't find one without the other!" Kerrill slammed down his fist on a leather-covered card table. "Those girls are up to something, Fresnel, and if you don't find out what it is, you Harriers can go to hell before we pay you a single groat!"

Abel remained impassive. Doc would take immense enjoyment in schooling Georges Kerrill in just how he extracted payment due. He drained the last sip of espresso and stood. "Well then, it's good the ladies are at hand. Shall we?" Abel looked around at all the men.

Charvantes stared, and then gave a short laugh. "You seriously don't mean to visit the ladies?"

"Why not?" Abel asked. "They're right upstairs. The girl in question is there, and I need to get a look at her. To solve the case of the missing Guildmaster, I will need to understand why he had an interest in her."

TreMondi snorted.

"Now look here, Fresnel." Charvantes broke the silence, looking around at the others for support. "You aren't – that is, you aren't one of us. I don't think we should bother the ladies. They don't need to be disturbed."

Havartá raised a hand. "Lieutenant," he said, and Charvantes stopped in mid-protest. "Fresnel is right. We have to let him do his job as he sees fit. Shall we all visit the ladies? We can introduce Mr Fresnel, he can take his measure of the Mederos daughters, and then I'm sure he would be more comfortable taking his leave."

Abel schooled his face to reveal nothing, but on the inside, the small impoverished indentured boy he had once been, raged. You have more power and respect than they will ever have, he told himself, but he didn't believe it.

"Right. Let's visit the ladies," Kerrill growled. Charvantes led the way.

Chapter Seven

Elenor Charvantes, *nee* Sansieri, laid down the paper from which she had been reading aloud, and her guests all murmured their dismay.

"Jax says that it's but the calm before the storm," she said. "That many times a career criminal goes dormant before escalating his crimes and becoming ever more dangerous."

As the ladies all exclaimed, Yvienne sipped her tea. She and Tesara perched on floral sofas in Elenor's parlor, Tesara trying to hide her yawns behind her fist. It was Elenor's first intimate party as a married woman, and thus an important part of her development as a hostess of the highest of society.

Mrs Sansieri and her daughters were there, as were the first circle of Port Saint Frey merchant families. It's a wonder we're invited, Yvienne thought. Indeed, some of the more respectable guests eyed them askance, though everyone was polite enough. However, Inigho Demaris's mother was in attendance, and Yvienne was trying to formulate a way to talk to the woman about her son's business tactics. Mrs Demaris was a haughty, formidable woman, with scalloped white hair that towered alarmingly, and a double strand of massive pearls that glowed against her wrinkled neck.

"I think it's frightening," said Lily Sansieri, Elenor's younger sister. "It's gotten so one can't even enjoy oneself when visiting friends. I don't know how I can stand to have a come-out party, if there's a chance the Gentleman Bandit breaks into one's house and robs one's guests."

Yvienne continued to sip her tea.

"Jax says that the city should hunt him down once and for all," Elenor said. "I do hope they catch him before he hurts someone and makes such a grave misjudgment that he cannot come back from it at all."

"And I hope that it's as the *Gazette* said, that he's gone on to greener pastures," Lily said, a bit ungenerously.

"Yes, let him fleece another flock," said the acerbic Mrs Demaris, and Lily flushed at the rebuke.

"I've been at two parties where he's made his appearance, and I got the distinct impression that he was a good man, if misguided," Elenor insisted.

Mrs Demaris snorted. "Elenor, you're a fool if you think these things don't escalate. And besides, Miss Tesara can speak first-hand to the Gentleman Bandit's demeanor."

Tesara looked startled, and Yvienne tensed. Had Mrs Demaris laid a trap for her sister? Tesara sipped her tea for a moment, as if to gather her composure. When she answered she was calm, and Yvienne's heart eased.

"It was rather frightening," she said. "But Elenor is right – I knew he wouldn't hurt me. It was only to prevent any of the gentlemen at the party from playing the hero."

Poor Mr Lupiere, Yvienne remembered. She had given him quite a fright.

"You see?" Elenor said, a mischievous if well-bred smile in her voice. "The mode of operation of our Gentleman Bandit is first and foremost quite well-mannered."

"Oh, surely you can't call him our Gentleman Bandit!"

cried a young lady, excitement bright in her eyes.

"Why not?" Elenor said. "He was well-dressed, and well-controlled, and kept everyone in line without resorting to crude violence. Even though he never spoke, his manner was gentle – except for his pistols, of course."

The hubbub rose once more at her quiet defense of the scoundrel. Under cover of the rising conversation, Tesara elbowed Yvienne with a barely perceptible nudge. Yvienne kept a straight face.

Interesting, Yvienne thought. Elenor had started out the conversation with *Jax says,* but she finished it with her own opinion. Yvienne knew little of the dashing lieutenant her friend had married – the Mederos sisters had *not* been invited to the wedding – but it had been made clear that if there were to be any opinions in the Charvantes's marriage, they would be Jax's. Elenor was not as entirely defeated as all that, thankfully.

"And the thievery," her mother interjected. "He wasn't there to dance, my dear. He was there to rob."

"Yes, but he was always a gentleman," Elenor persisted. She threw a glance around the room, and her gaze lit upon Yvienne. "Don't you agree, Yvienne?"

Yvienne smiled and set down her teacup. "Indeed, Elenor. From everything I've heard, he was a perfect gentleman."

"That's right, you never encountered him," Elenor exclaimed. "I wonder why, when we all have our stories of him, that you would be the only one who does not?"

One part of Yvienne noticed Tesara looking away as if lost in thought and uninterested in the conversation. Only her sister's hands, gripping the delicate porcelain cup so hard her knuckles were white, betrayed her. Another part of Yvienne wondered – did Elenor, shy, quiet, mannerly Elenor – *guess*?

"I was a governess during those six months and had no occasion to join in the revels," she said. She looked over at Mrs TreMondi, the bronze-skinned Chahoki woman who had fallen in love with and married Alve TreMondi of House TreMondi. "How are the girls, Mrs TreMondi? And Dubre?"

Mrs TreMondi looked at her, her smile bright against her earthy skin. "They are very well, Yvienne. They bade me tell you they wish you could come and teach them again. Even Dubre says he would much rather do maths taught by you than by the Academy Masters."

"I would love nothing more, Mrs TreMondi, but I am afraid that the business of House Mederos keeps me busy these days," Yvienne said. "Please tell the children I would be happy to show them about our offices if they would like another lesson in merchant economics."

"I am sure they would love such an excursion," Mrs TreMondi said. "May we call on you at your earliest convenience?"

"Of course," Yvienne said. It was as cordial as could be, except for the way the rest of the ladies cut their eyes at each other.

"All I want to say is, if the Gentleman Bandit ruins my come-out, I shall be cross," said Lily Sansieri, with an exaggerated pout. Since Lily, like all of the Sansieris, was vastly good-natured, this brought a laugh.

"Knowing you, Lils, you would ask him to dance and dinner," teased another young friend.

"Only if he took off his mask," Lily came back in an instant.

"I say, what if he *is* one of us?" one of the young ladies gasped.

Yvienne took note of who gasped and protested, and who did not – and mostly the mamas did not. Merchant women were not stupid – they were merchants themselves, and like Alinesse ran their homes as well as their Houses. If I were a gambler like Tesara, she thought, I would wager that one of these women has already speculated that the Gentleman Bandit was a lady.

She glanced again at Mrs Demaris. Under cover of the general merriment and scandalized excitement of the younger set, Mrs Demaris was expounding at great length to Mrs TreMondi. Seeing her chance, Yvienne excused herself from her sister, and went over to talk with her.

"How do you do, ma'am?" Yvienne said, sitting next to her.

With a polite air of relief, Mrs TreMondi turned her back to them and engaged Mrs Havartá in conversation.

Mrs Demaris eyed her with a hawkish glance. "Well enough. And that's all the small talk I can abide. I hear you are running things now," she said. "Probably for the best. Your father was coasting, my dear. Better for everyone to acknowledge it. And your mother lost her fire."

"I do my best," Yvienne said, irked, even though inwardly she agreed.

"Hmmph. False modesty. You've got the brains and the knack. So what do you want with me?"

"What is Inigho's real game?"

Loud giggles from the other end of the parlor gave their conversation cover. As the young ladies sat down to a childish game of lottery tickets and the other mamas chatted, Mrs Demaris and Yvienne Mederos talked business.

It was a gambit designed to impress Inigho's formidable mother and flatter her to think she was privy to her son's business dealings. Or not flatter exactly, Yvienne thought, but to assure her that Yvienne knew the old woman was not out of the game yet but was a full partner in House Demaris.

As she expected, Mrs Demaris's old eyes gleamed.

"Every merchant's game is to make money," the old woman said. "But you mean with the contract. That was my doing – an attention-getter, no more."

"It worked. Of course we won't sign it, it's ridiculous." Yvienne waved it away as if the idea were a bothersome gnat. "But it gave me food for thought."

"He's a good man," Mrs Demaris said, quite unexpectedly. Yvienne experienced a start of surprise. "He's not pretty, but he's got brains, I'll give him that. And depths, my dear. He has depths."

What on *earth*? Stunned, Yvienne said, "Are you *matchmaking*?" The contract was a matchmaking overture?

"Why not?" Mrs Demaris said. Her voice dropped, and she and Yvienne sat head to head. "A connection between our two Houses – you wouldn't have to worry about the reputation of House Mederos anymore."

How absurd, Yvienne thought. Uncle Samwell had been right about the contract – but for the wrong reasons. "I'm flattered," she said, shaking her head. "But I'm not ready to form that kind of connection."

Mrs Demaris snorted. "Girls these days. What's the delay? You'll have to marry someone, and what are your choices? Amos Kerrill?"

They both looked over at Mrs Kerrill. This unprepossessing woman, mousy and tired, was entirely caught up in the game the girls were playing. She had seven other children besides Amos, and it was widely known that her husband bullied her terribly. Yvienne knew what Mrs Demaris was trying to convey – the apple wouldn't fall far from that tree. They turned away from the unsuspecting and unfairly targeted lady, and back to each other.

"I have nothing against Inigho," Yvienne said. "Except

for that ludicrous contract. Anyway, I have no intention of marrying soon, and when I do marry, I intend to consider the needs of my House as well as the needs of myself."

Odd, she thought. She had never once considered marriage or her requirements for it. She had only known that she would marry someday. But I do have requirements, she thought, and it would be foolish not to consider them.

"Girls," Mrs Demaris said. "Heads full of nonsense. I hadn't expected it of you."

Yvienne ignored her disdain. "I have a business proposition for Inigho," she said. "Will he be interested, do you think?"

"He's a merchant," Mrs Demaris said. "Of course he'll be interested."

"Then I will send to his office for an appointment," Yvienne said.

"I'll tell him to dress for company," his mother said, wryly.

A rap at the door caught their attention, and the men filed into the room following Jax Charvantes. The women greeted their husbands with a general air of merriment, and under cover of the hubbub Yvienne scanned each one. Six months ago Tesara had been captured by Trune and paraded in full view in front of many of the men in this parlor. All of those men were now arrayed before them.

She looked across the parlor at her sister. Tesara's gloved hands were clenched in her lap, a small, pursed smile her fixed expression. *Prisms and prunes,* Yvienne remembered. Their old nurse Michelina used to tell them that. A lady arranged her features in a pleasing fashion by mouthing the words *prisms and prunes* for the correct effect.

Her sister's hands were glowing through her gloves. Yvienne froze. No one was paying attention to the younger Mederos daughter, but if anyone looked at her...

Yvienne dropped her teacup. It tumbled to the floor, splashing the dregs onto her skirt and the embroidered pouf that she and Mrs Demaris had been conversing over. She leaped to her feet.

"Oh dear!" she said. "Elenor, I do apologize. I'm so clumsy. In front of the gentlemen too," she added with as much distress as she could muster.

"Oh," Elenor said, flustered, because she had risen to greet the gentlemen, and now had to attend to her guests.

"Never mind, dear," said Mrs Sansieri, and she gestured to the servant to clean the small spill. The older ladies all clustered around, clucking with disappointment at the disaster, and all giving advice to prevent stains. Their daughters were bright-eyed with suppressed laughter. Oh, the gossip to come, Yvienne thought. She exchanged glances with Tesara. There was no longer any sign of a glow, and her sister gave the tiniest nod. She breathed a sigh of relief.

"Our fault, our fault," boomed Mr Havartá in a joshing way. "Come now, ladies, we didn't mean to cause a fuss."

Then the last man filed into the room and Yvienne had the distinct feeling that her day had gone from bad to disastrous.

"Ladies," Mr Havartá said. "May I present Abel Fresnel? He's a Harrier, come to investigate the doings of last year. Abel Fresnel, the treasure of Port Saint Frey."

The Harrier looked out of place in the fine company of well-dressed merchants and lovely ladies. He glanced over at Yvienne, took in the mess of tea on her skirts and gave a brief nod, which she returned, having the distinct impression he knew exactly what she had done.

As hostess, Elenor came forward to meet him. Jax Charvantes hastened to intercept. "My wife, Elenor Charvantes."

Elenor went to curtsey, just as Abel stuck out his hand, instead of bowing. The room was charged with a shock that had nothing to do with Tesara.

"Oh," Elenor said, and instead of finishing her curtsey, she did the polite thing to make her guest feel at ease. She reached out and took his hand.

Such a simple thing, thought Yvienne, and yet so much happened. Everyone was frozen around them, the young girls bright with laughter and shock at the scandalous false step, the mamas disapproving. The men verged on shock too, but also anger, and of them Jax Charvantes was almost apoplectic with fury at Abel's transgression.

In a second it was over and everyone could breathe again. Yvienne looked from Elenor, breathless and red-faced, to Abel, whose expression was one of a man bemused, to Jax Charvantes.

Yvienne felt something akin to pity. In his eagerness to ruin House Mederos, Jax Charvantes had to watch his wife fall in love with another man.

Chapter Eight

The Port Saint Frey Constabulary warns all citizens that any attempt to take advantage of Fog Season with deceit, mummery, fraud, banditry, robbery, burglary, or other felonious activity will be met with the stiffest penalties. §§ *The* Iderci Empress *has been sighted off the coast of the Emerald Islands, according to the Canterra mail packet just docked; House Iderci has beat the local speed record by two days, set by the* Lupiere Hycynthia. *House Lupiere was not available for comment.*

THE GAZETTE

Bravo, Papa! Yvienne thought upon reading the news. She had been hoping for such a report in the two weeks since her parents set sail. Her father must be ecstatic. He was no doubt chalking up the ship's speed to his advice to the captain. She scanned the rest of the paper, making mental notes of the commodity and stock prices, and reading the advertisements for shoes, tooth powder, harnesses, stays, and in the help wanted notices, household help. There was always a shortage of housemaids.

She looked up from the paper as her sister entered the breakfast room. Tesara was dressed in a warm nightgown, a voluminous bathing robe, and slippers. Yvienne snickered.

"Don't make fun," Tesara complained. "I'm freezing, Vivi. Can we have more fires?"

"Have some coffee. And Mrs Francini has made the best porridge. I swear, I thought Mathilde's was the best I had ever tasted, but I think that was because it was so soon after that nasty slop we were served at Madam Callier's. Mrs Francini puts whiskey in hers."

Tesara slid into her chair with difficulty. She helped herself to porridge, steaming under its cover, and Yvienne poured her coffee.

"You know we can't have more fires," Yvienne continued, but she could sympathize. It was dreadful being rich and poor at the same time. She was working on expanding the company business and it was starting to pick up, but for now fires were an expense that had to be limited. *At least we have enough food. And we can pay our staff. And business is growing, though if that blasted Harrier would just leave town, it would pick up faster.* His mere presence was making potential partners skittish, or in the case of Inigho Demaris, opportunistic. Inigho had accepted her offer of a meeting, at least. She would make him explain himself. The match might have been his mother's idea, but she had no doubt the contract was all Inigho's.

Tesara sighed, blowing across her coffee. "I know. I'm only complaining for form's sake. Black sheep, you know."

"They're away. You don't have to keep doing it," Yvienne said, her voice softened. It wasn't easy for her little sister, and never had been. She had always been a bit of a disappointment to their parents, who couldn't understand her scattered nature or her dislike of anything to do with business. It was utterly impossible to tell their parents about Tesara's unusual talents, both her singular power or her card-playing gifts. They would deny the first and disparage the second, as if anything that Tesara touched was of no value. It was the same with Uncle Samwell, she realized with a pang. She herself had been guilty of the same attitude toward him. Two black sheep, both the youngest in their respective families. When had anyone ever had confidence in them?

"What?" Tesara said, at her long silence. Yvienne just smiled and shook her head.

"Nothing. I'm a bit distracted this morning," she said.

"It's the cold," Tesara agreed. "You simply can't concentrate. Your mind is slowing; your very thoughts are freezing…" She shrieked and batted away the toast that Yvienne threw at her.

The door opened and they both turned to look as Uncle Samwell staggered into the room, wrapped in a loud bathing robe, a bath towel wrapped around his shoulders for extra warmth.

"Yvienne, what are you going to do about the fires?" he grumbled. He squeezed into a chair at the end of the table, reached a long arm over to the covered bowl of porridge and gave the contents a hard stare when he lifted the lid. "Good God. Has there been another fraud?"

"It's lovely and it's good for you," Yvienne said, her voice tight. Why couldn't he have slept in, as he had been doing?

With great deliberation Samwell recovered the porridge, and poured himself coffee. "I'll breakfast at the docks," he said, stirring in three lumps of sugar and a dollop of cream. "I'm surprised, Vivi. I expected you to manage things better. Or no – did you give over the household duties to Tesara?" Tesara stuck her tongue out at him, which he missed, but she otherwise slumped back into her robe like a disgruntled cat.

"Speaking of households, I heard an interesting tidbit at Aether's," Samwell went on, after taking a sip. "Vivi, are you fixing your interest on Inigho Demaris?"

Tesara turned to look at her, shock and horror in her expression.

Yvienne rolled her eyes. Oh, those Names – the worst gossips in the world. It was part of the reason the principal investors and insurers in Port Saint Frey were so wealthy, but she wanted to box their hairy old ears. She had no intention of letting Uncle Samwell know for sure she had an appointment with Inigho Demaris later that week.

"Never you mind," she said. "Eat your porridge, uncle. It's good for you."

"Vivi, they haven't been gone two weeks. You don't need to turn into your mother quite so soon."

"Apparently I do," she snapped.

"Seriously, Yvienne. Or rather, you can't be serious," Tesara put in. "Married?"

Yvienne made a face. "You two are terrible. I'm not planning to marry him. He proposed–"

"Ah hah!" they chorused.

"–a *business* arrangement, which you, uncle, had a hand in. I am proposing a counter offer – strictly business – to get better terms."

Uncle Samwell slammed his flat hand onto the table, making the crockery jump. "So you see? It was my doing. I told you, you underestimate my value to the family."

"If by value, you mean bringing the business deal to my attention, yes, of course. But it was impossible to sign without negotiations."

"Well, I knew *that,*" Samwell muttered.

The girls exchanged glances.

Yvienne drained the last of her coffee and stood. "You two

finish breakfast. Albero and Mrs Francini have the monthly household accounts to go over so I'm off to the kitchen."

"See if there are sausages," Samwell called after her.

"Eat your porridge," she called back, and closed the doors on his groan.

At her approach Albero and Mrs Francini stood up from the kitchen table. Yvienne waved them back to their seats. Noe was somewhere else – she made a mental note to see if the girl lurked around anywhere.

"More coffee, Miss Yvienne?" Mrs Francini asked with her usual good cheer.

"No, thank you, Mrs Francini. I've had a cup with breakfast. The porridge was wonderful."

"It's just the thing to hold back the weather," Mrs Francini said. "I'm going to get a start on the noonday meal, so if you don't mind, I'll be at the stove while you two have your talk. I'll put in my two groats when necessary."

She turned her back to them, leaving Yvienne and Albero face to face. He was about three or four years older than Yvienne, far too young to be a butler, but he was steady and grave and took the responsibility well. Nearly seven years before, he was a skinny young footman, but by the time they had come home from Madam Callier's Academy for Young Ladies, he had grown a few inches and filled out.

She assumed he had forgiven her for her ruthless actions the night she rescued Tesara, but asking him about it would have only embarrassed the both of them. He seemed to have overcome it, maintaining his steady composure. She gave him a friendly smile.

"So what is the household report?" she asked him.

He turned the ledger around.

It was all meticulously presented. Alinesse had assured her that the household was well-managed between Albero and Mrs Francini, who rubbed along together like an old couple. Yvienne went down the list, running her finger along the expenses and the income.

"We did have a question," Albero said, hesitant. He pointed to the notation next to one of the entries. *Misc funds.* The notation appeared with some regularity down the neat columns, adding up to a tidy sum. "Madam Mederos asked us about that, and I didn't have an answer."

Mrs Francini turned around, and Yvienne knew at once that they had discussed this before confronting her. "I felt that bad, not knowing where the money had come from, and all I could tell her was that it came from you," Mrs Francini said.

Yvienne nodded, nary a flicker in her expression. "Oh, of course," she said lightly. "Mama asked me about that too, and I completely forgot to tell you what I told her." She stopped, heart hammering.

"And that was?" Mrs Francini prompted, when Yvienne said nothing more.

"Oh! Yes, of course. How silly. You see, that's from my governess days. Sometimes, Mrs TreMondi paid me extra wages. On the days I stayed over for astronomy lessons, or tutored Dubre TreMondi in maths so he stayed at the head of his class at the Academy."

There was a tiny pause, and then Albero and Mrs Francini both nodded. "Of course," Mrs Francini said.

"That makes sense," Albero said, with a judicious nod.

"Right," Yvienne said, thrusting down her guilt at lying to two of her favorite people. "Anything else?"

"No, that was it," Albero said.

"Good. All looks in order," she said. "Thanks, Albero and

Mrs Francini. Now I wanted to ask you both; you've taken on the tasks of a housekeeper between the two of you. Do we need to engage a professional in that capacity?"

She hoped they would say no. Adding staff would mean channeling more of their ill-gotten gains through the household, and she didn't want to lie more than she had to. But she couldn't understaff the house, not if it meant overworking her cook and butler.

The look that young Albero and wise Mrs Francini exchanged suggested a wordless communication. Mrs Francini said, "It's a very good idea, Miss Mederos. But Albero and I think that until your mother and father come back, and with the household so quiet, we can make do as we have been. When the House comes back into her own, then we can go to full staff. And I have no problem with training Noe in all her tasks, although she's a bit flighty, but then girls are these days."

Flighty was the least of Noe's faults, Yvienne thought, smiling with relief.

"So long as you both agree," she said. "Perhaps we can hire temporary staff as needed if anything comes up. But that brings me to another item. I'd like to shut off the southern rooms, including the solar, since it's Fog Season, as well as the third floor. Have a last fire burned to take the wet off and then cover the furniture."

"We'll have it done," Albero said. "Which reminds me, did Madam Mederos tell you what she wanted with the dumbwaiter?"

"Yes, and I've meant to ask what you think. I do think Mama might have taken a quite unreasonable dislike to the contraption, which if it worked, would be an asset to the household, would it not?"

To his credit, Albero's expression did not change. He had

seen her clamber inside it six months ago. It had been an asset back then too.

"Well, miss, when it worked it was quite useful. It has been jammed for the last six months." Albero looked away with a studious expression, and after a moment she realized that he was trying to keep from – *laughing*? Mrs Francini just looked at the two of them, and Yvienne bit her lip, trying to keep her composure.

"Did you ever see if you could determine what was wrong?"

"No, miss. I looked in the shaft and tugged on the ropes, but that was all. There was a bad smell, making me think food was left in it, and I mentioned as much, but Madam said only to keep it shut. She, ah, added that she didn't want to even have to think about the dumbwaiter any further. I didn't push the matter."

Wise of Albero. "I understand," Yvienne said. They couldn't afford to have the dumbwaiter taken out, and Alinesse didn't want it to be repaired. It was hard to navigate those waters. "Well, now is the time for us to act, and Mama had given me instructions. I don't like the idea of something potentially useful broken. Shall we look into it? Can you have the craftsmen who installed it come and take a look?"

"I will do, miss."

"Thank you, Albero. And you too, Mrs Francini. I'm looking forward to lunch."

"Roasted vegetables with anchovies and wine," Mrs Francini said with immense satisfaction.

Chapter Nine

Dear Tesara,

There was a space, as if Jone was using it to think, to show off his hesitation. Tesara had read the letter many times in the two weeks since the *Iderci Empress* weighed anchor.

I have much for which to apologize. My silence and my absence in the past six months cannot easily be excused or explained. I will try my best because you, above all, deserve that.

When we became friends again after so many years apart, I was the happiest I have ever been. We were more than friends – comrades in arms, perhaps, together against an unfeeling world, finding laughter where we could. With Mirandine, we were the three comrades, best of friends, best of – anything.

But I also began to dread seeing you – and Mira – because I knew – I have always known – it could never last. My family situation is such that my life and my choices were never mine to make. It would be easy to blame my mother for it, but I beg of you to understand and pity her because in her youth she was as constrained as I, as thwarted as I. Her life was not her own, and therefore neither would mine be.

It was her demand that I break it off with you, and though you think I am a coward, it was the right thing to do. You would never be happy in my world, for my world does not bring happiness, only decay, anger, frustration, and eventually, despair. I could not do that to you, darling – can I call you darling? I will, and if you do not like it you can say so in a letter back to me and I will receive it and understand. But now, when I can speak to you without your protest, I will call you darling, even as I state you can never be my darling.

I know – I know you think I have chosen Mira in your place. I have not. For while I could not bring you into my dreadful family, I could also not bring myself into Mira's. She is damaged, Tesara, damaged beyond repair, and she is brittle and ready to break. Though her last name is Depressis, she is a Saint Frey, through and through, and our union would be monstrous. I told her this. She ignored me. She went behind my back to my mother and told her that she would see to it that we married. It was a betrayal beyond anything I have ever imagined.

Too much, Tesara thought. It was as if the reticent, charming Jone Saint Frey had discovered that pen and ink had loosened his tongue beyond all discretion and consideration.

None of this is to excuse me. Nor will I be surprised if it does not fully explain. But I felt that my life was at a point at which I had to choose between harming a girl – you! – I had come to hold most dear to me, perhaps by fulfilling her greatest wish – and harming myself by choosing Mirandine Depressis.

Do you love me? Or does this letter grossly overstep and overstate the feelings I have thought you have held for me? If so, I apologize for presuming so laughably upon your friendship. And so tormented am I that I both want you to love me and hope you do not, that you are appalled by this letter and rightfully want to tear it up, because it will mean that I did not break your heart after all.

And so, I take the coward's way out. I will not choose. The options are disgusting to me. When you read this letter I will have sailed on the Iderci Empress *for a voyage of many months, perhaps years. When my contract is up on the* Empress, *depending on which port I find myself, I intend to either continue to sail, to put to use the hard-won skills with which I have supported myself, or, if the sea does not become me, to settle in some far-off country. I will be a Saint Frey no longer.*

And when I write you next, if you decide to answer, I hope you will answer that you can find it in your heart to forgive me at the least, or love me at the very most.

I am yours, forever,
Jone Saint Frey.

No matter how many times she read the letter, she felt a confusing onrush of emotions she could not parse. She should have been ecstatic over Jone's letter, or at the very least, smug. Was it not the point of a merchant girl's existence, to be courted by an eligible young man, to marry, and by investment of time, energy, and cunning increase the wealth of both their Houses? Six months ago, her parents had wanted her to consider the suit of Colonel Talios, for heaven's sake.

They would have frowned upon Jone's declaration of love, for certain – his family was hardly wealthy, for one, and she was hardly noble, for another. But her parents' disapproval could have nothing to do with her own feelings, which were all doubt and confusion.

Every time she read the letter and relived the kiss, her confusion deepened. I'm nineteen now, she told herself. Far too old to be acting like a silly, immature girl. But this felt too fast. She missed Jone and she missed their adventures, and she missed Mira too, but why did Jone have to say he was in love with her? It ruined *everything*.

She sighed. She hadn't written to him; it made little sense because no matter whether she wrote a letter and carried it down to the next mail packet that day or in six months, it would still take the same amount of time to reach him. And she didn't know what to say.

A rap came at the door and Tesara hastily shoved the letter into her dressing table drawer. "Come in," she called. Yvienne ducked in, and closed and locked the door behind herself.

"We have a problem," her older sister said without preamble. "Albero and Mrs Francini know the money we've been giving them from my escapades last summer isn't on the up and up. Mama had been asking about it, and I think they wanted to make sure they wouldn't get in trouble for a discrepancy."

Tesara sighed. If it wasn't one thing, it was another. "What did you tell them?"

"I said that it came from extra governess wages. But we can't keep giving it to them, now that I'm no longer governessing. And with the Guild investigation ongoing, we can't put it in the House Mederos account, right when an influx of monies would look suspicious." Yvienne bit her lip, her brow wrinkled. "I had hoped to be able to continue doling it out through the household account. Much the safest way to dispose of it."

"Oh, I can think of many ways," Tesara said with an impish look. She ticked off on her fingers. "Twenty-one, Seven card lady..." If I had access to a gaming house, she thought, I could turn that money into a fortune.

"Hush, you," Yvienne said. "But that brings me to another idea. You said that Mrs Fayres deposited the bulk of your winnings in your account. So a large amount of money won't be an anomaly. We need to put it in your account, and keep it there until people stop looking for it."

No one audited the personal accounts of the Bank of Port Saint Frey, or at least not of the merchant houses. The lesser merchants, the shopkeepers and tradespeople, made noises about that, but the Guild thus far had kept a stranglehold on the privilege.

"Easy enough," Tesara agreed. "How much is it?"

"Twelve hundred guilders."

Tesara nodded judiciously. "Most of that was from the Iderci salon, as I recall." It had been surprising to see the Gentleman Bandit break into the genteel gambling party that the fabulously wealthy Iderci family had thrown last summer. It had been astonishing to recognize her sister, dressed in men's clothing with a handkerchief across her face, and watch as she held the room at bay with two pistols and an air of complete aplomb. While Yvienne held Mr Lupiere hostage with a gun to his head, she had made Tesara gather up the money from the gambling tables, all without speaking a word, then fired one shot into the wall and fled into the night. Twelve hundred guilders was about right. "I'll take it to the bank this morning, after I dress," she said.

"I'll have Albero send for a hack," Yvienne said. "I don't

want you to walk around town with that much money."

"I don't think we have to worry about another Gentleman Bandit," Tesara pointed out with a grin. She flexed her fingers in a claw. "And even if we did..." She let the words trail away.

Yvienne gave her a look, but evidently decided to take it as a joke. Even though, Tesara thought, I am serious. But there was no need to worry her sister more than usual.

"That's settled then. I'll have a purse for you when you're ready to leave," Yvienne said.

A muffled noise outside the bedroom door caught their attention. Yvienne held a finger to her lips. Tesara listened, but there was only the one sound. With a quick motion, Yvienne pulled the door open, almost bowling over Noe, who was standing there with fireplace tools in a bucket.

The maid shrieked and jumped back with a rattle of firedogs, tongs, whiskbroom, and dustpan. "Miss Yvienne!"

"Oh, hello, Noe," Yvienne said, as if she had not nearly knocked the maid off her feet. "Come to clean the fireplace?"

"Yes, miss. Mrs Francini said that Miss Tesara doesn't like the smell of cold ashes." Noe glared at Tesara for good measure, as if her troublesome, sensitive nose was such a bother.

"But I'm afraid now is a bad time," Tesara said, in no mood to try to placate the girl. "Perhaps later."

Noe heaved a sigh, dipped a curtsey pointedly to Yvienne, and stomped off, her tools clanking. Yvienne closed the door behind her and leaned against it.

"I think you're right – she really doesn't like you," Yvienne said.

"More to the point, Vivi, do you think she heard?" Tesara said.

"Oh, most definitely. If she hadn't been trying to sneak,

she would have made quite a rattle with all that stuff. She was trying hard not to be heard."

"So what do we do? Sack her?" Tesara cast her memory over their conversation. "If she heard everything, she knows a lot and can guess the rest," she said. "What a bother, Vivi." Her heart sank. They had such rotten luck with housemaids.

Yvienne sighed. "I suppose we must, though I hate to do it. I'll have Mrs Francini keep a close eye on her for now, and make sure she can't cause any more mischief for today."

Tesara dressed quickly in her warmest clothes, camisole under her corset, a dress of thick dark red wool over a fine underdress, flannel stockings that had to be tied carefully or they would droop in the most annoying fashion, and oiled half-boots. She buttoned them up with the buttonhook and stood, shaking out the skirts. Her long overcoat of fine blue wool, her scarf and kid gloves, waited for her by the front door. She grabbed her small netted purse and looped the cord over her wrist and trotted down the stairs.

Yvienne and Albero were waiting in the foyer. Yvienne came over and under the pretext of a sisterly kiss, she slipped the fat wallet into Tesara's purse.

"Don't be gone too long," she advised. "You know how badly Fog Season settles in your lungs. Wrap up in your muffler."

"Yes, Mama," Tesara said, teasing. "Oh, Albero, tell Noe that now would be a good time for her to clean my fireplace ashes."

"I will let her know, miss. She's assisting Mrs Francini at the moment."

At the sound of a hack rolling up the circular drive, Albero gave a pleased hmmph.

"Goodness," Yvienne said. "Did you give the boy an extra guilder? He must have run as if on winged feet."

Albero paid the Edmorency's gardener's boy next door to send messages and hail cabs, an arrangement that pleased everyone concerned. Now he merely raised his eyebrow and said, "I'll be sure to reward such industry in the future, miss."

Albero helped Tesara into the ancient hack, which looked as if it were held together with rust, moldy fabric, and peeling paint. The horse looked equally as ramshackle, and the only sense she got of the driver was that he was a large man, swallowed up in an even larger greatcoat with a hat low over his eyes to keep off the drizzle.

"To the bank, please," Albero told the driver, and Tesara settled back against the seat.

Chapter Ten

The hack swayed and bounced on extended springs as it rumbled down the steep hill toward the city, at one point tilting alarmingly with a bounce. Tesara braced herself to keep from falling forward. As a child, she used to love the feeling of the carriage tilted at an extreme angle, and would beg Coachman Jone to make the horses take it at a gallop. To his credit, he never once gave in to her pleading.

The fog closed around the vehicle, and Tesara, peering out the window, could see little from her vantage point.

At the bottom of the Crescent, the carriage leveled out, and Tesara relaxed a bit. She flexed her fingers experimentally, and a bit of power coursed between them. Her fingers, crushed by Madam Callier when she was a child, ached as always – a Fog Season would always have that effect on them now, she thought. But it did little to dampen her power any more.

Then the carriage began to climb again, the horse surging against the harness. Tesara stopped flexing her fingers and frowned. Where was the cabbie going? She looked out the window again, but the fog was so thick, she could barely make out buildings, let alone signposts. It appeared they were in an alley off the main street. What on earth – was he taking a shortcut? She tsked and rapped the ceiling.

"Excuse me," she called out. "The most direct route is to go down Mercantile Row."

There was no response. Tesara rapped harder. The hack jerked to a stop. She pulled on the handle, but the door remained locked.

Oh. Oh, indeed. Tesara braced herself against the back of the seat and yanked off her gloves. Fear and nervous excitement gripped her. Once before she had been locked in a carriage. This time, she would fight back.

The driver pulled open the door, holding a pistol in one hand, with a pair of irons in the other, ready to slap around her wrists. He loomed over her, his face indistinct under a broad-brimmed hat and muffler.

"Now, my dear, you can either be a good girl and sit still," he said, "or I can lock you up and stuff a gag in your mouth. Your choice."

"Neither," she gritted, and pushed the power out through her fingers.

The man was blown backward; with a loud crack, the pistol discharged, shooting a hole in the ceiling of the carriage; and the horse reared and bolted, dragging the carriage behind him. The man fell away from the door and Tesara was tossed around as the cab ran over him with a bump and thud, reeling from side to side. She grabbed for a handhold, and was jounced without mercy.

With a last final jump, the cab tipped over, and Tesara rolled off the seat against the door of the carriage, banging her head and her elbow. The horse dragged the equipage a few more steps and finally came to a halt. Shaking, her face scraped and bleeding, Tesara got to her feet. She pushed open the door, now above her, and stood on the seat to pop her head out, looking around. Dark buildings loomed over her in the fog, but she had no idea where she was.

Blast and damn. Anger gripped her, taking over fear. She grabbed the purse, made sure it was tightly knotted, and pulled her way out of the carriage, sore and bruised. Tesara clambered down the muddy wheel to the ground. She stopped, listening, but heard nothing but the dripping of the rain. If the driver was nearby, assuming he was not dead or badly injured, he had not caught up yet. She was sickened by her memory of the man run over by the wheel. Could he have survived that?

If he had, he was in for more pain. She was furious at the attack, her heart and her fingers buzzing with electricity. She slowed her breathing, trying for calm. The horse was trembling and snorting. It had run into the end of the alley in its wild panic, and now was blocked by an old brick wall looming out of the fog, trapped by the overturned carriage.

"Whoa," she said to the horse, patting his neck, and the poor creature flinched, reacting to the electricity in her fingers. "Sorry, pet, sorry," she said, snatching her hand back. She felt dreadful leaving the poor thing, but unharnessing him would take too long, and she couldn't right the carriage, not by herself. "I'll find help, I promise," she told him.

She hurried down the alleyway, limping at first, but soon moving faster. There was no sign of the cabbie.

The alley opened into a street, and she got her first sense of where she was – near the small tradehouses north of Emery Place. She dodged into the first establishment she saw. The men working there looked up in shock at her sudden appearance. I must look quite wild, she thought. Her dress and coat were torn, her face raw and stinging, her hair a mess, and she had no gloves.

"Miss! Can I help you?" said the manager, a young man in shirtsleeves and suspenders.

"I'm so sorry to bother you," she said, trying to gain some control over her trembling voice. "My cabbie tried to rob me at gunpoint. He fired a pistol and the horse bolted, and the cab tipped over and I came here."

"That's dreadful!" the young man exclaimed. "Are you hurt? Should we call for a doctor? Bynge! Slyere! Go fetch the horse! Who was the cabbie, miss? Did you get his city number? He tried to rob you? What a scoundrel. We'll send for the constables."

"Yes, I think you should. It was quite dreadful." She felt a moment of grim satisfaction that the constables would deal with her driver, if they could find him. She let the young man lead her to a chair in his office. The workers all stared at her, until the manager told them to jump to and get back to work. They jumped to.

"Tea, miss? Or brandy?"

"Neither, thank you. Just a moment to pull myself together. You've been very helpful," she said. "Do you have a washroom? I must look a fright."

"Not at all," he said gallantly, but he pointed her to a door at the back of the office. "There's a pump for water; let me help you."

The washroom was dim, lit only by the somber daylight coming in through a high window, but she managed to straighten her dress, pin her hair up, and wipe away most of the mud on her hands, from when she clambered over the wheel. There was a pump outside the door, and the young manager pumped diligently. The cold water gurgled up the pipes, so cold it bit, but was refreshing at the same time. She looked down at her fingers – red with cold and buzzing with power. Her trembling slowed, and full understanding of what had just happened sunk in.

There was only one explanation. Despite every attempt to keep Noe on a short leash, the housemaid had wasted no time in informing her contact that a very large sum of money was en route from the Mederos address to the bank. We must stop underestimating our enemies, Tesara thought. She looped the purse strap around her wrist, feeling the reassuring weight of its contents.

She came out of the washroom to find the young manager hovering anxiously. "We've sent for the constables. In the meantime, is there anyone we can send word to?"

"Yes. I must send a message to my sister."

Chapter Eleven

Tesara sat down at the manager's office desk – where the name Ravietti was written in prominence on the door and the stationery – and scrawled a few lines to Yvienne, then sealed and sanded the letter with hands that still shook a bit.

Vivi, the cabbie tried to rob me. I took care of him but he must be in on it with Noe. I'm waiting for the constables at the Ravietti warehouses.

The young manager – he gave his name as Christofre Ravietti – sent a messenger boy with her note up to the Crescent.

"The constables will be here soon," Mr Ravietti said, when he had dispatched the page. "They'll get to the bottom of this and find your man."

Even though she had turned down refreshment, young Mr Ravietti, wise beyond his years, brought a tray with both tea and brandy, and then stoked the small fire in the grate, bringing welcome warmth to his office. "Is there anything else I can do for you, miss?" He watched her anxiously. She gave him a brilliant smile, though chagrined that she had made a conquest of the susceptible young man.

"Mr Ravietti, you have gone above and beyond the call of duty for me. I thank you for calling the constables. I'm afraid we will have to take over your office for the interview."

"It would be my honor, Miss…?"

"Mederos." She saw his face alter slightly in recognition of her notorious surname, but he continued gallantly.

"Miss Mederos. And then you will allow me to carry you home afterwards in my carriage."

"Mr Ravietti, I have imposed upon your kindness enough," she protested. "I could not possibly ask you to drive me all over town."

"You can hardly be expected to take a public hack, miss. I would be honored to give you a lift home. I have a carriage right here at the office stable."

Tesara took a deep breath and gave in. "I thank you, sir, for your generosity."

He took her hand and pumped it enthusiastically, and then let her be, saying the constables would be in shortly. And in truth, she admitted to herself, she did *not* want to set foot in a public cab, not any time soon. She poured herself some tea and laced it with a splash of brandy. She drank and coughed, and only then came to terms with what had just happened.

The cabbie had *shot at her.* Fury gripped her, partly borne of reaction. First she trembled, then her feelings calmed, and at last became ice cold.

If we ever cross paths again, Noe's unknown accomplice, she thought, the next time I won't give you the chance to get the drop on me.

Abel watched from the mouth of the foul alleyway as the constables converged on the overturned hack and the trembling horse. They would not find the cabbie. Abel had watched the big man pull himself to his feet, groaning and cursing, finally limping away, furtively looking around for pursuit. Most likely, Abel thought, the man feared the younger Miss Mederos was coming back to finish him off.

That's what I would be afraid of.

If he hadn't seen it, he wouldn't have believed it himself. Abel had been watching the Mederos house when the rickety cab drove up and the young lady got in. Concealed by the fog and rain he had jogged alongside the cab and attached himself to the back like a limpet as it headed down the cobblestone hill. Consequently he had a ringside seat for the attempted abduction and Miss Mederos's counterattack. She had handily defeated the man, and it confirmed Doc's intelligence that the girl was an unnatural. No wonder he wanted her, Abel thought. Untrained, she had a powerful talent. Once Doc got his hands on her... Abel felt a sickening lurch in his belly. It's not my concern, he told himself. The girl would survive or not – his job was to bring her to Doc and that was enough.

If the plethora of ten-groat novels were to be believed, the random abduction of well-bred, wealthy young ladies was a common hazard. Abel knew better. Some other faction knew the younger Miss Mederos had powers and had made a move. Abel needed to grab the girl and fast, before whomever it was made another attempt.

Chapter Twelve

After Tesara left in the hack, the rain came down in earnest. Such was Fog Season, Yvienne thought – drizzle and fog and rain. She went off to her study, and had barely settled in to review the House books when Albero knocked on the door with a most puzzled expression.

"Miss, a hack is here, and he says *he's* the driver the boy reserved."

Yvienne could feel the blood drain from her face. Struggling for calm, she said, "That's unusual, isn't it?"

"Yes, miss. And I don't like it. Not after everything that's happened." His flat declaration confirmed her own fears.

"Nor I, Albero. I wish there were a way to warn my sister."

"I can send the boy for the constables," he said, "but what would we tell them?"

She nodded, thinking hard. Noe had heard them discussing the money. Noe knew Tesara was going to the bank. Noe had not wasted any time. *I should have tossed her from this house the moment I caught her listening at the door.* Well, she was about to rectify that situation. She said, "Where's Noe?"

Albero's confusion deepened. "Noe? She told me she was going on an errand for Mrs Francini. I'll ring for her, and she can explain."

As expected, Mrs Francini had not asked Noe to go on an errand and was baffled by Albero saying she had.

Uncle Samwell chose that moment to return to the house, damp but self-satisfied, reeking of spirits, coffee, and cigars.

"What's the fuss?" he asked, when he found them gathered in the study.

"Noe is missing," Yvienne said. "And Tesara may be in a bit of trouble."

"The girl has a knack," Samwell said.

"Noe's things are still in the servants' sitting room," Mrs Francini said. The kindly woman's expression was angry, and her countenance appeared unused to the emotion. "She must be intending to return. I'll send her packing, Miss Yvienne. This is beyond flightiness."

"I counted the silver last night, but I'll count again," Albero said, the first thought of a competent butler.

Yvienne totaled the ways into and out of the house, and she went running to the solar, the others following in her wake. Sure enough, the portofinestra doors that led to the garden were unlatched. Of course, she thought. We just closed off this part of the house. No one would see Noe sneak out this way.

She and Albero exchanged glances. "She's never had a key, miss, that I know of," he said. "And the fact that she's left the door unlocked means that she hasn't had a chance to borrow one or have a copy made." He blanched. "I hope."

"Oh!" Uncle Samwell said, handing over a crumpled bit of paper from his waistcoat pocket. "I was so astonished by you all it completely slipped my mind. A runner was at the front door when I came in. Cheeky bugger wouldn't go 'til I gave him a groat and he looked at me as if he expected a guilder."

Yvienne wanted to scream, but settled for giving her uncle a glare and tearing open the letter. She read Tesara's note. She didn't say she was hurt, but then, Tesara wouldn't want her to worry. She passed the note to Albero and Mrs Francini, and then Uncle Samwell. The latter gave a long, low whistle.

"Sounds like a housemaid's ring," he said. "I've heard that Cramdean's involved in that one."

A sound at the glass doors caught their attention. It was Noe, and it was just her bad luck that when she stepped inside the house through the portofinestra, breathless, wet, and disheveled, everyone was standing there waiting for her.

Noe's expression went from shock to shame to defiance, her face red with embarrassment. She straightened her back and clasped her hands together, but she said, "I know, I know. You're disappointed in me. You've given me a chance, and see what I did. I've let you all down, treated you all so badly. Well, I don't care. You can sack me all you like, and I won't care."

"It's not being turned off without a reference that you're facing, Noe," Yvienne said. "You're an accessory to a crime." She held up the letter. "You told your accomplice that my sister was going to the bank, didn't you? He was waiting at the hack station at the foot of the Crescent. You just had to run down there and give him word that the youngest Miss Mederos was going to make a deposit. A sturdy girl like you could make it down there in five minutes; maybe ten to fifteen minutes to walk back up. I know; that hill is quite steep."

Noe tried to interrupt but Yvienne bored on.

"All you had to do was find a pretext to run down there, and you could be gone as long as necessary. Neither Albero nor Mrs Francini would question, because they trusted you."

"Miss Yvienne, I–"

Yvienne was relentless, fury rising in her. "And you knew no one would be coming in or out of the solar, because we were closing these rooms off for the season. My only question is, why did you come back? Was it because you knew that there would be more where that came from? And all you had to do was leave the portofinestra doors open in the solar for easy access *to my home*?"

She finished on a shout, her voice cracking. Everyone jumped, even Noe.

Silence. Albero broke it. "I'll call for the constables," he said, his voice quiet.

Struggling to keep her calm, Yvienne turned away without saying anything else, heartsick and furious all at once. Behind her, Noe began to cry.

"Miss, I don't know anything about the cabs. Miss, please, you can turn me off, but I didn't – I couldn't – whatever's happened, that wasn't me."

Yvienne turned around. Noe was sobbing, gulping down tears.

"Where did you go?" she asked, expecting a lie.

Noe gulped again. "I – I did go to tell someone about the money, but I don't know anybody at the cab stand, and it was someone else, and he makes me do it, miss. I swear."

"The money?" Albero said.

"The *money*?" Uncle Samwell repeated.

"You've been spying on us, haven't you?" Yvienne said. "Running around the house, trying to learn our secrets? Who are you telling, Noe? Have you already given him a sample of the goods in this house? If we look among your things will we find missing spoons?"

Noe was out of words. She was trying hard to stop crying, which was good, as it was the one thing that was apt to put Yvienne even the slightest bit on her side. I cannot abide crying, she thought, because I stopped crying when I was fourteen, the day my family lost all its money.

She looked at Noe, really looked at her. The girl was only a few years younger than Tesara, perhaps sixteen or seventeen. At that age, Yvienne was at Madam Callier's, doing the same scullery work for her room and board. She and Noe had the same reddened, rough hands from the caustic soaps and boiling water used for cleaning. She had escaped; Noe would not. In a few years, the freshness that remained of her childhood would be burned out of her, her hair turned drab, her teeth rotten, and her cheeks hollow from deprivation. I was a Gentleman Bandit, robbing my peers, Yvienne thought. Was I so different from Noe?

"Who is he?" she said, her voice far more gentle than before. They all looked at her, at her change of attitude. Noe gulped.

"I don't think I should tell you that, miss," she said, wiping at her eyes. Her nose was redder than ever but the rest of her complexion was wan. "He's – not a good man."

"No, I imagine not," Yvienne said. "But I won't allow him to continue on like this, corrupting perfectly decent housemaids. You're one of us now, Noe, and I won't have any more nonsense like this."

There was a ringing silence. Noe made to speak, then subsided, lips parted as if speech were stolen.

Samwell said what everyone else was thinking. "Vivi, you've run mad. Sack her and call the constables. Going up against the dock gangs isn't a good bet for business."

"Maybe it's time the dock gangs should know they shouldn't go up against me," she snapped. There was another ringing silence. "Noe, you have been warned. You're lucky this time this wasn't your doing. But if anything like this happens again, I will have no scruples about sending straight for the constables. Have I made myself perfectly clear?"

This time Noe managed a response, her voice quiet. "Yes, miss."

Chapter Thirteen

"So it wasn't Noe after all?" Tesara said, after young Mr Ravietti had driven her home.

"Apparently not," Yvienne said. "I could be a fool, but I believe her. Someone else is after you."

They sat on the floor in front of the fireplace in the sitting room, as they had done as children, toasting bread and cheese over the fire on long forks. Tesara's hair was in a braid draped over her shoulder, and Yvienne had let hers out of the prim bun she always wore. Her hair was dark and dappled in the firelight – Tesara's had turned from white blonde as a child to a light golden brown. Her face stung, but she had put Miss Gentian's Salve on the scrapes, and the soothing balm quieted the pain.

The two junior constables had taken her report, writing down her description of the cabbie with great excitement. Tesara had given an abbreviated recital of events, saying only that the cabbie had held her at gunpoint and fired his pistol to cow her, but frightened the horse into bolting. She omitted her own defense. After getting assurances that the City Constabulary would get their man, young Mr Ravietti drove her home in his understated, yet comfortable, modern curricle drawn by a well-kept carriage bay. He handled the reins with great competency and no little pride, but was refreshingly un-showy about it. She had a notion that he would have wrapped her in Qin traders silk and laid a hot brick at her feet if he thought she would accept it. He was sweet and earnest, and she was exhausted and grateful.

The reaction from the attack had drained her – the explosion of power had left her limp, even sleepy. This felt as if something was taken out of her, even as she knew she had learned an important part of managing her unusual talent. The power required to attack on the fly was more enervating than if she had been able to prepare and center herself. As a child my power was naïve, she thought. And it came without question and I used it without a thought. But now when I need it most, it requires careful handling. It's not the power that's draining. It's the control.

While she was thinking about it, Yvienne was considering her answer. Her sister set down her toast on the plate but she didn't bite in right away, though the smell of the cheese and warm bread was heavenly. "I keep wondering why the cabbie would try to handcuff you," Yvienne said. "That made no sense until I realized – it wasn't a robbery; it was an abduction." She gave her sister a long look. "And I can think of only one reason they would be after you."

Someone who knows. The memory of the ships, sliding down the side of a giant wave, slowly toppling over into the sea, made her shudder. *They know what I've done. They know what I'm capable of.*

"Trune," Tesara said. He had kidnapped her six months ago and tried to force her to use her power at his bidding. And the cabbie – she remembered him now. It fell into place. "Oh, Vivi. The cabbie was the *coachman.*" Tesara shook her head, sickened. The brute of a coachman had done Trune's dirty work six months ago. "They've come back."

"Trune," Yvienne agreed. "We all thought it was Noe, of course. She was the obvious suspect. But Trune must have had someone keeping an eye on the house. They knew that when Albero sent the boy that we were ordering a hack for one of us. If it had been me, they would have used me as leverage. They just got lucky." Her voice was dry.

"How does he dare? He's been sanctioned by the Guild. If they find he's returned, he'll go to prison." Tesara felt a rising sense of anxiety. "We must go back to the constables, Vivi, and tell them what we know."

"We could," Yvienne said slowly. "But what would we tell them?"

"He tried to kidnap me! Again!"

Her sister was silent for a long time. Finally, she said, "It's bad enough the Harrier is here, poking into our business. If the constabulary investigates, what will they find?"

They will find I sank the fleet. They would find out that Vivi was the Gentleman Bandit. An investigation by the constabulary could sniff out secrets best left hidden.

"So Trune can operate with impunity," Tesara said, her words laced with bitterness.

Yvienne pushed her cheese and toast around on the plate. "Not necessarily. The Harrier's mandate is to investigate the Great Fraud and Trune's whereabouts. If we tell him that Trune's back, then we let the Harrier get his man."

It was an appealing idea, but… "Can we trust him?" Tesara asked.

"Maybe," Yvienne said. She met her sister's eyes. "That is, I don't. I think he's got ulterior motives and I think he suspects that we have secrets too. But yes, if we give him Trune, maybe he'll leave us alone."

"And then we'll be free of Trune, once and for all," Tesara said. She hoped it was true, wished it to be true. With Trune in gaol, she could finally be free of the constant worry of being exposed.

"In the meantime, we have to be careful. Trune *will* try again," Yvienne said.

"If he does, I don't care who finds out what I can do," Tesara replied.

She expected her sister to object, but to her surprise and satisfaction, Yvienne just said, "It's about time he was taught a lesson he didn't forget."

Indeed, Tesara thought. It was entirely time for former Guildmaster Trune to stop underestimating the Mederos sisters.

Chapter Fourteen

Dear Mr Fresnel,

I have information that will be of use to you in the matter of the Great Fraud and the disappearance of Guildmaster Trune. I will come see you at 11 o'clock on Saturnes day at the Hotel Bailet.

Signed,

Y. Mederos

Abel scanned the letter from the elder Miss Mederos that the worshipful clerk brought to him that morning. The stationery, having been recently in her possession, yielded a few clews to her temperament, though not much could be gleaned. Abel received an overall impression of caution and distrust, but no dissembling. She wasn't lying – she did have information. It also revealed something else.

She thinks Trune had something to do with the attempted abduction. It was a guess, but Abel hadn't spent years under the tender ministrations of Doc Farrissey only to make unsupported guesses. The younger Miss Mederos had already been abducted once by Trune. He knows about her powers, Abel thought. Trune was the other factor in the game.

"Mr TreMondi will see you now, sir," the nervous House TreMondi clerk said as he poked his head into the anteroom where Abel had cooled his heels for fifteen minutes. He followed the clerk into TreMondi's office.

Alve TreMondi looked up at Abel but didn't bother to get to his feet. Where the office of House Mederos was sparse and functional, House TreMondi was simply magnificent, from the expensive desk with its gleaming inlays, the carved molding, even down to the baseboards. The paint was cream, the furnishings dark wood, the paintings pastoral, and the only indication that money was made on the premises were the clerks at their standing desks, studiously head down at their books, silent but for the scraping of their pens and the ticking of their adding mechanisms. The nervous clerk scurried away once he had deposited Abel into TreMondi's clutches.

As Abel made a swift analysis of the office, TreMondi made a wordless inspection of Abel, designed, the Harrier knew, to throw him off his guard.

"Fresnel," TreMondi acknowledged at last. He waved a hand at the chair in front of the desk. Abel sat. "I'm glad you asked to see me," TreMondi went on. "I've been meaning to ask for an update." He offered Abel a cigar, which the Harrier accepted, and with great ceremony TreMondi made a production of clipping the end and lighting it. Abel leaned over and touched TreMondi's fingers as he took the cigar and puffed at it, the acrid smoke curling like a disembodied warm tongue inside his mouth. All the while the touch activated his extra sense, and he felt as if he could taste TreMondi himself, the way a snake scents its prey.

Oblivious, TreMondi leaned back in his leather chair and luxuriated in his cigar, putting on a show of his fine sensibilities.

TreMondi. Mid-thirties. Merchant with a Chahoki wife and three half-Chahoki children, and as a result he inhabited a sort of twilit position in the society of Port Saint Frey. The other men of his set spoke of him with admiration and some sexual envy – he had "tamed" a fierce Chahoki woman. And the man had a self-satisfied air, reflected by his office. Alve TreMondi liked to surround himself with fine, rare possessions.

TreMondi had been in on the fraud from the start and had perjured himself in the official investigation after the whole thing was blown wide open by the Arabestus broadsheet. He had liked the idea of it, getting one over on one of his fellow merchants, and he liked being that sort of impish fellow who had won in an underhanded way, the more underhanded the better.

It explained the Chahoki wife: a way to thumb his nose at the society in which he moved, because it would force the other merchant families to accept his unusual wife.

He better watch his back, Abel thought. If her Chahoki family got wind of his motives, he'd be lucky he didn't end up with his manhood cut off and stuffed down his throat. They were a prickly people and didn't take kindly to jokesters.

"I'm making progress," Abel said. "It's a sticky situation but we'll un-stick it."

"We?" TreMondi said.

"The Harrier organization. I may be solo on this job, but rest assured I have the full force of the company at my back."

TreMondi nodded. "Well, we hired you Harriers for a reason; we should get our money's worth. And since you work for the Guild – and by extension, me – I'm disappointed in a report as vague as, *making progress*. You have to do better, Fresnel."

Abel refused to be baited. "To that end, Mr TreMondi, can you answer a few questions?"

"Again?"

"Different questions."

TreMondi gave a full, put-upon sigh. "Very well."

"What do you think Trune wanted with the younger Miss Mederos?" Abel asked.

TreMondi snorted. "Really, Fresnel? Have you Harriers taken a vow of celibacy, too?"

Of course that would be the first place TreMondi's thoughts would go, Abel thought. But there was some underlay in TreMondi's response that told him TreMondi himself didn't believe it.

"Bit out of character for the man, don't you think?"

TreMondi's laugh was a bit too loud, too forced. "When it comes to pleasures of the flesh, it's in every man's character." He leaned forward. "Even you, Fresnel." He sounded pitying, as if to say that a man as poor and nondescript as Abel could only dream.

"Any chance Trune wanted the girl for something else?"

TreMondi snorted. "Can't imagine what that could be. She's a troublemaker, that one. Some females, they persist in tempting fate – and tempting men. Her fall from society was to be expected. It's a shame. Her older sister is nothing like her."

"Yes, I understand the eldest Mederos girl worked in your house as a governess," Abel said. "Why did you allow that?"

"It was my wife's idea. She wanted a governess for the girls rather than send them away to a seminary. My son goes to the Port Saint Frey Academy, of course. It's traditional, and I wanted Dubre to have all the advantages that I had." An emotion flickered over TreMondi's face, and Abel identified it before even TreMondi was aware of what he was feeling.

TreMondi had just had a moment of empathy for his son, a seal among the sharks, and some self-doubt as to whether he had done the right thing by forcing him to go to the school. Then the moment was gone, and the smirk was back.

"Was she a good governess?"

"Fresnel, even the smartest girl in Port Saint Frey can't teach my middle daughter how to solve for *x*. But yes, as governesses go, she was a good governess."

Another flicker crossed his eyes – a sudden memory, an interesting thought about the suitability of Miss Yvienne Mederos. Abel called him on it.

"What?"

TreMondi hesitated, discretion warring with desire to tell.

"She's... got secrets."

You don't say, Abel thought with weary sarcasm. The whole family was a powderkeg of secrets.

"What makes you think that?"

"She would stay over some nights to teach the children astronomy. I let them use my telescope under strict orders not to break anything, and she knew how to use it – apparently she had one as a child. A good one too – we talked about lenses once and she knew enough to flaunt her knowledge."

Another flicker – annoyance at being shown up by the formidable Miss Mederos. "Anyway – one afternoon her uncle was jawing on and on about her down at the coffee house where he sponges off the Names, and he said she had taught astronomy the night before at our house. But she hadn't. I would have known." TreMondi laughed coarsely. "I hadn't expected it of her. Her sister, yes. She's out of control. But Miss Mederos is a good girl, or so I thought. I warned her about it. I told her that her tainted reputation would brand her as a soiled dove."

It was hardly likely that Yvienne Mederos's pluck and backbone would drive her to the streets. Whatever she was using her cover as governess for, it was not to tarnish her virtue.

TreMondi leaned forward suddenly in his chair. "I'll tell you one more thing, and then I need to get on with running my business. Maybe, yes, maybe Trune got ahead of himself. Maybe he did some things that weren't quite on the level. But he was a damn fine Guild liaison and magistrate, and he knew how to keep everything sailing smoothly. Maybe what happened to House Mederos is a small price to pay. I'm not saying it's right, but I'm not saying it's wrong, either. I'm just saying that since Trune disappeared and everyone got all up in arms about "legality" and what's "right," this city has been embroiled in trouble after trouble. Think on that, and when you find Trune you'll find he has his own side of the story. It's not all black and white, Fresnel."

"You said Trune was good at his job," Abel said, ignoring TreMondi's desire to get rid of him. "Were you friends?"

TreMondi snorted. "He was the Guild *liaison*, Fresnel. Don't be an idiot."

Abel gave him a level look, not speaking, and TreMondi flushed and looked away. After a moment, just so the man got the point, he said, "Just thought you might know where he is." He allowed a hint of roughness, of untutored unsophistication, of street tough, in his voice. To save face TreMondi would chalk it up to a rude countryman who didn't understand fine class distinctions between *merchants* and Guild *liaisons* but he wouldn't discount the threat.

"No," TreMondi said, his voice tight. "I don't know where he is."

He was lying. Abel waited. TreMondi broke first, one of those men who couldn't bear the silence. "I mean – I don't for sure. He might be in town, but as I said, we weren't friends."

"If he might be in town, where might he be?"

"Haven't the foggiest," TreMondi said, yet tenseness and anxiety shaped every syllable.

Keep him talking. The longer TreMondi sweated, the more information Abel got. It had gone beyond touch. The truth exuded from his pores, manifested itself in the smallest of muscles around his eyes, the set of his shoulders. Sometimes Abel registered the information he received from his informants as words in his head; more often, it was an emotional click of rightness, as when he made an intuitive leap.

"He's in town under an assumed name, isn't he?" Abel said, and TreMondi snorted elaborately and leaned back, and the truth screamed out at Abel.

As suspected, Trune was back, had rented a house, was lying low. He could see the pillars and the brick siding, all of it revealed in TreMondi's subverbal communications that had nothing to do with voice, and everything to do with language. *Only humans think they talk just with their mouths, boy. You learn to read the rest of it, and you'll always know what someone is saying.*

"This has been fun, Mr Fresnel, but I am a very busy man," TreMondi said, no longer able to maintain eye contact. "I must ask you to leave."

Abel snubbed out his cigar on the tray, and stood, shrugging into his coat.

"Thank you for your time, Mr TreMondi. I appreciate how forthcoming you've been."

TreMondi reacted with wide eyes and Abel didn't elaborate. He let himself out, flipping up his collar against the drizzle.

Find the house with a brick facade and pillars, a red roof and black shutters, and he would find Trune. Once he had Trune, the man would no longer be a threat to his second objective. Once Abel had Trune, he could concentrate on taking the girl.

As Yvienne hurried down Chandler's Row toward Alastra's and her meeting with Inigho Demaris, she wondered again if she had done the right thing by writing a letter to the Harrier. Everything about the man screamed duplicity. He would ask all the right questions, she thought, and they would lead back to the sisters. On the other hand, he was here to investigate Trune, and the sooner he had his man, the sooner he would go back to where he came from. But I won't underestimate him, she thought. If he ever nosed out Tesara's secret, or her own, for that matter, they could not afford to be lenient. Yvienne thought back to her sister at Elenor Charvantes's party. Tesara had been as tense and wound up as a hot-blooded thoroughbred before a race. All of those men had been present at Trune's, who sat and ate and drank while she served them, no doubt lasciviously – Yvienne found that she herself was clenching her fists. She forced herself to unclench them. No, the Harrier would do well not to underestimate the Mederos sisters, and she welcomed a good fight.

She turned the corner to cut across Emery Place. Across the plaza she could see Alastra's, the warm, inviting, rain-streaked windows glowing with lamplight and hinting at the delights within.

The world of the finest dining establishment in Port Saint Frey was a far cry from the world of kidnapping coachmen, nefarious Guild liaisons, and dangerous Harriers. Relax, she told herself. Enjoy this. This was important too. House business was as pressing a concern as revenge. If she focused on the latter, as she wanted, there would be no House left to avenge. However, Inigho Demaris had better not try anything underhanded, she thought. She was not in the mood for anyone else to try to take advantage of her family.

Then she gave herself a mental shake. No need to frighten poor Inigho. The man only had trade on his mind.

"Tea with friends, miss?" The host at Alastra's gave Yvienne a polite smile as she entered the fine, quiet establishment. The host boy closed the door behind her, cutting off the weather, and held out his hand for her wet coat and umbrella. She shed them both along with her hat, and smoothed back her hair. She hoped she didn't look like a drowned rat but suspected that she rather did.

There was a table of young misses, many of whom had been at Elenor's luncheon party the other day, enjoying Alastra's famed tea and cakes and hot spiced wine on a miserable day. She could understand why the host had made the assumption.

"No, I've an appointment. Under the name Inigho Demaris," she said.

He didn't bat an eye. He ran his finger down his ledger and beckoned to the errand page. "Please show Miss Mederos to her table."

Yvienne followed the boy. She smiled at the shocked girls when she passed the table and she could feel their attention upon her as the page led her to an empty table in the corner of the restaurant. Inigho hadn't arrived yet. She sat gracefully and thanked the page with a tip, and he beamed a gap-toothed smile at her.

The tablecloth almost glowed in the low light, and the water goblets sparkled. When she had sent word to the Demaris office that she wanted to schedule a meeting with

Inigho, she had expected to meet him at the Demaris House offices. Instead, the secretary sent an errand page with a message that directed her here.

Matchmaking, she thought. She sipped from her water glass, sitting as erect and calm as could be. She hated being on display, she hated not knowing Inigho's game, and she hated the gossip that the misses of Port Saint Frey were about to unleash regarding her. Once they told their mothers who they saw in Alastra's, Alinesse's wish that her daughters live retiringly while she was away would be shot to smithereens.

There was Inigho. He looked across the dining room at her, spoke briefly to the host, and then made his way alone through the sea of tables.

The misses all goggled after him, turning their heads as one.

He smiled when he reached her, and it was a smile of relief and pleasure. Of course, she scolded herself, standing to greet him. What did you expect – a nefarious snicker and a twirled moustache?

"Miss Mederos," he said, clasping her hand. "I'm so pleased you came out to see me on such a rotten day."

"Not at all, Mr Demaris. Life must go on, even in Fog Season."

There. The banalities were out of the way. He sat, chatting as she gave him a swift once over. His mother's assessment was correct. He wasn't pretty. He was about thirty, his hairline receding, and his face an oddly ungraceful mix of features as if the Great Maker hadn't decided how to put this one together. This is just business, she reminded herself. Business she could handle.

"I've not lunched yet and I'm famished. Got caught up in things at the office. You?"

"I have not either, and breakfast seems so long ago." Even Mrs Francini's simple, hearty breakfast porridge could not keep her whole long past midday. "In this weather there is no end to my appetite."

Good God. Would he take that as a double meaning?

He said only, "Oh, I well know. Choose something hearty from the menu and I'll have the captain's lunch."

Yvienne ended up choosing oyster chowder and biscuits.

Alastra started them off with a complimentary beef broth to cut the chill, and they both sipped.

"So, after meeting my mother, you still came to see me," Inigho said. "I apologize; she has her motives, and they are all ulterior."

It was said with teasing affection.

"I admit I was curious before I met Mrs Demaris," Yvienne pointed out. She gave him an arched brow look over her cup of broth.

"Ah, yes, the business contract. Not my finest hour. Can I blame my mother once again without acting the complete scoundrel?"

"Why did you write that contract?" Yvienne said. He looked a little surprised at her bluntness. "Do you truly want to do business with House Mederos?"

"Yes." He dropped the familiarity, and all of a sudden Inigho went into business mode, like a lazily swimming shark sighting a seal. "We're primarily an overland shipping company, but in order to bring in my goods to my customers, we're at the mercy of the shipping families. You're a shipping family. If you bring in what no one wants to buy, you've gone to great effort for what may be very little demand. Then you have to unload goods at a discount. It's done you well so far, I admit, but even before the Great Fraud, you were slipping."

So his mother had said; apparently House Mederos was dinnertime conversation for House Demaris. For a moment outrage stiffened her spine, even as she identified another emotion: exhilaration.

"Even if – and mind you, I say *if* – there's a modicum of truth to what you say, I'd like to point out that House Mederos has done very well at anticipating demand. You might even say that we specialize in making a market where there had been none." She felt a sharp pang of nostalgia. That was so long ago, even longer ago than when the Fraud laid waste to a mighty merchant House. Inigho was right. House Mederos had been slipping.

A uniformed waiter came up to them, removed the broth, and replaced it with their meals. Yvienne almost swooned at the aroma of the chowder, rich with cream and broth and fruits of the sea, and the biscuit was almost as tall as one of Mrs Francini's. Inigho's captain's luncheon was an epic platter of lobster and steak, with mashed potatoes swimming in gravy, and roasted carrots and parsnips. It was Alastra's specialty, and well-matched to the restaurant's clientele, who were mainly captains of industry, not sea captains.

Inigho tucked in, and Yvienne followed suit. She would never spurn good food, not after years of starvation. Inigho broke the silence and continued their conversation.

"What if I told you I could guarantee a pre-sold cargo, provided House Mederos meets contract terms and comes in at an agreed-upon delivery date?"

"I would say that's how you bamboozled my Uncle Samwell," Yvienne shot back. Inigho grinned. He was enjoying himself as much as she was. If she wasn't careful, she was going to end up liking him.

"I like your Uncle Samwell. He's a good sort of fellow, and his heart's in the right place."

Yvienne said abruptly, "Inigho, in all seriousness, why House Mederos? Is it because you think we're desperate?"

His easy grin faltered, and he looked taken aback. At his next words, she reddened – only then did she realize that she had called him by his first name. Then he leaned forward, intense.

"Yvienne, I'm not exaggerating – your House has been running on its reputation for years. We've all noticed it. So if it were your father still running things, we wouldn't even be talking." A sudden, wolfish smile flickered and was gone. "Well, I had my plans, but never mind. But you. I've been watching you. In the past six months you've done more to restore House Mederos's fortunes than anything your father did in the previous six years. You retrenched, consolidated debt, came through on some very lucrative deals, and I have no doubt you will return the House to its former glory within a year. I also know that you know shipping. If anyone can bring my cargo from Malenthia or Grand Harbor, it's you."

He sat back and she didn't say anything for a moment. She was acutely aware of her heart pounding, and she was hard put to regain her composure. Foolish Yvienne, she thought, to be so overset by the simple fact that this man noticed. He noticed her deeds and her triumphs, he understood her trials. What her parents took for granted – "Vivi, run the office, will you?" – Inigho *got*. She gave a small, inadvertent laugh, and put up her hand to her mouth to stop it. He looked at her quizzically.

"Inigho," she said, and she could tell that he expected her to say *Yes*, and it almost made her laugh again. "I am flattered, but – we have no ships."

"Well, I thought of that. House Demaris could buy a ship, and we would pay House Mederos to sail it."

No better than hired help. Her laughter stopped. Her

cheeks warmed, and she looked down at her soup, running her spoon through the dregs of her chowder. Don't be angry, she warned herself. Be dispassionate. Consider the offer.

"What?" he said, and she looked up. He was considering her. "Why not?"

Because it proves exactly what I suspect, that you think House Mederos is desperate and grateful.

"It is certainly possible with certain adjustments," she said, choosing her words. "As I not only have care for House Mederos's fortunes, I also have care for her reputation. And I fear that whether we sailed one ship or an entire fleet owned by another House, it would damage that reputation."

He raised an eyebrow and his reply was curt.

"Pride is costly, Miss Mederos," he said. "Are you sure you can afford it?"

Oh, are we back to surnames? Inigho Demaris did not like being turned down. Perhaps that was part of the hidden depths his mother spoke of.

"I will not sell my House's reputation cheaply or at all," she said. "Mr Demaris, I will consider your offer. I think we can help House Demaris out of her dilemma, but I'll need more time and study."

"Not too long," he warned, albeit lightly. "Trade waits for no one."

"We'll speak further. Send over your full proposal to the office and I'll review. I'll have an answer no later than Freyday."

"Fair enough," he said. "And now, continue to eat. There's no reason we can't be friends, you know."

There's every reason, she thought, but he was right. Whatever came of this – a business partnership or something more – she liked Inigho.

They chatted over the rest of the meal, very generally, but

she could tell a lot about him from the idle conversation. He loved trade. His eyes lit up when he spoke of the family business, of House Demaris's expeditions across the Desert Sea to the Chahoki empire. He quizzed her about the overseas shipping business, and they traded notes on the business gossip of the city. They even talked about the Great Fraud and the business with Trune. House Demaris was a Guild member in good standing, but Inigho had not been at the dinner that night. *Else I would not think of doing business with him.* He expressed frustration that the city had let Trune slip. Yvienne couldn't resist.

"What do you think of this business with the Harrier?"

"The Guild didn't make any friends among the constabulary with that decision," Inigho said. "I've heard that Renner himself is annoyed. But I can understand the Guild's point. Trune embezzled significant funds and that's the Guild's money. I'd like to see him found and brought to justice, and if it takes a Harrier, then that's good enough for me."

It was the most enjoyable lunch she had had – ever. She regretted its conclusion, over tiny cups of bold coffee that made her head buzz and her heart pound. And finally, it was time to go.

She set her napkin next to her bowl and stood, and he stood too. He reached out his hand and she clasped it, merchant to merchant. The misses will be swooning, she thought. His hand was warm and firm.

"I'm glad we're going to be in business together," Inigho said, and his smile was back, crinkling the corners of his eyes. "You'd be a stubborn adversary."

She smiled too, but with more reserve. She would have to find other ways to test Inigho's character. That flash of temper – if the man couldn't even take the mildest of setbacks, would he be a good business partner?

He followed her out through the dining room, the misses all pausing in the midst of gathering their belongings and purchases to watch them go, and while he scrawled his signature next to his account, the maitre d' helped her into her damp coat.

"Can I have my carriage take you anywhere, Miss Mederos?" he said formally. "It's a wet, nasty day."

Why not? It wasn't as if walking alone would quell the rapturous gossip.

"Thank you, Mr Demaris. I'm going to the office, so a lift would be appreciated."

Inigho was all solicitousness. The carriage came round, drawn by two wet, stamping horses, their backs and harness covered with waterproofed rugs, and driven by a similarly uniformed coachman. He handed her in and hopped in after her, and she sank down with a sigh. Walking was all well and good, but a ride in a well-sprung conveyance was a luxury. When we are restored, she promised herself, she would make sure the family owned a well-made carriage. They barely bounced over the rough streets.

They spoke but little during the short ride. Both were comfortable in their own thoughts. When the carriage pulled up in front of the Mederos waterfront office, Inigho paused with one hand on the door handle.

"You know what my mother wants," he said. "I want you to know you shouldn't feel pressured, one way or another, about that. This is strictly business."

With sudden daring, Yvienne smiled. Why not? No one could see.

"Perhaps," she said. "Or perhaps not." She leaned forward and kissed him full on the mouth.

Inigho was stunned for a moment and then he put his

arms around her and pulled her onto his lap so they could kiss more thoroughly.

The busy people of the waterfront, if they weren't hurrying to get out of the fog and rain, might have thought it odd that the Demaris carriage stayed still for so long outside the Mederos offices, the patient coachman and the horses standing in the rain, the horses now and again shaking droplets from their blinders. But they would have seen nothing amiss when Miss Yvienne Mederos, the eldest daughter of House Mederos, exited the carriage as demurely as any merchant's daughter, and hurried briskly into the warm office.

Chapter Fifteen

Albero came back into the foyer, closing the door behind him. His cheeks were ruddy from the chill and his dark hair and his coat had silver droplets on them. He is quite the handsomest butler in Port Saint Frey, Tesara thought.

"The cab is here, Miss Yvienne, Miss Tesara," Albero said. "And yes, I checked the driver thoroughly," he added before they could ask.

"Thank you, Albero," Tesara said, drawing on her gloves and setting her warm cloche on her hair, tucking her bun underneath it. "I doubt very much it would happen again." All he and Mrs Francini knew was that it had been an attempted robbery. There was no need to frighten them with the news that Trune had returned, and he was after Miss Tesara again.

"Can't be too careful, miss."

"No, indeed," Yvienne said. She was dressed for the office, her wool coat over her arm, wearing a dark blue wool dress that set off her coloring to its most advantageous. She carried a fur muff that sagged. She was armed, Tesara knew. They were sharing the cab; Yvienne to the office, and Tesara to the bank, to finally deposit the incriminating funds acquired by the Gentleman Bandit. Tesara half-hoped that

Trune's coachman would try again, but she knew he would not. He was surely planning his next attack, though.

Tesara shook her head. "He won't try anything, and if he does..." she flexed her fingers in a sign that only Yvienne could see. "Anyway, we should go. Don't you have an appointment with the Harrier?"

Yvienne nodded. "And the TreMondis this afternoon for an economics lesson." Her expression softened. "I'm quite looking forward to it. Their father is dreadful but the children can't help that. They are sweet."

"Oh dear, it's true," Tesara said. "Governessing *ruined* you, Vivi. It's sad, but there it is. Now the truth is out – you are a soft-hearted childminder."

Yvienne made a rude noise. "Just because you never liked our governesses doesn't mean all children should share that fate." Tesara watched as Albero helped her into her coat, as correct as always, except there was a flicker of something between them as Yvienne turned to him to smile her thanks. Tesara raised an eyebrow, unnoticed by the two of them.

"We can share the hack as far as the Esplanade, and then I'll go on to the office on foot," Yvienne said. "I like to walk past the shipyards anyway. There are some glorious ships taking shape." She sounded wistful.

"Soon we'll have the Mederos fleet back," Albero said.

The sisters didn't look at each other. "Yes, indeed," Yvienne said, her voice light. "Thank you, Albero. See you at dinner."

"Have a good day, Miss Yvienne, Miss Tesara."

Despite her certainty that Trune wouldn't try another attack, Tesara felt a pang of anxiety as the cabbie drove them down the hill, negotiating the steep, slick street by setting and releasing the brake and talking the horses through it.

She and her sister faced each other, their coats filling the cab with material. It was raw and cold. Her sister looked careworn in the gray daylight.

"How goes the House?" Tesara asked, her voice low, though there was little chance they could be heard by the driver. "I know you think I don't have a head for business – and I don't – but if there's anything I can do, you must tell me."

"We need more business," Yvienne admitted. "Father took out two loans before he and Mother left, and the interest is not onerous, but I'd be happier if we had income from new ventures. That's why it's so important for me to work with Inigho – I mean, House Demaris – on this contract."

Tesara narrowed her eyes. "Uncle is right. You *do* like him."

To her horror Yvienne's expression turned impish. "A little. Maybe. We've kissed," she added with a full-on grin.

"Vivi! My rule-abiding, prim sister kissed someone?"

"What?" Yvienne maintained wide-eyed innocence. "It was just a kiss. It was lovely though. He's rather good at it."

Tesara couldn't help laughing. Correct, older Inigho Demaris good at kissing… She was reminded of Jone's kiss. It was nice, but she didn't think it lovely. In truth, she had been so astonished that it was only until it was over that she had time to think about it.

And it doesn't matter, she thought. Jone has gone to sea, and I much preferred him as a friend than as a beau.

The carriage slowed, and Tesara caught her breath. Yvienne tensed. Then the carriage made the correct turn, and they both relaxed. The coach merged into traffic along the Esplanade, and the wheels rumbled over the stone causeway, the roadway smoothed by generations of foot traffic and horse-drawn carriages. At the Bailet Hotel, the cabbie pulled up.

"All right then. Be careful," Yvienne told Tesara. She gathered her things.

"I will. If Trune or his coachman tries it again, he won't have any easier of a time." She demonstrated, running her finger across the thin window frame, a curl of fire trailing along it. "I am very good at controlling it now." She snapped her fingers and the fire disappeared, and with it the slight queasiness.

Yvienne gave her a long look. "If anyone else finds out–"

"No one will find out," Tesara said. She gave her sister a kiss on the cheek. "Make the Harrier believe you."

"I will," Yvienne said. "See you at dinner."

"See you at dinner."

The Bailet lobby was dark, with only small table lamps to provide light for the patrons. Men and women in traveling dress waited amidst their luggage, and the bell rang for the bellhops with intermittent genteel tones. Every wing-backed chair was occupied, and none by the Harrier. Yvienne went to the front desk, where a correct young man gave her as intimidating a smile as his sparse mustache and spotty cheeks would allow.

"May I help you, miss?"

"I have an appointment with the – with Mr Abel Fresnel," Yvienne said. "On House business."

There – that was enough to make the youngster jump to. He snapped his fingers, and a young page materialized out of nowhere.

"Tell Mr Fresnel in Room Twenty-three that he has a visitor," he told the page. The little boy bounced off at full speed. "Miss, would you like to wait in the ladies' salon?"

Normally Yvienne would have preferred the lobby to being sequestered in a stuffy anteroom for propriety's sake, but today the option was welcome. She didn't recognize anyone at the hotel, but she had no interest in attracting attention.

She was pleased to see that she had the ladies' salon to herself. It was warmed by a small fire in the grate and lit by floor-to-ceiling windows that let in the gray, morning light. It was furnished with small uncomfortable chairs upholstered in an alarming floral print, a faded chaise longue, and a dressing table, presumably for the tired traveler to address her toilette. There was a pile of several outdated ladies' gazettes on an end table. Yvienne was alone for the moment, and she paced, trying to settle her nerves.

Then the door opened, and the Harrier entered. He gave her the same sweeping overview he had plied the first time they met. She had the distinct impression that he took more than her measure.

"Miss Mederos," he said, dropping the unsophisticated accent. "How do you do?" He reached out his hand.

Not so fast, Mr Fresnel. She wasn't Elenor. Yvienne curtseyed. For a second, some expression crossed his face – rue? amusement? – and was gone. She was struck again by his odd sort of portliness that belied the way he carried himself. He was still now, but he moved with a litheness that reminded her of an acrobat. He inhabited his body as if it were completely at his command. She decided not to waste any time.

"How do you do, sir. For the moment we have privacy, so we shall make use of it. Before I tell you, I demand your word that you will not tell anyone in the Guild that your information comes from House Mederos."

He raised an enquiring eyebrow. "And why is that?"

"It's enough that I demand it, sir, before I give you the information you need." She had no desire to bring any more Guild attention down upon her family. This interview was dangerous enough as it was.

He nodded. "I see I have no choice but to agree. Therefore, you have my word."

"We believe that Guildmaster Trune is back in town."

"Interesting," Mr Fresnel said. "And what is your evidence?" He took a small notebook and pencil out of his vest pocket, and waited.

"He sent his coachman to try to abduct my sister." She watched his reaction. She expected astonishment, but he was as calm as if she had been discussing an invitation to tea. He drew the rest of the story out of her, his questions to the point and unemotional. She knew, though, that he was taking in more than he wrote down in his little notebook than her simple answers.

"That must have been shocking. Was she injured? How was she rescued?"

"She was not injured, and she–" Yvienne stopped. *Fool!* She had almost told him that her sister rescued herself, thank you very much. "The coachman fired off his pistol, frightening the horse, which bolted, dragging the cab over the man."

He nodded. "And why do you think it was Trune, and not some other criminal? House Mederos has enemies, does it not?"

"We know it was Trune because my sister recognized the cabbie as Trune's man. As for our enemies, the threads all lead back to Trune."

"So why her? In fact, why again, Miss Mederos? Trune abducted your sister once before, is that right? That was the night the Fraud was revealed. You know," he said, musing, "I've never understood why he did that."

"Humiliation," she said, her voice low to keep it under control. "Hatefulness. Beastliness. We now know

Guildmaster Trune sought to destroy my family to keep the Great Fraud from being uncovered."

He nodded, judiciously. "But not you?"

"I beg your pardon?"

"He humiliated your sister, but not you, the eldest daughter. Why is that, do you think?"

Anger rose in her, and she knew he could see it and understood where it came from.

"You should ask him that, Mr Fresnel. I came here only to tell you that the man you were engaged to find is back in town, which should certainly help you uncover his whereabouts. I did not come here to be interrogated. Good day, sir."

She turned without waiting for him to respond, her heart hammering. She tried for poise as she crossed the lobby toward the entrance to the busy street, head high, all the while thinking, I have just made a dreadful mistake. She had the terrible feeling that she had told Mr Fresnel far more than she meant to.

Abel stood in the little salon a few moments longer. The image of her sister in a cab on her way to the bank had practically overwhelmed him, so strong had been Miss Mederos's anxiety. His line of questioning had been designed to bring out strong emotions and it had worked. It had been a rare case of not requiring touch to get the answers. All he needed was at his fingertips. He caressed the small note she had sent him, carefully folded and hidden in his palm. It had enabled him to forge a link. Whatever was top of her mind would be transmitted as powerfully as if she had shouted it at him – which, in a way, she had.

Tesara Mederos was at the bank and she was alone.

• • •

The bank of Port Saint Frey with its six massive columns rose above the street, blocking out the gray sky. A bulky doorman in his magnificent coat with gold epaulettes guarded the door, and customers came in and out, hurrying in the miserable weather. Abel kept watch from across the street, his hands in his pockets and hunched against the rain, watching and waiting. He knew he was barely visible in the dour weather. Strictly speaking, to go unseen was not one of his talents, but he had a well-developed knack that was aided by his unprepossessing appearance. No one noticed him, even those pedestrians who brushed past him on the sidewalk.

Finally, the door opened once more, and Tesara Mederos came out, wrapping her muffler around her throat. Abel timed her steps. He would wait until she reached the broad avenue. He would intercept her just as she turned the corner. The anesthetic-soaked handkerchief was in his pocket. It would be the matter of a moment to cover her mouth with it, and with her reeling and half-senseless, support her to his rented carriage, a miserable nag between the shafts. No one would notice them.

And then she stopped, and his well-timed plan went straight to hell.

Elenor Charvantes and her bastard of a husband came out of the bank at the same time as his quarry. Abel cursed as she looked directly at him, and he knew she saw him. He went into motion immediately, as if he were just arriving at the bank. Otherwise she would wonder what he was doing there, and his cover would be all for naught.

He drew abreast of Tesara. "Excuse me, miss," he said, angling to touch her. He couldn't take her now, but if he could but touch–

"Oh, I beg your pardon!" she said, giving him a glance

devoid of recognition, and she stepped out of his way. She looked back at Elenor, though, and her expression was distressed.

Elenor stopped dead when she saw Abel approaching, color flooding her cheeks. Jax's eyes narrowed in fury. Abel made a point to bow.

"Lieutenant Charvantes. Mrs Charvantes."

Elenor's color was still high but she had recovered. "How do you do, Mr Fresnel?" She made a point to curtsey.

Jax Charvantes grabbed his wife's arm, yanking her up from her curtsey, then pulled her along. Elenor gasped as she stumbled.

Tesara's raw anger was tangible to Abel, perhaps because he felt the same. He watched as the Mederos girl stepped forward, her fingers curling at her sides. Was he imagining it, or were her gloves aglow?

"How dare–" she began, her voice a low growl.

Elenor turned back, her face desperate, begging her wordlessly not to interfere. She glanced over at Abel too, pleading with him. *Stop her.*

Other customers on the broad steps were turning to look now. Elenor's face was white except for high color on her cheekbones. She turned and followed her husband to their carriage. The coachman handed her in, Jax followed, and the sound of a slap could be heard. The coachman whipped the horses to a trot, and they were off.

The Mederos girl clenched and unclenched her fists, then thrust them into her pockets, as if aware that her control was dangerously weak. She breathed hard, swallowing.

Nausea. He knew. His talents were different, but it had taken him the same way at first. She didn't know how to control her powers, and if she wasn't careful she would be destroyed by her untamed energy. Doc would fix that.

"How I hate that man," she said at last.

"Yea, verily," Abel said, and she started; she had forgotten he was there. They looked at each other. "This damnable weather," he added with an amiable smile that projected deference and sympathy. "Miss Mederos, I wondered if you cared to accompany me to the tea shop around the corner?"

She looked at him for a long moment. The energy still coursed through her. He waited, hands in his overcoat pockets, his unprepossessing face, slightly stout physique, and his receding hairline radiating harmlessness. He readied himself – as soon as he touched her he would have to overcome her. There would be no time for a second chance.

Her expression unreadable, she said at last, "No, thank you, Mr Fresnel. You have a pleasant day." She turned without another word.

Desperate times, Abel. He pitched his voice to carry but his tone remained neutral, disinterested.

"I know what's happening and I can help." The fog had almost swallowed her up but she stopped, turned, and faced him. All around them were the shrouded figures of hurrying pedestrians, but they were alone in the gloom, intently focused on one another. Abel continued.

"Every time you make it happen, your heart races, your stomach twists, and it feels like the shock goes inside you. Sometimes it feels as if there's more power than you know what to do with, and it frightens you."

"How–" She stopped. Swallowed. He could barely see her expression but he knew she was transfixed.

"You are in great danger, Miss Mederos. If you are not careful, the power will consume you. If you come with me, I can take you to someone who can teach you how to use it properly."

Doc would destroy her in the process, but that didn't matter. Better to be remade by Doc than to combust internally. More than her hands were glowing now. She radiated energy. She was trembling with the exertion to keep from lashing out at him. He feared what would happen if she lost control.

He reached into his pocket, handed her a card, careful not to touch her lest he set her off. She took the tiny scrap of cardboard, her attention still focused on him. He nodded at the card. "Doc Farrissey is the man you want. He'll teach you – everything. I can take you to him."

"I'll think about it," she said at last. "I– I have to go."

She turned and almost ran. She had virtually disappeared into the fog when he called out again, this time with more urgency.

"You know where to find me – I'm at the Bailet Hotel. And Miss Mederos, one more word of advice. *Don't use it on yourself.*"

She was gone. Abel stood alone in the fog and dripping rain, sweat rolling down his back, unpleasant in the damp chill. Her control had been extraordinary; he was lucky she had been able to constrain her energy. Such raw power; no wonder it was eating at her from inside. He let out another long breath.

"Abel," Doc was wont to say when was in a rare avuncular mood, "sometimes it's better to be lucky than good."

Yes, he had been very lucky right then.

Chapter Sixteen

HAS HE RETURNED?

Has Guild Liaison Trune, a man most wanted for engineering the Great Fraud of Port Saint Frey, returned from whence he fled? The word in the coffee shops among the venerable Names is that Trune is back and preparing to commit more mischief. Chief Constable Renner, however, says not. "If Trune were back we would have him in custody." He further stated that he thought repeating unsubstantiated rumors were a ploy by this esteemed publication to sell papers. For shame, Chief Constable!

THE GAZETTE

Interesting, Abel thought, reading the rebuttal in the most recent *Gazette*. Was the chief constable serious in his denial or was it a clumsy effort to lure the wayward Guildmaster out of hiding? Who else knew besides the Misses Mederos that the cabbie was Trune's man?

The Port Saint Frey Library kept all volumes of the *Gazette* bound in large heavy covers. The librarian gave Abel a stern once over before showing him to the reading room. The gloom of Fog Season was dispelled with cheerful reading lamps. Abel found a place at the end of a long desk and took off his overcoat, planning to settle in for the day.

There were only a few patrons at the library. One, an old, whiskered fellow dressed in rags, dozed at the other end of the table, snoring intermittently. He snorted awake, giving Abel a hard, considering look. It was not at all the look of a homeless drunkard. Abel gave him the same look back, and the old gentleman responded with a disdainful *hmph*, and shook himself back to sleep.

The librarian came back, lugging a heavy book with a wooden spindle for a spine. She set the book down.

"Leave it here when you're done. We've got people who can file it properly."

"I will. Thank you."

She gave him another stern look over her spectacles, and for good measure left him with the same derisive noseful as the old man.

Abel began leafing through the last year of the newspaper, its leaves of broadsheet yellowed but still legible.

The usual stuff – notices, shipping news, weather – impacted the city's livelihood far more than reports of distant war. Abel skipped over the weather. He noted a few interesting tidbits in passing. A dock war was brewing, according to the notes some intrepid reporter took on some skirmishes. It didn't sound as if the constabulary was aware of what was going on under their noses. There were some interesting notices under Household Help: someone was running a ring of light-fingered housemaids, if the slang were the same in Port Saint Frey as it was in Great Lake.

There. Under Homes to Let, he ran his finger down the list of available houses and homes that were no longer on the market.

> *Let to Mr Elfinnier, with wife and three children, a cook, and a housemaid, on Breque…*

Let to Mrs Finanetti, widow and weaver, on Talifieri Ave…

Let to Mr Caravellito, a single man, with no household, on…

There were seven houses let in the past month to single gentlemen. Abel copied them down in his little book, his quick notation indecipherable to any not in the Harrier organization. He would make quick work of running down these leads and identify the house TreMondi had shown him in his mind. It was possible that Trune had come back to town earlier than that, but Abel didn't think so. Trune would need but a few weeks to suss out the habits of the Mederos sisters and make the snatch. Furthermore, he would know that all the leases were accounted for in the Gazette each week, so a nom de guerre was in order. He would have Trune in a few days at most, and once he handed him over to the Guild, he would deliver the Mederos girl to Doc. The aborted attempt at the bank was a mere setback. He was more prepared now.

Abel began leafing through the rest of the papers, skimming for more information on the Fraud and its players.

The cheeky campaign of the Gentleman Bandit began just after Saint Frey's Day in the spring and he struck early and often in the weeks that followed. One of the first to be hit was a lively party of young merchants. In a town such as Port Saint Frey, there would always be feckless young idiots with more money than sense and no sense of self-preservation. Easy pickings for a daring thief.

There were many such reports of the audacity of the Gentleman Bandit. He had been described by witnesses as a neat, slender fellow, equally at home in the drawing rooms of his victims as they were. He wielded two pistols, wore a mask, had either handsome blue eyes or piercing black ones, depending on the particular bent of romanticism of each witness, and never spoke. "But his gestures were as eloquent as any speech," claimed one young lady.

At the Iderci salon, he held his pistol to the head of one merchant – ah, that was Lupiere, Abel noted – and forced a young lady to gather up the guests' valuables. Abel's attention sharpened at the description of the young lady in question – *daughter of a disgraced house.* Abel read the reporter's breathless description of the night – at the villain's direction, the girl had gathered up the valuables and then was used as a human shield before exiting through the garden doors.

> *The young lady in question rose to the occasion, throwing off the doubts about her honor and honesty. With great fortitude she pointed the direction the evil-doer had taken in his flight. "There! There! He flees down the alley!"*

And yet he slipped the net once again, Abel thought. Imagine that. So which Mederos sister would be at a salon at the Iderci mansion that night, to be in position to grab the cash and pass it off to the Gentleman Bandit? TreMondi said Yvienne Mederos was using her position as governess to cover for other activities. Acting as accomplice of an armed robber was certainly more like her than walking the wharves, as TreMondi suspected. But even that was unlikely. Whatever Yvienne Mederos had been up to at night when she was supposed to be teaching astronomy to her charges, it was not playing second fiddle to a two-bit pretty-boy thief.

That was not her style, Abel thought. Yvienne Mederos *ran* things – she wasn't anyone's sidekick. And it was her sister who was the society gambler, who upset the good ladies of Port Saint Frey because she won their pin money from them. And it made sense, he thought – if Tesara Mederos collaborated with the Gentleman Bandit, it made sense that he was there on the fateful night. No doubt they planned a sweet take, and it was only when Trune turned the tables that things went bad.

Abel felt as if he were on the verge of putting all the pieces together. He looked into space, not really seeing the shelves upon shelves of books in the reading room and through the doorway into the rest of the stacks. He felt eyes upon him and turned to the old man who gave him another beady-eyed look, like an impudent crow. Then he lolled back into sleep, his snores sailing into the rafters.

Something else impinged upon his concentration; voices, albeit hushed, at the front desk – one familiar.

Shock coursed through him, shock and anticipation. Even as he told himself to move, to hide so she couldn't find him, he stayed stock still, hands on the newsprint, as the voices grew louder.

"I know I saw the advertisement for watered silks in last week's *Gazette*, but Cook used it to wrap fish," Elenor Charvantes was saying brightly as she followed the librarian into the reading room. She had on an overcoat of deep brown that accentuated her gold locks and pale pink cheeks. Her eyes were the color of a twilight sky. She looked straight at Abel. He looked down indifferently, but he could feel his face heat. With barely a pause, she finished, "And I just need to find out which shop had them. I can't rest, you see, until I know."

"He has the *Gazettes*," the librarian said. Her peremptory tone indicated that she expected Abel to abandon whatever frivolous research he was doing for the benefit of Mrs Charvantes.

"I simply can't rest," she repeated, her color high but her eyes fixed upon his. Abel nodded.

"Of course," Abel said. "If you would allow me." He turned the volume around so it faced the seat opposite. Elenor nodded with great dignity and turned to the librarian.

"Thank you," she said, and sat. The librarian turned on her heel and left them to it. The old fellow kept snoring.

Abel leaned forward, his fingers steepled so he wouldn't touch her. Elenor closed the portfolio and opened it from the beginning, leafing slowly and carefully, skimming each and every ad. He kept his voice low, just above a whisper, so that his words were as light as air and almost as soundless. She followed suit.

"You haven't rested?" he said.

"No. They are watered silks, you see."

"A priceless fabric. Do you make your own dresses?"

Her cheeks flushed even higher. "Is it a failing if I do not? A merchant's daughter is not a lady, Mr Fresnel. We are well-acquainted with the price of hard work and the value of labor, and we also know that it's better to pay for expert hands than to ply our own at a trade for which we are ill-suited."

She was beautiful and sad, and she had followed him here. No doubt she thought it was coincidence. Abel knew better. This was his doing. He had forged this link with her in that single ill-fated handshake. An unintended consequence of his skill; some of Doc's Harriers exploited it. He could tell himself he had not wanted this to happen, but he knew he was lying.

He wanted to wind his fingers around hers, and with his other hand pull her toward him, and know everything about her, including her desire. He kept his hands where they were.

"I don't devalue you," he said. Her eyes flicked up to him, and back down at the old newspapers, and she licked her finger and turned the page. "You aren't flawed."

A laugh. "I'm human, Mr Fresnel. Of course I'm flawed." Bitter, now. "And I pay for my clay feet every day of my existence."

"He's a fool," Abel said.

"I was the fool," she said. "He showed me who he was from the start. I chose not to believe. He could not possibly be how he presented himself." She shook her head. "And here I am, paying for my firm misconception that no one could possibly be that – indifferent to kindness."

"I'm another kind of mistake," he warned. "Worse than the wrong husband."

"At least I will have chosen you with my eyes open," she said. She looked directly at him. She reached out and took his hand, closing her fingers around it.

Abel stiffened as he was flooded with her need and desire, battering against his own, and emphasizing it, as his particular talent was wont to do. How long had it been since he'd allowed himself to open up to a woman? How long since he had felt anything other than indifference? For this very reason – that his energy, amplified by Doc's ministrations, would also amplify desire – he had kept himself shut off from love.

She's a mistake too, he told himself. Don't do this. He twined his fingers around hers. Mindful of the old man, he didn't lean forward to kiss her sweet, inviting mouth. He guided her hand back to the page and placed it there.

"I'm at the Bailet on the Esplanade. Room Twenty-three. I'll leave now."

He did, leaving her behind, throwing a glance at the

old man. The old codger hadn't moved, and by that Abel knew he had heard every word.

He had been pacing in his room for half an hour, hoping she would show up, knowing it was foolish to hope, wishing with all his body that she would come, and with each passing minute more and more sure that she had come to her senses for the both of them. He cursed himself, cursed her, hated his weakness and hers, and wished Jax Charvantes to the devil for having the nerve to abuse and berate his hopeful young wife.

A small knock came at the door and he took two giant steps to the door, wanting to throw it open and drag her in, but his hard-won caution came to the fore. He palmed his small pistol and opened the door a bit. There she was, wet and bedraggled, a scarf over her fashionable bonnet and long overcoat, concealing the wealthy young woman beneath it all. Her eyes were wide and large in her cold wet face, but they burned with exhilaration. He opened the door and pulled her in, closed it behind her and gave in, kissing her with abandon. She gave a little cry against his lips and pressed herself against him.

They shed their clothes in a fury and fell upon the narrow bed.

Everywhere his hands touched her he could feel her overwhelming emotion and the outline of her thoughts. All of it was focused on him, on her own need, on their total desire. Abel was consumed.

Chapter Seventeen

"Miss Mederos!" Idina TreMondi, the younger daughter of Alve TreMondi, called out to Yvienne, waving excitedly from down the street from the Mederos office. Standing in the doorway, Yvienne waved back, keeping as cheerful a mien as possible. The TreMondi family, all warmly dressed against the damp weather, hurried down the wet cobblestones toward the open office door. It was a scramble to get everyone inside, chased by a nasty squall off the harbor, and their entrance was a confused tangle of umbrellas, and breathless thank-yous, and *please just put your coats here*, and *I'm so glad you could come*.

With waterproofed coats hung up and umbrellas left in the portico and the front office full of the TreMondis, their mother, and their current governess, Miss Clairett, the office seemed rather smaller than Yvienne had ever noticed before.

"This is where you work?" Dubre demanded, turning in circles, his eyes wide with awe.

"This is it," Yvienne said. "We have a view of the harbor, and we log all the ships that come in, and their cargo. Then when our cargo comes in, it goes straight to our warehouses, and thence to the buyers."

He peered out the window at the harbor, barely visible in the slashing rain. "Which are your ships?"

"Ah, that's a story," Yvienne said. "Some say our ships are at the bottom of the ocean, sunk by a massive storm. But, in fact, our ships were stolen and their cargo diverted, and now my mother and father have sailed off to bring them back. Tea, Mrs TreMondi?"

She had been predisposed to like Mrs TreMondi when she had first met her, but now Yvienne wondered how much the woman knew. Her husband was at the house that fateful night. As part of the Guild's inner circle, he had to have some hand in the fraud that hobbled House Mederos, though he had not been found guilty.

She was gratified to see Mrs TreMondi's expression turn pained at her forthright explanation, but the woman made no other acknowledgement.

"Thank you. Tea would be lovely on a day like today."

"And hot cocoa for the children," Yvienne said. The office had a small pot-bellied stove that kept off most of the chill and served to keep a kettle on for the clerks and the family. She turned to it to busy herself.

"Mrs TreMondi, should the children have cocoa twice in one day?" said Miss Clairett disapprovingly, perhaps because she knew Yvienne had been her immediate predecessor. Establishing her territory, Yvienne thought. Immediately the younger children began to tease.

"Oh Mama, it's so cold!" Idina objected.

"I don't need to have cocoa at bedtime," Dubre said.

"I will have tea, if I may," said Maje, the eldest. She looked the most like her father, and it seemed as if she had already formed a deep attachment to the forms of etiquette that guided Port Saint Frey society. Poor kid, Yvienne thought.

Mrs TreMondi immediately waved away Miss Clairett's concerns. "Oh goodness, it won't harm them any. In Miss Mederos's office, she may feed the children as she pleases."

That was interesting – Mrs TreMondi was most particular regarding her children's diet.

"I certainly don't mean to corrupt them, but as hot cocoa in Fog Season is my favorite indulgence, I'm afraid I can't set a good example," Yvienne said with a laugh. She stirred the cocoa, added a dollop of cream to each, and handed round the cups. "Now you all sit here and I will tell you everything about what we do." She looked over at Miss Clairett and saw the woman give the cocoa tin the merest glance, but in that glance. Yvienne saw longing. She was older than Yvienne by about ten years, a stick-thin woman with mousy hair and a plain mouth. *She is me, were I to have finished my years at Madam Callier's, with no prospects save my own brains.* She continued with her introduction to the business of House Mederos, but with no further word she handed over a cup of cocoa and cream to Miss Clairett, and turned away before the woman could object.

"If you have no ships, what does your House do?" Dubre asked.

"Dubre, you are being very forward in your questions," Miss Clairett said nervously.

"No, it's quite all right, Miss Clairett. They are here to learn," Yvienne said. "We still handle cargo for other companies, and we buy and sell commodities on the exchange. And we will get our ships back, and build new ones, and then it will be as if nothing ever happened." She looked straight at Mrs TreMondi. *Take that back to your husband, if you dare.* Mrs TreMondi could not hide her emotions – a flare of anger narrowed her eyes.

"So House Mederos was not injured by the Great Fraud, after all."

"Injured? Yes. Defeated – no. Nor will we ever be."

"And yet, the Houses accused of taking part in the fraud – they may be diminished by this act. If there were no lasting harm, should there be a lasting punishment? Would not House Mederos wish to forgive its old enemies for the sake of trade that benefits all?"

Ah, Yvienne thought. House TreMondi got grabby, and got its fingers burned. Was Mrs TreMondi asking for leniency?

"I think that is up to my parents to decide, Mrs TreMondi." *And the seas would boil away to desert before my mother would ever forgive.*

"My people have a law," Mrs TreMondi began. "That if the victim agrees, a certain payment could be made to make them whole again. It's quite common, and very useful, to forestall any grudges that could impact future generations."

Did Mr TreMondi know that his wife had come to make a deal? Everyone was silent, watching them – the children were very aware that something serious was happening, and Miss Clairett had an expression of sincerest horror.

"I don't know that Port Saint Frey could adopt the laws of a foreign nation," Yvienne said at last. "The fraud against my House was a criminal suit, and in such matters the city brings the charges. The Houses involved broke the laws of the city. As for influencing the Guild or the Houses involved, that would be my parents' decision, not mine."

"So it's out of your hands," Mrs TreMondi said. She set down her cup. "It has been most enlightening. Most enlightening. Children, we've imposed on Miss Mederos's hospitality far too long. We must be going."

"But we've only just got here!" Dubre cried, receiving a fierce glare from Maje.

Over Dubre's outcries and Idina's pleas, Miss Clairett hastened the children into their fine waterproofed coats. Young Maje curtseyed to Yvienne and thanked her.

"Thank you for your visit," Yvienne responded. "Please come any time for as long as you like. And how is your music progressing, Maje? I do admit I miss hearing you play. You are quite talented."

Solemn Maje gave her a genuine smile. "I'm playing for Papa's birthday party! Perhaps you will come then! It's to be a great party."

Mrs TreMondi gave a laugh that she tried to cover up. "Maje! Papa's birthday party is to celebrate Papa, not you! Miss Mederos, I apologize–"

"Not to worry," Yvienne said as cheerfully as she could muster. *The only way I would come to Alve TreMondi's birthday party is as the Gentleman Bandit.* Now there was a tempting idea. She thrust it back down where it belonged.

There came a jangling at the door, and Inigho Demaris poked his head in. "Hello, Yvi– Miss Mederos," he began as he took in the crowd. His eyes lit up. "A party!" he said.

"Inigho, come in out of the wet," Yvienne said. "Mrs TreMondi, may I introduce Mr Demaris?"

"Delighted," Inigho said. He bowed to her, droplets falling off his walking cape.

"Very nice to meet you," Mrs TreMondi said. "I had the pleasure of extended conversation with your mother at Mrs Charvantes's salon the other day."

"Talked your ear off, did she?" Inigho said frankly. "I'm sorry. And who is this?" He bowed to Maje as the eldest daughter and though she reddened, she managed a very correct curtsey.

"Maje and Idina were my pupils during my governess tenure," Yvienne said without batting an eye. "Dubre escaped my clutches only because he went to the Academy."

"Ah, an Academy boy, are you?" Inigho said. "Do you boys still carve your name in the pine grove on the west side of the pitch? You'll find the initials *ID* about five feet up, shot out of a crudely drawn cannon."

He turned to Yvienne. "Miss Mederos, I saw you were working and thought I would pop in and discuss that contract."

"Of course," Yvienne said.

"And we really must be going, as you have work to do," Mrs TreMondi said. "Come, children. Miss Clairett. Miss Mederos, please consider our conversation if you will. Mr Demaris, my regards to your mother."

With that, the tumult of their arrival was reversed, with coats and umbrellas acquired and unfurled, and the family trooped out of the office, leaving Yvienne and Inigho alone amidst cups of cocoa on the desk and side tables.

"Well," Inigho said finally. "About that contract that we need to discuss." He moved closer to her. "Are your clerks in?"

"They've gone to their dinner," Yvienne said. She felt a flutter in her abdomen. He pulled her toward him.

"Good," he said, his voice almost a growl. "We'll get down to business without them."

He was so good at kissing, Yvienne thought, melting in his arms so thoroughly that she didn't hear the door open behind her again. She heard the little shriek that Miss Clairett gave, though, and she and Inigho jumped apart to see the governess staring at them, a single glove in her hand. "I–" she began, and then thought better of it, fleeing.

"Shit," said Inigho, in a most unmerchantlike way, staring after her. "Yvienne – I am so sorry."

Yvienne sighed. "No, it's not your fault," she said. She smoothed back her hair and straightened her waistcoat and skirts, feeling unfairly irked at Miss Clairett.

It's just my luck.

Chapter Eighteen

There have been no further dispatches regarding the rogue cabbie preying on fares; the city force is silent upon the subject. The Chief Constable has given no official statement on whether his officers have given up all hope of apprehending the villain, or even if the attack were a figment of the unknown victim's overactive imagination, as the Gazette's sources strongly suggest. When asked if the report was in question, the Chief Constable, with his admirably straight jaw and erect bearing, responded only that the thing was under investigation. We think the Chief has not forgiven this reporter our earlier impertinence. ~~ No word of any ships, and we are all anxiously awaiting news of the Iderci Empress. *In lighter news, are nuptials pending between the young heiress of House M and House D? – we are not sure what her parents have to say of such events, as they are off on an extended voyage.*

THE GAZETTE

That was quick, thought Yvienne with a sigh. Miss Clairett had wasted no time in spreading her news regarding the independent Miss Mederos. She set aside the morning paper and crunched into her toast, pale gold and soaked in butter and preserves, and the only thing better than Mrs Francini's biscuits.

Face it, she thought. You knew that just taking lunch with Inigho would set the city whispering all by itself. But she had hoped for a bit of respite before the full force of the Port Saint Frey society gossip mill descended on the family this time.

"Thank you," she said to Albero, who had replenished her coffee. As usual, she was the only one up. She had a meeting with the family solicitor, Dr Reynbolten, to go over Inigho's contract, and then a meeting with Inigho himself, in his office this time. She felt a shiver of excitement at the coming meeting. Stop it, she scolded herself. Then she had to speak with Noe about her handler.

Albero put the coffee back on the sidebar and straightened a dish unnecessarily, then stood at attention. He had little enough to do with just a household of three, and when he only had to serve one member of the house, he clearly felt at a loose end. She felt sorry for him.

If I married, then we could fill the house, she thought. And just as suddenly she half-laughed, half-recoiled from the idea. The thought of it, marrying to keep the butler busy! And the idea of marrying Inigho; she had to admit she was far from taking that step.

"Albero," she said, banishing the uncomfortable thoughts, and he jerked to attention, hoping to be of service.

"Yes, miss?"

"I only wondered what was happening with the dumbwaiter. Any word?"

"It was installed by the Alcestri family, which runs the trades' guild, Miss. I've sent word and they promised to have someone up here today to look at it."

"Good. You know, the odor has gotten worse, I've noticed.

I'm afraid we may have vermin."

He wrinkled his nose. "We noticed that too, miss. The house under the previous owner was not well-run."

"Squatters very rarely look after things properly," she said. Even she could hear her mother's voice in her words, but she meant every bit of it. No doubt Trune jammed the dumbwaiter out of spite before he fled for his life and reputation.

"Yes, miss," Albero said. "Is there anything else this morning?"

Yvienne drew a breath. "Please send for Noe, Albero. I'll speak with her here."

He hesitated a fraction and then nodded. "Yes, miss."

To her credit, Noe did not creep. She entered with her head up and her eyes on Yvienne, though her face was pinched and red around the nose. She bobbed a curtsey. Albero closed the doors behind her and left them alone. Yvienne looked at the girl for a long moment, really seeing her. Noe had been skinny when she first came to service in her house, but with Mrs Francini's good cooking she had filled out and her cheeks had warmed. She was still slight but her eyes were clear, and though she was quick to irritability Yvienne had seen her smile once or twice, brightening her eyes and her complexion, before her double life was revealed.

Now she was as mousy and quiet as when she first came.

"Noe, I don't wish to make this any more uncomfortable for you than it has to be," Yvienne began. "You shan't be sacked, not if you do your work and listen to Mrs Francini and Mr Renarte. We'd like you to stay, just not to steal from us, or tell the family secrets."

"Yes, miss. Thank you, miss."

Yvienne cocked her head, eyeing her. Noe was dutiful,

nothing more. Caught between two masters, she thought. It must be dreadful for her.

"Have you spoken to your handler about being caught?"

"Yes, miss."

"And what did he say? Are you in danger in any way?"

"He – no, miss. Malcroft said that if I was stupid enough to get caught, and you were stupid enough to keep me, then we could go on as before."

"He expects you to continue to work for him?" Despite herself, Yvienne's voice rose in surprise. "I must say, that's fresh. Well, that's simply not on. From now on, you'll live in. Mr Malcroft can have you back when he comes to see me."

She allowed herself a moment of self-satisfaction until Noe's look of horror impinged upon her. Yvienne rolled her eyes. "What?"

"If I don't go home, miss, my mother and father and the rest – he'll..." Noe fell silent. Yvienne sighed. She had not thought of that, but of course, it made perfect sense. Noe's family was being held hostage to her ability to produce the goods. Clearly, she needed greater leverage to tip Mr Malcroft over to her side. She needed to think on this.

"All right," she said. "For now, say nothing more. But I warn you, Noe. You work for me now. Your loyalty is to *me*. Not this man. Is that clear?"

Noe nodded, her expression by turns wary and skeptical. Yvienne understood; could a merchant's daughter protect the housemaid from the dock gangs? *I hope so, Noe. I surely do.*

"You may go. And tell Mr Renarte to come in, please."

Yvienne watched her leave, and the butterflies in her stomach intensified. *What am I doing?* No, she thought stubbornly. It's what this city is forcing me to become. The

Harrier, and now this – if the society of Port Saint Frey had wanted a demure Yvienne Mederos, they should have backed off.

By the time Albero returned, she was back to her old self. "Albero, could you send the gardener's boy to fetch a cab for me? I have to travel to the solicitor's offices and I have documents to carry."

The city hack was comfortable and dry, the cabbie resigned to Albero interrogating him and giving the cab a once over, but making no complaint once a half-guilder changed hands. Albero handed Yvienne up into it, and passed her case of documents after her. She settled in, he closed the door, and she drew one hand from her rather moth-eaten fur muff and rapped on the ceiling of the cab. The horse started off with a lurch and then almost immediately came to a halt. For a second she gripped the pistol, but the door opened and Uncle Samwell flung himself inside, his hair a tousled mess, and his overcoat half-buttoned.

"Glad I caught you, missy," he said. He adjusted himself to fit in the tight space. "You can just have him drop me off at the docks."

Yvienne's breathing slowed, and she made sure the pistol was entirely concealed.

"Good morning, uncle," she said. "No breakfast?"

"I am on a reducing regimen." He patted his belly proudly. "Coffee and a cigar. Keeps me whole the entire day."

"Uncle," she said, tired of his nonsense. "Why are you here?"

"I need to keep an eye on you. What would your parents think if I let you go on the way you've been?"

"Really."

"Really. Look, I know you think you're running things,

but you're as headstrong as that sister of yours, and you need a guiding hand." At her look, he elaborated, "This business with Inigho. You don't want to make a mistake. The man's clever."

The hack tilted as the horse trudged down the steep hill with the brake on. They bounced over the cobblestones. Remind me to investigate other street paving options, she thought. In a hilly city like Port Saint Frey, smoother roads would be welcome, and many merchants had a sideline in providing goods and services to the city.

"You're the one who presented me with the contract," she pointed out, her voice wobbling along with the bouncy hack.

"I never thought you'd take it seriously," he said, which made her roll her eyes.

"Well, you don't have to fear – I've rewritten most of it."

"It's not the contract I'm worried about," he said. "It's you and Inigho. You're not thinking of forming a personal connection? Not that I trust the *Gazette*, but the word at Aether's is you and him are sparking."

That the Names were betting on the relationship between herself and Inigho Demaris was stomach-turning. This was worse than gossip. She glanced at her uncle. He was serious, concerned.

"Setting aside your revolting slang," she said, "what if we were? Would that be such a bad thing?"

"I just don't think he'd be a good fit with the family," he said, looking earnest. "Face it, Vivi, we're different. House Mederos and House Balinchard aren't like other merchant houses. Inigho might take issue."

Meaning he'd take issue with you, she thought. She had to admit, though, he had a point. Inigho would get along with Alinesse; she was most like his own formidable mother. And no doubt he and Brevart would be correct and mannerly with each other. But how would Inigho get along with Tesara? They would have to keep her powers a secret from him. And it was one thing for the family to treat both Tesara and Uncle Samwell with disdain, as they did – but Inigho would be an outsider and it would be terrible if he did. Love me, love my family – could any man do that?

And how would Inigho get along with me? The kissing was nice, but marriage was more than kisses.

"I think you can be at ease," she said. "I'm certainly not planning to form any connection with Inigho – or anyone else – any time soon."

He refused to be comforted. "Well, but that's just it. You might. And then it will all go bad, Vivi. Believe me."

She had to laugh, but she was also irked. His persistence was beginning to irritate. "Uncle, I believe I can choose my own husband without your help. But I'm not even anywhere near that point."

"In fact, it would be better if you didn't think of it at all," he said. "For Tesara, at one time, she would have done the family good by marrying. But you shouldn't bother. I've seen married women. They lose all perspective. It would be a shame if all you thought about was your house and your children. Look at Alinesse – she lost all sense of fun."

"I'm sorry that my hypothetical marriage would be such an inconvenience for you," she said, her voice dripping with wrath.

"See? That's exactly what I mean."

"Uncle, let me make one thing clear, since you think you have a say in my future. I will marry whomever I want, whenever I want. And you will say nothing more about it."

She rapped the ceiling of the cab so hard dust rained down on them. The cab jerked to a halt. Yvienne flung the door open and the cold wet air rushed in. "Out. I wish to be alone."

He stared at her, and then heaved his bulk out of the hack. He turned back to look up at her, his pink-rimmed eyes wet with injury.

"I don't know what's come over you," he said. "You used to be the sensible one. Now you're as flighty as your sister."

"Good day, uncle." Yvienne jerked the handle of the door from his hand. "Enjoy your coffee and cigar."

She pulled the door shut, rapped the ceiling with more restraint this time, and settled back in a huff. He was incorrigible.

I should marry Inigho. It would serve uncle right. Then she sighed. She had hidden depths, but rebellion against her own good sense was not on the cards. Uncle Samwell was safe from a family interloper, at least for now.

Left hand. Right hand. Tesara splayed her hands against the cold glass panes of her bedroom window, marking the crooked fingers, the condensation slicking on her palms. The damp felt good, as if her blood always ran hot now. Then in an instant, the condensation dried up, and her hands were also dry, the water wicked away. Her fingers throbbed with power, and the familiar queasiness came back.

The Harrier was right.

It's getting worse. She hated to admit it, but it had become undeniable. The power was getting harder and harder to control. Every time she used her talent, it sickened her a little. Even against the lieutenant, even against Trune's coachman, whenever the energy built up inside her fingers, it made her queasy. She had become more adept at controlling it, but at a great cost – it took more effort than ever.

She had been hard-pressed to control herself when she met the Harrier outside the bank, and his quiet, dead-on analysis of what was happening had almost destroyed what little control she had left.

We can train you, he said. So the Harriers knew about her talents. Presumably there were others like her, and that was intriguing. Tempting. But at what price? she thought. What would the Harriers want from her in return? She imagined that it would be something like what Trune had wanted – to make use of her powers. She wanted none of that.

And then what had he meant – "don't use it on yourself?" Why would I be so foolish? she thought. The idea of it sickened her.

"I don't know what to do," she whispered, resting her forehead on the window. She couldn't tell Vivi. It would only worry her, and she had enough on her plate, what with running the House. She had no one to talk to.

A knock came at the door. She withdrew her hands from the glass, leaving an odd imprint as if her hands had indented the pane, and called out, "Yes?"

"Miss Tesara?" Albero said. "There's a letter for you in this morning's post."

She opened the door, and the young butler handed her a single letter with a formal red wax seal. She took it carefully, avoiding his fingers lest she shock him. "Thank you. Has my sister left for the day already? I thought I heard a cab in the drive."

"Yes. She had an appointment with Dr Reynbolten and with Mr Demaris. Your uncle caught a lift too." Before she could ask him, he added, "I checked the cab and the driver thoroughly."

Her mouth quirked in acknowledgement. "Of course," she said. "I knew you would. I'll be down in a moment. I do apologize for being late to breakfast again. I know it makes more work for you."

"Miss Yvienne instructed me that slugabeds should fend for themselves for breakfast," Albero said, a slight smile lifting the corners of his mouth. "But Mrs Francini would never allow it. If you can keep it secret, would you like to come into the kitchen for your coffee and toast?"

"My lips are sealed," Tesara promised. "I'll be down in five minutes."

Alone, she slid the paper knife under the edge of the seal and opened the letter.

Madam Saint Frey is at home to Miss Tesara Mederos today at 11 o'clock in the morning.
Signed,

The signature was unintelligible, the scrawl shaky and weak.

It was a demand, not an invitation. Tesara's heart sank. What on earth did she have to say to Jone's mama? How could she tell her that she, Tesara, had received a letter from her wayward son describing his determination to seek a life at sea? Not to mention, she thought, that he declared his love for me.

Don't go.

It was tempting to just ignore the summons. Who did old Madam Saint Frey think she was? But despite her self-righteous indignation, she had to admit, she was curious. She had never met Jone's mama, even though she had been a guest at her salon. Perhaps she could sit and hear the old lady out, allay her fears if she could, try not to give away Jone's secrets, and make her escape as soon as was polite. It would be her one good deed, and it would take her mind off the Harrier's offer.

The instant she stepped out of her bedroom, she gave an involuntary, "ugh!" The house was not only cold and damp due to Yvienne's no extra fires dictum, there was a dreadful smell, and she covered her nose with the ends of her rose shawl.

"Ugh, Albero," she said to the butler as they both headed to the kitchen, Albero with a tray of breakfast things. "Has something gone wrong with the water closet?" Of course they would have plumbing issues, with their parents on a six-month sea voyage.

"No, miss," he said. "It's the dumbwaiter. I fear the damp of Fog Season has accelerated the rot. Miss Yvienne has instructed us to bring in the Alcestris to fix it."

"Worse than that," she said, wrinkling her nose. "It smells rather like the Academy, when a squirrel died in the walls of the dormitory. I hope they can fix it."

She followed him down the shallow steps to the kitchen. Already it was warmer here, and the smells of coffee, tea, and Mrs Francini's lunch preparations overwhelmed the odor from the dumbwaiter shaft. Tesara breathed in deep. Albero pulled out a chair at the wooden table and she sat.

"I'm sorry, Mrs Francini. I'm not used to keeping Vivi's hours."

"She's a go-getter," Mrs Francini said with brisk cheer. She set down a cup of coffee in a big mug, and a pile of toast dripping with butter. Tesara took a sip and sighed with pleasure. Perhaps it was her imagination, but coffee tasted better in the kitchen.

"What are your plans today, Miss Tesara?" Mrs Francini asked over her shoulder. She was whisking a roux on the stovetop.

"Oh, very little. Just some bits and bobs of errands. I'll need a cab this morning – half past ten, please."

"I'll let the boy know," Albero said.

The massive old mansion, far larger and more ancient than the modern merchant townhouses, sprawled on a cliff overlooking the sea. It rose higher than any other building in Port Saint Frey due to this vantage point. It even overlooked the soaring spires of the Cathedral in the central city.

Welcome to the Port of Saint Frey,
Where men trade with a wink and a nod.
Here the merchants look down on each other,
And the Saint Freys look down upon God.

She had the hack leave her below the drive and she walked up the rest of the way, covered by the fog. The last time she had attempted this walk, she was wearing dancing slippers and a silk gown and cloaked in desperate bravado. This time, her warm Fog Season attire offered more physical protection but she was far more vulnerable to self-doubt. It was entirely possible that Jone's mother, with her reputation for selfishness, would simply refuse to see her, that it was enough to vindictively call Tesara out in dreadful weather to make her point. That would be a relief, she thought. Then she could say she had tried, and all of the attendant awkwardness would be avoided.

Tesara stood before the massive door of the Saint Frey House. She steeled herself and lifted the heavy ring, banging it against the rain-stained oak. The knock reverberated with a hollow echo. Then there was only the sound of the dripping of the eaves. She waited, wondering if she should knock again or go around to the kitchen and peer in the window, when finally she heard the sound of the door being opened. Slowly, as if it were so heavy that it took three sturdy footmen and a kitchen boy to move it, it swung open to reveal the dark entrance, and Tesara and the butler regarded each other.

He was old and white-haired, and stern. She almost completely lost her nerve, but retained the presence of mind to announce herself.

"Miss Tesara Mederos to visit Madam Saint Frey," she said.

He squinted down at her, and she had long enough to notice that his fine coat and trousers were threadbare, and there were stains on his impressive necktie, a relic of an earlier age. Poor Jone, she thought. House Saint Frey hadn't lost their money as suddenly as House Mederos had, but in turn they had little chance to earn it back.

"Come in, Miss Mederos," the butler said. "Madam Saint Frey has been waiting for you."

Resigned to her fate, she followed the man into the house.

The last time she had stepped foot in the Saint Frey's home it had been illuminated for a large party, and she had taken no notice of the structure of the great room, being far more preoccupied with the crowd of brightly dressed guests, the music, and the dancing, and with Jone. This was the Fairy Hall the day after, when the magic had been extinguished and the elves all gone under the mountain. The Saint Frey hall was dark and cold, and smelled of a fireplace that hadn't been lit in days. The only light came from the high windows on either side of the door, and it was a gray, gloomy light.

The butler gestured to a dusty, threadbare chair in the foyer and she sat, sliding a little on the fabric. Once it had been a fine seat, embroidered with roses and greens. Now tufts of fluff poked up. Tesara shifted her weight to avoid most of the fluff. The butler made off at a measured pace and she was alone.

If he had to walk to the other side of the house to tell his mistress, she could be there for a long time. Tesara got up and began looking around, restless.

The hall had a desolate air. Most merchant townhouses had a genteel foyer for their guests, with a mirror and a narrow table, and two precisely set chairs, polished and dusted. Here the single chair was an afterthought, and in its state of disrepair, possibly an after-afterthought. Cold steeped up from the flagstones into her feet as she paced, and she was mindful of a clammy draft. There was a huge painting over the cold fireplace, but it was so dark she could get no more of an impression than that of a ship in a roiling, dark sea.

Tesara looked away at once. Even just looking at representations of waves could set her off. She needed to concentrate.

"Hello, Tesara," came a familiar voice.

Tesara started and turned. It was Mirandine.

The fashionable girl stared back at her through the gloom. Her dress was of the very newest mode, accentuating her long lines. Despite the cold, clammy air, her bared arms were a rosy bronze. The sweet scent of tobacco wafted over to Tesara. Mirandine took a long draft on her cigarillo, and then dropped it and ground it out on the flagstones with a dainty silk-covered shoe.

"Welcome to the house of the dead," Mirandine intoned. She came forward out of the gloom. Now Tesara could see that her dress was actually a tunic over long, drapey trousers of gray rose, a fashionable silk Tesara had just seen in Madam Courget's window.

Tesara cocked her head. "What are you doing?" she said at last.

"Here?"

"In general. Mirandine, you're acting as if you're in a stage tragedy."

"I am in a tragedy," Mirandine said, sounding more like herself. "You would be too, if you were shut up in this house."

Just like that the mood was dispelled. She led Tesara over to a large bow window and threw open the mildewed velvet curtains. A powerful cloud of dust rose, setting them both coughing, but the dimness gave way grudgingly to gray daylight. They sat on the threadbare cushion of the window seat.

Tesara inspected her friend. Mirandine was as beautiful as always, her lips painted red and her eyes lined with kohl, but there was strain at the corners and her forehead wrinkled with concern.

"Why are you confined here? Why haven't you gotten in touch with me? And why are you–" she gestured "–acting like this?"

"Well, I could ask much the same of you, but I'll answer first. I'm shut up here because Mama Saint Frey has threatened to off herself because of Jone's disappearance. I haven't gotten in touch with you – and mind you, you can pen a letter too, can you not? – because I thought the Mederos family was far too busy restoring its fortunes to bother with the likes of me. And I'm acting like this because I thought I might take it up. Papa Depressis has been carrying on with an actress and she said that I was a natural for the stage."

"What?!" Tesara could not believe her ears.

"No, it's true. Apparently all the historical drama we had to learn at school paid off."

"I meant about Jone's mama. She isn't really going to kill herself, is she? She can't. Mirandine, I know where Jone is."

She had a slight sense of satisfaction at Mirandine's shock. She hurried to explain. "He's at sea. I saw him on board the *Empress* when my parents sailed. And he sent me a letter, explaining everything."

"Oh, Tesara, this is marvelous news!" Mirandine seemed genuinely happy. "Do you know what this means? I can finally leave my post!"

"And that Jone is all right," Tesara pointed out.

Mirandine made an impatient face. "I always knew that. I had faith in him, dear boy. He had to get away from that woman, somehow." She waved an elegant arm to illustrate.

"*Is* that why she asked for me?" Tesara asked. "Her letter was quite… terse."

"It must be, but she doesn't confide in me," Mirandine said. "I must admit, I'm rather surprised that she called for you."

"That makes two of us," Tesara muttered.

"And Jone didn't confide in me either," Mirandine said, and something in her voice made Tesara look at her in the dim light. It took her a moment to realize that it was hurt that sounded in her sophisticated friend's expression. Then Mirandine gave a tinkling laugh. "Oh, Jone. When I see him next, I'll scold him. What did he say?"

Tesara didn't miss a beat. "He didn't say much. He told me he wanted to seek his fortune. He didn't want to be Jone Saint Frey of Port Saint Frey any longer." She smiled at a memory. "When I saw him aboard the *Empress,* he already looked like a sailor."

"Jone with muscles. Who would have imagined?" Mirandine opened a cigarette case and selected another cigarillo. "Did his letter mention me?"

"Only in the most general way – about the good times we had last summer."

"Ah."

I hate this, Tesara thought crossly. Why did Jone have to put me in this position? "When did you start smoking?" she asked, to try to avert more uncomfortable questions.

"About the time Jone proposed to me, so I expect about, mmm, four months ago."

Tesara stared at her. "Oh," she managed. That was not how Jone had put it.

"Yes, I had the same reaction. I can't imagine why he did it – unless his mother put him up to it. I always thought he loved you. And it wasn't as if I wanted to marry him. We've been good friends since we were kids, you know. Best cousins. The slightly awkward, slightly fast, not like the rest of the family set."

Mirandine lit the cigarillo but did not smoke it, just watched the smoke curl into the gloomy hall.

"So he proposed – did you accept? I mean..." Tesara stopped.

"I did. I didn't mean to, but when one's cousin proposes, and one loves the cousin like a brother – well, it doesn't sound likely but yes, I said yes. I didn't want to hurt his feelings. As soon as I did, I could tell he regretted it. I think he thought that he had done his duty, and if I had been thinking I would have said no, and he could have gone back to Mama, and told her, 'well, I tried.'"

"Ah," Tesara said. "That never seems to work."

"No, it doesn't." Mirandine smiled her brilliant smile, and Tesara could have sworn her eyes were bright in the gray daylight. "But now you're here to save the day. You can show Mama Saint Frey the letter, and she'll know Jone's alive and well and becoming muscular and tanned, and I can go home to Ravenne."

"Miss Mederos," said the butler and they looked at the

man as he loomed out of the shadows, a skeletal figure clad in black, only his white hair and old gray face showing above his collar. "Madam will see you now."

"Jolly her up, will you, Tesara? I'll be here."

Tesara followed the butler down the dark hallways, the sweet smell of tobacco trailing along behind her as if Mirandine trod along in their path.

As soon as Tesara stepped into Madam Saint Frey's sitting room, she was reminded of Madam Callier's Academy for Young Ladies. But it wasn't the strong-willed, wicked headmistress she was thinking of, but of her old nurse, Michelina, when she died their first year at school. The room had the same sickroom stink to it, as if the sheets had not been washed in a long time. The fire burned hot, and Tesara felt uncomfortably warm in her coat, which the butler had not taken when she arrived, and for which she had been thankful in the drafty hall. She dared not take it off here, and she remained standing ill at ease, as Madam Saint Frey waved a languid hand to her manservant.

"Savain, light the lamp in the window, please."

"Yes, madam." With the same stiff, slow care, the butler set up the lamp, filled it with camphene from a metal tin, and lit it, the camphene oil sweet in the odorous sick room. It was almost too much for Tesara; she swallowed the nausea that rose up at the combination of thick, cloying smells, and put her sleeve against her nose and mouth to gain control. The lamp shone in the window, a beacon of light in Fog Season. Sitting as it was in the window, it barely lifted the oppressive twilight of the sitting room.

At another wave of Madam Saint Frey's languid hand, the butler backed out of the room, closing the doors.

Jone's mother sat up on an ancient chaise longue. Despite

the immense heat of the room she had a rug across her legs. She wore a pink silk robe, and her unbound hair was twisted in a thick loose braid that trailed over her shoulder and down the front of her gown. Her hair was surprisingly full and shiny, a warm chestnut brown. With a shock, Tesara identified what it was – a wig.

Tesara remembered her manners and bobbed a curtsey.

"Ma'am–" she began, but Madam Saint Frey held up a hand. She closed her eyes, as if listening to an inner voice. Tesara kept from rolling her own eyes. The sooner she relayed her message the sooner she could make her exit. "Ma'am," she repeated in a rush, wanting nothing more than to get out of the stifling room. "Your son sent me a letter – he is aboard the *Iderci Empress*, and he's sailing round the world. He doesn't know when he will return, but you may write to him by packet mail."

"You wicked, wicked girl," Madam Saint Frey intoned.

"I– I beg your pardon?"

"You will never marry him," Jone's mother declared in throbbing tones of high emotion. She shook her fist, as if it held a fistful of dice, and then sank back, her arm draped across her forehead. Her outburst had caused her wig to shift, and a bit of gray, tangled hair peeked out from beneath the chestnut tresses.

"He was meant to marry his cousin Mirandine," Madam Saint Frey went on. "And then he met you, a good-for-nothing merchant girl, of no consequence to a Saint Frey, and all of a sudden, a Depressis was not good enough for him. As if the bloodlines of the Saint Freys could stand to be so polluted. I hounded him, I tell you! I harangued, I argued day and night and I told him of your true nature, and he still would not budge. I told him I would have old Savain thrash him, as he used to do when Jone was a child, and do you know he laughed at me? He laughed!" Her eyes flashed again. "And I am happy he's gone! Happy, because it means he will not marry you! I would rather my son, my flesh and blood, my *name*, be gnawed by the leviathans of the deep than throw away his name and his nobility on you!"

She gasped, her tirade leaving her breathless, and sat back triumphantly. She smacked her hand against the upholstered chaise, raising a cloud of dust.

Tesara stood like stone. What a ridiculous old woman; she felt nothing for her except sadness. She had driven her own son away in her madness and need, and her insults were pathetic and absurd. It was stupid to have answered her summons. Nothing she said would get through to Madam Saint Frey; she clearly wished to wallow in her grief and indignation.

"I see," she said at last, and curtseyed again. "Good day, ma'am. I wish you well. I will not return."

She turned on her heel and fumbled for the doorknob. It didn't budge. Frowning, Tesara twisted the giant knob again. It was locked. She was shut in with a madwoman. A flash of panic ran through her and she turned back to Madam Saint Frey.

"Madam," she said, fighting for calm. "Ring for your manservant."

"Insolent girl! I will not be ordered about. You will leave at *my* pleasure."

Tesara's tone turned to ice; Alinesse's daughter would not be denied. "I cannot imagine, madam, an instant at which my presence *is* your pleasure. Release me, ma'am, and I won't pollute your home any further."

Madam Saint Frey stared her down. "You little fool. You've no idea of the net you're tangled in. You'll wait here until it's time for you to be taken away."

Confusion, followed by realization, overcame her. Of course. Whatever her feelings about the unsuitable nature of merchant daughters, Madam Saint Frey had no qualms about dealing with the Guildmaster. She had been sold.

Tesara ignored the madwoman on the chaise and cast about for a way to escape her prison. She wiggled the doorknob again, to no avail. She crossed the room in two steps and went over to the window where the little beacon cast its light onto the city – no doubt the signal to Trune or to his henchman that his quarry had been run to ground, she thought, bitter. What a little fool indeed. She and Yvienne had underestimated Trune after all. Furious, she plunged the lid down on the lamp, extinguishing the flame. The room was plunged into a deeper twilight, only the fire on the grate providing any light.

"No!" cried Madam Saint Frey. "How dare you!"

"Madam, if you do not call for your manservant to release me, I will dare much more," Tesara said. She was coldly angry now, and her hands trembled. Madam Saint Frey's frail condition be damned – she would use her powers on her if that's what it took to escape. Of course! *Tesara, you idiot!* She whirled and thrust her hands at the ornate doors. With a whoosh, she pushed air at them. They rattled, but did not budge. Despairing, Tesara tried again, and this time, the air impacted against the door with a boom that shook them but they did not shatter, or blow off their hinges. Sweat sprang out on her forehead and the now-familiar nausea rose in her throat. She stopped, waiting for the physical reaction to subside.

At least they will hear *that* downstairs, she thought. She hoped.

Madam Saint Frey glared at her. "I demand that you listen to me!" she cried, and full of anger she picked up the tin of camphene oil from the table next to her and threw it petulantly on the fire.

With a whoosh, the fire roared up, and flames licked out of the fireplace. Soot and smoke billowed in its wake. Jone's mama shrieked at what she had done, scrambling off the chaise with more alacrity than Tesara would have thought she possessed. "See what you made me do! Put it out! Put it out!"

Tesara snapped, "You blasted madwoman!" She grabbed the drapes from the window and pulled them down, choking at the dust, and threw them over the fire. Surely the heavy velvet would suffocate it, she thought. And at first the flames were extinguished, heavy dark smoke leaking around the fabric. She had a moment of relief, and then to her horror the fire caught again, fueled this time by the desiccated, shredded fabric. Coughing, she stepped back, one arm over her face. Madam Saint Frey was backed against the wall, shrieking at the approaching flames.

"Open the door! Open the door!" the old woman sputtered.

"I would if I could!" Tesara shouted back. "You idiot! That's why I said to call for your man!" She yanked again at the doorknob, and this time, to her horror, it came off in her hand. Oh my God, she thought. The door wasn't locked. It had jammed, due no doubt to the general disrepair of the household. Unless the butler or Mirandine were standing right outside the door, the fire could quite easily go unnoticed until it was too late.

Madam Saint Frey's answer was to wail louder.

How high up were they? Tesara ran to the window and despaired – they were high over the rocky cliffs. Her powers were one thing, but she couldn't fly, not even without Jone's mother to save. She had a special affinity for fire, because somehow fire and light and waves and air were all related. But she didn't need to call *up* a fire – they had quite enough fire at the moment. She had to extinguish it.

She spared a glance for Madam Saint Frey. The woman was terrified, struggling for breath, and her long chestnut wig was beginning to smoke from errant sparks. Tesara grabbed her and pulled her close to the window, dragging the wig off her head and throwing it across the room. It snaked along the ground, smoking, and looking alive.

Despite the danger Madam Saint Frey shrieked at the insult, clutching her gray, balding locks. "How dare you?" she cried out. "You terrible low-bred girl!"

Tesara ignored her. She tried to lift the sash but the wood frame had swelled after so many years of wet weather and neglect. She still had the doorknob in her hand. She swung hard, and it shattered the window with a satisfying crack, glass falling outward over the cliff. Cold air rushed in. The small lamp teetered on the windowsill and then fell over the edge. She hoped savagely that it clunked Trune or his coachman on the head when it landed.

Now they could breathe, but so could the fire. And they still couldn't get out.

Think think think. She had to be able to stop the fire.

She closed her eyes, feeling the heat against her face, hearing the crackling of the approaching flames. But she also felt the growing energy in her fingers. She didn't need to push air at the fire, because that would just feed it.

She had to pull the air *away* from it. She had to create a vacuum, and seal the fire inside. She and Jone's mother would be sealed in too, but perhaps they could be revived once the fire was extinguished.

The searing flame made it hard to concentrate but Tesara closed her eyes and began to pull. Her nausea increased, and she forced herself to ignore it. She had to work delicately; she had to pull the air, but not the fire. She worked at the edges of the flames even as they licked closer to her and Madam Saint Frey. It helped to imagine a dome pressing down from the ceiling, and the air escaping beneath it. She lowered the dome over all of them, the smoke and the lack of air making her desperate to breathe. Madam Saint Frey crumpled beside her with a look of ghastly distress. Tesara fell to her knees, choking for air even as she pulled it from the room. As she lost consciousness, she imagined the fire dying along with them.

Chapter Nineteen

All in all, Yvienne thought, returned from her visit with the Mederos attorney and Inigho Demaris and his advocate, it had been a most successful meeting. Dr Reynbolten had been entirely helpful in going over the prospective contracts, and Inigho had been the perfect gentleman while he was also the picture of a smart merchant. He had only once let his wolfish nature slip, during negotiations over a particular clause, and she found herself sparring warmly for her House's rights, and at the same time wondering what it would be like to continue their acquaintance. If her intellect was focused on the contract, her body was most agreeably intent upon the other game they played. If I am not careful, she thought, I am in danger of losing my head *and* my heart over this man.

Now she settled down in her study with a cup of tea and paperwork, her stockinged feet up on an embroidered footrest, going over the rest of the House business. This had been a little-used room when her parents were here, more of an architectural afterthought than a study, or a solar, or a breakfast room, or any other of the named rooms in the large house. Yvienne claimed it for her own after her parents set sail, because it hadn't seemed right to make herself at home in their offices. Her study was a cozy room, filled with old charts and almanacs, and warm wool rugs from other climes, and end tables that invited one to set down plates of scones and tea cups and curl up on the sofa and doze. Even without a fire, it was comfortable, because the thick drapes held in the warmth.

There came a knock at the door, and Albero poked his head in. "The Alcestris are here," he announced.

"Oh, thank heavens," she said, throwing on a shawl against the chill held by the rest of the drafty house. She thrust her feet into her shoes. "Hurry, Albero. It will be splendid to be able to breathe in this house once again. Where's Tesara?" She would want to be here for this moment, she was sure.

"She's out on errands, Miss Vivi."

Ah well, they could celebrate when she returned. They all would – the smell had truly permeated the house. It had, if anything, worsened, now that they had opened the elevator shaft several days ago to try to assess the situation. It was a combination of rotten food and death, and mildew and must. She covered her mouth and nose with one end of the tasseled shawl and hurried after Albero.

The two Alcestri brothers and their sister stood at the dumbwaiter shaft, looking up and talking amongst themselves. They all looked remarkably alike with dark eyes and dark hair and aquiline noses. The physiognomy was only slightly more female in Miss Alcestri, because her brothers' faces had a feminine structure about them. They were a wonderfully handsome family.

"You can't imagine how grateful I am to see you all," Yvienne exclaimed. "Miss Alcestri, thank you all for coming to our rescue."

"Of course," Miss Alcestri said. "We were surprised it failed – the engineering was superb. But retrofitting is a tricky business. We'll soon have it set to rights. Of course, you'll have to engage another tradesman to stop up the hole where the animals get in. That's what the smell is, you know – a nest of squirrels, no doubt."

"It's wonderful how they get into houses," said a brother, peering up at the shaft. He gave Yvienne a look. "Them and rats. The smallest opening and they worm right in."

"We'll take care of it," Yvienne promised. She steeled herself and peered up at the shaft. A rush of fetid cold air whooshed down at her and thick twisted rope cables disappeared into the darkness above. The shaft was as narrow as a chimney, set in between the walls. She could scarcely believe she fit in the dumbwaiter car. Though I was half-starved back then, she reminded herself. The younger Alcestri brother squirmed in next to her, holding up a lantern, pressed up tight by her.

"Here, let's take a look," he said, and opened the brass window over the glass. Now she could see further up the shaft – the bottom of the dumbwaiter loomed above them. Something caught her eye.

"Wait – move the lantern slightly to the left," she ordered, forgetting the ill-mannered nearness of young Mr Alcestri. Now she could see something half out of the dumbwaiter. It was large and it was stuck.

"That's no squirrel," Yvienne said. Horror dawned.

"Where is that?" Mr Alcestri asked. "Second floor?"

"Caught between the second floor and the attic," Yvienne said. She squirmed to get out, and for a second they were stuck, until he held her still with one arm and backed himself out first.

"All right now, Miss Mederos," he said, and she ducked out, and looked at them, indecision in their faces.

"Well?" she said. "What are we waiting for? To the second

floor, people. Hurry."

They thundered after her up the stairs to the blank surprise of Noe, who was descending with the carpet sweeper. The door to the dumbwaiter came out in what was once Trune's office, now restored to Alinesse's study. They slid open the panel in the wall, and looked up. Yvienne grabbed the lantern and thrust it up the shaft, peering as it illuminated the darkness. They were closer now, and she could see a bulky coat and trousers. The smell of decomposition was stronger, and she had to fight the reflex to gag. She pulled her head and shoulders out of the shaft and faced the others. They were all somber.

"Albero," Yvienne said. She had trouble speaking. "Go send the gardener's boy for a constable. Give him a note – do *not* tell him – you know what to do. Then come right back." He nodded and ran. She covered her mouth, and then regained her composure. Miss Alcestri laid a comforting hand on her arm. "Miss Alcestri," Yvienne said. "How do you propose we manage this?"

"Well," Miss Alcestri said, "Ludo is the smallest. We can access the shaft from the attic. Ludo can climb down and see what – I mean, how – we can best extricate – well. Ludo?"

No one could speak of it. How extraordinary, Yvienne thought, that none of them could *speak* of what was caught in the dumbwaiter shaft.

Ludo nodded bravely. His big brother patted his shoulder. They had to go down to the back of the house and up the servant stairs to reach the final flight to the attic. No one spoke. Old trunks and broken household furnishings loomed in the twilight under the eaves. The only light came from the fanlights under the gables at the end of the attic.

Here there was no concealing door – the cables were attached to a massive pulley system bolted into the attic ceiling between the rafters. Ludo, encumbered by a formidable toolbelt, stepped between the timbers and began to shinny down the cable. They heard a thump as he landed on the top of the dumbwaiter, and a strangled noise of disgust.

"Hey," he called up a moment later. "I can free him. I'll attach the rope, and you'll have to haul him up."

"All right, Ludo," his sister called. "Icci, the rope."

The elder Alcestri brother quickly dropped the thin, strong rope down the shaft.

"Ready," Ludo said. "He's free. He's, uh, dead weight and there's a lot of him, so – I'll guide the body from here, and you pull."

Yvienne ranged herself behind the Alcestris. Albero burst into the attic, breathing hard, eyes wild.

"Sent the boy on the double," he said, and without another word he got in place behind her. They gripped hard, pulling slow step by slow step, with Ludo shouting instructions, his voice hollow and strained. Finally she could feel the body move more smoothly, and they got into a rhythm, pulling hand over hand as the rope coiled behind them.

"Almost there," Ludo shouted, and Yvienne caught sight of the massive four poster bed, carved of mahogany, a relic of her grandparents' life.

"Tie the end of the rope, quickly," she said, and Albero, proving that every young man in Port Saint Frey dreamed of the sea, tied a sailor's stopper knot as if he did it every day. Now they could pull without worrying about losing the body, or Ludo.

Finally the dead man appeared at the top of the shaft. Miss Alcestri and her brother ran forward and pulled the body out and laid him on the floor. As one, they all gave cries of disgust and horror. Shinnying up the rope came

Ludo, all but forgotten.

Yvienne took a deep breath to calm her heart and edged forward. The dead man was dreadfully decomposed, but there was no mistaking his features.

It was Uncle Samwell's old friend and nemesis, Barabias Parr.

Chapter Twenty

The gray light of Fog Season could scarcely be distinguished from noon or evening. Abel lay entwined with Elenor Charvantes, the second assignation in as many days. She drowsed in the crook of his arm. He cursed himself for a fool. This was too dangerous; Doc would kill him if he knew. And though he was not afraid of Jax Charvantes for himself, he knew the lieutenant would be brutal to Elenor if he found out.

He was restless, jumpy. As carefully as he could, he slid out from under her and left the bed, the cold air a slap against his nakedness. In the bed, Elenor murmured, but continued to doze. Abel went to the window and looked out. It was midday but the streetlamps of the fog-shrouded city were nothing but smears of light in the mist.

Some other light caught his eye. Red and yellow flames from across the city, high on the western headland. Abel frowned and looked closer. Fire.

"Aren't you cold?" said Elenor sleepily behind him.

"It feels good," he said, without turning to her. What could be burning so high above the city?

"What are you looking at?" She was fully awake now. Her bare shoulders almost glowed in the dim lamplight. Her hair had fallen from its prim bun and was tousled and wild. She was lovely and he was an idiot. She got out of bed, wrapped in the blanket, and peered out the window. Her gaze sharpened. "My God. That's the Saint Frey place." Almost as soon as she remarked upon it, the fire dwindled, and finally disappeared. The mists closed in as if there were nothing there.

"Oh, my goodness. I hope no one was hurt. Madam Saint Frey lives alone, mostly, but I understand her niece has been living with her lately. Oh, there are the bells. The firetrucks are on their way."

Abel could hear them now too, the clangor rising up to the third floor of the Bailet. Elenor put her arms around him, pulling him inside the blanket with her. He closed his eyes, the sensation of her desire overwhelming him, overpowering his nerve endings.

"I've often thought that it would be a wonderful thing if my friend Tesara married Jone Saint Frey," Elenor mused, her cheek resting against his shoulder. "They've always liked one another. He could get away from that awful mother of his, and Tesara would be happier, I know it. But then again, I haven't seen Jone in society at all these past months. But they used to be thick as thieves at the salons, not six months ago. I'm sure his mother put her foot down – the Saint Freys tend to look down upon merchant families."

Interesting, Abel thought. Interesting that a girl who had extraordinary capabilities and powers should like a boy who had not been seen in society for months. Interesting that his mother should stand against the match. And interesting that her house should catch fire.

"I have to go," Elenor said, sighing against his skin. He turned to face her, and she rose on tiptoes to kiss him. He felt himself helpless under the onslaught of need, hers and his.

"Elenor," he began, knowing it was no use.

"I know. It's not safe. I know. I won't come back here. We'll think of something else." She was trying to be brave; he could tell. She gave him a smile, touched with rue.

"We will," he promised, cursing himself for his own weakness. He had to end it, for both their sakes, and at the same time he knew he would not be able to withstand her.

She dressed quickly and wrapped herself up against the cold, her scarf muffling her face. He made sure the hall was empty before she left his room and scurried down the hall to the stairs.

Abel dressed and went downstairs to the Bailet dining room for an early lunch, nursing a glass of beer along with a thick garlic and beef stew, and instead of wondering how to find Trune and kidnap the Mederos girl, he spent his time trying to determine the best way to protect Elenor Charvantes from her brutal husband, and still be able to see her. And still, in the back of his mind, he wondered about the fire at the Saint Frey mansion, so quickly put out, and its odd, almost inconsequential connection to Tesara Mederos.

Water trickled into Tesara's mouth and she coughed it out, her throat so constricted she thought she would never breathe again. She could hear nothing, see nothing, could only feel the cold compress at the back of her neck, the horrible constriction of her lungs and throat, the smell of vomit and blood and soot.

She heard voices as if from far away, dreadfully stretched out and odd, as if they were songs from a distant land. Someone sat her up and thumped her back and it helped a bit as the pain in her lungs and chest cavity eased. She was still unable to see or hear.

Dear God, if I live, can I stand to live like this?

• • •

When she woke again, she could see and hear, though her head still buzzed, and her vision was hazy. Tesara looked through the film in her eyes at an indistinct ceiling. She reclined in a bed, propped up against a pillow. It was musty and the sheets were clammy. She moved a languid hand over the coverlet, and sensed that her hands were bandaged. There were people in the room with her, though she could see nothing but shadowy blurs. Someone with a firm touch that was not unkind spooned a vile-tasting liquid into her mouth. She coughed and almost cried out at the pain, but managed to swallow.

"There. That will take care of her for now while you transfer her. You must keep her quiet and make sure she has bone broth to warm the humors," came a voice, albeit one that sounded as if the speaker dwelt at the bottom of a well. "We won't know if she will retain her sight and hearing – only time will tell."

I'm going *blind*? Tesara tried to cry out and even the small sound she was capable of tore at her throat as though sawing at it with a serrated knife.

"Thank you, doctor." That was Mirandine, speaking from the bottom of the same distant well. "You've been most helpful. She will be well cared for."

The doctor harrumphed. "She should be in hospital, not in this drafty old pile. Are you sure you don't want to bring her to my surgery in Ravenne?"

So she was still at Jone's house. And Mirandine had sent for a doctor from Ravenne? Ravenne was twelve miles away. What about Dr Melliton? He had taken care of all the illnesses of the Mederos family since she and Yvienne were in leading strings.

"I'm afraid we can't," Mirandine said. Something about her voice alerted Tesara. Was Mirandine worried? "I've engaged a nurse. She will be taken care of. Thank you for coming so far, doctor, and on such short notice. Let me make sure you are well compensated. And I'm sure I have no need to tell you that your discretion is of the utmost importance."

They kept speaking to one another, but they moved away, and Tesara couldn't hear the rest of the conversation. Tears leaked from the corner of her eyes. She was going deaf and blind. She was dying, and Yvienne would never know where she was.

Mirandine returned, sitting on the edge of the bed, just out of Tesara's sight. She smelled of tobacco and scent.

Tesara tried again to speak. "What?" There was the same knife edge, and she gave up.

"Oh, good. You're back among us. You're at the Saint Frey house for now," said Mirandine. The girl moved to where Tesara could see her and sat at the edge of the bed, her stylish trousers rumpled. She was no longer play-acting and her eyes held strain. She took Tesara's hand. "By the time we smelled the smoke and broke down the door, you were both unconscious but the fire was out. Did she set it?"

Tesara nodded.

"I thought so. She was always one for the grand gesture." Mirandine sounded bitter. She fumbled for a cigarillo and a match. Tesara watched with faraway horror. She worked her throat and managed to ask,

"Alive?"

Mirandine turned to her, the smoke curling up from the cigarillo. "Yes, but she's worse than you. We thought we lost you both. When we opened the door it caused an explosion of air. If the fire hadn't already been out it would have caused a conflagration. What happened in there? No, don't answer that. Your voice can't handle it."

Tesara moved her bandaged hand in pantomime.

"Oh, of course!" Mirandine scrambled for paper and a pencil. Tesara looked around, blinking to clear her vision. The room was like the rest of the house – grand, shabby, ill-cared-for, clammy, and falling down. But it had been kept up in its way. There was a chest of drawers and a wardrobe and sports equipment in the corner. She could make out a bat and a leather ball. Someone had also hung a pair of boxing gloves and pugilist's bag in the corner. She turned her head the other way and there were schoolbooks on a desk, through which Mirandine was rifling for paper and pencil. She was in Jone's room.

How extraordinary, she thought, still far away. Does Jone's mama know? She wondered if the woman would have allowed such a liberty if she did know. If she could smile she would, but she could still barely breathe.

Mirandine handed her the paper and the pencil and *Principles of Geometry* to lean on. It was hard to grasp the pencil with only her fingertips, but Tesara made do.

does my sister know?

"Not yet," Mirandine said. "We haven't had the chance to send word."

what date

"The afternoon of the fifteenth."

So she had been gone for hours. Vivi would be worried. She hadn't told her where she would be.

I need to go home

"Tesara, that's not possible right now. You're very ill, and–"

Tesara made a wordless noise of frustration and jabbed with the pencil, her letters jagged and dark.

send word to my sister to come for me

"Tes, listen. You're alive, and you're safe and sound. Just be patient. I've sent for help. We'll have you out of here soon."

Tesara underlined her last sentence.

"No!" Mirandine stood up and threw the cigarillo onto the floor. "There's no time. We have to get you out of here."

Tesara stabbed her pencil at the page, writing furiously, fighting an insistent languor that grew with each passing moment. She thrust the paper at Mirandine's face.

My sister will be worried. Tell her that I'm alive. Tell her, Mirandine.

"I will. I promise. But Tes, Jone's mama did a terrible thing, and the first thing we must do is remove you from the House. You have to be patient and come along without a fuss, please." Mirandine tried to smile as if she were pleading with a child.

Tesara tried to think but she was completely muddled. She tried to write, but her hands could barely lift the pencil. *Is is Trune?* she scrawled. What had the doctor given her?

Mirandine had no time to answer. The door to the sickroom opened and Savain the ancient retainer came in. "The carriage is ready for madam, and the gentlemen you hired are here," he said in his old, quavery voice.

"Oh, at last," Mirandine said, almost breathless. "Be a dear and have them come in with the litter."

"Yes, miss."

Wait! Tesara wanted to cry out. Instead, she grew duller

and duller, unable to think with any clarity. They were moving her, but to where? How would Yvienne find her?

"This is for the best, Tesara," Mirandine said. "I promise you, they're carrying you to safety. Soon you'll be safe and warm." She dropped a kiss on Tesara's cheek and then straightened. "Savain, to the carriage, please, with madam. I'll take care of Miss Mederos."

Though Tesara remained awake as the burly gentlemen transferred her from the bed to a stretcher, she could do nothing more than lie limp and helpless. They carried her through the long passageways of the Saint Frey house, descending down short stairs and turning corners, the torchlight throwing odd shadows on the walls and ceiling. After a while the air grew cold, and she shivered, though she was warmly wrapped. They stopped as someone fumbled out keys and unlocked a creaking, heavy iron gate, and then the rest of the way they were in a rough tunnel, the pathway rocky. She could smell the sea, and she knew that waves crashed just outside the limit of her damaged hearing.

Limp, paralyzed, Tesara was manhandled into a boat. She lay in the damp, wrapped like a spider victim, as the men settled at the oars, pulling hard out to sea. Tesara stared up at the overcast night sky, unable to see anything, and salt water and tears intermingled on her cheeks.

Chapter Twenty-One

A GRUESOME DISCOVERY AT HOUSE MEDEROS!

The troubles of the trading house Mederos continue apace. Engineers from the engineering firm of Alcestri & Family discovered the body of merchant Barabias Parr, last seen six months ago after a devilish dinner party hosted by none other than the fugitive Guildmaster Trune. The dinner party was held at House Mederos during its brief heyday as Guild headquarters and Trune's own residence.

The Gazette has spoken with attendees of the dinner party who were shocked to discover the nefarious doings of Trune had potentially extended to murder.

"Trune had clearly gone off the rails," said one distinguished merchant who asked not to be identified while the Guild investigates. "As soon as I and my colleagues saw which way the wind blew, we wanted nothing more to do with him. Parr, on the other hand, had thrown in his lot with Trune. See where that got him."

When asked if they had left Parr at the house at the end of the dinner party when it all descended into chaos, our source frowned and said he thought that Parr had exited with the others.

There has been no comment from the putative head of

House Mederos, Miss Yvienne Mederos, the eldest daughter, nor from a member of the distaff House, Samwell Balinchard. It is known that there was bad blood between Parr and Balinchard, owing to Mr Balinchard's unique approach to investment partnerships.

THE GAZETTE, EVENING EDITION

Yvienne almost leaped out of her seat when Albero came in with additional fortifications of tea and sandwiches. She and Uncle Samwell sat in the parlor, curtains drawn, under siege from the reporters and the idly curious massed outside the gate.

"Any word?" she asked. He shook his head, his expression as somber as her own, and her heart sank. Oh, Tes, she thought. Her sister had not come home all day. It was now nearing ten o'clock at night, and they had heard nothing of her.

"I have a bad feeling about this," Samwell said, though he was not so shaken that he could not help himself to a sandwich.

Once word escaped that the constabulary was called to the Mederos house to investigate a murder, the news spread like fire unchecked. The extra edition of the paper only incited the crowds. Some enterprising fellows had climbed upon the top of the spiky, iron fence that surrounded the house, propping themselves up on ladders and peering towards it with spyglasses, waiting for movement from the occupants.

"None, miss. We've sent out discreet inquiries but we don't want to draw more attention and so it's hard to get a straight answer." Albero looked both determined and worried. He was losing some of the correctness with which he comported himself. If Yvienne didn't know better, she would even have called him scruffy, though to an outsider the only indications were ruffled hair as if he had swept his hand through it, and a tiny bit of fluff on his chin from a shaving mishap.

"Did she give you any indication of where she meant to go today?"

"She said errands, Miss Yvienne. I didn't think – I should have asked more questions," Albero said, looking guilty. She felt a pang because she so badly wanted to shout at him that yes, he should have asked more questions, and failing a satisfactory answer, locked Tesara in her bedroom like an autocratic father in a ten-groat novel.

"No, of course not," she said. She pressed her fingertips to her temple. "If only there was a clew – something to tell us where she might have gone."

Albero gasped. "Miss Yvienne! She received a letter in the morning post. I just now remembered it."

It was their only lead. Yvienne ran up the stairs to her sister's bedroom, followed by Albero and Uncle Samwell, passing a wide-eyed Noe on the stairs, hoping against hope that her sister had left the letter behind.

And there it was – as if it were of absolutely no consequence, the letter with its scarlet seal lay on Tesara's dressing table amidst her hairpins, a comb, and other odds and ends of her daily life. Thrusting away her guilt at reading her sister's mail, Yvienne unfolded the letter. She scanned the curt summons with growing fury. How dare Madam Saint Frey speak to a Mederos that way?

"Is it helpful, Miss Yvienne?" Albero asked.

"What's the girl gone and done this time?" Uncle Samwell said.

Yvienne folded the letter and tucked it into the small purse at her waist. "Somewhat helpful," she said, trying to sound reassuring. "She seems to have answered an invitation to the Saint Frey mansion early today. Albero, perhaps you could call a hack for me? I will go fetch her." At the expression of horror on the face of her butler and her uncle, she demanded, "What?"

"Vivi," Samwell said. "Haven't you heard?"

"There was a fire, miss," Albero said. "In all the commotion around here, we never had a chance to tell you. The Saint Frey mansion had a fire, and Madam Saint Frey was removed to Ravenne, clinging to life."

Yvienne found she had trouble breathing.

"Miss Vivi," Albero went on, sympathetic and adamant, "shouldn't we call the constables and tell them she's missing? There's already been an attack on her. I don't think we should do this ourselves."

"Yes, of course," she said. "That would be a good idea, except for one thing, Albero." She met his trusting, open face with as much honesty as she could muster. "You see – knowing Tesara, she may have caused that fire. So I don't know that calling the constables would be very helpful in that case."

"Miss Vivi!" he said, shocked to his core. Samwell only grunted, and said, "Nothing's beyond that girl."

Albero refused to give up. "Be that as it may," he said, quiet but firm. "She's our Tesara, Miss Vivi."

Our Tesara. The quiet way Albero said it cut to Yvienne's core. This was not butler to employer, but friend to friend. Dare she say it – family to family? It warmed her, and she gave him a rueful smile, laying a quick hand on his sleeve.

"I want to find her as badly as you do, if only to scold her within an inch of her life. But if the report of the fire was so thorough as to include Madam Saint Frey's whereabouts, I wonder that it was silent upon Tesara's? If she– if she were injured, or… no doubt we would have had news of that. There would be no stopping the press from reporting it."

"Hadn't thought of that," Uncle Samwell grunted. "The *Gazette* would have been on it."

"So we can only hope that she had nothing to do with the fire, but if we send the constables snooping in that direction, well… they might think her guilty first and deal with the truth later."

Albero nodded but reluctantly. She could tell she hadn't convinced him.

"You know, she's probably found a game and is head down winning money," Samwell added, a clumsy attempt to comfort.

"I devoutly hope so," she said.

"So what do we do?" Albero asked. "Miss Vivi, there has to be something we can do."

Yvienne knew exactly what she was going to do, but as none of it could be imparted to her butler and her uncle, she tried to be encouraging.

"I know it's hard to wait. It's the hardest thing. But Albero, I trust Tesara to… well, to be foolhardy, yes, but she has inner depths. We'll follow all the evidence, and we'll find her."

"I say!" Samwell said. "I could go to the docks. Do my usual. Ask around."

"No!" Yvienne and Albero shouted together. Yvienne closed her eyes and wished for strength. "Uncle, please. We must not let anyone know that Tes is missing or that she could have anything to do with the fire. The House needs no more bad press."

"See, there you go again," Samwell grumbled. "Always assuming the worst. I just think it's best to put the right story out, not the sensational one they'll be bound to come up with. The paper says there was bad blood between Parr and me. Not at all. We had a simple misunderstanding, and it wasn't even my fault after all."

"Nevertheless, we must not give them any more fodder in our direction."

At least for the moment the paper was assuming that Parr's death was at Trune's hands. At what point would the city begin to consider House Mederos a suspect?

"I don't know, Vivi," Samwell said, still grumbling. "I don't think much of your reasoning. But if you don't want me to try to find out what happened to Tes, well, it's on you."

"So it is, uncle," Yvienne said, trying to hide her own sudden stab of self-doubt. No, she told herself. Uncle would just blab and they would have more problems than before.

She peeked out behind the drapes. The crowds remained clustered at the front gate. She hoped that the bad weather would chase them off, but no – the intrepid watchers had set a fire and clearly settled in for the night. Gawkers, she thought, and shook her head. Didn't they have anything better to do?

She reread the letter from Madam Saint Frey, trying to find additional clews and failing. Oh Tes, she thought. What have you done?

Chapter Twenty-Two

Yvienne made sure that her bedroom drapes were drawn tight before setting down the candle on her dressing table and kneeling beside her bed. She pulled out the boy's clothes from under the mattress. They were clean and serviceable, but she had filled out in the past six months, owing to Mrs Francini's good food. She had curves now where before, still half-starved from her stay at Madam Callier's, she had been flat as a board. It would be the matter of moments to let out the waist and hem of the trousers and she would have to take the additional step of binding her bosom to fit into the shirt.

Twilight and darkness fell early during Fog Season. What better disguise than a messenger boy who melted into the crowd? Tesara was last seen at the Saint Frey mansion. It was time to find her and bring her home.

A knock on the door made Yvienne start and she hastily shoved everything under the covers.

"Who is it?" she called, standing in front of the bed. Noe's voice came through the door.

"Mister Demaris to see you, miss."

"At this hour?" she said, aghast.

"He apologized, miss, but he was most insistent. He said he'd come up himself if we didn't let him in."

Oh, for heaven's sake… he was acting like a lover in a play in a Milias theater. Yvienne screwed up her eyes and clenched her fists. When she relaxed she said, "Thank you, Noe. I will be right down."

Inigho was standing by the fireplace in the parlor. He came toward her, hand outstretched, concern writ all over him. Noe had taken his coat, and rain spattered his hair and his shoes. "I was at business in Ravenne when I heard. I came as soon as I could," he said, pressing her hand in a way that made her heart sink. It was meant to be comforting but it was the sort of thing that a man with a romantic interest did, and she had no time for that now. And I never did, she thought with sudden clarity. Uncle was right. Inigho would never in a million years understand her family or approve of her sister – and how could she tell him about her activities as the Gentleman Bandit?

"Nonsense," she said, shaking his hand in return, hoping to convey a hearty co-equal friendship. "You needn't have come at all." She sat on the sofa across the room and indicated the chair opposite, but instead, he perched on the other end of the sofa.

"We're friends, Yvienne. I'd come to any friend in need."

She didn't bother to contradict him; the kisses had obscured the matter. See – this is why I should never act impulsively, she thought, and stifled a sigh.

"It's just that now you're fodder for the newspaper," she said. She smiled. "I would rather not wish that on anyone."

"Eh," he shrugged. "Today's news is tomorrow's fishwrap. So tell me what happened. I can't believe what I've read in the *Gazette*."

Yvienne gave a brief summary, omitting Tesara, and he reacted with shock and dismay.

"I am so sorry," he said, when she finished. He put his

hand forward as if to hold hers again, but she drew back and he stopped himself with a rueful expression. "I can't imagine how dreadful that was for you. No doubt the tradesmen spilled everything to the paper."

"Don't malign the Alcestris," Yvienne said. "They were most helpful. Anyway, it was bound to come out, and I don't know that they were the source."

"But that you had to assist in pulling the body up – I don't count that helpful, Yvienne."

Impatience welled up in her. "Inigho, that is the least important concern I have right now. Have you come for a reason other than sympathy?"

His eyes widened at her sharp words. "I came to offer what help I could," he said, with undertones of injury.

"For which I'm grateful," she said, and this time she reached out and pressed his hand, and he returned the clasp. "But we're fine, really. And you said it yourself; tomorrow's fishwrap, eh?"

He smiled, but he said, "You know, there is something I can do. The Guild has hired a Harrier, you know, to investigate Trune's disappearance. I'm sure I can send the man over here. He'll figure out who murdered Parr and stuffed him in the dumbwaiter in a hurry, I should think."

Good God. "That is very kind but entirely unnecessary," she said, struggling for words. "I think we know who the murderer is, or was – Trune himself."

"Perhaps, but it's best to be sure," Inigho said. "I would almost certainly believe that, and I'm sure I would not be surprised if the investigators come to that conclusion. But what if it's someone else, someone who had a grudge against the Guild and the man himself?"

He stopped suddenly and reddened. "I– I didn't mean..." He faltered to a halt.

"We didn't kill Parr," Yvienne said, and this time she made no attempt to modulate her tones. Fury rose in her, fury at his stupidity and blindness and complete wrongness for her, fury that any hope that she might have had in his direction was all misplaced. "But as long as we're discussing the old days, Inigho, where were you the night of the fateful dinner party, when my sister was humiliated and endangered by Guildmaster Trune and his cronies? Where was House Demaris six years ago when my family's business was stripped from us?"

He shot to his feet. "House Demaris was not involved," he said. "You can't seriously believe–?"

"But you can believe my family capable of murder!" she snapped back. She stood too.

"I never said–!"

"You didn't have to! It was in your face!" She pointed out the window. "They all think it! Every single one of them thinks House Mederos got a bit of revenge six months ago, and why not? We were wronged, Mr Demaris, brutally wronged. But we did not kill Barabias Parr and leave him to rot inside our own walls!"

He straightened. "Yvienne..." He stopped. His expression became cold. "You're distraught," he said. "It was a mistake to come. I meant only the best. Good day, Miss Mederos."

She refused him the courtesy of a reply and watched in silence as he took his leave. When the door closed behind him, she let out her breath and sank down on the sofa. Doubt and fear hammered at her. She didn't have time for this. She needed to find her sister.

Doc was not going to be happy, Abel thought, even though he himself had taught Abel to trust his instincts. Half of those instincts said this was a wild goose chase. But the rest – the conversation that night at the Bailet bar was all about two stories: the discovery of the dead body at the Mederos house, and at the other end of the city, the fire at the Saint Frey mansion. The gossips didn't need much encouragement to talk about either family to a stranger in town, and each time, two names kept on coming up together – Jone Saint Frey and Tesara Mederos. He taught her to gamble; the student had outstripped the teacher. Now she visited private gaming clubs, and made a pretty penny. And Jone was rumored to have proposed to a cousin – the niece who was staying at the mansion.

It was the off-duty constable who proclaimed he had seen the dead body in the dumbwaiter that gave Abel's instincts the final push.

"Must have sent the sisters into hysterics," Abel said, as he signaled the barkeep for another round for the copper.

"Nah," said the constable, pleased as punch to have impressed a Harrier, of all people. "Miss Yvienne is cool as a cucumber. Nothing fazes her – the smartest girl in Port Saint Frey."

"And the younger sister?" Abel prompted.

"Oh, didn't see her. Probably out spending daddy's money, what's left of it." He laughed raucously.

The clock of the cathedral struck eleven as Abel sat on his bed and unlocked his trunk. He slipped out of his clothes, hurrying because of the cold, and drew on his night gear. Gone was the slightly portly young man with the nondescript face and the thinning hair, the portliness effected by a bit of padding in his waistcoat. He was slight and wiry, muscle and skin over bone. Abel pulled on the black garb, painted eyeblack around his eyes, and drew on the mask. He attached a toolbelt with his pistol, a small flask of anaesthetic, and a twenty-foot length of deceptively thin, fragile-looking rope. He drew on padded slippers with roughened soles and gloves of the same texture, and snuffed the light in the lantern. He let his eyes adjust to the darkness.

In a second he was out of the window. The cold and the wet slapped at him through the fabric, but Abel was soon warmed through, every muscle moving smoothly and professionally as he clambered up the side of the old hotel, catching handholds and footholds with ease. He eased himself onto the roof and surveyed the dark city. Even in the fog he could see lights below, smeared with mist, and the great swooping lighthouse light from Nag's Point. It swept over him like an accusing eye and back out to sea.

When the light swept back over the hotel, Abel was gone.

Sneaking out of one's own home was unnecessarily difficult, Yvienne grumbled. She couldn't let herself out the front door, due to the crowd of gawkers and reporters. The kitchen door was likewise secured as Albero had set the bell to ring in his room if anyone tried to open it. It was a thoughtful detail, which proved what a good butler he was. No burglar would rob House Mederos under his watch. And she couldn't leave by the parlor doors that led to the garden, because Uncle Samwell, with new-found purpose as guardian of the House, was sleeping in the parlor.

Yvienne resorted to the window in her parents' lavish bedroom. It was down the hall at the other end of the house, with a balcony overlooking the back garden. The vast apartment occupied half of the second floor. It included an en suite bathroom and water closet. The first thing Alinesse had done when they returned to the house was sell the old furniture that had presumably been polluted by

Trune's soiled physical presence and character, and bought all new on advance. Yvienne couldn't blame her, but the new pieces, an enormous bed, two massive wardrobes, a vast dressing table, and a variety of end tables and chairs, depressed her. She was nostalgic for the bedroom of her childhood, when she and Tesara had been allowed to jump on the bed, or sit with their mama while she dressed for an evening out, watching in awe at Alinesse's transformation from formidable mother into an even more formidable and splendid stranger.

Yvienne threaded her way through the furniture, and only barked her knee once on a wayward end table. Rubbing it and cursing under her breath, she hobbled over to the portofinestra to the balcony. She slipped out between the doors, and even through her wool trousers and jacket, the cold slithered to her skin. She shivered and tugged the cap down tighter over her hair. Should she have worn a muffler? No – it would only get in her way. She resisted the urge to tug at the binding over her bosom. Even with its help, the shirt strained over her shape, but the jacket helped, and as it was dark, she had no doubt that, at first glance anyway, she could still pass for a boy.

There were no outside stairs. Yvienne would have to climb down the iron railing to the garden. It occurred to her that by leaving the window unsecured for her return, she was allowing an enterprising burglar – or reporter – entry. Conscientiously, she reached back inside and locked the window doors so that when she pulled them to, they latched behind her.

She took a deep breath and swung her leg over the railing.

Chapter Twenty-Three

Yvienne was no longer shivering by the time she made it across the city to the Saint Frey mansion. The clocktower in Cathedral Plaza had rung the twelve o'clock chimes. The city slumbered under the blanket of fog. From her place in the shadows along the drive, she couldn't even see the city, the fog had rolled in that thoroughly. The lighthouse searchlight swept over the top of the fog as along the top of a low-lying cloud. The only noise came from the ever-present drip drip drip of water on ornamental trees.

The mansion was dark. Yvienne's night vision was hard-pressed to discern any distinguishing features of the house, such as a front door. Not that she would be going in that way. She darted across the drive and skirted the front of the house, making her way by guess and by feel along the rough stone walls.

When her fingers encountered a window that gave a bit to her probing, she pulled out a thin metal shim, and worked at the slit in between the sash and the sill. In seconds she had the latch undone. Yvienne paused, holding her breath, then pushed up the window. It groaned, but it gave. She squirmed inside.

It was utterly dark and utterly cold. Yvienne scratched a

match and it flared against her fingertips. She lit the stub of candle she had brought, holding it high above her head. As the darkness gave way the room took shape. A parlor.

In a trice she had a candlestick and fixed her small light in it. It was time to find Tesara.

Fifteen minutes later, she found herself in a burned-out room, its doors having been forced open. The room had suffered a great conflagration. The furnishings and drapes were reduced to tatters and ash, and the smell was dreadful. The window had been smashed, no doubt to give trapped people a few minutes of air. *Oh God, Tesara.* Panic seized her, and she thrust it down. There was no time for that.

Yvienne looked around, trying to discover some evidence of Tesara being in the room, but her candlelight was too dull and the room far too destroyed to give up any clews.

She stepped on something soft and stifled a shriek, then looked closer, holding the candle at a better angle. What she first thought was a dead animal was a tangle of burned hair. A pet? She nudged it with her boot, and then all of a sudden recognized it. A wig. Yvienne shook her head, and with one last glance around, she left the room.

Another bedroom down the hall contained a bed recently occupied, and her interest increased. Yvienne replenished her candle with another, and the light had a bit more life to it. She set the candleholder on a bedside table. This was a masculine room. The bed was unmade but recently slept in, judging by the cleanliness of the sheets – no dust or clamminess as she had seen in the other bedrooms. She lifted up the blankets and sheets and looked under the mattress, and then under the bed for good measure, but found nothing.

The room held a measure of warmth, and she checked the fireplace. Sure enough, some coals still breathed. She took a poker and fished through the ashes, pulling out half-burned cloth. Blood and salve coated the bandages, and they stunk of soot and burned flesh. Whoever had been in the house fire was taken here to recuperate. When they changed the bandages, they just cut them off and tossed them aside. Because they were in a hurry to get away, she thought.

By the warmth of the fire, she had missed them by a few hours.

She prodded at the fireplace again and pulled out a half-smoked cigarillo. She went with renewed urgency back to the bed, shaking it out. She plucked at a few hairs on the pillow, and she lifted them up and held them to the meager light. They were sorrel with highlights of chestnut and gleaming gold. Tesara's hair had the same striations of color.

And there was something else on the bedside table, a pencil. Yvienne began to look for paper. There it was, crumpled in the sheets and almost indistinguishable from them. She smoothed it out.

does my sister know?

Chapter Twenty-Four

Yvienne didn't know what made her suddenly excruciatingly aware of the oppressive emptiness of the house, but all of a sudden she whirled around and stared at the doorway. Beyond it was darkness, and she and the room were illuminated in a pool of light. With great deliberation she pulled her pistol from the satchel at her side.

If she snuffed the candle, it would take crucial moments for her night vision to return. She had to place her trust that whoever watched her from beyond the doorway would be at the same disadvantage. She blew out the candle and dodged to the side.

From the moment Abel followed the burglar into the house through the window, he had taken the man's measure. The burglar was slender, about his height, and armed with an old-fashioned pistol. He was good with a lockpick, for sure, but he was a talented amateur, no more. Self-taught, not trained by a dock gang or organized housebreakers. Abel knew better than to get cocky, though – many a professional had come to an embarrassing end because they had underestimated beginner's luck. He followed at a safe distance as the bandit blundered through the house. If anyone had been home, he would have alerted them within five minutes of breaking in.

When the burglar snuffed the light, Abel moved in. He followed as silent as an owl on the wing. The man's breathing and furtive movements were like shouts. He heard him cock the pistol, and he ducked and rolled, fetching up against the man's legs.

The pistol went off harmlessly into the ceiling, and plaster rained down on them both. The struggle was brief. The burglar went down hard and Abel had him secured on his stomach, wrists captured in one hand and a knee in his back, bracing himself for the coming flood of insights.

Instantly images flashed – Miss Mederos in her office on the docks, in Elenor Charvantes's parlor, her kissing someone. All of her secrets flooded through him in quick succession and, overwhelmed by the emotional maelstrom, Abel's grip loosened in surprise.

Miss Mederos threw her body over, struggling to get her knee up at the most vulnerable portion of his anatomy, but though they were of a size, he was stronger. He held her down. They stared at each other in the darkness. He could feel her heart beating like a rabbit's. She worked to control her breathing. She did not struggle for the sake of it; her muscles were taut, and she was ready to act if he gave her an opening, but she did not squander her strength. She spoke, her voice challenging and firm.

"Who are you? What are you doing here? Where is my – where is Tesara Mederos?"

Abel didn't answer. Yvienne Mederos would stop at nothing to rescue her sister. He could still see the world through her eyes, a residue of the effects of touching her for the first time. Oh, he thought. Oh. He was a fool – the answer had been right under his nose the entire time.

Yvienne Mederos, a demure governess by day, a clever Gentleman Bandit by night. Of course the sisters were in it together. Of course the younger sister collected the money, misdirected the pursuers, and was duly rescued in the end. He got no sense of the same power in Yvienne Mederos as he had experienced with her younger sister and felt a curious relief. He did not have to bring her to Doc. Go, he thought. I'm giving you a gift. Save yourself.

He disguised his voice; or rather, he spoke in the dialect of one raised in the slums of Great Lake.

"Yer in grave danger. You don't need to be comin' round here no more."

"Where. Is. Tesara. Mederos?" she growled, and he could feel fury and impotent rage radiating off her.

Time to go, Abel. He fumbled for the small flask at his belt. Still holding her down, he tilted the flask above her nose. She coughed and squirmed and twisted, but the clever stopper was engineered to leak a small bit of fluid when tilted. In less than a minute she was out.

He checked her breathing; it was even and deep. Satisfied she would wake up with no ill effects other than a pounding headache, he sprang away and melted into the darkness.

Yvienne moved slowly, chilled and disoriented. It took several minutes before she knew where she was – on the cold floor of the Saint Frey mansion – and why she was there – to rescue Tesara, but that she had been overcome and drugged. Her head ached like the devil, and she had a rotten taste in her mouth. The man had thrown her to the ground as if she were nothing to him, and she winced. She hadn't even *seen* him. It had been like being hit by an invisible force. Only the very real sensation of hands on her wrists and a knee in her back, of sweat and the smell of garlic-beef stew on his breath, identified her attacker as human as she. And then he had drugged her. It was the final outrage.

She wanted nothing more than to go home, but she had not yet found her sister, and clearly she was not the only one looking for her. Tesara had been spirited away, but was she safe? She fumbled for the candle and with shaking hands relit it, taking several tries to light a match. She glanced at the dark hallway outside the candlelight. The darkness pressed on her, and she couldn't tell if she was alone, or even how long she had been out.

If she found Tesara, so would he. The best thing she could do was to walk away for now. At any rate, it did not appear that Tesara was still here.

She said out loud, her voice trembling but startling in the silence, "If you harm her, if she is endangered in any way, I will find you. And I will kill you. I swear."

She was ashamed by how weak she sounded, how impotent. Only silence answered.

The walk across the city was colder and harder this time; Yvienne shivered and wrapped her arms around herself, alternating with blowing on her hands. She strove for alertness but was so tired and demoralized it took all of her energy to creep along steadily, sticking to cover whenever she could. The Clock Tower chimed three in the morning, and here and there an early rising tradesman – a baker or a blacksmith – had begun stoking their ovens, the red glow and bit of heat emanating out of the gloom.

The crowd outside the Mederos gates had cleared at last, vanquished by the cold and, gauging by the bottles scattered carelessly under the fence, the last of the gin. Yvienne fumbled with the key to the small side gate, but she had no strength to climb back up the wrought-iron balcony to her parents' bedroom. Yvienne stood sick and shivering at her own kitchen door and rang the bell. It took a long time, but finally she heard the door being unlocked and it opened a crack, a candle shining light over the front portico. When Albero saw who it was, he opened the door and pulled her in. He was in a tattered nightrobe, his hair stuck up all over his head, and his chin was stubbled.

"Miss Vivi! You surprised the dickens out of me!"

She couldn't speak. She just nodded at him. He took off his robe and put it around her – he wore a long nightshirt and his ankles were hairy. His robe was still warm. It barely dented her chill.

"Let's get you upstairs," he whispered, and with one arm around her shoulders he guided her, holding the candle high to lead the way. "Quick now, into your room. I'll light a fire for you and you change into your night things – I won't look, don't be foolish. I'd call Mrs Francini, but I don't think you want her to know about this."

"Not really," Yvienne managed through chattering teeth. He knelt in front of the fireplace and soon had a blaze going. The chill retreated somewhat. With shaking hands Yvienne unbuttoned her shirt and her trousers and got into her nightgown. She laid her wet clothes out to dry, and shoved the gun under the bed with a quick glance over her shoulder. Albero was still poking at the fire, giving her time. She got into bed, pulling the covers over her, and said, "I'm ready."

He turned around then, and took his robe, belting it over his nightshirt. When he had regained some semblance of butlerhood, Albero said, "Miss Vivi, you know you can tell me what's going on."

She nodded and gestured at him and he sat down on the

edge of the bed, his presence comforting.

"I went to find Tesara at the Saint Frey mansion. She's not there and the place is empty. There was the fire, too, and evidence that she was there, possibly hurt. There were bandages and they were thrown into the fireplace as if they had to leave in a great hurry. But someone else was there – he overcame me, and drugged me, and I was out for hours."

"Overcame! Did he...?" Albero's voice was low with anger. She shook her head.

"Only my pride and a few bruises," she said. "I don't know why he was there, but he told me I was in great danger and not to come back."

"You didn't recognize him?"

She shook her head, and then all the pain, the exhaustion, and the fear overwhelmed her and she began to cry. She wept into her hands. "I'm sorry, I'm sorry," she managed. "I'm half-dead, Albero, and you are so good to me. To us. To this House. I don't know where she is, and I don't know what to do."

He lifted his hand as if to pat her leg, but settled for patting the coverlet instead.

"Send for the constables," he said. "Miss Vivi, you must see now that it's the best course."

"No!" For a thousand and one reasons, she thought, involving Tesara's gift, her own extracurricular activities, the dead man found in their walls, and the Harrier.

He didn't protest. "You need to sleep now, that's what you have to do. We'll find her. If they bandaged her, they can't want harm to come to her, can they?"

It heartened her as it was meant to, even as she knew that whoever had her sister could still mean her great harm. He rose from the bed, and said, "Good night, Miss Yvienne."

"Good night. Albero. Thank you – for everything."

It was a long time before she ceased shivering and could stop castigating herself for her failure. She had been cocky; she had been outgunned and out-maneuvered, not just by the dangerous man but by Miss Depressis. Finally she warmed enough to lose herself in sleep. As her eyes closed and she was lulled by the crackling of the fire, she remembered that there was only one restaurant in town that specialized in garlic-beef stew.

The Bailet, on the Esplanade.

Chapter Twenty-Five

What happened at the Saint Frey mansion last night? The Gazette has learned that the high mansion, the seat of the founding family of our fair city, suffered a great conflagration that afternoon, but the Fire Guild insists it knows little of the disaster.

"We were alerted and sent out trucks," the Fire Marechal said in an official dispatch. "However, the fire was out before we arrived, and representatives of the household said that they had no need of our services."

Eagle-eyed gents o' the city, who ask not to be identified, say that in their perambulations around our fair metropolis they saw a strange red glow coming from the mansion and wondered that it might be a devilish apparition.

Could the fire be related to the ghastly discovery at House Mederos? Or does it have aught to do with that other scourge of the city, the Gentleman Bandit? Did someone try to cover his tracks?

No one answered at the Saint Frey mansion when an intrepid reporter knocked on the door to ascertain the truth. The Gazette will continue its investigation and report back.

THE GAZETTE

"Miss Yvienne, the chief constable is here," Albero said through her bedroom door. Yvienne stifled a groan. Of course he was. It was eight o'clock in the morning, and she ached from head to toe. Her eyes had dark circles and her face sagged. She had an abominable headache. She sat at her dressing table and pushed at her cheeks, trying to raise a smile. All she achieved was a ghastly grimace.

"Did he say what he wanted?"

"He said – he said he wanted to speak with Miss Tesara."

"Oh God," she said.

"Yes, miss," Albero said, his voice grim.

"All right. Have him cool his heels in the library, and I'll be there–" when I'm jolly good and ready, she wanted to say. Or, eventually. What she settled on, was "–soon."

"I'll stall him, miss," Albero promised. He paused and then said in a very different tone, "Miss Vivi, are you all right?"

She smiled wearily and pressed her forehead into her hands. "I'm fine, Albero. Don't worry."

She heard him leave, and then she pushed away from the dressing table and got into a simple lightweight wool daydress in a deep red that normally would complement her complexion but that morning she hoped would only mitigate the damage of her late night adventures. She unbraided her hair and brushed it out, then put it up again with swift, competent fingers. She drew on fingerless gloves, rolled up her stockings and buttoned her boots, and when she was done, after pinning her purse to her waist with all the tools of a lady of the house, she set out to see why the chief constable wanted to talk with Tesara.

Chief constable Renner stood at her approach, setting down the book he was perusing. Albero had set him up with a pot of coffee and laid a fire and the coffee smelled wonderful and the fire was cheerful and crackling. Chief Renner was a large man, over six feet, and splendid in his uniform. His dark thinning hair was combed over a large pate, but on him it was not vain at all. His uniform was as circumspect as he – black, with narrow gold braid on the shoulder and a medal here and there.

Yvienne took a deep breath and gave him a smile, approaching with an outstretched hand.

"Good morning, Chief Renner. Albero, thank you. Could you please bring me coffee as well? And if Mrs Francini has scones, that would be lovely."

"I'll send a tray right up, Miss Mederos," Albero said, and closed the door.

Yvienne gestured to the chair Chief Renner had been sitting in. "Please." She sat on the sofa opposite. "What can I do for you, chief?"

'I'm sorry to bother you, Miss Mederos," Renner said. "I told your gentleman I wanted to speak with your sister, but he insisted I speak with you."

"As head of the household, I do appreciate your coming to me first," she said smoothly. There came a discreet knock and then Noe peeked in with a tray of coffee and scones, steaming and emitting an aroma of butter and sugar. "Thank you, Noe."

Noe gave the chief a scared little peep and scurried out after dropping the tray on the side table as if she were afraid of being arrested there and then. For his part the chief stared hard after her, as if mentally sizing her up before returning to his errand.

"So, now may I speak to your sister?" Renner prompted. Yvienne busied herself with her scone and cream, and sipping her coffee. "Miss Mederos?"

"Please help yourself, Chief Renner. Family manners today."

"I know when someone is stalling, Miss Mederos," he said, without taking her up on her offer. His voice was gentle, but firm.

"Oh. Well, in that case, Chief Renner, no, you may not speak with my sister."

He raised an eyebrow. "As the representative of the city and responsible for the safety of all the citizens of Port Saint Frey, I must insist."

"And I must also insist. You will not speak with my sister. But if you tell me what it is you wish to ask her about, I'll be happy to relay the information."

He paused only the slightest. "We wish to take your sister's statement regarding the discovery of the body of Barabias Parr."

"I've given House Mederos's statement, chief constable, so that won't be necessary."

She continued to look back up at him with as amiable an expression as she could manage, her mouth pursed in a smile and her eyes blinking with mild curiosity. Chief Renner was a stolid man. He did not budge.

"Miss Mederos, I don't think you understand the gravity of your situation. You are obstructing city justice and city law and you face severe sanctions. You are also trying my patience. If I have to come back here with a warrant for your sister's arrest, I will do so. I'm sure you can see that it's much better for your sister to simply talk with me in as friendly a manner as possible, so as not to embarrass anyone."

"I see." Yvienne nodded. She sipped her coffee, buying time, thinking furiously. What did the chief know and why did he think Tesara had anything to do with Parr's death? Just like the *Gazette*, he was being fed information, leading once more to the framing of House Mederos. She went on the offense. "Chief Constable Renner, yours isn't the only patience that has been sorely tested these last few days. You are being awfully diligent about the law and the obstruction thereof now, although I don't know where you were six years ago or even six months ago. Regardless. I agree with you that we can't have people going around applying the laws willy-nilly. Therefore my sister will come and speak with you at headquarters in three days, after we've had the opportunity to converse with our lawyer. I trust you can hold out that long, sir?"

His eyes narrowed and he glared down at her. "Two days, Miss Mederos. You have two days to produce your sister. If she isn't at headquarters at four o'clock on Sunday this week, you both will be arrested."

She could tell there would be no bargaining. She said in a tight voice, "Very well, Chief Renner. Sunday."

After seeing Renner out, Albero returned to the library where Yvienne waited by the fireplace, her stomach clenched with sick-making anxiety. Mrs Francini and Noe clustered around him, and she gestured them all in.

"Oh, miss," Mrs Francini said, wiping her hands on her apron, and with only the smallest *tsk* at the untouched scones. "Is Miss Tesara coming home soon?"

She shook her head, omitting any tale of last night's escapade. "Albero, where is my uncle?"

"In bed, miss."

"Roust him, then. I want him down here, in his dressing gown if need be."

Albero nodded and gestured to Noe. The housemaid went to the door but Yvienne said, "No. Noe, stay here." Noe turned and looked at Yvienne. "I have another task for you. This Mr Malcroft running the housemaid's ring – bring him to me."

Noe and Albero both drew in their breath. Noe gained her voice first. "Miss, he's – a dangerous man. I don't think that's a good idea."

I need a dangerous man. Last night proved that. If she were to find her sister and protect her house, she needed all the help she could get, over and above an enthusiastic butler, a diligent cook, a bumbling uncle, and an untrustworthy housemaid.

"Nonetheless, Noe, you will do as I ask, because if you do not, I will report you to Chief Constable Renner."

Noe gave a small gasp, and her eyes went wide. Yvienne remained implacable. I no longer have time for a soft heart, she thought. I will make use of any weapon that I can.

"Yes, miss," Noe said, with only the faintest expression of fatalism. "I'll go now."

"Good." She wondered if Noe would return, and thought with grim humor that it might be best for the housemaid if she didn't. The maid gave her a small curtsey and made her exit.

Albero ran up to get Samwell and he came downstairs, disheveled and grumbling, tying his robe around himself. He brightened at the sight of the coffee and the scones.

"Any news of our girl?" He took another look at Yvienne. "I gather not."

"That's why I've woken you," she said. "Put on your thinking cap, uncle. Why would the Saint Freys mean Tesara harm?"

Samwell looked hard and thoughtful. He poured himself coffee and helped himself to the cream and sugar.

"Word at Aether's is that the boy – Jone – ran off to sea, and his mother was right unbalanced because of it. Well, she always was, but this was the final straw. Jone was supposed to marry his cousin, Mirandine Depressis, but becoming a sailor put paid to that idea, what? And I heard that he was sweet on our Miss Tes. What if Madam Saint Frey decided to put Tes out of the running?"

There was a shocked silence. Mrs Francini spoke up first. "She's a mad old woman, but she's not a murderer. I did some catering for the family at one time. There's never been a whisper of anything like that at all."

"Type of woman like that, she just has to lift a finger, and she has old retainers to do her dirty work," Samwell contradicted. "And then there's the fire. Bit of bad luck on her part that it nearly brought down her house, but I doubt the old bird ever tried to plan a murder before."

"Mr Balinchard!" Mrs Francini said with a gasp.

"Stop. Stop," Yvienne said. "All right. The chief constable was just here. He's looking for Tesara and wants to question her regarding the case of poor Mr Parr. So we can't go to the constables for help. For now, at least."

"We can't just leave her in the hands of – of whoever has her," Mrs Francini objected.

Yvienne said, without looking at Albero, "It has come to my attention that she is no longer at the Saint Frey's. So now we need to find out what they… where she is now."

She clung to her few hopes. She fingered the notepaper with Tesara's writing. Tesara was alive. Her wounds had been tended. Whatever the Saint Freys intended, she could only hope and pray that they did not mean ill. If she let her fears overwhelm her, Yvienne thought, she would drown in them. She turned her attention back to the task at hand. "So we have to be very diligent about turning over every stone in search of her. All of her haunts, all of her acquaintances – uncle, this is your particular area, I believe. The friend of yours – Colonel Talios? – had an interest in Tesara at one time, correct?"

"A passing fancy. But he's attached to Mrs Fayres – it's not likely he'll know something different."

"Tesara gambled in her establishment," Yvienne reminded him. "She was turned away because she won too much money. I know that in many of these private clubs information is currency. Could you broach the colonel and his lady on the topic?"

"Ah." Uncle Samwell looked embarrassed. He grimaced and set down his scone, looking as if he had lost his appetite. "There was a bit of bother at Fayres's one time – well, I won't go into details, but the colonel had to strike me off the guest list."

Yvienne suppressed a shudder. She couldn't imagine what he had done – then she thought, no. I simply don't want to try.

"All right, uncle, you win. Go talk to the Names. But for heavens' sake, be discreet!"

He brightened. "I won't disappoint you, Vivi. If the Names don't know it, it's not worth knowing."

"Well, feel them out, won't you?"

He saluted with coffee in hand. "You have my word."

She turned to Albero. "Albero, go down to the Conch and Sail and see if there's any news, anything at all, no matter how silly the gossip. Uncle, you have your orders. Mrs Francini…"

"I'll do what I do best, Miss Vivi. I'll cook."

"Miss Yvienne," Albero said. "What will you be doing?"

She braced herself. "I think it's time to call in the assistance of professionals," she said. At his expression, she said, "No, not the constables – the Harrier." She would confront Abel and find out what he was doing at the Port Saint Frey mansion. She would make him talk.

"Vivi!" Uncle Samwell said. He was not the only one shocked. She raised a hand.

"I know. But he's been conducting his own investigation, and he might have news of Tes before we do. I may be able to convince him to throw in with us in this matter."

After all, she thought, there could be only one reason he was at the Saint Frey mansion that night – for some reason, the Harrier was looking for her sister too.

Chapter Twenty-Six

Tesara was engulfed in flames. She struggled to put out the fire, but her powers were useless. Madam Saint Frey – no, it wasn't Jone's mama, but someone else – grabbed her hands and pulled them into the fire…

She woke, gasping with terror, her sore throat cutting like a knife so that her only cry was a hoarse mewl. Her hands throbbed and stung, despite the salve and the bandages. The nightmare faded away, and she concentrated on slowing her breathing, willing the pain to subside. She had soaked through her dress – no, she realized, looking down at herself – she was no longer in her dress but in a nightgown, lightweight and flimsy. She had been changed while unconscious.

After the journey by rowboat she was carried onto shore, still wrapped in a cocoon of wool blankets and a tranquilizing draught. Whatever tincture Mirandine's doctor had doused her with made her so woozy she couldn't object, and so she merely lay there as they carried her into an old carriage and she was driven off and away.

Now she was ensconced here, somewhere in the city. Her room was utilitarian. A bed. A nightstand with a ewer and basin. A water closet in the corner. Whitewashed, barren walls. Sloping ceilings, indicating an attic room. Two shutters, also white, closing out the view.

Mirandine was nowhere to be found, and she could only hear muffled noises from the lower floors and the sounds of a busy city outside the shuttered windows. Somewhere a clock struck two solemn notes. That and the pale light leaking through the shutters told her it was afternoon. Tesara sat up in bed, resting on her elbows, wincing as she put pressure on her bandaged hands to push off the covers. Moving slowly, she swung her feet to the floor and stood. She was weak and dizzy, but the dizziness soon passed. She held onto the bedpost and when stable, shuffled over to the window, placing her hand against the shutter. She could feel the cold wet weather of Port Saint Frey against her bandaged hand, but the shutters were nailed tight.

Just to keep busy, she tried the doorknob with her bandaged paws, unsurprised to find it locked. She listened for the sounds of occupation, but the house was quiet. Interesting, she thought. Perhaps if no one was around during the day, she might be able to get out. She cast around for something, anything, to cut through her bandages, to access her power if she still had it. She tried her teeth, but succeeded in tearing off only a corner of tough cloth. Tesara knelt beside the bed and looked for a piece of broken metal from the bedframe, but it was all well-kept, nothing jagged. Her gaze fell on the ewer.

She picked it up, holding it between her wrists. It was heavy, solid, painted with roses and greenery. There was already a crack running down the side. Tesara took a deep breath and raised it high over her head. It was awkward, the slick surface slipping between her bandaged hands. She retained enough of a grip to throw it at the floor.

The ewer broke with a satisfyingly loud crack, but it

only split in half. Bother and thunderation, she thought. She picked up the most promising half and threw it on the floor again. This time, it shattered.

Tesara held her breath. She could hear footsteps coming up the stairs. Hastily she scrabbled among the shards and found one with a pointy edge and razor sharp sides. The footsteps came closer, and then someone was at the door with a key. Tesara shoved the shard under the mattress and stood just as a matronly woman with a nurse's demeanor came in.

"What happened?" the nurse said.

"I'm awfully sorry," Tesara croaked. "I picked it up but–" She made a vague gesture with her bandaged hands.

The nurse looked at her askance, but said, "Were you hurt?"

Tesara shook her head.

"Well, I see you're up and about and feeling better. I was told to let them know. I'll have to keep you here for now, but I'll be back to clean this mess up."

"Wait!" Tesara croaked, but the matron slipped back out and locked the door behind her. As soon as she was gone, Tesara scrabbled for the shard again, palming it. If the nurse were gone to tell "them" she was awake, "they" might want to move her again.

She was standing upright when the nurse returned. With her was Mirandine.

"Goodness, you look better," Mirandine said, hiding what to Tesara's eyes looked like concerned shock. She swept into the room, wrinkling her nose at the broken ewer and the messy sickroom. "Ready to go home, I expect."

"Yes, rather," Tesara said.

"Look, I know you're upset. I would be. But it was for

your own good." Mirandine drew out a thin case and selected a cigarillo.

"If you smoke in here, I shall vomit," Tesara said.

Mirandine stopped in mid-strike and peered at Tesara over the cigarillo. Then with a displeased click of her tongue, she set the cigarillo back in the case and closed it. "I can see your temper hasn't improved," she said.

"I beg your pardon. Kidnapping makes me waspish."

"Now who's being dramatic? We merely removed you from the drafty old pile to someplace cozy to recuperate. And tonight, we'll take you home. You should be happy."

"Mirandine, please stop your ridiculous fictions. I want to go home. Now."

"You can't." Mirandine turned to the nurse, who took the hint and left, closing the door behind her. But not locking it, Tesara noticed. "With any luck no one will know you're here. Believe me or not, you are in grave danger."

"Well, yes. Madam Saint Frey tried to burn me alive. Then I was rendered immobile and kidnapped and carried off here, after I saved her life, mind you. So yes, I do think I'm in grave danger."

"Not us." Mirandine lowered her voice and drew closer. "Tesara, my aunt is a difficult woman, but even she recognizes that she... she has much to apologize for. When she described what happened, and that you tried to save her, she broke down and confessed. You see – she lured you to her house. She said it was revenge for stealing her son."

"What did Trune offer her to turn me over to him?" Tesara's voice was flat.

Mirandine sighed. "She didn't say. When we pulled you both from the fire, she tried to confess something. Savain and I didn't really listen, because honestly, Tesara, she rarely makes any sense anymore – she just seethes with rage and hurt. She was divided between asking us to go back for her hair and sobbing in confession that she had done something dreadful and that the awful man had forced her to do it. Savain filled me in on the details. When he said that Trune was on his way, I knew I had to whisk you away. Thank God the Saint Frey ancestors thought of a smuggler's tunnel underneath the house."

"Where am I?"

Mirandine turned up the palm of her hand, and the small box of matches was stamped with two names elegantly intertwined. Depressis-St. Frey. "It's… it's part of my marriage portion. Papa gave Jone and me a townhouse to start our married life together. I thought, well, it's mine, and private, so it would be the best place for you to recuperate. When it's dark, we'll take you home, and your enemies will be none the wiser."

"I have an even better idea," Tesara said. "I'll go home now. Don't bother to call me a hack. I can manage," she added, with stuffy grandeur. "I imagine my sister must be very worried."

Something flickered in Mirandine's expression – hurt. Tesara felt a pinprick of shame. Then the hurt turned to sulkiness, and Mirandine went to open the cigarillo case, but remembered and put it back in her purse. "Well, you can't go home in daylight and that's final. It's too dangerous. Trune may have missed you at the Saint Frey house but he will no doubt track you down. You're safe here. He may even have a guard on your house."

A chill swept over Tesara. Of course. What was she thinking?

"Then I have to leave at once, Mirandine!"

"No," came a new voice from the doorway. Both girls

turned toward it, and Tesara felt a leap of fear. "You won't be going anywhere, Miss Mederos. Thank you very much for your services, Miss Depressis. I'll take it from here."

It was Trune.

Chapter Twenty-Seven

It had become natural for everyone in the household to eschew upstairs-downstairs divisions and convene in the kitchen. They all sat at the long, scarred worktable, surrounded by wonderful aromas and warmth, and united by a shared mission – to find Tesara.

No luck, Albero reported, after a midday recon at the Conch and Sail. The servants' gossip was about the Mederos family, and he was plied with many offers of spirits and beer if he would only spill the details on the scandalous house. As for the fire at the Saint Frey mansion, there was plenty of avid speculation but no true news. There was no word of the wayward Mederos daughter in any of it.

Uncle Samwell had no more success. He returned from docks smelling of the sea, cigars, and brandy. "You know, Vivi, I am beginning to think the Names' reputation is entirely overrated," he said, disgruntled, as he helped himself to a tot of the wine Mrs Francini used for cooking. The woman gave him a steely glare and he gave her an abashed look in return. "Just a whole lot of nonsense about the Harrier and – well, never you mind," he added. "Gossip unfit for anyone. I gave it up," Samwell went on. "I ended up in conversation with a fascinating gentleman from out of town. Most sympathetic," he said.

Yvienne's heart sank to her toes. "Oh, uncle," she said. "Oh, no." He looked at her, surprised. "What did you tell him?"

"It wasn't like that," he protested. "I didn't tell him a thing. He just said I looked full of trouble and bought me a drink, and I told him, in a most general way…" his voice trailed off as his memory came back to him. "I might have mentioned that Tesara was missing," he said. "And I might have talked about Trune, but vaguely, quite vaguely. And we talked about the Harrier…"

He sat down heavily on the bench. "I've ruined everything," he said. He dropped his head in his hands. "Oh Vivi, can you ever forgive me?"

She sighed. "The damage is done, uncle. Are you sure he was a stranger? Did he give his name?"

"Never saw him before. And he was a medical gent – he said just to call him Doc."

Only Noe, it seemed, had any success. Shortly after the other two had returned with disappointing news, the maid came panting back to the house, letting herself in the servants' door.

"He said he'd come, miss!" she said with triumph. "I told him what you told me, that you would send for the coppers, and he said he'd come only to teach you a lesson." She faltered a bit at that, but Yvienne had to laugh.

"At last, someone calls my bluff," she said. "Good work, Noe." To her surprise the maid brightened at her praise, and despite her distrust, Yvienne thawed toward the girl. Poor thing, she thought. When this was over, she would do everything she could to extricate Noe from her handler's clutches. "Right," she said out loud. "Now, let's seal this deal."

• • •

At five minutes before the two o'clock hour, a large and wide figure loomed in the doorway of the kitchen entrance of the townhouse. Yvienne remained seated at the kitchen table as the dockside thug stepped over the threshold, ducking his head under the low lintel. Albero, Mrs Francini, and Uncle Samwell ranged themselves around the kitchen, with Noe crammed into the corner, making herself small. The only one obviously armed was Mrs Francini, with a formidable rolling pin. Yvienne had her pistol in her lap, under the table.

Noe's ringleader scanned all of them with admirable aplomb that just masked a vee of concern between his eyebrows. He was a large and imposing figure, made even more imposing by his wet great cape, large boots, and broad-brimmed hat. His black eyes were keen. He was rough-skinned and tanned, and obviously had spent time at sea as well as along the docks. His nose had been broken at least once, and there were red veins alongside it that indicated a fondness for drink. He grinned, and his teeth, though yellowed, were straight, and he had all of them. He looked directly at Noe, and she shrank back in fear, all her earlier confidence drained away.

"Well, Noe," he said. He removed his worn leather hat and slapped it against his great cape. "You brought me here. And I don't like playing games, not with the quality. So tell me true – are we playing games now?"

"No– no," Noe stuttered.

My turn, Yvienne thought. "How good of you to come, Mr Malcroft," she said. "As you will soon learn, I have a proposition for you that I think you will find it prudent to accept. You halt your activities as the head of the housemaid's ring, and work for me. If you choose not to accept..." She put her hand on the piece of paper in front of her. "I've called you here to say this little game of yours ends now. Noe has signed an affidavit and will swear to that effect in court that you are running a housemaid's ring, and furthermore that you have implicated the dock boss Cramdean in your wrongdoings. That affidavit is with my lawyer. If anything happens to any of us here, or to Noe's family, it goes straight to the chief constable and the courts. You can play dumb all you like, but if you try anything you will spend a great deal of time in gaol, where no doubt you will be at the mercy of Cramdean's inside men and their boss's displeasure."

His expression darkened. Yvienne kept her breathing easy, though her heart was racing, and her hand on the pistol was wet with sweat. He looked straight at Noe again, and she swallowed hard.

"You stupid little cow," he said. "You think they'll be able to protect you? You better say your prayers, little girl, because when I get through with you, you'll wish it was Cramdean you were dealing with." He jutted his chin at Yvienne. "She's nothing but a fine bit of silk and lace, playing at her daddy's business, and she'll turn you off at the first sign of trouble."

Yvienne felt a great swelling of anger. "Mr Malcroft," she said, her voice soft. "Do you know who House Mederos is?" She stood up, though he still towered over her, and she cocked the pistol and pointed it at his nose. She didn't know who gasped – Albero, Samwell, Mrs Francini, or Noe.

It got the man's attention most thoroughly. He was almost cross-eyed in keeping his eyes on the pistol. He held up his hands and took a step back.

"Let me remind you, Mr Malcroft, with whom you are dealing. We ruined Guildmaster Trune and drove him from this town. We took down the Merchants' Guild and we restored our family to its proper place. House Mederos rid this city of the corruption and filth at the top, and there is nothing to stop us from ridding it from the filth at the bottom. Do you want to go back to Cramdean? Be my guest. But you take this message to him if you dare. House Mederos will not rest until Cramdean and his ilk are served as thoroughly as we served the Guild.

"And *I am House Mederos.*"

There was a thrumming silence. She could practically see the man's calculations going on in his head as he weighed his two fates – throwing in with her or returning to Cramdean and trying to explain what had happened. After an interminable interval, Malcroft broke. He glanced down at the paper on the table.

"All right, all right," he said, smiling an obsequious smile. "All right. No need to get hasty. How can I help House Mederos?"

She gestured with the pistol and he fumbled backward and sat down on a stool by the door, looking like a chastened and overgrown schoolboy.

"First you can acknowledge here that Noe is no longer a part of your gang and her family will face no repercussions from you."

He glanced at Noe. Something passed between them, some communication that Yvienne could not read. He returned his gaze to her and nodded.

"Second, you work for me now, Mr Malcroft. Not Cramdean."

She pushed the paper over to him, wondering if he could read it. He could, and she saw the comprehension in his expression as he scanned through the contract, his eyes widening at the terms. She nodded to Albero, and he produced a pen and ink. Malcroft wrote a credible signature and pushed it back over to her.

For a second there was something shrewd in his expression although it was gone in a flash. But I saw it and won't forget, Yvienne thought. Contract notwithstanding, she had no doubt he had no intention of being bound by it. She lowered the pistol and released the hammer, and he let out his breath.

"You'll be amply rewarded, provided that you don't return to your old tricks," she said. "If you double-cross me or steal anything, then we turn you over to your old master." In response, he crossed his heart and yanked his ear. "Welcome to the team, Mr Malcroft. You are now head of security for House Mederos."

Chapter Twenty-Eight

The small gamekeeper cottage clung to the cliffs overlooking the rough sea along the lower Crescent, and a bit of smoke curled up from the chimney into the fog. Abel could smell the wood smoke. It was a pretty place, well-kept. This was Elenor's idea. The cottage was part of her portion, given to her by her parents on the eve of her wedding. The small note, delivered to the hotel front desk, was written on her personal stationery and in her elegant hand, and it told him to come to the cottage that afternoon at two o'clock. *As we discussed,* the note said, and left it at that. So she had come up with a safer place for them to meet, since there were too many prying eyes at the hotel.

He was going to break it off, gently but firmly, and he would not touch her or sleep with her, or take her with him, no matter how much she pleaded. This affair had cost him too much already, and the note on her stationery – for God's sake, he wanted to scream at her. Even the smallest bit of commonsense would have told her that was a foolish decision. She's young and inexperienced, he thought, and he felt a pang. A more sophisticated woman would have known how to keep their affair a secret. Instead, Elenor was barely older than a schoolgirl, and this was her first affair of the heart.

You idiot, Abel told himself. He had to extricate himself, for her as much as him. He was overwhelmed by her desire every time they were together, and it clouded his senses. He could no longer untangle his emotions from hers, and their desires fed on each other, until he was spent with the effort to keep his sense of self intact. Doc would kill him if he knew that Abel had let himself become entangled with a woman, losing himself in the process, undone by the very sensitivity that gave him such an advantage as a Harrier.

At least the ever-present accursed fog hid his approach. He went down the path to the cottage, noting the pretty winter roses and the curtains at the window, which shifted as he neared, as someone lifted them from the side.

The hair rose at the back of his neck and he stopped.

Abel, you idiot, he told himself again, but this time he put his hand to his pocket and palmed his pistol as he resumed walking forward. Elenor was young and she was inexperienced but she wasn't stupid. He was the stupid one, for taking the note at face value. He was walking into a trap.

As stupid and brutish as Jax Charvantes was, it was too much to hope that he had come alone to ambush Abel. He could expect at least two and possibly three men lying in wait. The problem wasn't going to be the ambush – it was the aftermath, in which he faced Doc and had to confess that he had not only lost the target, he had become embroiled with another man's wife, and failed to complete his mission.

At least you know who the Gentleman Bandit is. Which gave him some leverage, he acknowledged, as he knocked on the door of the cottage and braced himself for battle. He might not have the girl now, but he had a hold over her sister, and he could deliver both of them up to Doc.

If he survived the next half hour.

The door opened, and he faced Jax Charvantes. Not only was he flanked by Alve TreMondi, Amos Kerrill, and a couple of mates from the Navy, behind them stood Elenor, sobbing brokenly, with a purpling bruise across her cheek.

Abel moved first, in the style of eastern fighting that used feet and fists. Jax's bullies were big but inept, and Amos Kerrill was soon screaming in pain on the quaint rush-strewn floor, holding his broken knee. One of the sailors was efficient at seaman brawling, and pummeled Abel with savage brutality, but he was fouled by his own eager mates before he could get more than two or three solid hits.

Jax Charvantes saw the way the fight was going and grabbed his wife by the arm, and holding the muzzle of his pistol against her temple. She screamed.

"Stop," Charvantes said, his voice pitched to carry over the mayhem.

"Abel," she sobbed, and he halted. The two remaining bullies held him with his arms behind his back, and one had him with a chokehold. It still wasn't enough, and he could have extricated himself, but for the poor girl with the gun to her temple. Elenor tried to catch her breath, and managed brokenly, "Jax, please. Please don't hurt him."

"Don't you goddamn plead for him!" Charvantes shrieked and she sobbed harder. "You need to beg me to take you back!" He thrust her from him and she fell to the floor, crying. He looked at Abel and cocked the pistol and aimed it at him. Ah, Abel thought, curiously calm. At least Charvantes had the courtesy to not hold a cocked pistol at his wife's head. *I should have known. I should have expected.* But everything in Port Saint Frey had upended him, from the moment he arrived in town. A Gentleman Bandit who was a woman. Her sister, with vast power. And this ordinary girl, who had taken his heart by storm.

When Jax, instead of shooting him, smashed Abel across the face with the pistol, the Harrier wasn't surprised at all.

Chapter Twenty-Nine

Tesara pulled out the pottery shard and grabbed Mirandine, pulling the girl in front of her. Mirandine shrieked. She was as light as a bird; under the drapey silks and languid air, she was skin and bones. Tesara held the girl against her, the shard at her throat.

"Get back," she ordered Trune. *Oh, I wish my hands weren't bandaged.* Nausea be damned; she had blasted Trune once six months ago, and she longed to blast him again. Her fingers throbbed with pain, and she knew that her power, though muffled by the bandages, was beginning to gather.

Trune smirked as if knowing she was hobbled and he was safe. He looked the same as she remembered. Tall, saturnine, with deep lines grooved into his face. His hair was swept back and artfully oiled, and his collar points gouged dimples into his cheeks. His black coat was impeccable, his trousers crisp and lined, and his shoes gleamed. He looked good for a fraud, a cheat, a disgraced collaborator, and a thief. *He has not suffered at all.* Her heart sank.

"Don't be a fool," he said. "I know you won't hurt her."

Tesara dug the shard deeper into Mirandine's throat, and the girl whimpered. "Tes, please," she whispered. Mirandine sagged against Tesara but there was an expectant tightening of her muscles. Tesara braced herself and pushed as hard as she could, both with her muscles and her power, throwing Mirandine forward. The girl windmilled in an ungainly way, and crashed into Trune, managing to tangle both of them in her long trousers and silk scarves. Trune staggered backward, pinned against the wall by the leggy debutante, and they both screamed and cursed.

Oh, well done, Mirandine! Tesara bolted, darting between Trune and the door. He grasped for her with long, knobby fingers, but missed, and she ran down the stairs, praying Mirandine could keep him tangled for as long as it took.

Tesara kept her head and her balance, even though she was still sick and shaky. Down to the next landing, and she slid on stockinged feet to the next flight. From the sounds upstairs, Trune had disentangled himself from Mirandine and was pelting after her.

Tesara pushed through the door at the bottom of the stairs and burst into the kitchen. A cook looked up at her in surprise, and so did the nurse, who was adding something from a brown bottle to a bowl of soup. The nurse reacted first.

"Hey!" she shouted, rounding the table. Tesara grabbed a battered pot off the wall and threw it at her. The nurse batted it away with a forearm and came at Tesara with a snarl.

"HEY!" the cook shouted louder at the abuse of her cookware. Tesara grabbed a knife from the butcher's block and scanned for her escape. She feinted toward the pantry; the nurse went the other way round the work table to cut her off; and Tesara jinked right with a flash of satisfaction. She burst into the hall just as Trune came down the stairs, trailing torn silk, followed by Mirandine. He screamed in frustration and reached for her as she slithered sideways, just barely evading his grasp.

Heart bursting, wheezing for air, Tesara put one hand out and pushed open the double doors into the dining room. Behind her Trune recovered, and grabbed her nightdress, yanking her backward. He turned her around, gripping her forearms so hard that she lost the knife.

"I've got you now," he gritted, and his face was so close to hers she could see the red veins around his nostrils and the spittle at the corner of his mouth.

A great welling rose up from below her abdomen. The power exploded in her like a soundless sun, and for a moment all went still, all except for Trune's widening eyes as he experienced the great expansion of her power. First the bandages loosened, and then the scraps blew off her hands in tatters. Tesara's eyes bored into Trune's and she lifted her released fingers only the smallest bit.

The explosion was like a thunderclap between her palms. Trune flew backward through the doors, carrying them off their hinges. The great exultation of energy threw Tesara backward too, and she landed painfully on her behind, knocking the wind out of her lungs. She struggled for breath and hearing, and a part of her wondered at the predicament she now found herself in, once again undone by her own strength.

Then with a whoosh, breath and senses came back to her. Tesara looked up at a ring of faces looking down. A respectable butler bent down to help her to her feet, and she waved him away. She could still feel the buzzing that suggested she was not finished yet – or that her power was not finished. He stepped back with alacrity, as if aware of the danger. She struggled to her feet and looked around.

More servants appeared – a charwoman, a footman, and a groom, staring in shock and curiosity. Tesara noted them while she took in the rest of her surroundings, taking stock.

With the doors blown off, she could see across the hall into the kitchen. The nurse and the cook were covered with soup and soot. The blast had blown the pots and pans off their racks and had killed the fire, from the looks of the smoke rising out of the ovens.

But most important of all, Trune lay on the hall floor, blood coming from his head, but groaning. It sickened her to see it, even more than any momentary jubilation.

The clanging bell of the fire department and the constable wagons caught her attention. Tesara held up her hand, fingers trembling, magic sparking.

"Don't follow me," she said.

The butler nodded nervously, and with a gesture held back the brave footman and groom who looked ready to play the hero for the constables.

Tesara fled back to the kitchen and out into a tiny garden. There was a locked gate leading to the alley. With a flick of her fingers she pushed air at the gate and it snapped the sturdy iron links as if they were made of thread. She began the long walk home, trembling with the effort to control her powers. Her skin crawled, itching from the inside, and she thought she would go mad. She was hungry, dizzy, weak, and in pain. She stumbled against the wall and vomited, retching until it felt as if her stomach must come up too.

Home. I must go home.

She had to warn Yvienne.

Chapter Thirty

"Right," Malcroft said, rubbing his hands together with cheerful glee. "Show me around. What are the defenses of the place?"

For the love of Saint Frey, what have I done? Yvienne's heart sank. In the resounding silence as everyone stood about, uncomfortable at the new situation, Malcroft rolled his eyes.

"Now look, I only signed on because you had my bollocks on a leash. Only fair to hold up your end of the bargain." He gave her a wink, which caused Albero to sputter in fury and Yvienne to be torn between laughter and a blush. She chose the former.

"Mr Malcroft, you are absolutely right. Let's begin the tour."

As they all trooped through the house, including Mrs Francini, who professed a keen interest as she said she hardly got to poke her nose out of the kitchen, a statement that Yvienne noted and filed away, Malcroft scanned the house with the expert eye of a house breaker or estate appraiser, causing the young butler to sputter again.

"First, we need to put pins in all the window latches," he said, demonstrating with a simple piece of metal he drew from a pocket in his voluminous cape. "None of your run-of-the-mill thieves will get through that.

"Next, we need to set up patrols, inside and out of the house," he added. He looked at Uncle Samwell and Albero. "Just the two of you? No coachman or gardener? Just as well. Too many, especially amateurs, and it can be worse than nothing."

"When it comes down to it, you can add me to your roster of guards," Yvienne said.

He gave her a keen, assessing look. "I don't think so," he said. "No. Can't have you in the thick of it."

"He's right," Mrs Francini said. She folded her arms over her bosom. "Miss Vivi, you are our employer. You need to let us get on with our jobs." As Yvienne protested, she cut her off. "No. I'll brook no opposition. You are the face of House Mederos and you need to know your place."

Malcroft gave a low whistle of admiration. "Mrs Francini, if there is no Mr Francini in the picture, allow me to apply for that position."

"Oh, go on," Mrs Francini said, but she was pleased.

"I yield to Mrs Francini's evident good sense," Yvienne said, knowing when she was beaten. "Carry on."

They reconvened in the foyer. Malcroft was serious now. "Noe told me some of your problems. Wayward little sister, old enemies, new enemies, and the chief constable on your tail. Now I can't do nothing against him – that's beyond what you're paying me for, and if he knew you hired me it will make it go worse for you. So who are these enemies and what should we expect from them?"

"Our old enemy is Guildmaster Trune," Yvienne said. "We know he's back. He made one attempt on my sister so far, and now that she is missing we fear he may be involved in her disappearance. Our new enemy may be the Harrier, engaged by the Guild to uncover Trune's whereabouts but with some interest in Tesara himself. As the Guild has implicated House Mederos in that disappearance, the Harrier has been troublesome." She stayed mum about the Gentleman Bandit. "I know that Trune has a manservant who is his bodyguard and muscle. The Harrier is dangerous by reputation and I believe it is well-deserved."

"Harriers always get their man," Malcroft agreed. "They can be nasty little buggers. Did you know they don't hire 'em if they're over five foot seven?" He didn't wait for an answer. "All right. That gives me some idea of what I have to work against. I need to go back to my flop and get my kit. Trust me on that?"

"No," Yvienne said. He acknowledged that with a sly wink. "But I'm sure if you keep our agreement and its consequences in the forefront of your mind, you will behave. Albero and my uncle will go with you to help carry what you need. How long will it take?"

In the end, it took an hour to fetch his kit from his home in the squalid Hell's Soup Pot, as the part of town near the warehouse district was known. Uncle and Albero came back wide-eyed and impressed, helping Malcroft carry a sack of implements – brass knuckles, a weighted truncheon, and a lovingly hand-crafted spiked mace that looked as if it was made by inmates of the Port Saint Frey gaol.

The real treasure was a long gun covered in a narrow sock. When Malfcroft pushed the sock off, Yvienne was struck silent. It was a gleaming, gorgeous Chahoki repeating rifle, the likes of which made her own pistol look as serious as a child's pea-shooter.

"May I?" she asked.

He didn't look surprised, merely handed over the rifle.

It was heavier than she expected, and she held it pointed away, inspecting the mechanism. It was fascinating and simple and entirely deadly, and the source of the Chahoki's great strength. The gunsmiths of Ravenne had been making their own version of the Chahoki cannon, as it was known, for years, but there was nothing like the original workmanship. "I would like to use it sometime," she said, before she looked up at all their frozen stares. She had forgotten that Miss Yvienne Mederos was a proper merchant's daughter. For the moment, the Gentleman Bandit had taken over completely. She handed back the rifle with a sense of reluctance.

"Aren't you happy to be using your powers for good, Mr Malcroft?" she said, and he rolled his eyes in response. "Right," she said. "I'm off to visit the Harrier at the Bailet."

"You just said he was an enemy," Malcroft pointed out.

"It is rather complicated, I agree. But he may have news of my sister, and as you are well aware, I have no problem with unconventional allies."

"Fair enough," Malcroft said with a grin.

"Is it safe to go alone?" Albero asked, worry creasing his brow.

"I think it's best," Yvienne said. "Plus, I need you to watch Malcroft, watching the house."

"My wounded heart!" Malcroft protested. "I signed a contract."

"Yes, you did. And I will thank you to leave the silver where it is, and stop testing the locks on the cabinets. When this is over, you will be well-compensated for your time."

The Bailet lobby bustled with travelers, as a coach had just come in from the north, its six-mule team being unharnessed and led around to the stables at the back, while the redcaps and baggage handlers unloaded the luggage from the top of the equipage. Rather than alert the clerk to her presence, Yvienne took advantage of the chaos to slip up the stairs to the rooms.

The card the Harrier had given her on his first visit to her office was creased, smudged, and well-worn. Yvienne took it out while she knocked on Room Twenty-three, waiting in the dimly lit hall. The hotel was well-appointed but gloomy, the oil lamps hardly turned up. She went to the window at the end of the hall to look at the card. It was printed and engraved, and said simply,

ABEL FRESNEL
DETECTING MAN
HARRIER AGENCY, GREAT LAKE

She flipped the card over and there were notations on the back, as if someone had jotted down a code, but it was unintelligible to her. She shrugged and walked back to his room, and knocked again. There was no answer. After five minutes of knocking and waiting, she gave up. Another fruitless errand, she thought, heading back down the stairs to the lobby. She glanced at the clerk at the desk and walked over. He looked up without any recognition.

"Excuse me," she said.

"Yes, miss?"

"You have a gentleman staying here – a Mr Fresnel? May I leave a message for him?"

The very correct young man's expression changed to one of distaste.

"Mr Fresnel is no longer staying at the Bailet, miss," he said. "And might I say that… that, good riddance to him?" His throat bobbed.

"I'm sorry – did you say he is no longer at the Bailet?"

"Yes, miss."

How odd. Had he finished his investigation? It made no sense.

"Thank you," she said to the clerk, smiling with as much goodwill as she could muster. He gave her a judgmental look in return, and she barely kept from rolling her eyes. The Bailet had once been the best hotel in Port Saint Frey. Perhaps supercilious clerks were the remainder of its long-waned mystique.

As she went back through the lobby she caught the eye of a large, well-dressed gentleman checking in. They gave each other civil nods, and she had the impression of a formidable countenance and great strength. Yvienne even turned back to look at the man, and he watched her as she left. She flushed and hurried out into the weather.

Naturally there was no hack to be had. It was late afternoon, and the drizzle fell harder as the day darkened, and the lamplighters began their shift. Most people were hurrying home after a long day of business and commerce, and all the hacks were occupied. Yvienne resigned herself to walking.

On the long walk home, she remained deep in thought. Where now? Tesara was last at the Saint Frey mansion. The fire was out; the mansion was empty. The city gossip was mum on the subject of Trune. And now the Harrier had left town. She stopped suddenly, oblivious to the jostling crowds, a chill going through her that had nothing to do with the weather. Had the Harrier left because he had completed his mission?

Had he taken her sister with him?

Yvienne hadn't even really heard the newsies' cries for the afternoon edition until they impinged upon her consciousness.

"Fugitive from justice! Attacks on the quality! Read all about it!"

Yvienne fumbled into her purse, pulling out a half-guilder. "Here. Right here, boy!"

The cheeky urchin in the ragged clothes gave her a gap-toothed grin and thrust the broadsheet at her. Yvienne stopped with her back to the brick wall of a sundries shop, under the awning to keep the rain off the fresh ink, and read.

FUGITIVE FROM JUSTICE!

The younger Miss Mederos is wanted by the Constabulary of Port Saint Frey for questioning in the matter of the fire at the Saint Frey mansion, according to our sources. The girl has been involved in a series of attacks in the city, including most recently an unusual affair at a private townhouse in the West Side. A cook there described an assault on an unnamed gentleman and said it was a young merchant lady with alarming tendencies.

"She had no respect for other people's belongings that they use to do their jobs," the outraged artiste said. "And she hurt that poor fine gentleman something awful." Cooks are not to be insulted, as anyone who has ever wished to dine well has always known. We fear for the residents of the house until Cook's bruised feelings are salved.

The owner of the house, a young lady of the Depressis family who is connected by blood and a rumored engagement to the Saint Freys, was seen venturing to the Chief Constable's offices in what our ladies in the Home Department said was a most advanced mode of dress. Will trousers take Saint Frey by storm next season?

THE GAZETTE

"She's alive," Yvienne breathed, garnering glances from passers-by. She barely registered the attention.

Tesara was alive, but she was on the run.

Chapter Thirty-One

Tesara came to consciousness wedged under the protective embrace of a rocky outcropping on the western headlands. Her throat was still thick with pain and, to top it all off, she shivered with aching muscles. She pushed herself upright to find her nightgown drenched, bedraggled, and covered with dirt and vomit. She could smell the sea and hear the distant crash of waves, but her world had narrowed to a small patch of mist-shrouded rocks spattered with white and green lichen. The distant bell of a warning buoy clanged; a gull answered with a raucous cry.

After her encounter with Trune at Mirandine's house, she had been hounded by the city's constables, chased from hither to yon, until finally, now that it was coming on to evening, she had ended up on the headlands, hiding under an outcropping, curled around herself for warmth. In her panic, she had made her way there through instinct, rather than any planned design. She had sought concealment, not safety.

It had been a stupid idea, to follow that instinct. If she wanted to live, she needed to start thinking, instead of reacting. She couldn't go home. The constables would be waiting for her. She needed to find a place where she could get word to Vivi to beware and at the same time be concealed from prying and official eyes.

She thought of Trune and his machinations, his delight at finding her and his attempt to control her. She thought about Mirandine. Was she in league with Trune? But mostly she thought about the blazing strength of her power, when she knocked Trune backwards, the great expulsion of energy that was like a volcano erupting in her soul. She couldn't control it any more if she wanted to. And she didn't want to.

The anger was good; it sustained her for the cold walk back into town.

At four o'clock in the afternoon, Mrs Fayres's establishment was locked up and silent. It would not come alive for another six hours. Tesara stood shivering on the wet portico, and rang the bell, waiting. There was no indication of life within. She gave the bell another push. Finally, she thought she heard footsteps, and a moment later the door was pulled open. It was one of the burly gentlemen who served as security during the gaming.

"Yes?" His voice was deep.

Tesara tried for a charming smile and knew she managed only a ghastly grimace. When she first spoke she made only a wordless croak, and had to work her throat to get the words out. It felt as if she had swallowed glass shards.

"Is Mrs Fayres at home to visitors? Please tell her that Miss Mederos wishes to see her."

He frowned and then made his decision. "Wait in the foyer."

She followed him in thankfully, and sank down on the spindly chair just inside the entranceway, before hopping up after remembering where her nightgown had been. It was too late. She had left a bottom-shaped smudge on the beautiful embroidered cushion. Tesara closed her eyes in despair.

Footsteps again. The burly gentleman took one look at the cushion and gave a deep, disgusted sigh. "Follow me."

She had never been inside Mrs Fayres's inner sanctum. Tesara had expected a suite draped with silk and strewn with gifts from the colonel and her other admirers, decorated with frills and a giddy sensibility. Instead, she was led into a crisp sitting room. There was a fire crackling merrily in the fireplace, a wall lined with books, a massive desk with several ledgers, and a beautiful world globe on its stand that would have turned Yvienne green with envy. A maid was setting out a simple evening tea of soup and greens. She took one look at Tesara and exchanged speaking looks with the burly gentleman.

"Mrs Fayres said you should help yourself to tea, miss," the maid said, casting a dubious glance at her.

"I– I probably shouldn't sit," Tesara croaked. "I just need to ask a favor of Mrs Fayres." Perhaps if she could just borrow stationery to send word to Yvienne…

The world began to spin. Tesara grabbed the back of a chair. Oh no, she thought. Not now. She couldn't…

By dint of sheer willpower, she kept upright. "Perhaps I will sit after all." She managed to make her way onto a wooden end chair, hoping to mitigate the damage as much as possible.

There was a sound behind her and she turned with great difficulty. Mrs Fayres emerged from her bedroom, wrapped in a magnificent red robe. Her hair was loose over her shoulders, and despite the threads of silver, and the softer lines of her face, she looked more youthful than dressed in her usual fierce attire. She fought a yawn as she looked down at Tesara, as if she had been up all night and slept the day away – which, Tesara suspected, she likely had.

Mrs Fayres's first words were unexpected.

"Oh, kid," she said. She shook her head. "The entire city is looking for you."

Chapter Thirty-Two

Wet broadsheet clutched in her hand, Yvienne began to run. She lifted her skirts, muddy water splashing up from the streets and spattering up to her thighs. Her lungs burned and her side ached but she labored on, stopping now and again to press her hand against the stitch in her side.

She reached the bottom of the Crescent and had to walk again, but she was nearly home. At this hour, the fashionable street was still deserted, but that would soon change as the early evening bustle brought home merchants from their offices and took tired servants and tradespeople to their own homes and families. So the only traffic – a plodding one-horse flat cart – caught her attention. She stepped aside, almost in the line of trees that bordered the road. The fog concealed her, and she watched undetected as the cart loomed out of the fog up the hill.

Two men whom she did not recognize sat on the front seat, and the back of the cart was covered with a tarpaulin. The tarpaulin moved. It's a body, she thought. It has to be. Whoever it was, was still alive.

Tesara, she thought, sharp with panic. Yvienne kept to the side of the road and followed the cart up to the top of the hill, past her own house and the crowd at its gate. The

Crescent ended in a circle, where stood the Edmorency and Lupiere mansions. Past those houses was a narrow alley, almost a footpath, and it was this route that the cart followed. Yvienne made a decision and instead of crossing the open circle and risking exposure, she skirted the area and picked her way around the rocks.

Up here was the highest Port Saint Frey headland. The well-groomed houses along the Crescent, with their fine marble and brick, and elaborate wrought-iron gates, faced the wildness of the sea. The ocean crashed below, the surf a constant roar. Seabirds soared overhead in the mist, unseen, their raucous cries a call from a wild country. Yvienne was soaked through as she clambered over the rocks. She struggled on.

At the top of the headland, the cart stopped. At this height they were above the fog, and the air cleared, though the drizzle was constant. Yvienne perched behind a jumble of rocks and brush as the men threw back the tarp and pulled a man roughly out of the cart. Not Tesara, she thought with guilty relief. A moment later, she recognized the hapless fellow. The Harrier.

They manhandled Mr Fresnel's limp body over to the edge of the cliff and heaved him awkwardly into the air. A second later, she heard the splash.

Yvienne bottled up her shriek and was already moving, scrambling down the rock, half-sliding, half-scrabbling, angling toward where they had thrown him. Speed was of the essence and she no longer bothered to try for concealment. Down she slid, breath coming in gasps. When she reached the shore, and the dangerous upthrust rocks, she scanned for his body.

The cold saltwater had woken him up, because he thrashed listlessly, going under again and again, dangerously close to being battered on the rocks. Yvienne threw off her coat and hat and scrabbled at her boots, yanking at the buttons until she was able to draw them off and throw them aside. She ripped off the skirt, leaving herself in shift and shirtwaist. She stood up, took a breath, and dove in.

The cold water took her breath away, and she gasped. She had to work extra hard, but the surf helped her, driving Mr Fresnel into her. She rolled over on her back like an otter mother and held him against her chest. The waves rose over them and she coughed out water as he fought her instinctively.

"Stop," she managed. "Stay calm. Please."

To her relief, he could hear her. He settled down, fighting only a little when they sunk beneath the waves but he soon got into the rhythm of holding his breath when they went under and taking big gulps of air when they came up.

Yvienne was tiring but she kept at it gamely. She kicked and aimed for the side of the cliffs, around the headland. The waves helped again, the waves and the tide, carrying them against the steep cliff. And there it was, the sea cave that she had made her lair, so many months ago.

The waves were softer inside the dark cave, and the roar of the sea was muted. She grounded them both on an underwater shelf and she was able to half-sit, half-lean against the wet rock. She was shivering with the cold. She had to get the both of them up on the shelf, above the water, and into the dry part of the cave. She hauled him up as high as she could and squirmed out from under him.

"Wait. Stay."

She didn't know if he heard her but pulled herself free and climbed up onto the dry shelf. She bent down to pull Mr Fresnel up the shelf, hauling him up by his armpits. She was shivering hard, barely able to apply her strength to the task.

Again and again she almost lost him back into the sea, and it wasn't until he could feebly use his legs to push himself against the underwater shelf that she was able to get him onto land.

Chapter Thirty-Three

Abel came to with stinging cuts all over his body and throbbing pain in his ribs and his abdomen. He took stock of his surroundings while lying still, eyes closed. He heard the crackling of a fire and felt its distant heat. He lay on sand and was covered with a scratchy wool blanket, which was good because he was naked.

He could sense the presence of Miss Mederos and he gave up the pretense of unconsciousness to turn his head toward her. She had another wool blanket wrapped around her, but from her bare shoulders he knew she was also naked underneath. Her long wet hair was bound in a loose braid and hung over one shoulder. His clothes and hers were laid out alongside the fire.

"How do you feel?" she said.

"As if I were run over by a beer wagon," he said. She made a noise rather like a laugh. "Thank you for rescuing me," he added, and she lifted her shoulder.

"Not at all. Why did those men throw you off the cliff?"

"I expect it was because I had an affair with Elenor Charvantes," he said. He winced as soon as he said it.

He could see the shock in her expression change to anger. "Why would you *do* that?" she cried. She caught herself.

"You must think me quite naive. But God damn it, Mr Fresnel. She's a *friend* and he's a terrible man."

He didn't answer directly. "If it helps, I am very sorry for it," he said at last, knowing how weak that sounded.

"No, it does not help. It was beastly," she retorted. "Did you – do you love her?"

His silence was answer enough for both of them. She gave a long sigh and shook her head. "Never mind. I need you to help me find my sister," she said. "Why were you looking for her at the Saint Frey mansion?"

Self-trained, Yvienne Mederos was as smart and intuitive as any Harrier. He'd known that from the first moment he had laid eyes on her. He didn't answer.

"Mr Fresnel, I am quite angry with you, and more than capable of throwing you back into the sea. Do you know where she is?" Her voice caught. "Is she in danger?"

"I don't know where she is. But yes, she is in grave danger."

"Then help me."

Tesara Mederos wasn't the only one with special talents. Her sister's quickness was as valuable. *If I bring both of them to Doc, I can save myself from his wrath*. Maybe. Hating himself, Abel nodded slowly. "I'll help."

The little clock that Yvienne kept in the cave had long since wound down. She had a good sense of time, though, and calculated that it was now close to eight o'clock, nearly three hours since she pulled Abel Fresnel from the sea, built a fire, and undressed him and covered him with the old blanket. Her household would be out of their minds with worry. She found the extra clothes that she kept on a high ledge in the cave, wrapped in oilskin to protect them from the damp. She and Abel were nearly the same height and he was so skinny that she knew he would fit into her old Gentleman Bandit attire. And she had a skirt and shirtwaist that would do for herself.

"Can you move?" she asked him. He had been thoroughly beaten and even now was half-conscious. He roused himself.

"I can." His voice was thick and his eyes, as far as she could tell in the dim light, were unfocused. He tried to sit, the blanket sliding from his shoulders, and hissed at the pain.

"I'm afraid you'll have to," she said. "I can't stay."

"I can manage," he said again, and for a moment he closed his eyes. When he re-opened them, his expression was sharp. He was himself. My God, she thought. He managed the pain by sheer will. She felt sickened to think of the effort that took.

"Turn your back, please," she said, and he obeyed, lying down and turning onto his other side. Yvienne dressed while still half-draped under her blanket, working hastily to button her blouse. She had neither stays nor bandeau, but the warmth of the dry, slightly musty linen was heavenly. She flinched at the thought of putting on her wet boots, but she knew it had to be managed.

"Done," she said, when she had finished the buttons. She would have turned her back in turn, but while he might have managed his pain through extreme willpower, he could not knit broken ribs. She had to help him with the shirt, waistcoat, and coat, moving slowly but causing him pain nonetheless with every movement. He was so skinny, she thought, with a sympathetic pang. His hips jutted out from the waist of his trousers, and despite her anger at him she bit her lip at the sight of his abused torso. She helped him get his arms into his shirt, and then buttoned him up, her fingers grazing his chest in an intimate way.

"Sorry," she muttered, suddenly shy.

"No worries," he said. "Thank you for the dry clothes."

She looked directly into his eyes. They were of a height. "Why...?" she started, and then shook her head at herself. "None of my business."

"If it helps, and I know it doesn't, I knew it was stupid from the start."

It was so inadequate it infuriated her. "Yes," she snapped. "Very stupid. I pray you've come to your senses, sir. We have my sister to rescue."

Chapter Thirty-Four

The pain of the rough climb through the long cave to the surface made Abel regret every step. He moved like an old man, halting almost every few feet. Yvienne kept a slow pace, the lantern throwing light on the rocky walls as they squeezed through the passageway.

He wondered why she didn't just leave him. She didn't trust him; he saw it in her face, even in the dim light of the cave, and because he had touched her, he could read her as easily as if they embraced. But she read him too, with a quickness that was startling in its accuracy.

Or maybe I've just lost all of my abilities to conceal myself, he thought. Doc had spent years training Abel to efface himself so thoroughly his essential self all but disappeared. If it didn't hurt so much he would have laughed at how, in less than two months, he had sloughed off that carefully established protective skin. He was raw, vulnerable, and frightened, the same little boy he had been at the start of his apprenticeship. He didn't like feeling this way; it made him clumsy, angry, and prone to mistakes.

Abel felt fresh air on his face before he saw the cave mouth. Yvienne set the lantern down, extinguished the light, pushed aside the brush pile at the entrance, and helped him through it. Then she set the camouflaging brush back into place.

It was full dark now, hours having passed since that afternoon. Abel shivered. The fog had cleared, and a swath of distant stars shone down on them. The sea roared and the surf was white in the starlight. Above, he could see streetlamps of the Crescent, still a good climb.

She faced him, a dark shape in the faint light, and pointed to the west. "You take this path along the sea; the footing is good enough but in your state take care you hug the hillside. This will take you out to Kerwater Street and then you can find your way to the Esplanade and the Bailet, although they think you've checked out."

What? Abel had a very bad feeling come over him. His gear was all in that room. *Everything I own in the world.*

Her voice turned rough. "I must go home. My household will be worrying about me. I'll come to you later tonight. We need to combine our resources if we are to find my sister."

He nodded. "I have some leads. If the Guildmaster is back and he has your sister, we can track him. But we'll have to move fast."

"What leads?"

He didn't want her rescuing her sister without him. And in his state, he couldn't take Tesara alone, not if she were at her full strength, and not if she were a prisoner of someone else. So instead of answering, Abel said, "Miss Mederos, you saved my life. I owe you – immeasurably."

"Indeed. But I'm not sure, Mr Fresnel, whether acknowledgement of a debt is the same as a promise to repay it."

With that, she turned and began her long climb upward to the Crescent. Abel watched her for a moment, and then turned the other way, toward the city.

• • •

The elegant mantel clock in Mrs Fayres's dining room chimed eight. The elegant casino owner regarded Tesara over a simple dinner of fruits of the sea and sauced potatoes. The wine was excellent, a silvery white from Ravenne that tickled Tesara's nose and slipped down her sore throat. The bubbles captured the light and she had to work hard on tamping down the electric reaction in her fingertips.

She had been bathed and given clean clothes – a simple cotton gown that she suspected belonged to Mrs Fayres's maid rather than the splendid woman herself, and a warm shawl – and her hair was clean and up rather than falling in tangles around her shoulders. Despite all these advantages, she knew she couldn't rest and she couldn't wait.

"I've made inquiries," Mrs Fayres said, sipping her wine. "We've heard nothing about the return of the Guildmaster. Not that it means anything," she said, forestalling Tesara's croaking protest. "And, in fact, the complete stonewalling of our questions is suspicious. But we don't know where he is. Why would he be a danger to your sister?"

"Revenge," Tesara managed.

"I don't doubt it, but wouldn't he be more out for revenge against the Guild Council? They were the ones who threw him to the wolves."

"Complicated," Tesara said, after casting about for the least painful, least incriminating explanation. Mrs Fayres responded with a quick smile.

"I'm sure."

"Did you get the message through at least?" Tesara croaked. Tears leaked, and she dabbed at them with her napkin. They had tried all day, but Mrs Fayres had reported that the house was locked down, and with the crowd out front, plus constables surrounding the house from all points, there was no way to get a message through without attracting attention.

"We're trying now that it's night, and I should hear something soon," Mrs Fayres said. "And as annoying as the constables' presence is, surely they will prevent any mischief by Trune."

It hurt to snort a laugh, but Tesara managed. The constables had done little to prevent any of Trune's mischief in the past, as Mrs Fayres called it. What was to make them do their jobs now?

Almost as soon as Mrs Fayres finished speaking, a knock came at the door, and a burly gentleman entered. He leaned over and whispered in his mistress's ear, and she nodded.

"Thank you. And please tell my friends I will be down shortly." When he was gone, she said, "Well, and there you have it. Message delivered." She paused to contemplate her wine. "It's best for you to stay here tonight, Miss Tesara. Get some rest, recuperate. My staff will check on you periodically."

"Thank you," Tesara said, working her throat. "You have been most helpful and kind."

Mrs Fayres smiled, and stood. "I only ask that you don't tell anyone or my reputation will suffer."

As soon as she was gone, Tesara pushed back from the table. She drank some water, crisp and cold, so cold she almost wept at the pain, but it cleared her head a little. She flexed her fingers, feeling the power flicker through them. It didn't matter that she was sick, that her head ached, and her skin was so sensitive that even the light gown was painful. None of that mattered, because Vivi was in trouble, and with the heightened senses her fever gave her, she clearly heard the burly gentleman whisper in Mrs Fayres's ears – *the young lady wasn't at home, ma'am, and the butler and uncle were alarmed.*

The first thing she needed was practical clothing. The cotton gown and the shawl were fine for a cozy evening spent indoors, but were not sufficient for a mid-Fog Season night. She had to find better clothes, warmer clothes. Fortunately, she knew where she could find some. She had been gambling at Mrs Fayres's casino long enough to know that gaming wasn't the only entertainment.

Chapter Thirty-Five

The pain had receded somewhat, Abel was relieved to discover, by the time he made it to the Bailet lobby. The shock with which the night clerk greeted him took his mind off his lingering bruises.

"Mr Fresnel!" the young man said. "You're back!"

"Yes," Abel said, grim. "Were you expecting otherwise?"

"No... that is, I mean... your bill was settled up and they took away your things..."

That son of a bitch. His trunk had everything he owned, with all of the tricks of his trade. Jax Charvantes should have killed him when he had the chance. Abel would show no mercy now.

"Who told you I had checked out and wouldn't be coming back?"

The clerk looked helpless. He rang the bell on the desk, and Abel leaned against the counter, trying to make it look threatening instead of it providing necessary support. The manager came out of the back, an older gentleman with a neat spade beard and clad in a black suit with a string tie.

"Can I help you, Mr Fresnel?"

"Yeah, man. Who tol' you I wuldn't be back, and where the hell did you send my things?" He could feel the rage and helplessness welling up. The well-crafted mannikin Abel was gone, the wild, threatened kid in his place.

"I beg your pardon, sir," the manager said, stiff with outrage. "Master Kerrill said he was an associate of yours and that you had sent him to bring your things to his home, and that you would be staying at the Kerrill house from now on. You are here on Guild business, are you not? And quite frankly, sir, we do not enjoy your playing fast and loose with the reputation of this hotel nor with the respectable young ladies of this town."

"Do you still have a room for me?" he said, through gritted teeth.

The clerk made a move to look through the ledger but the manager stopped him. "I am afraid there are no rooms to be had at the Bailet," the manager said with crisp tones.

Abel removed his hands from the counter and stepped back. He doubted that Kerrill had found everything in the room, such as the wad of cash in the hidey-hole behind the mirror, or the vial of anesthetic drops that he had hidden in the window sill, after prying away a tiny bit of wood and replacing it so exactly that one couldn't see the joins.

"So you see, you'll have to ask Mr Kerrill for your things," the manager went on, his voice stern and unwavering.

Abel didn't bother to say anything more. He took his leave, and he heard the furious undertones of conversation between the manager and the clerk. He had no doubt that in short order Charvantes and his thugs would know he had survived his swim in the ocean. He needed a place to hole up and rest until he could come back to the Bailet and retrieve his belongings.

The crowd outside the Mederos house had dissipated. There were just a handful of stalwarts loitering outside the gate, and they had made themselves quite at home with a fire in a rubbish bin. Yvienne could only make out their silhouettes, their voices and laughter quite congenial, rising and falling in comfortable conversation. They passed around a bottle of what she suspected was strong spirits. She sighed. Were they vagrants or reporters or both?

She skirted the front gate and went down the alley, letting herself in by the kitchen gate, the key always at her side in her little purse. She closed the gate with care, but despite her efforts the gate squealed on its hinges as it always did.

"Stop right there," came a deep voice from the darkness and she obeyed at once. A tiny red glow and the scent of tobacco came to her in the next moment, and she could make out the large and reassuring bulk of Malcroft seated off to the side in the garden, his rifle across his lap. He stood and crushed the cigarillo under his heel.

"Thank God," she said, breathing easily for the first time.

"Yeah," he said, unimpressed. "Where the hell have you been?"

"A very long story," she said, and pushed past him.

She let herself into the bright and homey kitchen, blinking in the warmth and light, while Albero and Mrs Francini bolted from their seats, their words running over each other, both of them worried and careworn. "Miss Vivi! Are you all right?"

"We were so worried, Miss Yvienne! Where were you?"

"You're hurt, miss!" Albero added. "And your clothes... What happened?"

Malcroft came in after her, setting his rifle in the corner. The scent of tobacco and leather followed him in.

"I'll put the kettle on," Mrs Francini said. "And, miss, if you don't mind my saying, you have some explaining to do."

Yvienne sighed. "Mrs Francini, no scoldings please. These are unusual times, and this is an unusual house. Did you read the paper? Tesara is alive and causing mischief."

"We read it," Albero said. "But we still have no news of her whereabouts."

The front doorbell rang with alarming authority, startling all of them.

"At this hour?" Mrs Francini said.

Albero got up but before he could take two steps, Noe came clattering downstairs.

"It's the chief constable!" she gasped. "He's come for Miss Tesara!"

"You've run out of time, Miss Mederos," Chief constable Renner said. "Produce your sister. Now." He waited in the foyer and eyed her with steely demeanor, his medals and uniform as impeccable as always. Yvienne faced him with her arms folded, aware that she smelled and looked terrible.

"Why the hurry, Chief Renner?" she said. "You said we had until Sunday."

"That was before your sister attacked an unarmed man, leaving him severely injured, and also destroyed property in the process."

"Hearsay," Yvienne said. "And if it were true, no doubt the fellow deserved it."

He took in a deep breath as if seeking patience, and then turned to his men. He nodded his head at them and they took the hint, going outside and closing the big doors behind them. Only Yvienne and the chief were left in the foyer. I'm damned if I will let him into the house, she thought. She gave him a steely look.

"What happened to you?" he asked, his voice peremptory but rather as if he cared.

"I was pruning rosebushes," she said. The scratches were still raw and stinging.

He snorted a laugh. "You don't give up, do you? Do you know what happens to habitual liars?"

"Please don't tell me my face will freeze that way, chief constable. I'm no longer six."

"Keep it up, Miss Mederos, and you'll go to jail for your sister's crime if you don't turn her in."

"You have no cause to arrest me or my sister."

"We have a great many causes, Miss Mederos. But now I'm beginning to suspect something. You don't actually know where she is, do you?" A different expression came over him, considering something. "Why don't you just admit it?"

If she admitted that she didn't know where Tesara was, she couldn't protect her. What if Tesara *was* guilty of setting fire to the Saint Frey Mansion or of anything else, for that matter? She pressed her lips together, striving to radiate irritation rather than indecision.

"We can help find her," he said, and his voice was calm and soft. "If she's in danger, and she very well could be, we can make sure she's safe."

"Safe in gaol?" she snapped. "Chief constable, I'm not a fool. I'm tired of people thinking I am. I don't believe a single thing you say about my sister and how you intend to protect her."

He dropped the compassionate mask. "All right, Miss Mederos, I've had enough. You're coming with me. You are under arrest for crimes against the peace of Port Saint Frey including arson, vandalism, and battery. Do I have to handcuff you, miss, or will you come peacefully?"

"Those are trumped-up charges, and you know it," she shot back, knowing she was fighting a losing battle. Was it too much to ask that she had the chance to change her clothes?

"We'll let the magistrates decide that, Miss Mederos."

Albero and Noe, who had been lurking, burst into the foyer upon the chief's words.

"You can't! You can't!" Noe screamed, and she rushed the large policeman, her frail form dwarfed by his splendid bulk.

"Noe, stop it!" Yvienne snapped. Albero caught the maid and wrapped his arms around her, and she burst into sobs against his chest. Albero looked quite wild himself. Give him something to do, she thought. "Where's my uncle?"

As if on cue, Samwell came dashing down the stairs and into the front hall. He was dressed, but haphazardly, his waistcoat unbuttoned and his hair uncombed.

"Damn you, Renner, you know you have no cause here!"

"I have every cause, Balinchard, and you know it," the stolid Renner said.

"Albero," Yvienne said, surprised at her own sense of calm. "Contact Dr Reynbolten and have her meet me at the constable headquarters. And uncle…" she looked straight at him. "You're in charge of House Mederos. I know she – we – will be in excellent hands. Please take care of business."

Uncle Samwell gaped. His lips traced her words soundlessly. And then he beamed.

"Yes, admiral," he said, and he threw a salute.

Yvienne was not handcuffed. Instead, she was escorted respectfully through the front gates by Renner and his constables, past the crowd, creating a stir and causing a mad scrum of reporters to run after the closed wagon, shouting questions. Yvienne swayed inside the top-heavy box, trying to keep from panicking. Oh, Tesara, she thought. Please come home soon.

Chapter Thirty-Six

The upstairs hall at Fayres was quiet and dimly lit with glowing camphene oil lamps, and Tesara could hear the sounds of revelry getting underway. Downstairs, the casino and bar were beginning to liven up, and the clickety sound of the wheel, the dice, and the slapping of cards seeped upward to the rest of the house. Tesara crept from Mrs Fayres's apartment, shawl clutched around her, ready to lie through her teeth if encountered, and failing that, lash out with quivering fingers.

The townhouse itself was genteel enough. It faced the street, rising three stories above with an impressive brick front and a columned portico. Behind the townhouse was another building, once an old stable, now connected to the house via an upper hallway. Tesara had observed many male customers in the casino flirting with outrageously beautiful women who were too finely dressed and too sophisticated to compare with the soiled doves of the waterfront. She had heard the smirking whispers about *upstairs at Fayres*. She was no fool.

Somewhere a clock chimed the quarter hour – it was rising nine o'clock. Tesara hurried up the stairs, only to stop in dismay and back up a step or two to hide in the shadows of the landing. There was a burly gentleman standing at the door at the other end of the hall, arms folded, guarding the treasure behind. Could she brazen it out? She was reminded of Uncle Samwell's assessment, that she was coming into her looks, but it was laughable to think that she was anything like the beautiful women who captivated the customers. She looked like nothing so much as a precocious schoolgirl.

"Who's there?" the guard called out. "Show yourself."

She hesitated, then crept forward, crumpling the shawl in her fingers. "I'm so sorry, sir," she quavered, trying to get the words past her sore throat. At least it disguised her voice. "The mistress asked me to help with the hair tonight."

He looked her over in the dim lamplight and she spent an agonizing, sweating moment. Did he recognize her? Did he know about the pesky Miss Mederos who had arrived bedraggled and sick on the mistress's doorstep? Did the ladies of the night even need someone to help them with their hair?

"Are you new?" he said at last. Tesara nodded, hoping that it made her seem shyer than she was. He sighed. "All right. Go in."

He knocked once on the door and then unlocked it and let her inside. She gave an awkward curtsey and sidled past him.

Once inside, the door locked behind her, Tesara stared. The brothel was simply splendid. The parlor, for it could be called nothing else, was magnificently furnished, with thick velvet drapery and lacy things, and more brocade, and porcelain crockery, silver trays, and crystal carafes filled with wine and liquor. There were boxes of cigars laid out for the evening's guests. There were beautifully painted portraits of ladies in all sorts of undress, cavorting with fantastical creatures and mythical heroes. She stifled a laugh, because it hurt too much, and she thought it was a good thing she had a sore throat, because if she hadn't she would have fallen down laughing with tears streaming down her face.

"It does take one's breath away," drawled a lady on a sofa, reading a book, the author's name – Suristen – and the book's title – *The Madrigal of Grief* – picked out in gilt on the leather cover. She was the only person in the room besides Tesara. She sat up, adjusting her lovely silk wrap. She had masses of flame-red hair, and her lips were painted crimson, the same as her fingernails and toenails. "But what can you do – the gentlemen expect it, and they get very unsettled if it doesn't look this way. Once we asked Fayres if we could redecorate, and she said yes, but she warned us that profits would go down."

"Did they?" Tesara croaked.

"By a good twenty-five percent. We threw it all back up after two days. The customer's always right. What are you doing here?"

"I need help. May I borrow some clothes that the gentlemen may have left behind?"

The woman gave her a keen look. "They tend to exit clothed, you know."

"But not always in what they were wearing on the way in," Tesara pointed out. She had noted it on many an occasion, when an army officer or other notable did not want to be identified leaving either the casino or the back room.

"We may not have anything in your size," the woman said. "But I'll see." She raised her voice. "Lucielle, can you come out here?"

Lucielle was a primly uniformed maid. The red-haired woman explained what Tesara needed and she nodded, unruffled by the request.

"If the young lady doesn't mind rolling up her trousers, we can outfit her," she said, casting a competent eye over Tesara. "I think we've got some walking shoes that Estinne left behind."

"Good," said the woman. "But first, it is the custom of this house that nothing is for free. So what can you do for us, Tesara Mederos?" She gave Tesara a level stare.

Tesara had not given her name. Of course, these ladies were not shut away from the world. No doubt they took a keen interest in the doings of Fayres's establishment and of Port Saint Frey itself.

"I will be forever in your debt?" Tesara tried.

"Well, that sounds like a man, but no. Not good enough."

More ladies came out in various states of dress. "What is this?" one asked. "Fayres foisting off amateurs on us now?"

"It's the younger Mederos girl," the redhead said. "Fayres has been nursing her back to health. She wants us to disguise her in boys' clothes."

"Dear girl," said a woman with bobbed hair and a straight fringe across her forehead, "that never works."

Tesara thought about Yvienne and didn't contradict her.

"I don't have money, it's true," she managed. "But I have to go. I have to find my sister, before Trune tries to attack her."

The atmosphere in the room changed all at once.

"So it's true?" the redhead said. "He's back?"

Tesara nodded. "He tried to kidnap me." Again.

The ladies conferred in a huddle, whispers rising and falling. There were some strong words exchanged regarding Trune's character. She looked at their hard faces, taking in the knowledge that she had not been Trune's only victim. As Guild liaison and then Guildmaster, he had the ultimate power over all the guilds in Port Saint Frey.

What had Trune done to these ladies?

At last they stopped, and then the ringleader – the redheaded lady – gave her a skeptical look.

"You don't look as if you are in any shape to stop him," she said.

Tesara could not contradict her. She was sick, in pain, and practically trembling with power. Her head pounded with every heartbeat and her throat was sore. She had the worst ague of her life. If her power could do anything, she thought, it should help me now.

Whatever you do, don't use it on yourself. The last words of the Harrier came to her, and though she knew he meant it as a warning, it only emphasized that she could do such a thing, and that it might work. And it's all I've got, she thought.

She gave it a try, fingers trembling, seeking to turn her energy on herself. At first she swayed as dizziness overcame her. Then her head cleared, and her pain receded. She felt the strength buzzing in her bones, restoring her, dampening the effects of her illness but not curing her. It felt as if she had been jolted with electricity, awakening her muscles and bones and blood and nerves. At the same time, she knew it couldn't sustain her for long. She was drawing on the last of her strength to keep herself upright and in motion, and it was destroying her from within.

That's all right. I just need it for a while.

When she spoke again, her voice came out strong, and she stood a bit taller. "I can stop him. I will stop him. I won't fail."

She would spend the last of her power if it meant that she could stop him once and for all.

The redhead gave her a keen look, taking in the difference between Tesara a moment ago and the girl who faced her now. She made her decision.

"Right," she said. "We'll help, but remember, Tesara Mederos, that when it comes time to acknowledge the trade, that House Mederos will honor her debt."

"I promise," Tesara vowed, hoping against hope that Vivi would understand.

She could tell the ladies thought it was amusing and diverting to costume her, like dressing a living doll. She was outfitted in a pair of trousers held up with a belt and suspenders, and a white shirt that practically swallowed her, so thin she had become as a result of her illness and lack of food, and whose sleeves had to be rolled many times. She was given a warm wool jacket that came down to her hips, and a knitted scarf from one of the ladies – it was lovely and blue and the woman dismissed her thanks saying, "Goodness, girl, it's just a scarf. I make one a day, just to keep my hands busy."

Estinne's shoes fit with the help of extra socks. The crowning touch was a wool cap, with her hair tucked underneath it. The women oohed.

"Adorable," pronounced the redhead in the silk gown. "Now," she said, tugging at Tesara's scarf to straighten it, "there's one more loan, and this one is the most precious of all. Lucielle, call for Grivere, have him saddle up Persife. Stride saddle please. You do ride, don't you?"

Tesara nodded. "I haven't since I was a child, but one doesn't forget." She remembered her pony Daisy, and the scrapes they got into while riding in the park.

"Persife is my hunter, and she's spirited but honest. She's shod for the streets and she won't slip. If she gets hurt in your care, I will come after you myself, and you won't like that."

In a few minutes there came a knock from below, and they led Tesara down a back staircase to a solid door, which led to a narrow alley behind the townhouse. A groom held a robust bay mare who whickered at her mistress but stayed still for Tesara to be thrown into the saddle. The groom adjusted the stirrups for Tesara's shorter legs, and she looked down at her rescuers. She gathered the reins and felt the horse come together under her seat. It did feel good to be back in the saddle after nearly seven years.

"Thank you, ladies," she said, as heartfelt as she could. "And, um, if you could not tell Mrs Fayres–"

"We won't," the redhead said. "But you better go. Fayres has a way of finding things out."

She turned the mare in the tight alleyway, and boosted her into a steady trot, rising and falling in the saddle. The hoofbeats rang on cobblestone and, true to her owner's words, Persife never missed a footfall on the uneven surface.

The cold wet night air smacked at her cheeks above the scarf, but it felt good, bracing, despite the pain of her sore throat and feverish, sensitive skin. She turned the mare down the wide streets toward the Crescent, keeping to a trot because it wouldn't do to gallop through the dark avenues of Port Saint Frey, no matter how surefooted the mare was.

Hold fast, Yvienne, she thought, as she hurried home through the dark wet streets. I'm coming.

Chapter Thirty-Seven

Yvienne had barely alit from the constable wagon and been ushered inside the station when a streamlined carriage of the newest mode clattered up to the front of headquarters. Everyone turned to look. A large woman, followed by a tiny page, exited the carriage at full speed.

"Chief Constable Renner!" Dr Reynbolten boomed as she swept into the room, followed by a chastened junior constable, his undecorated uniform a match for his spots and his bravely attempted mustache. "How dare you detain my client? What is this? Have you lost your mind, sir? Arresting a daughter of House Mederos? On what charges? Let me see the charges. You have overstepped, chief constable! O. Ver. Stepped."

Dr Reynbolten was six feet tall, with broad shoulders encased in leg o' mutton sleeves in a dress of deep crimson, a tightly corseted waist, and demi-skirts that showed off riding boots and pantaloons. She wore the sash of the advocate's guild across her impressive bosom, and her chin rested on a froth of lace at her throat.

She cast a gimlet eye over Yvienne. "I thought I'd find your sister in here. Not you." She snapped her fingers. Her little page, a seven year-old boy, ran forward, lugging a record book almost as big as he was. Dr Reynbolten thumbed through the book. "Statute 10.5. Produce your proof now, chief constable, or release my client."

"Statute 10.5 doesn't apply in a Guild case," the stolid Renner said. "Stop intimidating my men, Claia, or I'll have you thrown out."

"I'd like to see you try." She shut the book with a thud. "For God's sake, Renner, she's the smartest girl in Port Saint Frey and the only sensible one out of the bunch. What do you have on her?"

"Obstruction of justice and conspiracy to commit arson and battery, and she is currently the lead suspect in the murder of Barabias Parr."

"Hmm." Another piercing, gimlet gaze. Yvienne looked her straight in the eye. "Everybody out. Not you," she said to the page, pulling him back by the collar. Renner and the junior constable filed out.

Yvienne sat on the hard wooden bench with her hands folded in her lap. "Thank you for coming, doctor. As you can see, we need your help."

"Yes, well. What on earth has your sister gone and done this time?"

Yvienne hesitated and glanced at the closed door. Dr Reynbolten waved a dismissive hand. "Renner and the rest know better than to listen in. Besides, he briefed me earlier today. Told me you're guilty as sin, and your sister too. Of what, I'd like to know. Just so I may defend you, you know."

"I don't think we're guilty of anything, doctor. It's another setup, clearly." She filled her in.

"So you don't know where your sister is?"

Yvienne shook her head. "Madam Saint Frey requested her to visit, but..." she thought fast, "when we went to bring her home, the house was empty."

Dr Reynbolten gave her a keen look. "Before or after the fire?"

"After."

"Hmm. Then, later, she was implicated in the disturbance at Miss Depressis's townhouse. For an innocent girl, your sister is cutting a wide swath, my dear."

"I think it's only fair to get her side of the story, doctor, before jumping to conclusions."

"Thinking like an advocate, Miss Mederos. If you care to give it a go, I can make an introduction to the University of Ravenne."

"That is most kind," Yvienne said. "However, I am called to Business, not Law. Do you know what happened at the Depressis townhouse? The newspapers were rather lurid."

"Weren't they," Dr Reynbolten said, her voice grim. "I'll see what I can find out. First order of business is to spring you on personal bond. I suspect Renner only wanted to soften you up a bit. He knows he doesn't have a shred of evidence of your involvement."

"As I know nothing of value, it was a futile effort," Yvienne said. Goodness, Renner was right. She was becoming an accomplished liar, except it was true she did know little of value, at least where Tesara's escapades were concerned. She had plenty of secrets of her own.

Dr Reynbolten gave her a look as if she didn't believe a word of it. "Right. Wait here. You should be out in less than ten minutes. We'll have to appear before the magistrates later, but for now you can go home."

She thumped the heavy wood and iron door, and the bolt was scraped back and the door opened a moment later. Then Yvienne was alone again.

The silence was a stark contrast to the bombastic presence of Dr Reynbolten. Mindful of her exhaustion, thirst, and hunger, not to mention the need to use the necessary, Yvienne fidgeted on the bench, hoping the advocate would hurry. All this time in custody was a dreadful waste. She needed to meet the Harrier and devise a plan.

True to her word, the door was unlocked and opened again, and Dr Reynbolten beckoned. "All right. You're sprung. Let's go."

It was nine o'clock. They were running out of time.

Chapter Thirty-Eight

Dr Reynbolten gave Yvienne a lift in her carriage and would have dropped her off in front of her home, but the vast crowd, refreshed after her arrest, put paid to that idea. The lawyer peered through the window shades and clicked her tongue.

"How long has this been going on?" she said.

"Since the discovery of Parr." Good God, had it only been that long? It felt as if they had always been there.

"And you didn't think to let me know?" Dr Reynbolten's tone was disapproving.

Yvienne lifted her shoulders. She was so tired, she could barely think.

"Would you prefer to stay at my townhouse, Miss Mederos?" the advocate said, after another peek out the window.

"I'd rather not let them chase me away," Yvienne said with a sigh. She peeked out the carriage window at the crowd, all quite jolly. "They have such… stamina."

"The appetite for gossip and rumor is unending," Dr Reynbolten agreed. "Do you have a gatekeeper?"

"No, but if your driver rings the bell three times and then twice, that is our signal that we have permission to enter," Yvienne said. Dr Reynbolten banged on the ceiling of the carriage, conferred with her driver, and accordingly the man pushed the large bell at the gate. There was a long pause while the crowd circled around, their excitement piqued, and then she saw the front door open and Albero ran out, hoofing it toward them, followed by Malcroft, standing at the front door, impressive rifle at the ready. Light from inside the house streamed into the courtyard.

The crowd began to shout. "The butler! The butler!"

An enterprising reporter jumped on the running board and yanked on the door. "Who's inside? Is that Miss Mederos? Can you give me an exclusive, Miss Mederos? Where's your sister? Is she an arsonist?"

Taken by surprise, Yvienne edged back into the seat, and the page crouched next to her. She put her arm around the little boy and he pressed against her.

Dr Reynbolten, however, remained unperturbed. "Reporters," she muttered. She yanked the door from the fellow's grip and held it closed against him. "Ah, here we go." Albero unlocked the gate and pulled one side open, giving them enough room for the horse and carriage. They began to trundle forward, the driver handling the nervous horse with aplomb. Yvienne could feel the crowd pressing in on them, forcing the carriage forward.

"Dr Reynbolten, they're going to follow us in," she said, with rising tension. She longed to jump out and defend her house.

"We'll see about that," Dr Reynbolten said. She reached into her enormous satchel, and pulled out a large silver-chased pistol. With a quick move she opened the door, pushing hard.

"Oof!" grunted the reporter as he was flung from the side of the carriage. Yvienne caught his shocked expression as he landed hard on the gravel.

Dr Reynbolten stood on the running board, and cocked the pistol, aiming at the sky. The shot rang overhead and the carriage lurched as the horse sprang forward. She hung on with impressive nonchalance. The mob shouted, and the carriage swayed but the crowd pressed forward.

The sharp crack of Malcroft's rifle dissuaded them. The horse reared at the sound of the second shot and came down, narrowly missing one fellow who had gotten out in front of the carriage. The singleminded crowd broke up as people screamed and scrambled backwards, pushing at each other.

Albero was able to close the gate against the invaders, and the horse half-trotted, half-galloped forward. Dr Reynbolten stayed on her feet, balancing half out of the door, as if she fired a shot from the running board of a carriage every day. The driver pulled up at the front door, the lawyer pulled herself back in, and she put her pistol back into the satchel. Albero opened the carriage door on the other side. He was a welcome sight to Yvienne.

"Miss Vivi!" he exclaimed. "We were so worried about you!"

"Thanks to Dr Reynbolten and you, everything is all right for now," Yvienne assured him. She gave him her hand, and he helped her out of the carriage.

"Come inside, Miss Vivi," Albero said, throwing a glance at the crowd. "Don't let them see you anymore."

Dr Reynbolten poked her head out the window at them. "Yes, stay put inside. I'll get to the bottom of this mess. Renner doesn't have anything on you, but if we can find your sister and get her story, that will go a long way toward making him back off."

Yvienne had her doubts about that – she was more and more convinced that Tesara was involved in everything of which she was accused – but she nodded. "Thank you, Dr Reynbolten," she said, conscious of her entire lack of intention to stay put. "You have been tremendously helpful."

Dr Reynbolten only gave her a keen look and pulled her head inside. They heard her bang on the ceiling and then the driver clucked to the horse and the equipage circled back to the gate.

Chapter Thirty-Nine

Yvienne watched from the steps as Albero let them out the gate and jogged back. He breathed hard but he looked immensely pleased with himself.

"That's that. It's good to have you back, Miss Vivi."

"It's good to be home," she said, clasping his hand for a moment. Slender, young Albero had toughened over the past months. He was unshaven, his hair uncombed – he looked most unbutlerlike. *Tousled becomes him.* Then she caught herself. The last thing she needed was to be mooning over the butler.

"Yes. Well," she said, releasing his hand and leading the way into the house, trailed by Albero and Malcroft. "Let's go inside and you can fill me in."

They closed the door behind her, and it was lovely to stand in her own foyer, surrounded by her family. There were Mrs Francini and Uncle Samwell, exclaiming their relief. There was Noe desperately wringing her pinafore.

"All right?" Albero asked.

"As well as could be expected. Dr Reynbolten is a treasure. Albero, I've quite lost track of time – ah," Yvienne said as the clock in the hall chimed half past ten. She needed to change into dry, warm clothes and head back out and meet the Harrier. She hoped whatever his leads were, they were true.

"Have you eaten, Miss Vivi?" Mrs Francini demanded.

"Mrs Francini, there's no time–"

"Nonsense. Downstairs. Now."

When Mrs Francini spoke in that tone, no one objected. They all trooped downstairs.

Yvienne had a crab bisque with sour cream, biscuits with butter and honey, and parsnips, along with copious amounts of water and just the slightest bit of wine.

Mrs Francini eyed her tartly, and when she had blunted the edge of her hunger, the cook said, "And now, my girl, you have some explaining to do. And I'll brook no nonsense from you as to how you are mistress of this house."

She looked at the array of faces, from Albero's earnest one, to Uncle Samwell's avid expression, Noe's nervous handwringing, and the curious expression on Malcroft's face. They'll just have to know the truth, she thought.

With as succinct a manner as possible she related how she had saved the Harrier and the kitchen exploded in shock. Every time she tried to continue, someone else would jump in with questions or more general exclamations and alarums. Finally she stood up and cried out, "*Enough*!"

Silence rang out.

"I rescued the Harrier and as a result he's on our side now." Malcroft snorted and she glared at him but continued, "He's going to help us. I will brook no more argument." To cut off further debate, she turned to Mrs Francini. "Thank you, Mrs Francini, for a lovely dinner; you have no idea how much you've restored me – and after I change into warm clothes, I'm going to find Abel Fresnel and he is going to help us bring Tes back. So now, if you'll excuse me, I'm going upstairs to bathe and change."

She looked around at all of them, a challenge in her upraised chin and her crossed arms. No one said a word.

While she'd been eating, Albero had stoked the boiler, so that when she went upstairs to take her bath the water gushing into the basin was almost painfully hot and steaming. Yvienne undressed, leaving her filthy clothes outside the door for laundry day. Thank heavens for Noe, she thought, dipping a toe gingerly into the bath. If the girl stays, she gets a raise. She sank into the tub with a long sigh. The water stung her scratches but was heavenly despite the pain. Yvienne sunk down until her nose was the only part of her above water, almost weeping with the deliciousness of it. She scrubbed at her hair until it squeaked, and washed furiously at the dirt and the salt and sweat that had caked her for so long. She closed her eyes for a moment, wishing she could sleep for hours, and finally forced herself out of the tub.

Tesara needed her. She couldn't stop now.

Chapter Forty

Still wrapped in the long towel, Yvienne peeked out the bathroom door. The hall was cold and mostly dark, only one lone lamp glowing by the stairs. Everyone was still downstairs, and so she tiptoed from the bathroom to her bedroom, hurrying to get into the warmth of her room where she could change into dry trousers, shirt, waistcoat, scarf, and wool socks. I will never wear a dress again, she thought, as she grasped the doorknob and pushed.

A hand reached out and grabbed her, pulling her into the room. Yvienne drew breath to scream when the hand went over her mouth, strangling any noise. She tried to fight but the damned towel thwarted her efforts, and she tripped and went down. Immediately the intruder fell down on top of her, hand still over her mouth. He kicked the door closed, and leaned in close.

"It's me. Don't scream," Abel said in her ear.

Yvienne went rigid with shock. The towel had fallen off her, and she was conscious of his clothed body pressing into hers. Turnabout's fair play, she thought. After all, she had seen him naked when she stripped him of his icy clothes after his plunge into the sea. A well of laughter bubbled up in her throat. He removed his hand and got up, throwing the towel over her, and she struggled to sit, holding the towel close around her.

They stared at each other in the dim light of the candle and the crackling of the fire, their own breathing the only sound. Yvienne strained to hear any noise from below, but there was none. If her guards downstairs had heard anything, they were in no hurry to investigate. She felt a moment of exasperation. What good were they after all?

"What are you doing here?" she whispered crossly. He looked terrible and smelled worse. How had he gotten in undetected? Of course – he had probably shinned up the balcony in her parents' suite.

"As you said, the Bailet hadn't a room for me anymore. I had no place to go."

"Excuse me. I just revealed to you a sea cave."

"Would you have gone back there to look for me?"

She would not. She would have thought he had given her the slip. At her expression he added, "I needed the one place you would be sure to find me."

She couldn't help it; she laughed again. "My bedroom? That would be the one place."

"And I needed someplace warm to recuperate." A fleeting expression swept across his face and was gone. "And I need food. Can you send up for a meal?"

His poor bruised and beaten ribs; his jutting hipbones. Despite herself and her vulnerable position, her heart went out to him.

She was about to say something when she heard footsteps. She froze. He put a finger to his lips, and got up, locking the door.

"Miss Vivi?" came Albero's voice.

"Yes, Albero?"

"Are you well? Do you need anything else?"

"Quite well. The bath was wonderful. Just what I needed." Abel jerked his head at the door, and she made a face at him. "But – I'm still peckish. Do you think Mrs Francini could send up some more of the soup? And are there any biscuits left? And… well, if there's any hot chocolate to take off the rest of the chill…" She sounded exactly like Tesara when they were kids, she thought, always begging for extra. And because she was reminded of her sister, she felt a pang of loneliness for her.

Perhaps Albero remembered too, because there was a smile in his voice as he answered through the door, "Of course, Miss Vivi. Hot chocolate, exactly the way you like it with extra whipped cream."

"Thank you, Albero."

They waited until his footsteps faded away. Yvienne let out her breath, only just aware that she had been holding it. She got to her feet, struggling to keep the towel around herself.

"Turn around, please," she whispered.

He did. She rummaged hastily for her dry, warm clothes, and got dressed, feeling the warmth envelop her as she drew up the socks and buttoned the shirt and trousers. Waistcoat on, she glanced over her shoulder. He was staring conscientiously at the far wall. "You can turn around." He did.

There was another knock on the door. Before responding, Yvienne threw on her jacket and then looked around for Abel.

He was gone. Stunned, she scanned the room again and again, and even knelt to look under the bed. Nothing. How–?

"Miss Vivi?"

"Oof, sorry. Coming." She got to her feet and opened the door. Albero came in with a tray, followed by Uncle Samwell bustling in behind him.

"Uncle!" she said, trying to keep her shock and annoyance out of her voice. "What–"

"I wanted to catch you," he said with pride in his voice. "I thought, while you're eating, we could go over some ideas I had for the business."

Was he joking? Surely he had to be joking. "Uncle, this is hardly the time for a strategy report."

"Nonsense. You sit and eat, and I'll do all the talking."

Oh, God. Poor Abel. Laughter welled up at the thought of him watching – from wherever he was – his breakfast being consumed right in front of him. And she was so stuffed, she couldn't put another bite in her mouth.

"I'll just set this here," Albero said, putting the tray on her dressing table. "Do you need anything else before I go?" He waited expectantly. Behind him, Uncle Samwell settled his bulk on her bed, which sagged in an unusual way, and he even frowned and shifted, trying to get comfortable.

It was time for drastic measures.

Chapter Forty-One

Yvienne drew herself up. It didn't take much to bring forth tears and a cracking voice.

"Do I need anything? Yes, I need something. I need... I need warmth, and quiet, and food, and my own bedroom, and not to talk to anyone or listen to anyone talking to me! My sister is missing, I was *arrested*, there's a mob surrounding the house, and I can't even have a moment to myself!

"It's Vivi do this, and Vivi solve that! Vivi, turn your sister over to the police, Vivi, dislodge the dead man from the dumbwaiter, Vivi, mislead constables and... and... there's a great big mob of reporters outside my house! What do I need, Albero? I need peace and quiet in my own bedroom!"

She burst into tears.

The two men stared at her in shock and horror. Albero responded first. He tapped Uncle Samwell on the shoulder and nodded at the door. Uncle Samwell hustled out in a hurry, not even looking back. To her dismay, Albero stayed put.

"You're right," he said. "You've had to bear a lot. I forget that – you're so capable, you see, it's like having your mother in charge." He handed her a handkerchief, and she wiped her eyes, at the same time stricken that he could liken her to Alinesse. Was that what she had become? A humorless, snappish woman? Had she missed girlhood completely? This time to her horror the tears were entirely involuntary.

Albero was quiet for a moment and then said, "I'll let you be, Miss Yvienne, but you should know, it's about time you saw us as more than just your household. We can do more. We can take some of the burden off your shoulders."

He stood there for a moment, hand lifted, as if he meant to wipe away the tears from her cheek but realized at the last moment that he was the butler, and she his employer. She was caught in the same frozen instant, really seeing Albero as a handsome young man, not just a correct and competent servant.

They came to their senses at the same time. Yvienne's face flooded with embarrassment, and Albero coughed, dropping his hand. He made as if to apologize, and then just left without another word. As he closed the door behind him, she sighed. *What am I doing?* It made no sense to have feelings for Albero. And she *hadn't* taken them for granted, she added, but she hadn't exactly thought of them all as partners, just… competent underlings, to be protected from her actions. Maybe she had brought some of this down on herself. Maybe asking them to help her find her sister was the first step in lightening the burden.

But she couldn't tell them the complete truth. If they were ever questioned by the police they would give her up in a heartbeat. She couldn't imagine Mrs Francini approving of her night-time scrapes. Rule number one of a successful household, she thought: never frighten the cook, especially one as superior as Mrs Francini. She sighed. Albero meant well, but no – she had to keep her secrets and Tesara's, if only to protect her household.

She realized she had been ruminating before the locked

door, and turned around. Abel stood there as if he had always been.

"How...?" she began. *He saw me with Albero.* Her face flamed again.

Instead of responding, he sat himself down at the dressing table and tucked in. "Get into bed. It will warm you up." She grumbled, but took his advice. Yvienne sat with her knees drawn up and her chin resting on them. It was satisfying to watch him eat; he took such pleasure in it.

"Tell me about these leads of yours," she said, as he tore into a biscuit and dunked it into the soup.

"To let notices," he said through a mouthful. "There are a half-dozen or so in the Gazette, of houses rented by single gentlemen with no families. There are two that I think we should start at. Twelve Bretenneau Bay Street off Cathedral Place, rented by a single gentleman named Astrielle."

She was shaking her head even before he finished. "Not Cathedral Place, unless Trune wants to be recognized. It's almost as fine an address as the Crescent, and the owners of homes to let have to permit their neighbors to approve of any tenants." Inigho and his mother lived on Bretenneau Bay. She had no doubt that Master Trune would not willingly beard that dragon in his rented den. "What's the other one?"

And the other is Forty-seven Kittredge Mews, rented by a Mr Gillien."

"North Town," she said. "It's respectable. Some of the most successful shopkeepers and tradesfolk live there." They weren't merchants, but they were the third level of the Port Saint Frey hierarchy, behind the judges and advocates and brokers. The Alcestris lived in North Town.

"Does it have pillars and red brick and a black roof?"

She looked surprised. "Yes, it does. It's a Carmagetti house, by the famous architect–" she could see she was losing him. "Kittredge Mews houses are all in that style."

"Then that's the one we want," he said.

"How on earth...?" She stopped when she saw his expression. He wouldn't tell her how he knew, and in any case, it wasn't important. Trune could easily hide there and send his man out to capture Tesara. For once, she thought, we have a real lead.

"Then what are we waiting for?" she said. "Let's go."

He gave her a quick smile in response to her eagerness, and it transformed his face from plain to charming. He liked what he did, liked the danger and the discomfort. Before she could stop herself, she grinned back. The Harrier and the Gentleman Bandit, she thought – two birds of a feather.

"You need to teach me that trick," she said.

His smile vanished. "What trick?"

"How you disappeared. I know you were under the bed, but I looked..." She trailed off uncertainly. Whatever she had said, it had set up an alarm for the young man. His expression, engaging but a moment before, had become if anything even more forbidding. A chill ran down her spine.

"You don't want to learn that trick," he said, with finality. "It comes at too high a price."

Left unspoken was the conclusion that he had paid dearly.

"All right," he continued, as if the conversation had never taken place. "I have to pick up my kit, so, let's say we meet at Forty-seven Kittredge Mews at midnight. Can you provide a distraction?"

She nodded. It was time Malcroft earned his keep. "We'll be there," she said. "Thank you," she added.

His expression was complex – regret, understanding, and something else so fleeting she almost missed it. "I said I would help you," he said, his voice gruff, edged with an accent that she couldn't place. "And I will. You saved my life and I pay my debts. But after that, we're square, right?"

Was he warning her of something? Danger tickled the back of her neck, but she only nodded. "We're square, Mr Fresnel," she agreed.

He got up without saying anything more. In a moment he was out the door, closing it behind him. Yvienne waited a second longer and then threw herself out of bed and opened the door. The hall was empty, the household sounds as before. Abel was gone as if he had never been there.

The warmth of the fire finally settled over her. Rain pattered against the windows. Only a few minutes, she thought. She had time for only a few minutes' worth of rest, until she could go out to find Tesara and bring her home.

Chapter Forty-Two

Abel crouched on the roof overhang outside his old room at the Bailet, a living gargoyle. He was spattered by the fine mist of a Port Saint Frey night. It stung his face and his bruised body even through his tattered clothes. He shunted the awareness far below the surface of his mind, concentrated on his breathing and the peculiar skill of a Harrier, to blend into his surroundings. Should any curious bystander on the street look up, they would not even notice that there was a deeper shadow above the eave.

A trick, Miss Mederos had called it, and perhaps it was, but it was hard-earned. Doc did not suffer slow learners, and everyone was a slow learner, even the bright, quick Miss Mederos. He didn't want to think what would happen to her, should Doc decide to bring her into his fold.

And the more time he spent in her company, the more likely he would bring her to Doc's attention. He needed to discharge his debt to her, and quickly.

The Bailet had not waited long to let his room. It was already occupied with a new guest. There had been a light in the window, long since extinguished as the traveler went to sleep.

The cathedral clock tower boomed eleven solemn notes.

Under cover of the noise, Abel slipped down from his perch and landed lightly on the windowsill. In an instant he had the window unlocked and pushed open, and he swung inside.

The shape in the bed muttered and stretched, but did not waken. Abel waited, then by feel he tugged at the bit of the sill that concealed the anesthetic. The wood came loose and he grabbed the vial, and tucked it into his pocket.

He checked the sleeper; no change, his breathing deep and artless. Abel made quick work of moving the mirror and grabbing the wad of bills, tucking it into his belt. He set the mirror back on the wall, looked into it, and froze.

Behind him loomed a presence in the darkness, large and menacing.

"Hello, Abel," said Doc.

Yvienne yawned as she brought her household plus Mr Malcroft together for one last kitchen summit.

"We'll need a distraction," she said. "Mr Malcroft and I will get into the house and search for Tesara or Trune. We know that Mr Trune has a very large coachman who does his dirty work. And according to the Let notices in the *Gazette*, the house was rented to a single gentleman with two servants. So there must be a butler."

"Maxis is the coachman, and Marques the butler," Albero said, and Mrs Francini nodded. They had both worked for Trune when he took over the Mederos home. "He's rather an insecure sort – a bully if he could get away with it."

"Never liked him, but he was a fine enough butler," Mrs Francini put in. "Now Mrs Aristet, the housekeeper – a proper barbarian, she was. No saying what trouble we'd be in if she were there."

Noe spoke up for the first time. "I know the police are not in your ledger right now, but if this is a trap, Miss Vivi, I think you need to engage them." She glanced at Malcroft and ducked her head nervously.

Malcroft merely raised an eyebrow, and to everyone's astonishment said, "She's right. Yeah, I know what you're all thinking but it takes a thief to know when it's time to call in the coppers. You're out of your depths here. No disrespect, Miss Yvienne."

"None taken, and I appreciate your honesty. I wish I could turn to the police, because I do trust them to do the right thing, if they have all the information they need. The problem is, my sister may be guilty of everything she's accused of. For good reasons, I hasten to add, but I doubt the police will be so understanding. I'd rather she come home first than be arrested." And if Tesara were arrested, if she struck out with her powers, it could go badly indeed.

"Miss Tesara is a lively girl, but she's not bad," Mrs Francini objected, which was rather sweet, Yvienne thought. At least one person thought the best of her disreputable little sister.

"We can't just walk up to the front door and demand Trune and his man hand Tesara over," Albero said. "Not unless we know what we're getting into."

"I can do it," Uncle Samwell said. He had an expression of resolve mixed with sickening fear. "I'll go, take a look around, use the gift of the gab to get inside."

Yvienne smiled, but gently. "I'm afraid not, uncle. You'll be too easily recognized."

"Miss Vivi," Mrs Francini said with a steady thoughtful look. "How many servants did the paper say?"

"Just the two."

Mrs Francini smiled. "Well, I can tell you that with

those two servants, they will need someone who knows her way around the kitchen. Neither of them had any skill in the culinary arts. And Mr Trune was always partial to my cookery. No doubt if I went in offering my services he would accept."

Yvienne shook her head. "Mrs Francini, it's far too dangerous. Trune will know you work for me now and he'll know you're spying for me."

Mrs Francini stood her ground. "I don't think so, Miss Vivi. For he fled before you engaged me. For all he knows, I haven't worked since that moment, although," she added thoughtfully, "it isn't likely that a cook of my caliber would not be snapped up at once. But there, Miss Vivi. That gives me an idea. I can tell him I have news of *you*." She sat back, obviously pleased with her own cunning.

Everyone was awestruck.

"Mrs Francini, you astound me," Malcroft said with great admiration, with his wicked grin.

"Oh, now," Mrs Francini said, but she was clearly pleased as punch at the stir she had made.

"I don't know that we want to risk the cook," Uncle Samwell grumbled, but he made no other objection.

Noe bit her lip. When she spoke, she spoke in a rush.

"Miss, I don't want you to think badly of me, because I am trying to be good, I swear, but – there's a two-person flip, miss, and if Mrs Francini wanted to, she could get their attention, and while she was distracting them, I could… get in and look for Miss Tesara. And in the meantime, you and Malcroft could come in the front and take care of the coachman and Trune."

Yvienne was conscious of the profound silence in the parlor, except for the ticking of the mantel clock and the crackling of the fire. My entire household, she thought, is made up of disreputable adventurers. And on the heels of that thought – and who else would work for a Gentleman Bandit?

"It's a thought," Yvienne said. "Though it could be quite perilous. You must both be very careful, and pull out at once."

Noe nodded and turned to Mrs Francini. "We'll have a signal. And all you have to do is make sure I get five minutes to get inside. Then you walk away in one direction, and I another."

Mrs Francini nodded, but she had turned very pale, as if she regretted her bravado. "We shall say, 'cheesy biscuits,'" she said. "For they are an abomination and will never be made in any kitchen I run."

Noe nodded.

"You don't have to do this," Yvienne said. She felt dreadful. "Mrs Francini, I'm so glad you want to, but you don't have to do it."

"If it helps bring Miss Tesara back, then I'll help," Mrs Francini said, with a firm nod of determination.

Yvienne sighed, feeling the weight of responsibility settle on her shoulders. It will be all right, she told herself. They would just be two upright, hard-working citizens of Port Saint Frey, and no one would look twice at them. "Right. Remember, caution first. Let's go."

At least, she thought, the Harrier would be there.

They gathered at the kitchen door, all crowded in their warmest clothes. Malcroft passed around a flask for luck. Yvienne took a swig and coughed, and even Mrs Francini had a tot, drinking the rough whiskey with remarkable aplomb.

"Uncle, Albero," Yvienne said. "Guard the house. We'll be back with Tesara soon."

Samwell saluted, and Albero threw a curt nod at Malcroft. "Take care," he said, stopping before he added, *of her*.

Malcroft nodded back. "If I hear 'cheesy biscuits' we're out of there faster than a lurcher on a hare."

Chapter Forty-Three

Yvienne stood across the street from Forty-seven Kittredge Mews and tried to get a good look at the house. She was dressed in sturdy tweed trousers and linen shirtwaist, with a short jacket over it. She had on warm walking boots, oiled against the weather. Her pistol was concealed in a special pocket that she had engineered herself, easy to access in the back of her jacket, where the garment ended in a small frill. She had practiced drawing it until she was satisfied with her ability.

The townhouse was a narrow brick building, its simplicity belying the classic architecture. The stairs up to the front porch were steep, and there was a dully glowing lantern above the door that illuminated the house number but little else. There was nothing to indicate anyone was at home. The street was entirely dark, fogged in, the lamp a smudge of light in the mist. Mrs Francini and Noe had gone to the servants' entrance on the side of the house and she and Malcroft had heard nothing since.

"Do you think they're inside?" she muttered, scanning the dark and silent house. Beside her, Malcroft shrugged, brushing up against her. He loomed in his overcoat, the rifle slung across his back. His overcoat concealed an alarming variety of weaponry including several knives and the truncheon, all arrayed for easy access.

"No reason why not. Noe's one of the best we've got. You don't have to worry about her. Er, that is–"

"Don't bother, Mr Malcroft," Yvienne said. "Noe's other activities are none of my business or concern right at the moment."

True to her word she tried to focus on the task at hand. Every nerve ending was alive, and her heart beat fast. She scanned the house and its surroundings, noting where the alley came out, the next door gate, and the way the street curved downhill toward the main circle. There was little traffic here, but not far away the city was lively. She wondered where Abel was, and she knew she would never see him until the time came for him to show himself.

"All right," she said. "It's time for me to go in."

"Alone?" Malcroft said, skepticism in his voice.

"I'll take the frontal assault. I want you to go back to the kitchen and help with the search for Tesara."

She didn't say that she wanted to face Trune herself, and best him once again. Now that she was here, the desire for revenge thrummed in every heartbeat. Trune needed to learn, for once and for always, that he would never be able to destroy House Mederos.

"That wasn't our plan, girl."

"If we storm in, it could put all of us in danger," she said. The way her heart was pounding, she thought he could hear it just standing beside her. She took a breath. "Malcroft, I know I seem like just a merchant's daughter to you, but I've gotten out of some rather serious scrapes. I'm not taking this lightly; trust me. Go ahead into the back. I'll draw Trune to the front door, and with a bit of luck, you can get in and out with our friends while I have his attention. Also, you'll be in a better position to take them by surprise than in a frontal attack, don't you think?"

He grumbled, but he finally said, "Agreed. But you heard Albero – if I don't come back with you, I'm in trouble."

She grinned for the first time that night, and she knew he could hear the smile in her voice. "At the first sign of danger you have my leave to break heads."

"Music to my ears," he said. Malcroft melted away into the darkness, his footsteps fading fast into silence. She was left alone in the wet street, the only sound that of distant water pattering down a gutter somewhere.

She gave Malcroft two minutes, and then gathered her courage and crossed the street. Yvienne padded up the front steps, and knocked, the brass doorknocker reverberating against the metal plate. Her shoulder blades itched and she was acutely aware of the Harrier somewhere in the darkness behind her, Malcroft behind the house, her sister and the other women in the house in front of her. She was the sacrificial lamb, the bait – and she knew that Trune could not fail to take it.

The door opened.

Trune's coachman. There was a second of dawning recognition, and then, even as she reached for her pistol, he grabbed her by the front of her tweed jacket and yanked her inside. In an instant he had her disarmed, her own pistol at her side, his arm across her throat. He pushed her in front of him to the genteel parlor, where a comfortable fire burned and the lamps cast a rosy glow on the well-stuffed furniture.

"Well, well, well," smirked Trune over by the mantel, sipping amber liquid from a crystal glass. "Not the smartest girl in Port Saint Frey, after all."

Yvienne glared at him over the coachman's well-muscled arm.

Chapter Forty-Four

Doc lit the small lamp on the dressing table, the low light casting a gentle glow. Abel stood rigidly, his heart hammering, sweat springing out all over him. He could smell it on himself, and he knew Doc would be disgusted at this most elemental of tells.

He watched as Doc carefully pulled on a pair of leather gloves, the ones with the brass knuckles sewn in. He unrolled a supple leather portfolio and laid out his kit – pincers, pliers, and a small, wicked scalpel. More alarming, there was the small wooden casket, a hand crank on the side. The lid was cracked an inch, and wire leads curled from the dark mouth.

"Abel, get me the handcuffs from my luggage, will you?"

Woodenly, Abel went over to the shabby carpetbag and pulled out the handcuffs. He knew what Doc was doing, softening him up, but he also knew that there was nothing stopping Doc. Doc had made him, and he wielded Abel so deftly he could even turn him against himself.

I can stop him.

No. It was a stupid thing to think. He couldn't win against Doc even at his peak, and he was exhausted, battered, weakened. Doc would win, just as he always had, just as if

Abel were still the seven year-old boy Doc had taken in and broken and remade.

He tried not to shake, and could not stop. He tried not to sweat, and only sweated harder.

"Thanks, son," Doc said, amiable as he always was, right before he turned fearsome. Abel had seen it before – the anticipation of great acts of violence calmed him. Doc took the cuffs and with a practiced hand slapped them around Abel's pliant wrist, fastening the other cuff to the bedpost. "Sit. Take a load off. You look terrible."

Abel sat.

Doc shoved the gag in Abel's mouth. "Shhh," he said consolingly. "Now this is going to hurt."

Yvienne was tied to a chair in the parlor, hands behind her back, the coachman's hand on her shoulder, further pressing her down. Trune laid her pistol on the end table and observed her.

"I've waited for this for a long time, Miss Mederos," he said.

She didn't bother to reply. Ten minutes, she thought. Ten minutes and Malcroft would burst in. He was in the house already, and had rescued everyone else, and was just waiting to break heads. The Harrier too, she thought. The Harrier was out there, ready to make his move.

"You thought you had me, didn't you? You thought that you could put me in my place. Well, see how that worked out. When we're through here, you will be where you ought to be – in gaol for your activities as the 'Gentleman Bandit.'" He made quotes in the air. "As for your sister..." his mouth screwed up in a twist of disgust. "That little freak of nature will be put to use, make no mistake."

Yvienne surged up and out of the chair, carrying it with her. She was gratified to see Trune start back in alarm. The coachman slammed her roughly back into her seat, but Yvienne kept her eyes on Trune. He recovered his composure, straightening his coat with a sniff.

"The smartest girl in Port Saint Frey," he said, his voice dripping with contempt. He checked his pocketwatch, then looked at her again. "The big brute and his rifle I understand, but you really sent your cook up against me? Or should I say, my cook. I hope you're happy. That poor dear lady will go to prison for her association with the likes of you."

Despite herself her eyes widened, and he laughed. "You are a foolish girl. You've played your hand, but I've won the match. You're done, Miss Mederos. You are done. So you may save yourself time, and pain, and tell me where your sister is."

So after all their trouble, wherever Tesara was, she was not here. Yvienne felt suddenly, entirely heartened, and at the same time, even more guilty for dragging her staff on a wild goose chase. She said nothing, staring up at him. He made a displeased *tsk*. "Come, Miss Mederos. It's *over*. I've won. Here you are; you're even *dressed* like the Gentleman Bandit. Renner will be ecstatic when I hand you over to him. By the time I'm done House Mederos will be in ashes and you might, just might, be able to run a sweet shop once you get out of prison."

She laughed. "Listen to me carefully, Trune, because I will say this only once. You are filthy, filthy scum. You think you've won? Think again, you miserable bas–"

He slapped her. The ringing blow made her cry out, and she could taste the blood on her lip where his signet ring cut her. She shook her head to clear it.

Trune was breathing hard, his eyes glaring and his face red and contorted. He clenched his fist and she winced despite herself.

"I'm only going to ask you one more time. Where is your sister?"

The mare was blowing hard as she made the last hundred feet up the steep hill of the Crescent, but her step remained springy as Tesara steered her toward the Mederos gate. There was a small crowd outside the gate, and she pulled the mare up before the streetlamps, staying in the shadows. She could see a small fire and people laughing and chatting, their voices rising and falling in comfortable tones.

She couldn't just ride up through the crowd to the gate. Well then, she thought. She dismounted, wincing at the pain and stiffness in her seat and legs. The boost of energy was fading, and she could feel the ague and sore throat begin to marshal their forces, the headache rising behind her eyes. She hung onto the stirrup for a moment until her dizziness cleared, and then she clicked to Persife and led the mare back along the alley to the rear of the house, to the garden gate. The small wrought-iron gate was locked, and she felt around for the battered old key under the loose brick where it had always been, and came up clutching it.

"Hey!"

She turned. The young man loomed behind her, his voice young and excited. He whooped again, causing Persife to start.

"Hey! She's here! Come and see, everyone! She's here!" He was beside himself with excitement and triumph. "I knew it! I knew you'd try to come home this way! Give me the story, Miss Mederos! What's the story about you and your sister?"

She was sick and tired, and ached all over. It had gotten harder to control her powers, taking more strength than she had. Trembling with effort, she faced down the impertinent boy.

"You want the story?" She could hear the approaching crowd. "Here's the story." Tesara put out her hand and pushed.

There was a crack of lightning in the dark, and the boy flew backward at the explosion of air and electricity. She was unable to restrain the impact, so he fetched up hard on his back in the alley. He stared up at her, his mouth and eyes wide open, insensate to the world.

Tesara nodded in satisfaction. "Tell that to your newspaper."

She unlocked the gate and led Persife through, just as the crowd came bumbling down the alley. As she was locking it up after, Albero came out the kitchen door, a poker in one hand and a lantern in the other. He took her in: in her men's clothes, the solid, well-bred mare beside her, and the tumult outside the gate.

"Miss Tesara?" he said.

She sighed. "I'm home, Albero."

He drew her in and hugged her, and she hugged him back. For the first time she had the most satisfying sense that it was all going to be all right. After such a long time and so much peril, she was home.

Chapter Forty-Five

Her sense of comfort evaporated when Albero and Uncle Samwell attempted to fill her in, interrupting each other, all the while Albero made tea and Samwell offered her brandy. She turned down the tea, and sipped water. It was both painful and refreshing, and she wanted to weep.

"Wait, wait," Tesara croaked, putting up a hand. "Tell me slowly."

Uncle Samwell took the lead. "They've all gone off to rescue you – Mrs Francini and Noe were to distract the household, and Vivi and Malcroft were to go in, pistols blazing, to bring you home."

"And they were looking for me where? Why?" And who was Malcroft?

"The Harrier said you were at a house in Kittredge Mews," Albero said. "He said that Trune was holed up there, that he had rented it under an assumed name, and used it as a base for kidnapping. That's where we thought he had you."

Of course. From Kittredge Mews, Trune could send out his coachman to abduct her, or he could travel easily across the fog-bound city to Madam Saint Frey, to compel or cajole her into turning over Tesara to him. And from Kittredge Mews in North Town, one could easily watch for a lamp at the window, high above the city.

"Where have you been, if you don't mind my asking?" Samwell grumbled, topping off his own glass from the bottle on the rough-hewn kitchen table. "Were you gambling? Fayres sent two of her housemen to ask for Yvienne, but they left when we said she wasn't here. Is that where you've been? I must say, Tesara, that is thoughtless, even for you."

It would take too long to explain, so she just shook her head, and set down her cup.

"I have the use of a horse, so I'll be going. If Vivi has gone up against Trune, even with this Malcroft – who is that, anyway?"

"He's one of Cramdean's but he's working for your sister now," Uncle Samwell said. "Good man in a fight, though one of a larcenous nature."

Her sister had fallen in with the dock gangs. It made as much sense as anything, Tesara supposed. "All right," she said. "We've wasted enough time talking."

"You're sick," Albero protested. "You can barely stand." That was true, and she stayed stubbornly put at the table, knowing that if she attempted to get to her feet she'd tip over. Tesara tried to brazen it out.

"I won't need to stand – I'll be riding."

It was a ridiculous argument, and he didn't bother to counter it. Instead, they were distracted from their disagreement by shouting at the kitchen door and the alarmed whinnies of Persife, tied to the garden gate.

Albero jumped up, hefting the poker, and went to the kitchen door. There was a flurry of shouting, and what looked like a skirmish, and then Noe burst through into the kitchen, stumbling over the threshold and landing on the flagstone floor.

"Albero!" she cried. "Something terrible has happened! They've captured Mrs Francini!"

Albero helped her to her feet and sat her at the table across from Tesara, while Uncle Samwell pushed the door closed and locked it, shouting back at the mob. The girl was sobbing, muddy, soaked through, and frightened. Tesara reached out and held her hand, trying to chafe warmth back into it, and the girl pressed her hand in return. Uncle Samwell fetched another cup from the cupboard and poured a healthy serving of brandy into it. Noe sipped and coughed, and color returned to her cheeks, though her eyes remained shadowed.

"What happened?" Tesara managed.

Noe told the tale in a straightforward way, sipping the brandy whenever her emotion overcame her, which was quite often. Samwell refilled her cup twice. She and Mrs Francini had approached the house as planned. They both went to the back door, with the simple idea of Noe hanging back in the shadows as Mrs Francini went up and knocked, to offer her services as a cook and informant. She would be interviewed by the butler, the plan was, while Noe slipped in undetected. "To find *you*, Miss Tesara," she had said, and there was only a mild rebuke in her voice.

Instead, the butler answered the door, called Mrs Francini by name with a great many accusations in his voice, and before Noe could creep out of the shadows, another burly fellow came to the butler's aid, and they grabbed Mrs Francini and pulled her inside, even as the poor woman shrieked "cheesy biscuits! cheesy biscuits!" at the top of her lungs.

Noe burst out of hiding with the intent of rescuing the cook, but the butler shone a lantern toward her, and shouted to the big man that, "there's another one!"

"And as he had a pistol, miss, I took myself home, as fast as I could."

"You didn't see Miss Yvienne or Malcroft?" Albero asked. Noe shook her head, her slender, workworn fingers wrapped around the cup. Uncle Samwell poured another finger of brandy and patted her clumsily on the shoulder. Tesara got to her feet, holding onto the chair back until the faintness subsided and the black dots that formed over her vision dissipated. "Right. I'm off."

"No," Albero barked. He straightened his shoulders, looking quite un-butlerlike, with a stubbled chin and wild hair. When was the last time he shaved? Tesara thought. Albero turned to the housemaid. "Noe, you've done enough, but you need to do more. Go and roust Dr Reynbolten and have her alert the constables and tell her Guildmaster Trune has returned and has Miss Vivi. Have her go straight to Kittredge Mews."

Noe looked determined. "That I can."

"Do it. And once you reach Dr Reynbolten, have her send Dr Melliton here to tend to Miss Tesara." He turned to Tesara. "You're going straight up to bed."

"I'm not staying in bed while you rescue my sister," Tesara said, even though she wanted nothing more than to stay in bed while they rescued her sister. Her heart was hammering so hard she thought it could be seen beneath her shirt, waistcoat, and jacket. Albero shook his head.

"Mr Balinchard and I will go. I know Marques and Maxis. Marques will be easy to cow, and the two of us will get the jump on Max."

"Let me at him," rumbled Uncle Samwell, and it would have been more convincing had his voice not held the faintest of tremors.

"Albero," Tesara said. Her voice was almost gone. "I have to go. I'm sick, but I still have special talents that we'll need, if we want to rescue my sister."

He looked at her skeptically. Noe gave her a bemused look. Only Uncle Samwell's gaze sharpened. She caught his eye and nodded at him, and his face was suffused with wonder. She had longed to tell everyone, and had imagined the dramatic day when she revealed all her powers to her family. Instead, with no fanfare, she raised her hand, and held it palm out. The energy gathered within her, even as she could tell that her burning fever was sapping her strength and her control. Still, it was simple enough to compress the air over the fireplace, causing it to blaze up and then die. With a quick twist she released the air and sent energy into the wood again, and the fire flared up.

Everyone in the room felt the pressure change and release, and everyone worked their jaws to get their ears to pop. Now they all stared at her, eyes wide. Uncle Samwell breathed something that sounded like, "I knew it."

"I can do things, Albero," Tesara said. "I can rescue my sister."

Chapter Forty-Six

Abel slumped in the chair, his lungs burning, trying to get a full breath from behind the gag. It tasted of vomit and saliva, because he had thrown up under Doc's ministrations.

"Now," Doc said, sitting back, and loosening his gag. "That was for disobedience and general incompetence. You know better, Abel. So you just answer the questions and don't try to play me for a fool. I've had my fill of that, dealing with that idiot Trune."

"I don't know." Abel almost couldn't recognize his own voice; it had become thick, gutteral. "I don't know. She disappeared."

Doc tsked. "Abel, Abel." He lifted Abel's chin, forced him to look up. "Come on, son. What are you doing?"

"I don't know," Abel whispered, looking at Doc. The big man had a little smile on his face, and his eyes bored into Abel's. Even in the dim light, even though the pupils had grown to subsume the iris, Doc's eyes were rimmed in an icy blue. Doc put the gag back over his mouth. An instant later he convulsed as Doc applied the electric current to his bare torso, cranking his machine. He had burns all over his body.

The current let up, and Doc sat down on the bed, head cocked to the side, as he observed Abel.

"I'm getting angry, Abel. Angry and impatient. You've made a mess of things, and I'm very disappointed. Give me one good reason I should go easy on you now."

He waited. He didn't remove Abel's gag though, and Abel braced himself. When Doc turned to the crank, he screamed through the gag, but he knew the sound was too thin and muffled to make it even to the hallway.

Even so, there came a knock on the door. Through Abel's haze of pain and anguish, he could hear the prosaic little sound, more of a tentative tap than a knock. This was not someone who had been woken from a deep sleep down the hall at the sounds of torture in Room Twenty-three, hammering at the door, demanding that they *keep your voices down, sirs, and be cognizant of the sensibilities of others.*

Doc stopped. For the first time in Abel's memory, he looked nonplussed. He could have handled a disgruntled guest. Not this cheerful sort of visitor.

"Who is it?" he said, his voice pitched to reach Abel's ears. Abel shook his head. Miss Mederos, come to demand his excuse for his absence? He had no idea.

The knocking came again. Doc set down his tools and went to the door.

"Who's there?" he said, manufacturing a sleepy yawn.

There was silence, then light footsteps hastening away, and in an instant Abel knew who it was. Doc must have too. He yanked open the door, and, moving fast for such a big man, darted down the hall.

Move, Abel, move! Abel bent at the waist, his arms screaming as he stretched forward, and plucked a scalpel from Doc's kit with his teeth. He worked it over his shoulder, and delicately dropped it along his back. It caught in his left hand, pricking his palm as he closed his grip around it.

Just as he caught it, Doc was back, dragging Elenor Charvantes with him.

There came a thunderous knocking on the door at Kittredge Mews. "What now?" Trune snapped. The coachman went to the window and peered out, positioning himself so he couldn't be seen by anyone outside the door.

The coachman turned and gave him a long look. "It's Renner. He's got a whole gang of constables."

Yvienne felt an extraordinary rush of relief.

Trune swore. "That fat fool. Always showing up when he's not wanted. All right. I can handle him. I didn't want to do it this way, but needs must. Let him in."

The coachman went to answer the door, and in a moment returned with Chief Constable Renner and two of his men. Renner took in the scene at a glance, and his face twisted with disgust.

"Former Guildmaster Trune," he said. "Before I throw you in irons, there had better be a good explanation for why you have Miss Yvienne Mederos tied to a chair in a rented house in North Town. And when I say a good explanation, I mean that the bar is quite high on this."

"On the contrary, you should thank me, chief constable." Trune was almost purring with self-satisfaction. "May I present to you the Gentleman Bandit of Port Saint Frey?"

Chapter Forty-Seven

The chief constable looked nonplussed. Trune went on.

"Yes, I know, you've come here to arrest me, but I think we can all agree that this changes everything, does it not?"

To Yvienne's relief, Renner did not look as if he agreed. Renner nodded to one of the constables.

"Untie her."

The constable went over to Yvienne, and after a moment's struggle with the knot he finally took out his knife and sawed through it. With relief she brought her hands forward and rubbed the wrists, moving her shoulders gratefully.

"Thank you, Chief Renner," she said. "I trust now you will arrest Trune for the Great Fraud and the murder of Barabias Parr."

"Not so fast," Trune said. He turned to his man. "Get the other one." The coachman did as he was told. In a moment the coachman was back with Malcroft, prodding him forward with a pistol at the small of his back. Malcroft looked bruised and battered, shocking Yvienne. How had the coachman managed to overcome him? Malcroft was the taller by a head and heavier by at least fifty pounds. Malcroft's head hung low but he managed to raise it dully. He caught her eye and gave her a wink.

Ah. She hoped he had a plan, because she had none. Still, she felt cheerful that they were at least in the same room.

"Malcroft Shy," Chief Renner said, giving him the once over. "What are you doing here?"

"I was just walking by, minding my own business, guvnor, when this fellow gets the jump on me," Malcroft protested. The coachman snorted in disgust.

Renner turned to Yvienne. "Do you know this man?"

She shook her head. "Aren't you distracted from your main focus, chief? May I remind you that I am – was – being held prisoner by a man most wanted by the Guild and the constabulary of Port Saint Frey?"

Chief Renner looked sour, as if he knew he was being redirected but he also knew she was right.

"Allow me to explain," Trune said, as if this was the opening he was waiting for. "Chief Renner, the night that I fled Port Saint Frey in fear for my life, I had been sorely attacked by this woman in the guise of the Gentleman Bandit. She attacked me in my own home, murdered my friend and business associate Barabias Parr, and drove me from the city. I came back here, at great peril to myself, to bring her to justice." He pointed dramatically at Yvienne. "Arrest this woman!"

The room went silent. The constable holding onto Yvienne gripped tighter, as if Trune's accusations emphasized the danger he was in. Yvienne was acutely aware she was dressed as a man.

"Trune," Renner said. "What are you playing at?"

"I'm merely pointing out what you should have seen months ago. This girl is the Gentleman Bandit who plagued the merchants of Port Saint Frey with her mischief in the six months previous."

Renner's jaw tightened. Idiot, Yvienne thought. Not the

best tactic to insult the chief constable's police work.

Renner gave Yvienne the once over. "Miss Mederos? Do you have anything to say?"

"Only that Guildmaster Trune has kidnapped my cook, Mrs Francini, and if he's harmed her in any way he better hope he's safe in your custody," she said.

There was another ringing silence. Renner turned to Trune. He didn't even have to ask.

"She sent the woman to spy on me!" Trune shouted. "And that's not the issue! The issue is that she's the Gentleman Bandit and a thief and a murderer!"

"And he is a man wanted by the police for the fraud against my family and the Guild!" Yvienne shouted back. "His ludicrous accusations are nothing but a smokescreen, chief!" She pointed at Trune. "Constable Renner, arrest this man!"

"Sir," reported another constable, just coming into the parlor, with Mrs Francini in tow. "We found her in the kitchen. She was tied up, sir."

"Oh, Miss Vivi!" Mrs Francini sobbed, running over to her. She was disheveled, her hair down around her face, and her overcoat and dress askew. Yvienne hugged her, glaring over her shoulder at Trune.

"How could you?" she said, low-voiced and furious. She helped Mrs Francini to a pouf in the corner of the parlor. She whispered against her ear, "Where's Noe?"

Mrs Francini's shoulder lifted in an *I don't know* gesture.

"Constable," Trune said, with the air of one whose control over the situation was slipping from his fingers, "never mind the cook."

"I'm afraid I can't do that," Renner said, not sounding apologetic at all. "Kidnapping is a serious business, Trune."

"Add it to his charges, chief," Yvienne said over Mrs

Francini's shoulder. Renner rounded on her, clearly at the end of his tether.

"So is banditry, Miss Mederos. Can you explain Mr Trune's accusations?"

"No," she said.

She could tell that he had to maintain a tight grip on his temper. "And can you tell me what brought you to this house this night?"

"No," she said.

He snorted a laugh before raising an eyebrow. "Of course not. Why did I even bother?"

"My lawyer has advised me to say nothing to you outside of her presence. If you would like to arrest me again, please do. We can discuss everything at headquarters."

Renner gave her a keen look. "Good idea." He nodded to his men. "Arrest them both."

Trune snarled. "Don't be a fool, Renner. You'll not cross the Guild in this."

At that moment the door banged open and Dr Reynbolten swept in. She took the scene at a glance, her sharp gaze alighting on everyone and causing the constables to look down as if they were guilty themselves.

"My God," she boomed. "My God. Renner, arrest this man as a fugitive from justice and the perpetrator of the Great Fraud."

"Doctor," Yvienne said. "I am quite grateful to see you."

Dr Reynbolten looked at her for a long moment. "I would not speak if I were you," she said, and turned back to Renner.

"That's just it," Renner said. "Trune's made some very interesting accusations. I think we need to hear him out."

"Balderdash," Dr Reynbolten said. "You've got nothing."

Renner turned to look at Malcroft. "We've got Shy, here. And you know what kind of record he has." Renner looked between Yvienne and Malcroft. "And if I find evidence that you two do have a prior acquaintance, it will go very badly for you."

She shrugged and shook her head. "As I said, I never met him before." She was very conscious of Mrs Francini's presence beside her.

Malcroft raised his shoulders too. "Same here, guv. No idea who she is."

"She's lying!" Trune roared. "They all three came here to waylay me and no doubt beat me senseless. The girl knows I can identify her as the Gentleman Bandit – she's here to silence me. She's masterminded the whole thing."

"This is most irregular, chief constable," Reynbolten said. "Release my client and arrest Trune."

"I can't do that. You yourself sounded the alarm tonight, Dr Reynbolten. Why was that? Who alerted you to the kidnapping of Miss Mederos? As an officer of the courts of Port Saint Frey, are you hiding knowledge of a crime from me, Dr Reynbolten?"

Dr Reynbolten snorted, but to Yvienne's ears, for the first time the supremely competent advocate sounded unsure. It was time to take matters into her own hands.

"This is utterly ridiculous, chief," she said. "Guildmaster Trune has been persecuting my family for years. He's deranged on the topic of the lawless nature of House Mederos, when we all know that he has committed crimes against us. Those crimes are fact, they are proven, and Guildmaster Trune was already tried and found guilty. Only by fleeing has he escaped punishment. Revenge led him to return. So you must do your duty and arrest him and bring him to his long-delayed justice."

Renner was silent through her speech. Then he cocked his head and looked at her. "What are you doing in this house, Miss Mederos?" he asked again.

"Don't answer that," Dr Reynbolten said.

Yvienne gave her a nod and fixed her gaze on Renner, her expression calm, her lips tight.

Trune's eyes gleamed. "I think we'll find with the evidence I have against you and your sister that the charges you speak of will be dropped. I didn't steal your ships, Miss Mederos. They were sunk by the hand of your unnatural sister."

Yvienne let out a long sigh, conveying a fraying patience. She turned to Renner. "Chief…" she let the rest of the sentence fall away, lifting her hands in helpless acknowledgement that they were dealing with a deluded man. "I don't know what to say."

The chief constable said nothing. Yvienne had gotten good at reading the stoic Renner over the course of their continued acquaintance, and a prick of alarm alerted her. Renner hadn't bought Trune's dramatic statement, but he hadn't discounted it either. I would not have considered Renner a fanciful man, she thought, but then again, Tesara had been cutting a wide swath through town the last day or so. Her antics had changed many a more stolid mind.

"I have an idea, chief constable," Dr Reynbolten said, after giving Yvienne a probing look. "I think this can all be sorted out at headquarters. You will arrest Guildmaster Trune on the original charges laid against him, as well as charges of detainment and kidnapping and assault of Miss Mederos and her cook." She waved a dismissive hand at Malcroft. "And for God's sake, can you let this poor man go while you're at it? It's utter foolishness that he's swept up in Trune's fantastiques."

Bless you, Dr Reynbolten, Yvienne thought.

"Chief Constable Renner, she's manipulating you,"

Trune shouted. "This man is a confirmed villain and he is a henchman of the Gentleman Bandit!"

A henchman, Yvienne thought. I have a henchman. She had to bite back a sudden giggle, brought on by a giddy sort of lightheadedness.

Renner made his decision. "All right, Claia," he said. "But your client rides in the police box with me and my men, not with you. And we're interrogating her before you get a chance to debrief her yourself."

"And Trune?" Dr Reynbolten challenged. "Aren't you going to arrest him? He's the only criminal here, you know. Fugitive from justice, perpetrator of the Great Fraud, and embezzler of Guild funds. Or have you forgotten?"

They all turned to look at Trune, including Malcroft, whose expression was both righteous and innocent.

"Chief constable, if you don't arrest this woman at once, I will bring you before the Merchant Guild!" Trune said in ringing, thunderous tones. His words fell on a silent room. The constables all looked at one another. Whatever had been their sympathy toward Trune at the beginning of the evening, it was clear it had waned. Maybe at one time the Port Saint Frey constabulary had been under the thumb of the Merchants' Guild, Yvienne thought, but those days were gone.

When Renner spoke, his voice rumbled with self-control. "Are you threatening me, Mr Trune?"

Trune struggled for calm. "I am merely pointing out, chief, that we are on the same side here, and this woman is not to be trusted." He jutted his chin at Yvienne. "Ask her. Ask her where her sister is. Ask her what her sister knows about the sinking of the Mederos ships."

Renner nodded judiciously. "All right. Miss Mederos, where is your sister?"

"Chief constable, on the advice of my attorney, I will not and cannot answer that question."

Dr Reynbolten smirked.

Trune gave an inarticulate howl. "She is a devil!"

Renner laughed. "Oh, she's an imp, all right. She's been so from the first moment we've spoken. But come now, Miss Mederos, what does your sister know about the sinking of the Mederos fleet?"

"The Mederos fleet did not sink, chief constable," Yvienne said. "The Guild had been defrauding merchants for years. The broadsheet Arabestus laid it all out, and the evidence was found in the Guild's own files. My parents sailed a month ago to meet our flagship, *The Main Chance*, and bring her home. She was re-flagged, you know."

Trune advanced on her and she took an involuntary step back, fetching up against Renner's solid form. "Your parents are on a wild goose chase, girl. That ship is at the bottom of the sea, along with the *Fortune* and the *Fortitude*, right where your sister sent them."

Chapter Forty-Eight

Shivering and feverish, Tesara pulled up Persife outside the house at Forty-seven Kittredge Mews. There was a crowd here too, and she gave an exasperated sigh. There were constables on guard, and the neighbors, some in their nightshirts and holding umbrellas against the ever-present mist, were standing about in hushed little knots, discussing the events of the night.

Tesara scanned the situation. Neighbors. Constables. The clanging of the firewagon bells, as if it were not enough that the constables were on the scene. And reporters. Of course. The scourge of Port Saint Frey, she thought. Can nothing happen in this town without them? She moved Persife closer.

"Hey," she croaked out to a man in striped pyjamas, a threadbare robe, and gumboots instead of house slippers. "What's going on?"

The man started at the outlandish voice coming out of the night, and looked twice at the boyish figure on the back of a well-bred horse. "The constables have the Gentleman Bandit cornered in the house."

An electric spark of alarm shot up her spine. Persife shied in response to Tesara's reaction, and it was all she could do to keep from falling from the saddle. She clutched the horse's mane and hung on.

"What are you doing here?" the man asked, but she was already reining Persife around. The mare charged forward and Tesara held on tight. For the first time that night she broke her own rule against galloping, and Persife burst forward as if she were running on turf. Tesara heard alarmed shouts over the clattering hoofbeats.

At the sound of the cries, Persife leapt sideways at the crowd. This time it was too much for Tesara's feverish, weakened state. She slid out of the saddle onto the hard cobblestones.

"Ow!" The sharp pain in her hip brought tears to her eyes. Persife kept running, and disappeared into the night, and Tesara felt a pang of guilt. She reminded herself that horses know how to find their way home, and Persife seemed bright. The redheaded woman would not need to come after Tesara over her horse.

"Are you all right, boy?" someone said, helping her up. The young man's eyes widened as he saw that Tesara was female. "…I mean, miss?" She winced, and nodded, rubbing her hip.

"Yes. Thank you. Most kind," she managed, and hobbled toward the house.

"You shouldn't go in there," the young man called out. "The Gentleman Bandit has the constables at bay!"

Tesara didn't bother to answer, busy scanning her approach. There were two constables on the front steps, and several more along the sides of the house, near the garden gate. The firewagon and its hellish bells came up the street, lanterns blazing, its team of six horses blowing hard at a fast trot. Men dropped off the wagon sides, carrying billy clubs.

Tesara cast around for a plan of attack and her gaze

focused on the lanterns held by the constables and those that were hanging off the wagon. She centered herself, drew in a breath, and blew gently along her hand, guiding and amplifying the breath with her power.

Hardly discernable at first, the small breeze she created gathered strength, and the lantern lights flickered and then whooshed out.

People cried out in alarm, and men cursed. Amid shouts of, "what's happening?" and "I need a light!" the constables guarding the gate on the side of the house hoofed it around to the front to see the cause of the hubbub. Tesara let them come forward and then darted back to the gate.

It was open. She let herself inside.

She waited a moment in the small kitchen, listening. There were sounds coming from the parlor at the front of the house, and she crept along the dark narrow hallway, following the light spilling out from the open parlor door. Now she could make out voices. Several men and her sister, Yvienne's voice low and bright and reasonable among the angry men.

Tesara centered herself again, and gathered her power, when someone pounded on the front door of the house.

"We're under attack!" came a muffled cry from outside. "Men on horseback, and they've got us on the run."

Now she could hear the chaos outside. There were shots being fired, people screaming, firehorses whinnying in terror. When she had doused the lights, it had set off a panic. Good, she thought. Easier to get Yvienne away. She centered herself again and went to push the air into the room, when something struck the back of her head. It was the last straw. Any attempt at control was lost. The last thing she remembered was her power, unleashed, shooting into the room and all of the lamps exploding.

Chapter Forty-Nine

Doc pushed Elenor into the room in front of him, keeping a hold on her arm and kicking the door closed.

"Sit," he ordered, pushing her at the bed, and she complied, her eyes wide and frightened as she took in Abel's state.

"How dare you, sir?" she said, with all the courage she could muster. "Who do you think you are? What are you doing to Mr Fresnel?"

"Quiet," Doc said, with hardly a glance at her. "If you scream or make any noise, I'll kill him. Do you understand?" That broke her, and she slumped, nodding. "What is your name?"

She hesitated, and then, "Elenor… Sansieri."

He looked at Abel. "Is she the one you slept with?"

No point in lying to protect her honor. Abel nodded. Doc made a face of disgust.

"Fool. Idiot boy. I didn't raise you for this." He glanced at her. "Do you know where the younger Mederos girl is?"

She shook her head, her eyes wide, pupils so big as to swallow up the color.

Doc looked her over, and shook his head. A gentle expression came over his face. "I'm sorry," he said, his voice filled with compassion. "You don't deserve this. Love makes all of us act against our own better natures."

To her credit, Eleanor remained wary, but she nodded. She never looked at Abel, keeping her gaze fixed on Doc. Working only with the tips of his fingers, Abel worked the scalpel at his wrists and palm. Slick, warm blood flowed from the cuts, the small abrasions stinging and sharp.

Doc tsked, a disappointed father who was pained by needed discipline. Elenor swallowed.

"I'm– I'm so sorry," she managed. "I didn't mean to distract him from his task." She sobbed.

The handcuffs slid over Abel's bloody wrists. He worked them over his palms.

"Shh," Doc said. He sat down on the bed next to her, taking her chin in his hand, looking deep into her eyes. "I understand. It's not your fault. A good girl like you…"

Elenor yanked her head away, her face transformed from tears to anger.

"Don't touch me, you monster!" she shrieked. She gave him a ringing slap.

Doc's eyes flew wide, and the second of startlement was all Abel needed. He pulled his bloody hands free and surged upward with a shout. In the instant in which Doc was about to snap Elenor's neck, the man had to go on the defensive against Abel. It was an infinitesimal space of a second in which Abel had to make his move, that shift from attack to defense.

Doc had trained him well to act in such fractions.

Abel flew at him. They fought without words: hands and feet kicking and slapping, a brutal dance. For all he was a big man, Doc was light on his feet, almost delicate in his bruising punches. Abel was like a bee and Doc a bull, but the bull gored him time and again.

Abel gasped, the pain in his ribs making it impossible to take a full breath, and at the same time he controlled his breathing and stayed calm, finding the place inside himself that gave him strength. Doc gave him training and brutalized his spirit, remaking him into a weapon, taking away his free will – except for the cool stone of himself at the core of his body.

With a powerful blow from his heel, Doc snapped Abel's leg, and he went down.

Abel cried out then, a single name, and Doc loomed over him, disgust and contempt in the man's expression, and by that Abel knew he and Elenor were as good as dead.

And that was when Elenor lifted the heavy lamp from the dressing table, spilling sweet camphene oil across the floor, and bashed it over Doc's head.

Hard on the sounds of rising madness outside the house, the lamps were extinguished with an explosive whoosh of wind from the hall. Many of the constables were knocked off their feet, shouting and cursing, voices pitched high with fear. Under the cover of the chaos, Yvienne moved. She grabbed a pistol from one of the constables and darted for the open hallway. She collided with someone rushing in, shouting, "I have the she-devil, sir! She's in the hall!" She twisted around him, elbowing him hard in the ribs with a sharp blow, and he bent double with an *oof*. She reversed the pistol and came down hard with the butt on his skull. The man went down with a thud.

Renner's voice rose above the chaos. "Somebody relight the God-damned lamps!"

Yvienne didn't know where Malcroft was and dared not call out for him. There was no light coming in anywhere, Tesara having doused the streetlamps as well as the lights inside the house.

She stumbled over a groaning body. "Tes?" she whispered. She knelt and helped her sit up, casting a look back at the chaos in the dark parlor.

"Vivi?" Her sister could barely speak.

Tesara was unbearably light, all of her childhood stoutness burned away. She was clammy and feverish, and Yvienne's heart sank.

"Here," said Malcroft, suddenly at her side. He lifted Tesara, making nothing of the slight burden.

"Go," Yvienne said. "I'll handle things here."

Carrying Tesara, Malcroft ran off down the hall toward the kitchen, as men bounded in the front door, and the chaos in the parlor came under Renner's control.

Under the chief constable's firm orders, the lamps were relit, the warm glow bouncing off the scene in the parlor. Yvienne watched from the dark hallway, a play unfolding in front of her. Everything in the parlor was knocked about, knick-knacks broken and paintings askew. A constable helped Mrs Francini to her feet, holding her steady. Trune was spitting with fury, berating Renner in a non-stop barrage of invective. His coachman stood behind him, stolid and grim. Dr Reynbolten looked astonished, but not shaken, scanning the room. The lawyer was the first to note that Yvienne was missing. She turned around, taking everything in, when she saw her standing in the hallway. They locked eyes. Yvienne came back into the parlor, emerging out of the darkness into the light. Now everyone turned to look at her. She handed the pistol over to Chief Renner; the hapless constable she had taken it from looking embarrassed in front of his superior. Renner took the pistol but absently; his expression was piercing, as if he were trying to get to the bottom of who she was with only his wits.

Trune's eyes bugged out. "Where is she?" he shrieked. "Where is that fiend of a sister of yours?"

Yvienne channeled her temper and let it forth as her weapon.

"Chief constable," she said, starting with a low voice and letting it rise in crescendo. "I have had *enough* of Guildmaster Trune's attacks and insults on my sister and my family! We have been the victims of his abuse for long enough! Now you, sir, must do your job and arrest this man for fraud, kidnapping, and murder!"

"You little bi–" Trune spat.

"ENOUGH!" Yvienne shouted. The anger exploded in her, and she was astonished by her own power. A kind of light came into her head, and a distant part of her marveled. *My goodness, does it run in the family?* But whatever Tesara could do, Yvienne could only use her particular gift, that of words.

"Enough," she said again. "Enough." She swept her arm out to the hall. "My sister is not here, as you all can plainly see. Trune's phantasm is the weather, the bugbear of his fevered imagination."

"Chief," said a constable in a low voice, as if afraid of attracting attention. "Malcroft Shy's escaped."

There came a groan from the floor, and Marques the butler came to. He was helped to his feet, and he moaned in pain, clutching his head. Even by the dim lamplight, they could see that his eyes were unfocused. Mrs Francini made room for him on the pouf and he sank down. She patted his hand, but a little brisk, still disgruntled. Trune practically leaped on him with eagerness.

"Here. My man will prove it to you. Marques," said Trune, his voice urgent. "Marques, look here. No, here," he sdai, as the man turned in an entirely different direction. "Marques, you said you had her. Who was she? Tell them who was here. *What girl was here, Marques*?"

Marques didn't answer for a long moment. Finally he turned to his employer.

"Girl?"

Renner's voice rumbled as if it came from the depths of the earth.

"Mr Trune. You are under arrest for fraud, embezzlement, kidnapping, and the murder of Barabias Parr."

Trune shrieked and fought but he was easily restrained, as was his coachman and the hapless Marques.

Dr Reynbolten looked at Yvienne and Mrs Francini and sighed. "Come on," she said. "I'll give you a lift."

Chapter Fifty

FIRE AND CALAMITY OVERTAKE PORT SAINT FREY!
GENTLEMAN BANDIT IS CAPTURED AND ESCAPES!
TORNADO TOUCHES DOWN IN KITTREDGE MEWS!
FORMER GUILDMASTER TRUNE ARRESTED AND DETAINED!
BAILET HOTEL BURNS TO THE GROUND!

A tornado was observed to touch down on Forty-seven Kittredge Mews last night, just one of many catastrophes that rocked the city. Several constables were guarding the house, said to be the holdout of the Gentleman Bandit, and in a desperate gun battle, in which shots were fired in exchange with the man, he escaped once again into the night. Witnesses said a mysterious youth – some say a girl – brought the bandit's horse for him to make his escape into the night.

The constables arrested former Guildmaster Trune, a fugitive from justice and perpetrator of the Great Fraud. Chief Constable Renner would not speak on the capture of the former leading light of the Guild and refused to say whether he had been in league with the Gentleman Bandit all along.

Several firewagons were called out to the Bailet Hotel on the Esplanade last night, and despite a valiant effort by the fire brigade, the establishment burned to the ground. The firewagons pumped water from the local water supply, and managed to prevent the spread of the conflagration. Most of the guests were accounted for, but rumors of a suspicious nature emanating from Room Twenty-three were said to be the source of the fire.

The hotel manager would not comment on the night's events, and was seen to harshly silence a clerk who appeared willing to discuss the terrifying scene.

The Gazette will continue to investigate until we get to the heart of these matters.

THE GAZETTE

Yvienne woke up to full daylight. She groaned and stretched, aching all over. It had been a long night, and she and Mrs Francini had not gotten home until nearly dawn, seated in Dr Reynbolten's carriage, which the lawyer drove herself.

Malcroft and Tesara had gotten home first, and Tesara headed straight for bed, with Albero and Uncle Samwell rising to the task of nursing her. Afterwards, Malcroft and Noe were nowhere to be seen, and Albero said they had been vague about where they were going but certainly appeared in a hurry to get there.

Yvienne did not expect to see them ever again, and only hoped they had left town safely and with rather less of the House Mederos' silver than could be expected under the circumstances, considering that she had not been able to pay either of them their contracted wages.

She sent Mrs Francini to bed, and the woman was only too glad to go. By the time Yvienne had gotten her sister into a warm nightgown, with a mustard plaster on her chest, her face washed in mint and lavender, and the worst tangles combed out of her hair, the clock had struck half past five. She had such nervous energy, brought on by exhaustion and exhilaration, that it wasn't until she realized that she was asleep on her feet, that she took herself to bed.

Her brain was still in a fog of weariness. Yet there was something different about the quality of the day that she couldn't put a finger on, and she puzzled over it even as she dressed in her robe, her muscles protesting, and fumbled for her slippers at the side of the bed with her toes. She slumped on the edge of the bed, staring at her left foot in a diamond of sunlight. At first she couldn't comprehend what she was seeing. Then Yvienne gave a shriek and scrambled for the window, pushing back the curtains.

The sun had broken through. Sunlight poured down over the land, and she could see out over the harbor, the blue sea with its whitecaps painfully bright on her fog-dulled eyes.

Yvienne cranked open the window, and the crisp air flowed into the room. She raised her face to the sun, almost weeping. She had never felt anything so good – it was as if the sunshine had gotten beneath her skin and was warming her from the inside. Even her aches were gone.

"Oh," she said over and over. "Oh."

She scanned the grounds by the gate. It was quiet for the first time in days. Trash hung on the gate, and there were two abandoned firepits, but no onlookers.

At last, another story had bumped theirs from the pages of the *Gazette*.

Still in her robe, Yvienne padded down the hall to her sister's room, leaving her bedroom door open to allow sunlight to pour through the second floor hall. She knocked on Tesara's door, then pushed it open.

Her sister turned at her approach. Tesara was propped up in bed, still so thin and pale, her fingers bony, and her cheekbones jutting out. Her hair, once white blond as a child and then a lovely golden brown as a young woman, was streaked with white and gray, and she looked startling, as if she were neither boy nor girl but somehow a mix of both. Her eyes were a darker blue than ever Yvienne had seen them. Yvienne eased down onto the bed and took her sister's hand, bracing herself for the inevitable spark. It had been happening all night long, and she could tell that it pained her sister whenever she flinched at the shock.

The room stank of the sickroom, a combined smell of unwashed body, the peculiar stench of fever, the rank aroma of the chamberpot, and the smells of mustard plaster and flannels and herbal tisanes, and medicinal powders.

"Do you need water or tea or another plaster?" Yvienne asked. Tesara shook her head to each suggestion.

"The sun is out. Can you believe it? Mid-Fog Season. I know we get these mid-season breaks, but it was so unexpected." Yvienne knew she was chattering, but she couldn't help it. "Do you want me to open the window?"

Tesara nodded, and Yvienne could detect eagerness. She cranked the window open, and once again sunlight and calm air flowed into the room. A few discarded handkerchiefs lifted up as the breeze caught them. Yvienne smiled, but then her gaze sharpened and she looked at her sister.

Tesara, even sick, had a beatific expression, her hands weaving about as if she were conducting a piece, leading the scraps of soft cotton in a gentle dance. Then she tired, and her hands lay at rest once again, and the handkerchiefs fell to the floor. Yviene watched her for a moment, but her sister had sunk back into sleep.

Sleep was probably the best restorative she could possibly have, Yvienne thought, as she straightened up the room, gathering up tea cups and strainers, and plasters, and other noxious nostrums. A putrid sore throat, which her sister appeared to suffer, could turn into a rheumatic fever if the sufferer did not rest, and last night's adventures could not have done her sister any good at all.

And what else had happened to her? It was clear she was no longer herself. The young girl had aged, and it was not just her hair or her shocking thinness. She had become someone quite different, and Yvienne knew that unless they were very careful, they would lose her.

And I am not sure that the creature she becomes will be my sister at all.

She made her way downstairs, still in her robe, and stopped short at the bottom when she saw Albero, still in his striped and tattered robe and his pajamas sticking out from under, his hairy ankles protruding from the lot. He was standing before of the open front door, head thrown back, drinking in the sunlight in front of God and all of Port Saint Frey, were anyone watching.

A note of birdsong came trilling in through the open entrance.

He must have sensed her presence, or else she made a noise, as he turned and looked at her. She set down her pile of sickroom trash and joined him. They both looked out at the glorious day. Even the gravel of the carriage drive sparkled under the rays of the sun, and distant sea birds wheeled over the tree-lined cliffs across the Crescent.

Albero sighed and sat on the front steps, sticking his long legs out in front of him. Yvienne joined him, and they leaned companionably against one another shoulder to shoulder, fuzzy robe to fuzzy robe. She lifted her face to the sun and the light.

A noise caught her attention and she turned. Uncle Samwell stood in the doorway, yawning and stretching. He padded over to them, and she scooted over to make room on the wide steps. Albero leaned back on his elbows.

"What do you reckon will happen to Trune?" Albero asked, gazing out at the dark trees and the bit of harbor that could be seen through the branches.

"He was escorted to headquarters for questioning," Yvienne said. "I hope that Renner throws him in gaol and the key in the sewer, but one can only hope for the best and expect the worst."

"Good riddance to bad rubbish," grumbled Uncle Samwell.

She doubted that Trune would confess to the murder of Barabias Parr, or for that matter that of Treacher the newspaperman, the first murder in this whole adventure, who had first tipped her off to the Guild's machinations, but perhaps Renner would be able to extract the truth from him.

"And what do you think will happen to us – this house?" Albero said, a note of worry in his voice. Yvienne sighed.

"We're not out of the woods yet. Trune accused me of being the Gentleman Bandit, and I am sure that Chief Constable Renner will follow up."

"Well," Samwell harrumphed. "I can't see Renner giving that credence–" he stopped when he looked at Yvienne and then Albero. "No," he said. He looked straight at Yvienne. "Vivi? How? I mean, what? How…?" His voice weakened and trailed off.

Yvienne sighed. If Samwell knew for sure, the entire city would know. "Don't be absurd, uncle. Of course it's a ridiculous untruth."

"Anyone would be a fool to believe it," Albero added.

"Well, you never know," Samwell grumbled. "I wouldn't believe it, but with Tesara's oddness, who knows?"

"And that must never be spoken of. Not even to Mother and Father," Yvienne said. "We must keep her secret so that she can recover in peace."

For a moment Uncle Samwell looked bitter.

"How is she this morning?" Albero asked.

"Better," Yvienne lied. "She's sleeping anyway."

They settled back into their own thoughts. Mrs Francini joined them, sitting next to Uncle Samwell, her small broad feet bare on the warm steps, her robe a splendid silk of butter yellow and pale green. Her hair was still up in a night cap, and she looked haggard and exhausted.

One by one the houses along the Crescent woke up, with servants walking to and fro on brisk errands, pausing only to catch the sight of the bathrobed tableau on the front steps of the Mederos townhouse and then hastening on. We'll be the talk of the town, Yvienne thought. Again. This time, the thought only made her sigh.

A creaking sound caught their attention, and they watched the postman appear with his rolling cart up the Crescent. He stopped at the front gate and busily sorted through his letters until he found the ones addressed to the Mederos house. In the act of putting the letters in the mail slot in the front gate, he looked up and saw the foursome on the steps. He froze, letters in hand, then dropped them and pushed off, the cadence of his creaking cart rising in a sort of panic. If Yvienne had the energy to laugh, she would have.

"Well," Mrs Francini said at last, leveraging herself up with a groan. "The kitchen waits for no one, and lazing about never got breakfast on the table or the washing up done."

"Mrs Francini," Yvienne said, rising to her feet too, the cozy moment forgotten. "Does that– does that mean you're staying?"

Do anything, she could almost imagine her mother and father saying, but whatever you do, *do not frighten the cook.*

Too late.

Mrs Francini took a breath and said, "It means I'm staying for now."

It would have to do. She would not do Mrs Francini the discourtesy of begging or pleading for her to stay on, no matter how much she wanted to. And the woman was right – there was still work to do.

"I'll help you in the kitchen," she said. "No, Mrs Francini, I insist. Albero, I place the household in your able hands, as always. Uncle, the family business could use your oversight and if you choose to breakfast at the docks, it would do us good to know what you find out."

He chuckled, and rubbed his berobed belly. "See there, Vivi? No wonder they call you the smartest girl in Port Saint Frey."

Sun-warmed sea air wafted in through the open window. Sunshine. It was Tesara's old affinity, and she could feel it warming her, strengthening her, even beyond the painful throat and the sweating and chills caused by her fever. The sun was so bright she had to keep her eyes closed, but she turned her face toward it, and felt its fire deep in her core.

Home. She was home. How long had she been gone? She couldn't even remember. With shivering aches she pushed herself upright and eased the covers away from her shoulders, pushing them down to her waist. She cracked open her eyes, and then, when they adjusted, she opened them fully.

Tesara knew better than to try any more of her talent. The tiny bit of control she had expended on the handkerchiefs had wasted all of her strength, and she had so much power that even in her weakened state she was buzzing with static electricity, and her veins carried more potent electricity to her heart. Poor Vivi, she thought – I shocked her good that last time.

Another knock at the door, and then Vivi crept in again, this time with a bowl of beef broth and tea on a tray.

"How do you feel?"

Tesara shrugged. She gestured for the cup of broth, and sipped it herself, rather than being fed. Yvienne watched her anxiously. *How can I tell her I'll be all right?* All she needed was sleep and time. But even though she knew she would get well, she would always be forever changed by the ordeal. Her power, combined with the fever and illness, had burned away everything extraneous from her. She was, now more than anything, just a framework that contained a vast amount of power, but a moment away from exploding.

Had I not been sick, Tesara thought, sipping at the tea, this wouldn't have happened. The sickness itself transmuted the power.

I don't feel frightened, but I know I should be.

She looked up at Yvienne, and her heart sank.

She might not be frightened, but Yvienne was.

What have I become?

Chapter Fifty-One

That day the post brought three letters. One, from Alinesse, carried the news that they had landed in Shad Harbour. The letter had come overland, via the express riders that began their stages at the edge of the Wilderness and then galloped across nearly three thousand miles of Chahoki Empire.

We scarcely docked when Father and I met with the port authority, and he brought us to the ship. Rather than prolong your anticipation let me tell you immediately: she is our ship. She is the Main Chance. *The keys that Father had for the cabinets in the captain's quarters still fit the locks, and we also brought the shipyard's plans, so after the port agent confirmed she was ours I sat to write this to have it sent home by express rider immediately.*

She is much changed and there was significant damage. At some point she was caught in a terrible storm, although the current captain said it had not happened under his watch. At this time the port agents say there is no word of the Fortune *and* Fortitude, *but I'm sure we will hear soon. Your father thinks they may have gone down in the same storm that damaged the MC, but I am optimistic that we will find them.*

I must say I am impressed with the port agents in Shad Harbour. They have been diligent in investigating our claim and are sympathetic to our situation. A young clerk by the name of Antoni Savaran has taken a personal interest and is investigating the Fraud from this end. I am sure we'll find out what happened to the* Fortune *and* Fortitude *soon. We will have our fleet back!*

I must close – I do not want to miss the mail coach. All our love, and we'll be home as soon as we can.

Love,

Alinesse B Mederos

PS. The crossing was quite peaceful – only one squall, and the rest fair winds and brisk seas.

*PPS. *You should meet him, Yvienne. I think you two will have a great deal in common. And he's quite handsome in his way.*

Yvienne shook her head and folded the letter back into the envelope. Trust her mother to matchmake, she thought. She wondered if Alinesse had told the promising clerk that she had a daughter who was quite nice-looking in her own way.

What was more vexing was that there was still no clear answer on what had happened to the ships. Yvienne was confident that the ship was the *Main Chance*. The blueprints and the keys were substantial evidence on their own.

And any ship could have suffered damage in a storm. It didn't *have* to be a storm that a twelve year-old girl thought she had created from her bedroom window six years before.

At any rate, Yvienne thought, the *Main Chance* lives. She didn't go down in a magical storm, and her presence was more evidence of the Great Fraud, though it was not conclusive enough to satisfy her. She would make sure that Dr Reynbolten received the letter.

The second letter bore the Demaris seal. Yvienne felt a pang of sadness and guilt, and sighed as she unfolded it. A few dried petals dropped out of the paper, exuding sweet, fresh scent. They were blue lupines from the mountains, also known as *forgive me* blooms.

Inigho was a man of few words.

I'm sorry. Friends? – ID

He was a good man, and her sadness intensified. She knew that if she wanted she could make a match with him. It wouldn't be one of love, but it wouldn't be one of indifference or expediency either. And it would have been a good, satisfactory life, she thought. Good, obedient Yvienne, making a brilliant match, once again meeting her family's expectations. But the other part of Yvienne, the Gentleman Bandit, could never settle for goodness or obedience, and if Inigho ever found out, he would never understand. She could never be with Inigho Demaris, and she could never explain to him why.

And then there was the matter of Tesara, or more exactly, Tesara's secret – a cloud over the household. It wasn't even that she didn't think Inigho could accept Tesara: he was a merchant through and through. First he would ask about the limits of her power, and then he would be thinking about ways to use it – to use Tesara – to make money. And that was exactly what Trune had wanted, and why Trune had been so eager to kidnap Tesara.

She wondered what happened to Abel and thrust that thought away. He was not her problem. In the end, he had not kept his promise, and it was just as well. His only reason for arriving at Kittredge Mews would have been to deliver her sister to their enemies, and the fact that he didn't show up meant nothing. Perhaps he had an attack of conscience. More likely, he watched the chaos of the night unfold and decided not to get involved.

The final letter was addressed to Tesara, with the initials JSF in the upper left corner. It was a simple letter, with no grand seal marking the noble lines of a noble family. Jone Saint Frey had adopted a new personality and character for his new life. Should she wait until Tesara was stronger to give it to her? Don't be ridiculous, she scolded herself. Neither she nor her sister needed that kind of protection, as if their sensibilities were so fragile. On the other hand, her sister was really very sick.

And very changed.

You must give her the benefit of the doubt.

She picked up the letter from Jone and then paused again, looking at the letter from her mother. More than anything Tesara wanted proof that she had not sunk the fleet, and Alinesse's letter cruelly did not provide that proof. Instead, it only offered more uncertainty. Yvienne made her decision.

She would give her sister the letter from Jone Saint Frey, but she would not give her their mother's. Not yet. Not until she was well.

And she would wrestle with the consequences of that decision when the time came.

While she was in the office, Albero knocked and poked his head in. He was back in his uniform again, as they all were – she wore a gray day dress with a faint pink stripe, and had dressed her hair simply.

"Elenor Charvantes is here. I've put her in the parlor."

"Elenor! My God." What could possibly bring Elenor to House Mederos? "How is she?"

"Sad. Agitated. Frightened." He made a deprecating face at his own forthright honesty.

"Of course," she said. She got up. "I'll see her at once."

"Should I bring tea?"

"I doubt tea will do it," Yvienne said, grim.

Elenor was pacing when Yvienne entered the parlor, whirling around at her approach. Albero had not misspoken – there were huge shadows under her eyes, and her face was blotched with tears. Her dress and overcoat were in disarray, and she had come out without a bonnet, exposing her fair skin to the sun. When Yvienne took her hands, they were trembling.

"Oh, Elenor," Yvienne said, drawing her to the sofa. Elenor sank down, covering her face in her hands.

"I'm such a fool," she said. "I am such a fool."

"You are not a fool," Yvienne said. She reached for the brandy decanter and poured them both a healthy portion. Elenor drank hers and coughed, laughing through her tears.

"Dear Yvienne. You're kind to say so. You, the smartest girl in Port Saint Frey. I'm just the prettiest, and it means nothing. My marriage – my mother and father – of all things, I regret bringing embarrassment to them." She turned to look at Yvienne. "You're the only person who can help me, and I can't imagine that you would want to. After all, my husband tried so hard to bring you down. You and this House. He was the one who brought the Harriers here, and who helped Trune return."

"How can I help, Elenor? You know I'll do anything in my power."

"I went to the Bailet Hotel last night to say good-bye. And–"

"The Bailet! It was burned to the ground last night!" Yvienne set down her brandy. "My God, Elenor, what were you doing there?"

Elenor looked straight at her, and gone was the fearful young woman. "I know, Yvienne. I burned it down."

Yvienne found that she was at a loss for words. "Elenor," she managed.

Elenor took a breath, speaking in a low voice. "I went to his room to say good-bye. I'm leaving Port Saint Frey. I cannot stay, not after causing so much shame. And..." her voice sunk further. "A man was there, abusing Mr Fresnel most abominably. He had him shackled to a chair and–and..." she couldn't finish.

And that was why Mr Fresnel was not at Forty-seven Kittredge Mews, Yvienne thought. "Did he hurt you?"

Elenor gazed into the distance at a horrible memory. "He tried. He would have killed me, Yvienne, were it not for Mr Fresnel. Somehow he got free and they fought terribly. That was when I picked up the lamp from the dressing table and hit the man with it."

"Well done!" Yvienne exclaimed, and Elenor smiled through her distress, but it was more of a twitch than a smile.

"We escaped, but in the chaos of the fire from the burning oil, I lost Mr Fresnel. He was so badly hurt, I'm sure he'll succumb to his injuries if we don't find him and bring him to hospital." She looked directly at Yvienne. "I know he was your enemy, but please help me find him. I just want to know he's going to be all right."

Yvienne nodded. "Of course I will help, Elenor."

Upstairs retrieving her overcoat she checked under her bed, feeling foolish, but there was nothing but empty floorboards.

Yvienne looked both ways down the hall and then ran to her parents' suite, but it too was empty, and the window to the balcony securely locked. Satisfied that Abel was not recuperating in her house, and a bit exasperated that he was not, she ran down the stairs. Elenor waited in the front hall, again pacing anxiously.

"Albero," Yvienne said. "Miss Elenor and I are going out for a walk." It was shocking to address a married lady by a girl's name, but Elenor seemed both pleased and regretful.

"Yes, miss," Albero said, as correct as if the night's escapades had been nothing more than a fever dream.

They walked along arm in arm, two young merchant women taking the air on a fine day. The length of the Crescent had a carnival aspect to it, the unexpected sunshine reviving spirits of everyone, servant and master alike. It would make it difficult to vanish down the trail to the sea cave, but Yvienne knew from experience that if one only walked as if one were allowed, one could go almost anywhere without notice.

Halfway down the Crescent, she steered Elenor onto the trail. At the girl's questioning eyes, she put a finger to her lips and only hurried her down the uneven ground. Elenor followed gamely, and the Crescent and the rest of the traffic was left behind them. Here the trail looked out over the blue harbor, the gulls wheeling and crying overhead, a fresh wind ruffling their hair and tossing their skirts. It brought color to Elenor's fair cheeks, and here, in the shade, they lost some of the comforting warmth of the sun.

The trail went down into the cliffs, behind the camouflaging shrubs, and Yvienne fumbled for the lantern and the matches.

"You've been here before," Elenor said, following in her footsteps into the cave.

"Yes," Yvienne said. "It's been my secret for some time."

Elenor said nothing more, and Yvienne could tell she was putting things together.

She knew before they even stepped foot into her lair that the cave was empty. The lantern light fell on the blankets and the firepit, glinting on the dark waters of high tide. The smell of the sea was strong, the sound of the waves muted but constant, a rushing noise like blood pumped by an unquiet heart.

"But... there's no one here," Elenor said, confused and disappointed.

Yvienne's keen eyes told her another story. The blankets had been folded, and the fire had been doused, and still smelled nastily of wet ash. And the clothes...

He had taken his clothes, leaving behind the boys' clothes she had lent him. Her mind must have played tricks on her; she swore she caught a whiff of his unfamiliar scent, and then it was gone.

"My mistake," Yvienne said. "I'm sorry, Elenor. I don't know where he is." Which was true, after all.

At the top of the trail, the air had gotten brisker and the clouds gathered. The small reprieve was almost over and Fog Season had returned. The cry of the gulls was more raucous than joyous, a warning rather than a celebration.

"Thank you," Elenor said, holding her coat tight around her. "I know you tried, and I appreciate it very much."

"What will you do, Elenor?" Yvienne's heart broke for her friend. Elenor took a breath.

"I plan to remove to Ravenne. I had a long talk with Mother, and though she pressed me to stay, in the end she gave me a letter of introduction to some colleagues of the House. I can work well enough as a clerk, and all anyone has to know is that I'm taking on a traditional year of apprenticeship with another House." A tremulous smile. "Ravenne has its own gossip and can hardly be bothered with mine."

Yvienne embraced her, holding her dear friend tight. "Write to me. Tell me where you land and find safe harbor. Promise me, Elenor."

Elenor nodded. "I will try."

"Elenor," Yvienne said. She tried to find the right words. "You did well."

She expected Elenor to say something self-deprecating as usual, but instead the young woman said, "Do you know what Abel said, when that horrible man had him on the ground, prepared to deliver the killing blow?"

Yvienne shook her head, forehead creased in confusion.

"He cried out for his mother, Yvienne, not for me."

They went their separate ways then, Elenor to the foot of the Crescent, Yvienne to the head.

Shivering, aching all over, Abel watched from the stand of trees as the two women took their leave. His few hours' sleep in the sea cave, rolled up in the wool blanket, warmed by the fire, had been too short a respite. He managed to bind his leg, but he was still tormented by the pain, and he needed a splint or it wouldn't heal straight. He needed rest and time and a place to go to earth, and he had none of those things.

Last night he had watched the Bailet blaze until it collapsed in on itself, and he had not seen Doc stumble from the building. He knew better than to believe Doc Farrissey was dead, but just maybe Abel had a head start. He had a few guilders in his pocket, salvaged from his stash in the room. He could catch the mail coach up the coast, and if he were lucky he could head east, through the Chahoki Empire. Not even Doc would be able to find him there, once he disappeared in the vast cities of the Great Plains and the horse soldiers.

Better get walking, Abel, he told himself, and supporting himself on a stick, he began the slow trek up the trail.

Tesara sat at her dressing table and listened as the wind picked up and a light rain spattered against the window, as Fog Season resumed after the short respite. Night had fallen, and a cold wind came in through the window and the shutters. She had a fire and it kept her room warm, and she felt almost well. She had gotten out of bed, and Yvienne had helped her to the water closet. She glimpsed herself in the mirror, and she winced. Gone was the stout rosy girl and the healthy young woman. Her hair had turned gray, and her eyes looked too big for her face. She took a pair of scissors from her dressing table and she cut her hair, clipping it round in a rough boy's style, and threw the rest in the fire, where it smoked and crackled with an abominable smell. Now her hair stood out from her head, but it pleased her to see less of it.

A knock came at the door, and Yvienne let herself in, holding a dinner tray. "Feeling bett–" She stopped short at the sight of Tesara with cropped hair.

"A little," Tesara managed. "Not ready to come downstairs. Thanks." She nodded at the tray. Yvienne's expression was a mixture of sadness and relief.

"All right. When you're ready. Just ring for me, if you need anything. And there's a letter for you."

"Thanks."

Yvienne let herself out. Tesara could tell without her sister even saying the words that she was hiding her from the rest of the household. Vivi, who was afraid of nothing, was afraid for her.

Tesara didn't fight it. She didn't want to be seen. The power continued its vibration just under her skin, and she could feel it fluttering in her heart, and pulsing with every breath she took. She had used her powers on herself and it had taken its toll, just as the Harrier had warned.

It was consuming her.

I once thought I was strong enough to destroy a fleet of ships from my bedroom window, she thought. All those years of useless guilt and shame. I was a foolish child; of course I didn't sink the fleet. I had nowhere near the power.

I could do it now, though. Oh yes, she could do it now.

She had to accept the Harrier's offer. If she didn't, she would destroy everyone she loved. She would travel to Harrier headquarters in Great Lake, and offer herself up, no matter the cost. She pulled out her writing desk and opened up the lid, taking out paper, pen, and ink.

The letter from Jone, in his well-bred handwriting, caught her eye. She picked it up. She knew what it would say without opening it. He would declare his love again, he would tell her of his adventures, he would complain once more about his mother and Mirandine – Mirandine who loved him fiercely, and who had tried to save Tesara from Trune.

Tesara held up the letter between her fingers, tears thick in her throat. "I'm sorry," she croaked. "But I am too dangerous for you, Jone Saint Frey." She breathed on it, barely pushing the air between her lips. The letter caught fire at the other corner, and it curled up. She held it until the last minute and then let the final scrap drop into her soup.

Then she pulled the paper toward her, dipped her pen, and began to write.

Dear Dr Farrissey…

Acknowledgments

As always, many thanks to my agent, Jennie Goloboy, for believing in the sisters and their story, and Marc, Lottie, Penny, Phil, and Nick, who, from the moment they welcomed me as the newest member of the Robot Army, have been professional and supportive and wonderful to work with. For Cryptopolis – the best little writer's group in Austin. And finally, for Louise Fitzhugh, author of *Harriet the Spy*, and winner of the best use of a dumbwaiter in fiction.

LOST GODS
They were trained from birth to kill. Now it is time to fight back.
MICAH YONGO

PALE KINGS
When the gods return to reclaim their world, the Five Realms will fall.
MICAH YONGO

DARIUS HINKS
the ingenious

MOONSHINE
JASMINE GOWER

THE QUEEN OF ALL CROWS
ROD DUNCAN

THE OUTLAW & THE UPSTART KING
ROD DUNCAN

The Islevale Cycle
D. B. JACKSON
TIME'S CHILDREN

The Islevale Cycle
D. B. JACKSON
TIME'S DEMON

JAINE FENN
HIDDEN SUN

The story so far...

PATRICE SARATH

THE SISTERS MEDEROS

"*A tale of magic lost and recovered, fortunes made and squandered, and broken lives healed.*"
LOUISA MORGAN, author of *A Secret History of Witches*